THE
KILL
BOX

Books by
H. RIPLEY RAWLINGS IV

Assault by Fire

The Kill Box

Red Metal (with Mark Greaney)

THE KILL BOX

A TYCE ASHER NOVEL

H. RIPLEY RAWLINGS IV
Lt. Col., USMC (ret.)

PINNACLE BOOKS
Kensington Publishing Corp.
www.kensingtonbooks.com

ORGANIZATION OF U.S. RESISTANCE FORCES

150th Cavalry Regiment
USANG
(West Virginia National Guard)

COLONEL DAVID NEPO

XO and Interim Commander
LIEUTENANT COLONEL TYCE ASHER*
* "Mr. Wynand"
* "Mr. Georgia-Blue"
* "Corporal 'Trigger'"

U.S. MARINE CORPS

Dragoons,
4th LAR Bn, U.S. Marine
Corps Reserve
Gunnery Sergeant Dixon
Staff Sergeant Diaz
(Quantico, VA)

U.S. NATIONAL GUARD (WEST VIRGINIA)

B Troop,
1st Squadron,
150th Cavalry
USANG
(Eleanor,
WV)

Company C,
2nd Battalion,
19th Special
Forces Group
Captain Ned
Blake
(Camp
Dawson)

U.S. NAVY

**Shock Trauma Platoon-
ALPHA**
JTF CAPMED
Fleet Surgical Team 10
Forward Resuscitation Unit
Commander Victoria Remington
(Bethesda, MD)

The 150th Cavalry Regiment

Colonel **DAVID NEPO** (Missing in Action): Commanding Officer, 150th Cavalry, West Virginia Army National Guard.

Major **TYCE ASHER**: U.S. Marine officer, wounded in Iraq, leads the regiment when the colonel is reported MIA. Lost left leg in combat in Fallujah, Iraq.

Gunnery Sergeant **CHARLES "TREY" DIXON III**: Called "Gunny," keeps the men in line and expects the troops to act like warriors 24/7.

Staff Sergeant **ALEJANDRA ENCANTAR CELESTINA DIAZ-PEREZ**: The squadron's heavy weapons expert.

Navy Commander **VICTORIA REMINGTON:** The raven-haired, impeccably well-educated navy doctor from Connecticut. The Italian Fury.

Captain **WILLIAM "NED" BLAKE**: U.S. C Troop commander, 19th Army special forces commander.

First Sergeant **BRENDEN HULL**: U.S. C Troop Staff Non-Commissioned Officer In Charge, 19th Army special forces commander.

Lieutenant **TOM BRYCE**: Marine Corps, Company D Commander 4th Light Armored Reconnaissance, the Dragoons.

Corporal **"TRIGGER"**: The 1st Squadron's Belgian Malinois. Military working dog. Been with the unit more than three years.

U.S. Civilians

LAWTON CUSTIS: Retired U.S. Army one-star general, manager of the Virginia AAF Tank Museum of Military History.

WYNAND: Bearded moonshiner and fixer who knows how to get things done, albeit often on the wrong side of the law.

GEORGIA-BLUE TEMPLETON: Nicknamed "Blue." Reliable and massively built mountain man sniper.

SUSANNA HOLLY: Mayor of the West Virginia town of Parsons, in her forties. Blue eyed, fit, red haired.

Russians

President **KRYPTOV** of Russia.

Army General **GRIGOR TYMPKIN**: Commander of the Eastern Special Liberation Army, formerly the Occupation Army, in the Eastern third of the Russian invasion.

Major General **VIKTOR KOLIKOFF**: Russian officer and mastermind of the invasion of the U.S., now the operations chief for all of the U.S. invasion but refocused by General Tympkin on his own priorities in the war.

The SPETS-VTOR: An advanced Russian computer system, short for *Spetsial'nyy Schetchik Vtorzheniy*, or "Special Invasion Calculating Machine."

Majors **PITOR PAVEL**, **IVAN DRUGOV**, and **DANILO QUICO**: staff officers to General Kolikoff.

Captain **CHRISTOV SHENKOV**: A Russian special forces commander.

Call sign:
Steppe Wolf.

Major **STAZIA VAN ANDJÖRSSON**, a.k.a. **STACEY VAN ANDERSSON.** An SVR special forces major.

Call sign:
Panther Chameleon.

Major **UINTERGRIN** of the Russian 27th Chem-Bio Brigade.

Il leone non può proteggersi dalle trappole e la volpe non può difendersi dai lupi. Bisogna quindi essere una volpe per riconoscere trappole e un leone per spaventare i lupi.
(The lion cannot protect himself from traps, and the fox cannot defend himself from wolves. One must therefore be a fox to recognize traps, and a lion to frighten wolves.)

—NICCOLÒ MACHIAVELLI, *The Prince*

PROLOGUE

Twelve years ago
Bethesda, MD

The man was vaguely aware of some sounds nearby. Voices, and a beeping noise. All else was a haze of confusion.

Where am I? came his first cogent thought. This was followed closely by a sobering second thought. *Wait . . .* who *am I?*

He heard some other sounds, like heavy sighs from a wheezing old man. Someone with a very raspy throat and an even drier mouth. Concentrating hard through the fog and confusion in his mind, he realized the noises were actually coming from him.

He smacked his dry, flaking lips and tried to open his eyes. They wouldn't budge. His world remained in relative darkness. He was vaguely aware of a dull beating in his chest and a throbbing in his head. Then he became aware that a pain was spreading out all over his body. At least, to his slowly awakening senses, it felt like it was spreading. He couldn't tell. Everything just hurt. Badly.

At least I know I'm alive, he thought with grim amusement.

"Ow," a voice said, and he recognized the sound. It was his own voice, but distant and somehow unfamiliar.

I can hear, he thought, trying to take stock, *so there is that.*

A few things were beginning to come back to him. Had there been gunfire? He remembered driving in a vehicle, then there was maybe a grenade going off.

No, he thought. *It was more intense than that. Huge explosion. Fireball. I was blown out of my vehicle. There was rapid gunfire.*

The feeling of confusion was now mixed with shock, and maybe some fear. The memories coming back were too rapid to comprehend but so vivid that he began to feel a pain in his stomach.

Then what? he thought.

He concentrated even harder now, but the harder he tried, the less he could remember. It was like turning on a car's high beams in thick fog on a dark night. When you flick them on, they just illuminate the fog and conceal everything behind it.

The beeping noise grew faster: *ping-ping-ping.*

Wait, I'm in a hospital. More rational thought was returning. A growing awareness of the here and now overwhelmed him.

He tried to open his eyes, but they were stuck shut. *Oh my God*, he thought, *am I blind?* He tried to move his arms, but they didn't seem to be working, either.

Alone and in his dark, hazy, pain-filled world, he remembered a man shooting at him. He'd shot back. In fact, he shot the guy twice without thinking and killed him. He could see the man's face clearly. The spittle on his mouth, the wild look in his eyes: a mixture of fear and determination. A look of sudden surprise as the two bullets caught the man full force, the body crumpling to the ground. From below, a knife cut across his own calf, and someone wrestled him down to the floor—a floor filled with spent brass shell casings, gore, and dead or half-dead bodies. A grenade exploded, right next to him. And then . . . nothing.

I was in a full-fledged battle, he remembered. He tried to move his legs, but, like his arms, nothing moved. *Dear God, did I lose my arms* and *legs?* A wave of terror passed over him as he thought, *I'm blind, and I'm limbless.*

The machine's *ping* was going even faster now.

Then he heard a door open.

"Hey, Marine, glad to see you're awake." It was a reassuring female voice. It brought him great comfort. "You've been through a lot."

He tried to lift an arm but still couldn't tell if it was moving. As if the voice's owner sensed the purpose of his awkward motions, she said, "You have bandages on both arms from where the doctors removed shrapnel. You had almost ten grams in you." He tried to lift an arm toward the bandages on his eyes. "You shouldn't mess with the bandages. You were very badly wounded, and the surgeons are still worried about infections. Just get some rest now. Everything is going to be just fine." He heard the door open again, and the sounds of the woman leaving the room.

She didn't get far. He heard another female voice outside the door. "Nurse, there was an alarm."

"Yes, doctor. I checked him, he's fine. He's just coming around."

"Good. This one is the Marine? The one from Fallujah."

"Yes, doctor. A combat infantry officer named Tyce Asher."

"I heard the Deputy Commandant came by and pinned the Purple Heart medal on him personally."

"Yes, a few days ago. Though he was unconscious through the whole thing."

"Okay. Pretty tricky coming out of a drug-induced coma like that. The heavy sedation leaves them immobile. He'll be very confused for the next day or two. Go ahead and get the next of kin over here."

"He has none. There was a Marine sergeant listed. Umm, Dixon is his name. He's the command rep and has been by a bunch of times. The sergeant was to be informed if he woke. He's staying at a nearby hotel."

"Did you tell him yet, about . . . ?"

"Not yet. I didn't have the heart."

"Okay. I guess I'll be the one letting him know we had to amputate a leg."

Two years ago
Paris, France

From the corner of the café, the man watched the three Russians pay their bill and leave. He folded his newspaper, downed the remainder of his café au lait, and continued following them. He and his French DSGE unit had been tailing them for the past few days. They hadn't been hard to track—in fact, it was pretty clear they were not trained in any kind of counterintelligence. Still, he stayed a respectable distance away as they entered the Paris Metro tunnel.

Twenty minutes later, the Russians arrived at the Quatre-Septembre Metro stop, the agent still tailing them. They walked to Palais Brongniart, the former Paris stock exchange. At the entrance to the Palais, they fumbled for their IDs, paid an entry fee, and went in.

The French agent signaled to his number two man across the street to hold his position, then reached into his raincoat and activated a concealed radio to call his headquarters.

"Chief, they have entered the Palais Brongniart."

"Why?" came back the one-word question from his superior.

"I have no idea, boss. Looks like the Paris consumer electronics show is going on here. Should I follow?"

"Agent, when three officers from the Russian army enter our country with fake passports, spend three days grossly inebriated and womanizing, then finally attend the premier global technology show, yes, I suspect this is something you need to be curious about."

The agent acknowledged, then proceeded into the convention center. He was immediately surrounded by barking robot dogs, swarms of drones dancing overhead in synchronized orbits, and everywhere beautiful ladies in slinky, computer-themed outfits standing next to signs or booths proclaiming the virtues of some groundbreaking piece of technology.

It took him nearly a half hour to locate the three Russian officers. He slipped casually nearby and watched as the three men looked to be closing a deal. They pulled out a credit card and paid for something on the spot, receiving a receipt in exchange. Then they left.

The agent called his partner to ensure he picked them up once they left the venue. His partner reported spotting them immediately. Then the agent went over to the vendor, flashed his badge, and demanded to know what they'd purchased. PlayStations, the man told him. Hundreds of PlayStations.

The DGSE man called his chief with the news, and his boss laughed. "Oh well, looks like a load of nothing. Russian army morale officers trying to keep the troops happy with some modern video games. Tail them to the airport and watch them board just to be sure it's not some elaborate ruse, then come back to base. We have more important matters heating up. The U.S. is getting froggy in Iran, and we need to keep an eye on a group of Iranian officials coming in tomorrow."

Twenty hours later, the three Russians had switched planes three times and were back in their uniforms, landing in Siberia. They each wore the rank of Russian infantry captain. As the plane's aft ramp lowered, the freezing Siberian winds whipping into the plane's loading bay, they covered their faces and wrapped their heavy coats around themselves. A Russian colonel walked up the gangway to meet them.

He didn't waste time. "Did you get them?"

One of the men spoke up. "Yes, Comrade Colonel Ko-likoff."

"All of them?"

"Three hundred brand-new PlayStations will be delivered to the special address in two months' time."

"Excellent, Captain Pavel." Colonel Kolikoff smiled broadly. "We will add them to the German computers we already have."

"What's next, Comrade Colonel?" one captain asked.

"Then, my dear Captain Drugov, the SPETS-VTOR will be one of the fastest military computers in the world. General Tympkin has something big planned for us."

"More computations for Ukraine?"

"No. More complicated. We are to plan a large invasion from start to finish."

Six months ago
Norfolk, Virginia

The woman looked sharp in her formal U.S. Navy "mess dress" uniform. Two of the security officers eyed her up as she stepped out of her Uber. She walked briskly toward the checkpoint outside the Norfolk Naval Shipyard. The breast of her starched white Navy dinner jacket was adorned with a simple row of three medals, and on her sleeve was the rank of a petty officer. Four gold braids, aiguillettes, cascaded over her shoulder, which the guards knew meant she worked for a four-star admiral. But what really caught their eyes were her legs. The slits on her skirt opened up with every step, revealing tightly toned, tanned calves with no pantyhose.

She flashed them a bright, confident smile. "Good evening, gentlemen."

The lead agent caught himself staring and put on an official tone. "Name," he said, pulling out a clipboard.

"Stacey Van Andersson." she said, accenting each syllable in her last name.

"Von A . . . what?" The unusual name caught him off guard. "What is that, Norwegian? Spell if for me."

"Finnish, actually. V-a-n A-n-d—"

"Okay, okay," he interrupted. "I found it. ID, please." He ran his pen over the names on his clipboard.

She opened up a small black patent leather purse and handed over her Navy identity card. The agent checked her name off the list and held up the ID to compare the photo with the woman. She widened her eyes and imitated the picture in her photo. She was pretty, very pretty. Light blond hair pulled up in a high braided bun and the sun-kissed skin of someone who enjoyed nature in her off-duty hours. Something caused the man to hesitate a little longer than was proper. Her eyes. One was an ice-cold blue, and the other a deep, impenetrable brown.

"Ahem." Someone behind her coughed meaningfully.

The agent was suddenly conscious of the gathering group of well-dressed diplomats and VIPs trying to figure out the reason for the holdup. He quickly waved her through the metal detectors and pointed to a sign that instructed everyone to surrender their electronic devices. Then he went back to checking in the new arrivals.

The woman entered the venue. A crowd of high-ranking officers dressed in their formal uniforms and civilians in sharp tuxedos and evening dresses were chatting freely and drinking champagne. The entire area was decorated with bouquets, red, white, and blue cloth bunting, and flags of all the U.S. states. Several foreign flags represented partnered nations' dignitaries who were also in attendance. Behind all of this, looming large and grey against the dark sky, a full twenty stories tall, was the hull of the latest American nuclear supercarrier, set to be commissioned the next day.

Stacey walked around a bit to get the lay of the land, then casually went over to one of many enormous potted palms brought in for the occasion. She set her purse down on the back side of a planter and pretended to adjust her uniform while she felt around inside the pot. She found what she was looking for. She smiled, thankful the shipyard employee had done his job. She cautiously fished out a slim black box the size of an iPhone with a crystal bubble on the top. Opening her purse, she gently pushed a worn red handkerchief to one side to make room, inserted the device, then snapped it shut.

Stacey searched the room for her target. The son of a former president, a known womanizer and playboy. Spotting him among a group of chatting dignitaries and ambassadors, she worked her way over. Grabbing a champagne glass off a server's platter, she looked for a spot to join their circle. There wasn't long to wait. The French ambassador's wife caught her husband eyeing Stacey, elbowed him knowingly in the ribs, then strolled off to look for something stronger than champagne.

Striking up a conversation with the ambassador in almost perfect French, Stacey kept one eye on the president's son, making sure to keep the slit of her skirt aimed squarely in his direction. He was unable to resist; it was only a couple of minutes before he moved in closer to speak with her.

"Pretty cool, huh?" he said, waving his drink toward the carrier.

She turned briefly from the ambassador, put on a flirty smile, and widened her eyes. "So, so cool!" she said, but then turned back to the French ambassador.

Not dissuaded, the president's son leaned in and tried again. "You know, I can get us a personal tour of the ship's bridge later. You interested?"

The French ambassador's wife returned and unceremoniously steered her husband away. The ambassador begged Stacey's forgiveness in flowery French but dutifully followed his wife.

Stacey shrugged and turned to the president's son. "You can do that?"

"Of course. The damned thing is being named after my dad," he said.

"Oh, so that's *you*?" she gushed.

He smiled, glad that name-dropping had worked. It rarely failed. He looked at all the adornments on her uniform and said, "Pretty sure I don't have to ask if you have the clearance." He turned to one of the secret service agents. "Hey, Tim, can you get the admiral to open the bridge for a private tour later?"

The agent looked at Stacey and frowned, but nodded, "Yes, sir. It's doable."

"Excellent." He leaned in and whispered in her ear while inhaling the scent of her hair. "Come find me later, honey." He reached down, patted her butt, then walked over to one of the wet bars for another cocktail.

Men are such simpletons, Stacey thought, *and the big shots are even easier to manipulate, especially the drinkers.* She lifted her glass in a secret victory toast to herself. *Or maybe I am just that damned good.* She downed the champagne and thought over the next steps of her plan.

Three months ago
West of Washington, D.C.

The U.S. Navy corpsman had to shout over the noise of rushing air as the Humvee ambulance sped down Route 66 at a breakneck pace. "Did you hear the Russkies sank one of our carriers?"

"What?" said the other corpsman, named Purvis. He'd heard the man, but he'd been ordered by their commander to count morphine ampules and didn't want to stop to talk. Partially he didn't want to restart the count, but also the counting was calming him down from what he'd witnessed that morning. Massive explosions, gunfire, and Russian tanks racing through downtown D.C., laying waste everything in their way.

"It was that new one . . . just launched a few months ago. The one named after the president," said the first man.

Purvis stopped counting and glared at the other man. His count had reached two hundred and thirty-something, but with the combination of the vehicle's motion, the other guy's constant chatter, and his own fright, his stomach was churning, and now he had lost count again.

"Who gives a shit right now?" Purvis said, restacking the loose ampules back into his unsorted box.

Purvis recalled back to that morning. Commander Victoria Remington had grabbed him and the other man and ordered them to follow her to the narcotics room, she'd told him to fill one box with morphine and another box with QuikClot. The other guy grabbed bandages and suture kits. When both men had balked at the order, she pulled them into a common room and showed them the live newsfeeds of the White House being attacked by Russian Spetsnaz. After that, he just obeyed and grabbed everything he could, and now he was here.

Purvis saw the other man hold his head in his hands and start sobbing gently, rocking back and forth.

"For fuck's sakes," said Purvis. He figured he probably better comfort the other guy, but he didn't even know the man's name. Then the vehicle screeched to a halt, and both men went flying—as did all the morphine and other unorganized medical gear. The back hatches were flung open, and Commander Remington was there, her pistol drawn.

"Get the fuck up, you two," she yelled, "and bring your medical bags." They obeyed, jumped out the back of the ambulance, and followed her. All six medical Humvees had halted behind them, and the navy personnel from those vehicles were likewise disembarking and following their commander to the front of their small convoy.

Two big pickup trucks were parked across the road near where several cars were rolled onto their sides in a drainage ditch. As the corpsmen walked up, they could see a few men walking around the vehicles and talking in animated tones.

"Hey!" Commander Remington yelled at the strangers, "do you need assistance?"

Purvis had seen her around Bethesda Naval Hospital. She was average height, perpetually tanned, and normally had a serious look about her that made him and others think she was bitchy. Pale blue eyes, raven hair, and the striking good looks of a model without being so skinny, she reminded him of Danica Patrick, including her widow's peak. But what most of the other corpsmen commented on was her chest size. It was grossly inappropriate for them to comment that way about an officer, but they were all in their early twenties and, like most young men, they just couldn't refrain from talking about the female form.

"Yeah, we got a few people here hurt real bad," said a man standing by one of the trucks.

Purvis thought he saw something, maybe the flash of metal, but then it was gone just as quickly. He was about to speak up, but he was too nervous thinking about what the crash victims were going to look like.

Victoria motioned for all the navy corpsmen to approach. "Okay, looks like a vehicle accident. Let's assess and assist, but stay sharp." Purvis had never really noticed before, but she had an Italian accent. It sounded kind of songful, and sweet, like the voice of his favorite Italian *Sports Illustrated* calendar model, Daniella Sarahyba.

The corpsmen followed her to the stricken vehicles in teams and started looking around for the wounded persons. When they were all within a few steps, the three strangers pulled out shotguns and aimed them at the navy personnel.

"Now, listen up, we don't want to hurt no one," said one of the men. "But we aim to take whatever you got in the back of them ambulances. So if you want to live, just stand aside and—"

Bang!

Everything happened so fast, Purvis hadn't even seen Commander Remington raise her pistol and shoot the man in the head. The man had propped his shotgun and his torso over the back of the pickup, and when he was hit, his head flopped forward but his body barely moved—other than the blood spraying out the bullet hole through his head and all over the other men like a fountain.

"Okay, now you listen to me!" yelled Victoria. "You are going to put those guns down and raise your hands. My men are gonna pick them up and toss them into the weeds. If any of you other *figlio di puttana* want to try something, I'll put a fuckin' bullet in your skull, too, *capisce*?"

The men had clearly not reckoned on this kind of a response. By the looks of things, the owners of the other two vehicles in the ditch had probably just given up their goods and been on their way. Two of the navy corpsmen moved the civilian pickups out of the way, careful to lay the dead man in the back of his own truck. Purvis and his partner collected up the shotguns.

"Holy shit, can you believe it?" the corpsman whispered to Purvis as they tossed the guns into the field.

"No," Purvis responded quietly. "But I also know our commander is one badass motherfucker."

Once they were all assembled again, Victoria yelled, "Mount up, sailors." Then, to the locals, she said, "Next time, think twice about how you treat your American brothers and sisters." And she spat toward them.

The men kept their hands up and nodded frantically. Purvis noticed Victoria still hadn't lowered her pistol. She kept it trained on them through the window, her finger on the trigger until everyone was mounted up and had driven off toward the mountains of West Virginia.

CHAPTER 1

Russian Occupation Zone
Union, West Virginia

Ghost breath, the exhalations from a panting boy and his father, joined a morning mist swirling head-high in the cool spring air. The early-rising farmer and his son led a team of horses up from watering them at a creek and went about hitching them to a wagon's harness. The sound of vehicle engines caught their attention. They dropped the tackle, looked up from their labors, and froze. A string of headlights was visible across the valley, making miniature halos in the fog. The farmers stood motionless and stared as the lights approached.

It had been three months since Russia had seized the U.S. centers of power. Life in the rural reaches of America had changed drastically and, somehow, not at all. On one hand, the markets were open, people were paying for and even stocking up on farm goods. But on the other hand, outsiders were showing up in increasing numbers in the valley.

Sometimes, lone opportunists came through to steal food from the farms. Mostly at night. The fields were still barren from winter, but the grain silos were full, and every farm for miles around had healthy stocks of chickens, cows, and pigs. More recently, roving bands of displaced families had been through asking for handouts.

Farmers and nearby townsfolk, who were mostly kin, anyhow, did what they had always done. From the Revolutionary War to the Civil War, through famines and the Great Depression, to the rationing of World War I and World War II—folks banded together. They watched over their own and their neighbors' property, and they locked and loaded.

About a month ago, a remnant U.S. military unit had come through fleeing south. The first U.S. troops the farmers had seen since the conflict had begun. At first, they were encouraged by the sight of U.S. military forces. They were running away from the strengthening Russian presence in the cities of West Virginia. They looked harried, skittish, and absolutely worn out. Their uniforms were in tatters. But what worried the farmers the most was that they looked scared. The farmers gave them some food, and then they melted away in full retreat.

The farmers grew alarmed when a Russian vehicle patrol or a pair of helicopters entered the valley. But the vehicles moved through fast and never stopped. Besides this—and like most citizens of the U.S.—contact with their new Russian overlords had only come through TV, radio, and over what everyone knew was a Russian-controlled internet. The broadcasts and available news had mostly been about staying calm, and orders were issued to remain sheltered in place from the West Virginia state governor.

Regardless, any approaching vehicles were reason enough to be cautious. The boy and the farmer could now see that the approaching headlights were some kind of convoy, and they didn't stick around to find out whose. They ran toward their darkened homestead, leaving the horses behind.

As the farmers ran, they didn't realize the real trouble had actually been hidden right under their noses all morning— even before they had woken up that day. An as-yet-unseen danger that lurked only thirty yards away from where they'd stood. Another set of eyes watched the boy and the man sprint away—but, unlike those of the watchful farmers, these eyes betrayed no fear at the approaching convoy.

The eyes belonged to a concealed, perfectly still form hidden amid the tall grass near a shallow stream at the edge of the farm. It was a sniper, clad from head to toe in a tan and green ghillie suit. The figure blended in perfectly with the mix of dried-out cornstalks and green rushes on a rise near the stream. Only a small hint of red showed from a handkerchief tied to the buttstock of a precision sniper rifle.

With a gloved hand, the sniper pressed a toggle switch mounted on the pistol grip of the Orsis T-5000 rifle. The button brought the Trijicon IR Mk III thermal sight out of standby mode. After a few seconds more, the heat-sensing sight had cooled to the correct temperature and, even with the mist, displayed a crystal-clear green image of the convoy's hot engines and tires. The hand relaxed against the forward bipods and pressed another button. This one activated an ultra–high frequency tactical radio on the sniper's back.

The sniper whispered into a boom microphone with a gentle female voice. "*Ya gotova. Nachat' podkhod.*" I'm ready. Commence your approach.

* * *

Sixty-six kilometers away, two Russian MiG-35UB ground-strike jet aircraft received the transmission and began a slow turn to the northeast, entering into a shallow dive that brought them onto an intercept vector with the vehicle convoy.

"Get ready," the flight leader said to his weapons officer over the intercom. Then he keyed his ultra–high frequency radio. "I copy, Panther. I'll have bombs on target in . . ." The pilot paused and waited for the weapons officer seated behind him to punch an update into the attack aircraft's telemetry computer. In moments, a digital bombing solution appeared on the leader's computer and in his heads-up display. He rekeyed the radio, "Two minutes, Panther."

"*Vremya vyshlo*," came the whispery female voice over the radio. Continue.

The weapons officer checked the attack solution once more, then sent it digitally to their wingman. "You will be early, Captain," he said.

"Fine," said the pilot, unconcerned. "Let's do this."

Marine Corps Staff Sergeant Alejandra Encantar Diaz-Perez was not supposed to be manning one of her own machine guns. She was, after all, the weapons platoon sergeant and the de facto commander of the vehicle convoy careening through the misty valley. But her boss had ordered her personally on this mission, and she'd never failed him yet. She also enjoyed the morning's cold wind against her face as she stood behind her gun. It was way better than coffee. It was the feeling of being alive and standing tall in the face of any danger, relished by most Marines.

Her M240's steel bipods scratched deep gouges in the

russet-colored metal roof as she constantly shifted the machine gun from one side to the next, scanning for trouble. The damage to the vehicle didn't bother the Bronx-born Latina one bit. She'd had her choice of vehicles when the unit, the 150th West Virginia Cavalry Regiment, had commandeered them new off the lot. That was just going to have to be the price of defending the U.S. The dealer they'd taken them from might someday give the U.S. a big bill, but she didn't care.

If the proverbial shit was going to hit the fan, Diaz preferred to be where she could blast a belt of ammo through her gun before she started issuing any commands. She'd been in combat a lot, and she knew fire dominance at the start of a battle was critical. Before the Russian invasion had even begun, the Marine Corps had started admitting women to the venerable men's club called the infantry. She wasn't the world's first female warrior and she wouldn't be the last, but she was determined to be the most badass machine gun leader in the Marine unit and even the 150th regiment they belonged to now.

As quickly as the numbers of women vying for entrance had increased, many of the women who had joined began leaving when the harsh reality hit that the infantry was nothing even most men relished. It was a terrible life: living in the dirt, constantly salt caked from sweat, always tired, usually on the move. But many other women stayed. They lasted through the pain and misery, and what's more, they shined. In the end, those ladies still left in the ranks of the infantry, much like their male counterparts, were tested and found to be made of incredibly tough stock. Staff Sergeant Alejandra Diaz-Perez, machine gun and weapons platoon sergeant in the Marine Corps 4th Light

Armored Reconnaissance Battalion, was made of exactly the kind of stuff the Marine Corps had envisioned.

Her mission directly from her boss, Lieutenant Colonel Asher, had been simple: "Go get us some ammo. As much as you can buy." She'd chosen the most backwoods roads she could find and had hit up seven small towns with known gun and hardware stores. Since the invasion, ammo had become exceedingly scarce—especially because most of the citizens used the same common cartridges as the military for their hunting and sporting rifles. Which, she'd discovered, made citizens all the more reluctant to part with their coveted stockpiles, even for U.S. dollar bills or the now-hated military promissory notes. A bit of cajoling had been necessary. Nothing drastic, just a patriotic speech or two about home and hearth and kicking the Russians out. When need be, Diaz's Bronx and Latina sides came out, along with a few tough words. Finally came the promise of actually paying them back once things returned to normal—a prospect that now seemed less and less likely, especially in the minds of a winter-and-war-weary citizenry.

A call went over their low-powered radios. The signal strength was dialed all the way down so it couldn't be intercepted by the Russians. Couldn't even be heard outside the valley.

"Weapons actual," came the broadcast, which was Diaz's call sign. "Air sentry reports seeing some black spots on the horizon. Direction, southeasterly."

The fine hairs on the back of Diaz's neck stood up, and at once she swiveled her gun to train it in that direction. Her eyes rapidly scanned the horizon above the Allegheny mountaintops looking for any sight of aircraft. There had been a lot of SPOTREPs, including a fair number of high-flying aircraft. On the ground it was mostly farmers or truckers speeding along the barren road. Spotting ground targets didn't worry her, but the Russians commanded the American airspace now, and when they flew over, there was little the Americans could do other than hide.

"Copy. Scanning now." Diaz tried to discern anything, but the intermittent ground haze and the predawn sparkle off the dew on the grass and trees made it difficult to spot anything moving.

Even though she didn't see anything, Diaz was a good leader, and she trusted her gunners enough to go into action. "Halt and gimme a herringbone," she said. The convoy halted in the requested herringbone. Every odd vehicle pulled off the road to the left, and the evens went right. Each vehicle was responsible for finding its own cover—a tree, barn, anything that broke up the pattern. It was an old tactic to mitigate any possible air threat. It spread the convoy out, made them less visible and less vulnerable. A holdover tactic left from the last time the U.S. fought another force that actually had enough aircraft to seize the skies.

A Russian missile or smart bomb fired from an experienced pilot could still ruin your day. Though the Russians invasion may have started with relatively green troops, after months of fighting in uncontested skies, their pilots were now beginning to understand the freedom of action their American counterparts had enjoyed in Korea, Vietnam, the Gulf Wars, and Operation Iraqi Freedom. There weren't even any active-duty U.S. pilots left alive who had ever experienced the harsher times at war when Germany and Japan had had enough airpower to force Americans to run for cover and hunker down in trenches. This wouldn't be the last war, and tactics were evolving rapidly.

* * *

The sniper watched the convoy scatter off the road. Something had spooked them; maybe the jets had been spotted. Too late to call them and rectify it now. She flicked a switch on the rifle's barrel, which flipped the night optic to the side, leaving the magnified day sight. Dawn had started to break and night optics were no longer necessary. She remained completely camouflaged and wasn't about to turn to see the aircraft. It had taken six hours of infiltration and setup to prepare a perfect sniper's nest, and it was "go-time."

She had already chosen her targets. Unconsciously, she rubbed her thumb over the red handkerchief for luck. It was time to begin her cyclic breathing.

Odin . . . dva . . . tri . . . she counted to herself as she inhaled, still tracking the lead three vehicles. Each was frantically trying to take cover, but it didn't matter; any tree, fence, or hedge was still well within her range.

A clump of blond hair, wet with dew and sweat, broke free from under her boonie hat. She ignored it, too deep in concentration.

. . . chetyre . . . pyat' . . . shest'. On "six," she breathed out and paused for a moment to let her crosshairs settle directly on the head of the driver of the lead vehicle. Then she lightly squeezed the trigger. The sniper rifle jolted upward. The combination muzzle brake and silencer meant barely a sound escaped. Just a loud *clack*, almost like a gate closing. The large caliber 9.5×77mm 375-grain bullet pierced the vehicle's windshield at 3,050 feet per second and continued into the driver's skull without deviating from its course.

The sniper registered the hit, though it was hard to

discern. There was frantic commotion near the vehicle, but she was already moving her rifle on to the next target and had begun her counting on an inhale. The third vehicle in the convoy was the ripest target. There were four men outside the vehicle staring up at the approaching planes, conversing and not moving around. They were confident in their camouflage and looked to be making a plan. Moving and active targets always presented ballistics problems. One of the men was pointing and looked to be giving orders. A team leader. She chose him.

She continued to breathe slowly and in a relaxed fashion until her count again hit *shest*. Then she paused briefly and calmly squeezed off another round.

Clack went the silenced, high-tech rifle, and another bullet zipped through the air.

It didn't miss. She had never missed. In training, maybe, but not in real life.

This one caught the pointing man in the neck. A neck shot maximized the effect of sowing chaos and fear. It worked. The man grasped his neck in horror, a stream of red blood spewing from the wound and spraying the other men.

From the corner of her eye, she could see the panicked rush of the soldiers around the stricken man, but she was already scanning the crosshairs back to where she'd mentally tagged the second vehicle in the convoy.

At first, she couldn't find the target, but then the bright red muzzle flash of a heavy machine gun drew her attention. It was concealed behind a wooden fence, but she could make out a figure on top of the vehicle talking over a radio, yelling at the vehicle crew and brazenly firing the machine gun. From her distance of about five hundred meters, she imagined she could hear the shouted call of "sniper" over the radio, and she enjoyed the confusion she was causing. She grinned but remained focused.

Ah, their unit's leader, she thought, *an optimum target.*

Her calculations were precise. She knew she had just enough time for one final shot. She counted upward again. *Odin . . . dva . . .* and fixed on her target. This time was going to be a head shot.

. . . tri . . .

Now she could see through her rifle's scope that the gunner was a woman.

. . . chetyre . . .

Unusual for the Americans to have a female leader. The sniper was all about strong women proving their worth in today's sexist world.

Oh well, she thought. *She still needs to die.*

She continued, but right as she hit *pyat'*, the roar of rocket launchers behind and above her interrupted the count.

"*Vy, zhirnye zhopy!* You giant fat-asses!" she shouted at the top of her lungs without looking up, her concentration all but broken by the jets' early arrival.

Clack! She squeezed the trigger out of her cycle anyhow.

Her brain registered a hit on the target as she was engulfed in smoke and fire from the MiG-35UB's exploding 122mm rockets.

The first jet streaked overhead now, dropping a load of low-release drag bombs. She could actually see the bombs falling off the aircraft and sailing toward the vehicles, twirling like dozens of maple tree spinners in a late fall breeze. Fifty feet from the ground, they each cracked open, becoming a shower of bomblets that rained down onto the U.S. vehicles. The hundreds of ensuing explosions carpeted the ground in fire. Then the second jet began its gun and bomb run, its own 122mm rockets hammering along the length of the convoy and adding to the cacophony and death.

Grebanyye piloty! she thought. *Fucking pilots!* The bright lights from the explosions blinded her, and she cursed loudly as she hastily collected up her equipment.

The second jet's bombs would come very soon. It was time to duck, then go. The pair of aircraft had mistimed their attack run, and now it was apparent they were going to be sloppy in delivering their ordnance, too. With the air alive with explosions, she kept to a crouch and was hefting the big Orsis T-5000 rifle in front of her, bending to grab her drag bag, when a deafening blast and massive blow knocked her off her feet, flinging the rifle from her grasp. It felt like someone had smashed a sledgehammer against a steel pole in her hands. Clods of earth flew through the air around her. She lay flat on her back, her hand and arm numb and her head buzzing from the concussion.

Fuckers! The pilots were off by more than six hundred meters. She didn't have a lot of time to be angry or to dissect the forensics of what had gone wrong, but she was certain it was their fault.

Covered in mud and frozen dirt, she rolled to her elbows and looked herself over. With no visible wounds, but still partially flashblinded, she used the bright explosions to look for her rifle. A meter away, she saw it. A piece of bomb shrapnel had slammed into it, peeling the barrel away from the wooden stock. Her precious rifle was ruined. Her heart skipped a beat at its loss—and not, as might be expected, out of fear at how close the pilots had come to killing her.

She calmed down considerably when a light from some

secondary vehicle detonations confirmed that her red hammer-and-sickle handkerchief was still securely tied around the splintered rifle's buttstock.

She slid to her knees with some effort and tried to rub some sensation back into her right hand and arm. She switched to her off hand and carefully untied the handkerchief, shoving it through the ghillie jacket into her bra and against her breasts. She gingerly pulled the small backpack over her good arm, stood while keeping a low profile, and snuck off through the thick grass, abandoning the rifle and her heavy drag bag. She took the third of three preplanned escape routes she had ID'd upon entering into her position. It was the one that remained the most hidden from the convoy's view.

But no one from the convoy saw her. They were fully preoccupied with burning and dying.

CHAPTER 2

Russian Pentagon
Washington, D.C.

One-star general Viktor Kolikoff tapped the computer monitor in front of him with the tip of his ballpoint pen. The loud *tap-tap-tap* made most in the room turn back to face him. Kolikoff was an exceedingly shrewd man, and they'd all come to dread his sniping during briefings. He always appeared at random in the back seats in their new headquarters, the Pentagon's so-called Iron Room.

Major Pitor Pavel was oblivious to the distraction and continued giving his morning intelligence briefing. "As you can see, the SPETS-VTOR predicts four or five more weeks of bloody battle in the eastern . . . Adirondack . . . Mountains . . ." His rate of speech slowed as he finally registered the noise. He turned around and realized the room was no longer paying attention, focused instead on his boss's incessant tapping.

Kolikoff launched in. "Major Pavel, we are already two months into the fight, and the 10th Mountain Division continues to hold out. Why?"

"Um, well . . . because that's what the SPETS-VTOR computer says they will do." Pavel said, using the name of the Russian uber computer.

SPETS-VTOR was actually an abbreviation for *Spetsial''nyy Schetchik Vtorzheniy*, which meant Special Invasion Calculating Machine. Developed in total secrecy, even from the rest of the Russian government, it had calculated several small battles with precision, including the half-invasion of the Ukraine. The biggest obstacle had always been the West barring Russia from purchasing the best and newest military-grade computer technologies from the best producers in the world. Without good computers, the plans it produced were innovative and strong, but two-dimensional. Every time they had tried to purchase the massive servers they needed, the West had blocked or embargoed the sales. Until a few years ago, that is, when General Tympkin had taken the program over. Kolikoff was saved from obscurity and found a way for Tympkin to beef up the computing power without getting noticed by the West, and even getting by the other Russian generals—who, for good reason, didn't trust Tympkin.

Kolikoff was the one who had come up with the idea to add civilian PlayStations. It was panned as ridiculous by most, but he had demonstrated to Tympkin that the devices had the absolute fastest and most modern computing power. His captains had secured the devices and secured themselves promotions at the same time. Then, devices meant to give their user fast, fun, and detailed war games could just as easily be turned to calculate fast and detailed war plans. What was there to lose? They were a cheap and simple alternative. When they were daisy-chained to the old German and Russian computers that formed the core of the SPETS-VTOR, Russia finally had computing power just below that of its Western military supercomputer counterparts. And thus Kolikoff figured out a way to fool the West.

From then on, Kolikoff had been given full autonomy,

and Tympkin tossed him an endless stream of global strategic challenges to chew on. Mostly, General Tympkin saw Kolikoff's work as a way to advance himself and gain access to the top brass by giving them in turn what they wanted: some great battle plans. Instead, the leaders saw a path to rid themselves of their old archnemesis, the United States, once and for all. The timing and the plan fell smoothly into the lap of a more-than-willing dictator. It was the perfect storm: a stainless and sublime battle plan, a narrow but irrefutably foolproof window during which to act, and a megalomaniacal Russian warlord who wanted nothing more than to see the U.S. in flames. A despot who saw the whole thing as a chance for him to finally ascend to his rightful place in history and liberate his nation from the perceived tyranny imposed by the Western superpower who had blocked their every global move for decades. Even Tympkin was surprised; he'd expected a promotion for his ingenuity, and instead they gave him a green light.

The invasion went forward, and the plan had worked. They'd plugged their SPETS-VTOR into the Pentagon and now had a supercomputer the likes of which the world had never seen. In recent weeks, Kolikoff and his team had been attempting to transition the bulky machine from its original purpose of calculating a shock invasion to providing useful data on fighting what had quickly turned into a protracted counterinsurgency of remnant U.S. military forces and an armed and angry citizenry.

Kolikoff continued his tirade. "You're failing to take something vital into account. What else could be contributing to the stiffening of the 10th Mountain's resistance?"

"They found some more ammo?" Pavel answered dimly.

"What, just lying around?" Kolikoff said scornfully. "Unlikely. But they do have more ammo. Why?"

Majors Ivan Drugov and Danilo Quico had already been snoozing in back when General Kolikoff had arrived, and now they tried to hide. The two majors were comrades in arms with Pavel, but they also knew when to remain silent. They could see Pavel's cause that morning was a sinking ship, and the last thing they wanted to do was to get into Kolikoff's debate cross fire. They'd learned it was usually best just to be quiet and let Kolikoff lead them down the primrose path to whatever conclusion he was trying to make. As intelligent as Kolikoff's input always was, his reasoning usually shot well over their heads.

"Sir, I can just say that we plugged all the variables into the SPETS-VTOR, and this is what it tells us," Pavel said.

Even though he tried to sound confident, Major Pavel regularly fell short. Nonetheless, he sometimes recognized his own inadequacies and was the smartest of the three.

The only one that showed any real promise, thought Kolikoff. The understanding that he had to teach them how to work the SPETS-VTOR if he didn't want to remain a one-man show was the only thing that stopped him from firing the lot of them.

He sighed heavily, speaking patiently, like a father to a child. "The SPETS-VTOR is only as good as its user. It can *not* interpret data that is flawed. You still must think, Pavel."

He waited, but seeing that there would be no flashes of brilliance forthcoming from any of his majors, he added, "Pavel . . . what is thirty miles from Fort Drum?"

Pavel turned back at the giant map on the large projected computer screen, squinted his eyes, and tapped his forefinger against his teeth in thought.

"Take your finger from your mouth and point to the *map*, man," said Kolikoff, his temper showing through.

There were chuckles around the room from the officers of the other headquarters organizations.

Pavel pointed to Fort Drum.

"Move your finger *up*, Pavel," said Kolikoff.

Pavel's finger traced a path north, past the Lake Ontario bays and into Canada, leaving a wet smudge on the big projected map.

"What is there, Major?"

"Canada, Comrade General . . ."

It was pretty clear Pavel didn't get the fact that Canada was the most likely source of weapons and ammo. Kolikoff wasn't even certain the man understood Canada was a separate country.

"Okay. That's enough for today," said Kolikoff. "Reconvene tomorrow for another intelligence and operations update. You are dismissed." The assembled men let out a collective sigh, then stood and milled around. Kolikoff worked on one of the SPETS-VTOR terminals while he listened to the officers talk about girls and the few bars and discos that had apparently opened in downtown D.C.

Things are becoming too routine, thought Kolikoff. *With the invasion behind us, the staff is becoming increasingly complacent with a comfortable occupation. Meanwhile, out there, our combatant forces are slowly losing ground to a growing insurgency.*

Dugway Military Proving Grounds
Salt Lake City, Utah

The forklift operator stopped and idled the engine but remained bolt upright in the operator's seat. His eyes, one of them swelling up fast, were fixed on the two men working the loading dock's crane. The forklift operator was dressed haphazardly in pajama bottoms, a winter parka, and snow boots. He had been ripped out of his bed only thirty minutes prior and ordered at gunpoint to follow. Now, he was trying with all his might not to look at the men who stood nearby with rifles trained on him and the two guys on the crane. The last time he had turned to stare at them, he'd received a pistol across his face from an angry Russian officer. An officer wearing black leather gloves and an odd pair of octagonal glasses. He was determined not to further provoke anyone's ire, especially the black-gloved officer supervising everything.

The guys on the crane were finishing up but looked to be behaving much the same as him, each hoping that concentrating on the task at hand would be enough to satisfy the Russians and that they would be left alone once the job was done. That's what they'd been promised, but the operator was starting to wonder if it was just a lie.

The crane men slowly lowered the last of the four cargoes they'd off-loaded that morning from the army loading dock. This time it was five special polymer barrels balanced on a wooden pallet. As the barrels touched down from the crane, the forklift operator increased the engine's revolutions per minute and drove forward, expertly loading and lifting the barrels. He then pivoted and swiftly drove back toward the depot and the awaiting Amtrak passenger train the Russians had apparently commandeered for some nefarious purpose. But he didn't get far before loud shouts came from behind him.

"*Stoyat'!* Halt, *Americanski!*" yelled a soldier.

He realized he'd moved out way too fast and came to an immediate stop. Too quick a stop, as it turned out. The polymer drums teetered precariously for a moment, their sloshing liquid cargo making them dance in tiny erratic circles on the wooden pallet as they bumped against one another. Apparently, the crane guys hadn't bothered to strap them down, such was their haste . . . and their fear. His eyes widened in horror that one might fall and burst open. If so much as one drop of their enormously toxic contents was released, he knew it would be instant death for him and everyone nearby. He had loaded and unloaded many such caustic and poisonous items before, but always wearing a hazmat suit, not PJs and a jacket.

After a moment, and to his relief, the barrels stopped their gyrations and settled themselves.

He'd been so focused on getting the job done as quickly as possible and not looking at the soldiers that he'd forgotten the unspoken procedure they'd developed for moving the barrels, vats, and crates that morning: wait for the Russian soldier.

The soldier panted up beside him, gave him a reproachful look, then stepped onto the pallet. This Russian soldier wasn't nearly as scary as the others. His look made the operator believe he didn't want to hurt him. It gave him hope that if he played by their rules, he just might survive this ordeal after all.

"Slow now . . . move slow, American," said the Russian, who now sat down on a barrel and stabilized the others with his legs.

The operator put the forklift into forward drive and continued toward the rail depot, much more slowly this time and keeping an eye on the soldier and the barrels. Even though it was literally below freezing, he felt a cold sweat break out on his brow and run down his back, soaking into his cotton pajama bottoms. It all felt like he was living in a nightmare. He chanced a glance at the soldier's AK-47 rifle and noticed what he believed were grenades strapped to the man's belt. He began to shiver, more from fright than the cold. The operator was young and had never before encountered imminent fear of death, and this new experience was beginning to slowly overwhelm him.

He drove the remaining fifty meters to the depot and up the loading ramp, then hoisted the barrels through the side door of the train's luggage car. In the relative darkness, he noticed the bespectacled Russian officer was standing there, watching him. A hand gloved in black leather rested on the grip of his holstered pistol.

He had just laid the barrels down gently inside the train when he heard the *pop-pop* of gunfire behind him. Unable to control himself, practically at his wits end, he twisted around in the seat just in time to see both crane operators tumble face forward off the warehouse loading dock. Each man had obviously been shot in the back of the head.

"*Vy duraki*! You fools!" yelled the officer in Russian.

The operator didn't understand the words, but this was the same scary Russian officer who had slapped him and had also been there when he and his roommates were dragged from their beds. That was when he'd first noticed the officer's weird wire glasses. He had held a printed list and asked for him by name. He coolly confirmed his ID badge and credentials, then hustled all of them here to the restricted army biological storage area. The operator wasn't inclined to think the officer was saying anything that could be good for him.

"Now you must drag the bodies here to the train. Remember, leave no trace," said the officer, again in Russian.

The operator still couldn't understand a word he was saying, but it sounded even worse. Angrier, this time. The operator began to tremble uncontrollably, all but certain that he would be next. He could hear himself whining and crying, though it all felt like an out-of-body experience. He'd understood when he'd taken this job working at the top-secret Dugway military chemical facility that there were risks. The risks of being exposed to some of the world's deadliest and most caustic chemical and biological compounds. But he had been trained and prepared for those hazards, and the pay was good. Exceptional pay commensurate with the exceptional hazards, but he was still just a civilian in a backwoods part of the country, not a trained soldier. He'd never counted on this.

"*Pristreli etogo pridurka!* Shoot this fool," said the officer in Russian to the nearest soldier.

It was the way the words were spoken that sent the operator into convulsions. He fell out of the forklift and onto the loading dock, wailing, utterly lost in panic. The Russian soldier pulled his rifle around but hesitated, looking back at his officer, a tinge of mercy on his face.

"*Tvoyu mat'. Davay bez svideteley!* Damn you. No witnesses!" The officer drew his pistol anyway and approached the whimpering man.

Major Uintergrin of the Russian 27th Chem-Bio Brigade did not suffer fools or cowards lightly. He'd been given a mission of the utmost importance, and he knew it was life or death. Including his own death, if he didn't succeed. Or so his ultimate commander, General Grigor Tympkin, had told him and his colonel personally and pointedly. There had been no resistance getting the train, or really from anyone here in the sparsely populated western U.S., for that matter. Things were peaceful and looked to be returning somewhat to normal, albeit with Russian governors. But according to his information, things on the U.S. East Coast were not going quite as well.

"You must succeed, or the success of the entire invasion might be in question," Tympkin had told them.

No, to accomplish the mission, a few of these idiot Americans must die, he thought. There was no time for hesitation or reflection. He needed to be as tough as his infantry counterparts. He walked over to the forklift operator, raised his pistol, and shot him in the head.

CHAPTER 3

Russian Occupation Zone
Union, West Virginia

Marine Corps Lieutenant Colonel Tyce Asher looked over what remained of his demolished convoy, and his heart sank to its lowest level ever. The sun was rising now, and he could clearly see the blackened, bullet-and-shrapnel-riddled remains of pickups and SUVs. He picked his way slowly over the carnage. When he spotted a machine gun or rifle near a destroyed vehicle, he called out to one of his personnel to come retrieve it lest it fall into the wrong hands. In most cases so far, the fires from explosions and burning fuel had cooked off ammo in the chambers of their weapons, rendering them useless, but he didn't want whoever was coming to assess the damage to get any intel from their wrecked convoy.

"Sir." He heard a shout from two Marines a few yards ahead. "I have a dead body over here."

Tyce had told the troops to inform him immediately if anyone found human remains. He raced over to the area as quickly as he could. Pulling up next to the man, he looked down at the broken and burned mess that had once been one of his soldiers or Marines. He couldn't tell which.

"Hey Marine, let's use the term fallen angel," Tyce said, quietly.

He was well aware of the effect of calling out "dead bodies," but he also realized, probably too late, that his reprimand had just served to make the Marine feel worse. But like a sniper attack, he now saw everyone popping their heads up from where they were searching to take a look. A few wandered over. Most just wanted to help, but there was also a morbid curiosity to see if it was anyone they knew.

Not good for morale, thought Tyce, *but neither was getting smoked by Russian jets.*

Tyce heard a barking from way up near the front of the convoy. It was Trigger, the unit's trained Belgian Malinois military working dog. The only thing that was even somewhat lifting his dark spirits now was the loyal pooch. Trigger had been with the unit for years. He'd even experienced combat in Iraq and Afghanistan.

Tyce couldn't be certain how the convoy was hit, but he'd seen enough of his own forces' air strikes on Taliban and Iraqi insurgents to be pretty sure this was a coordinated Russian air attack. The worst part about it was the reminder that skies were no longer friendly. He'd grown up during a period of military service when they been taught that in just about every kind of U.S. conflict, they could count on owning the skies. The initial Russian surprise attacks had all but neutralized this advantage, at least as far as Tyce knew. He'd gotten a few reports from his men on long-range patrols of aerial dogfights, but the reported outcomes had always seemed to end in a draw. It seemed that whatever American aviation was left was scarce, and the pilots had likely been ordered not to lose any aircraft. If only he could be as cautious. Fleeing when things looked grim wasn't in the cards for ground pounders.

Trigger's barking grew nearer and, in a flash, the dog sprinted his way around a few vehicles and found Tyce. He grabbed at Tyce's pocket and tugged a few times. Hard.

"Not now, Trigger," Tyce said, assuming the dog was going for the treats he kept there for times when Trigger was being a good boy.

He stared into the truck at the charred remains of two troops. His stomach churned, and his mind went through a flurry of thoughts. He reached in and felt across the man's neck. The man's throat was still hot from being burned alive, and parts of his skin collapsed under Tyce's touch, like a sooty log. It was terrible work, but it had to be done. Then, finding what he wanted, Tyce tugged upward on the metal chain. Reaching into his side pouch with his other hand, he pulled out a Leatherman tool and used it to clip the metal dog tag from around the fallen trooper's neck.

As he put the tag in his drop pouch, Trigger licked his hand, but Tyce batted him away and went back to work trying to find the second man's dog tag. A few Marines gathered nearby offered to do the work, but Tyce felt compelled to do the deed.

Once finished, he looked at both tags. Yep, he knew these men.

Shit . . . good men, he thought. *At least, they* were *good men, before I ordered them onto this mission.*

He tilted his head back and swallowed the emotions welling up inside. After all, he had personally ordered this mission. A pretty simple one, at least he thought it would be, to try and buy some meat and grain from farmers in the more rural parts of West Virginia and to get as much ammo as possible from a list of hardware and gun stores they'd compiled. Tyce nodded to the men waiting that they could now go to work pulling their fallen warriors out of the vehicle and looking for equipment. He walked off the road into the tall grass, lost in thought for a moment. Trigger followed him, barking and growling at him.

Navy Commander Victoria Remington appeared by his side. "Tyce . . . this is not your fault," she whispered when she was certain the men wouldn't overhear her.

Victoria was the unit's medical officer. A card-carrying Navy surgeon, she'd fled the D.C. area when the Russians invaded, looking to link up with the resistance—any resistance. She'd found Tyce and his mix-and-match outfit, most of them the remnant of the West Virginia National Guard 150th Cavalry Regiment. She brought two Navy ambulance Humvees with her, packed with supplies, drugs, and even a portable X-ray machine. She and her two corpsmen, kind of like nurses or surgical assistants all rolled into one, had proven their worth time and again.

"They knew the risks, and they did it all for the right reasons," she said quietly.

"Yeah," he grunted, trying to conceal his emotions. Her discretion was, of course, always appreciated. As was her sympathy with Tyce's seemingly perpetual penitence at any loss or injury among his troops. He was a fine leader, but he knew he took losses too personally. "Was this mission worth the risks?"

She didn't answer.

Tyce knelt down and petted the more than usually agitated Trigger. Holding the dog's head in his hands, he stroked his muzzle, which seemed to calm him a bit. "Find the wounded. There will be wounded. They may be unconscious, but my instincts tell me some *must* have survived."

Victoria looked at him dubiously but said nothing.

"The bombing patterns are uneven. They missed several vehicles altogether. Then your folks can go to work. Okay?" he said sounding hopeful. "I mean, you know, within the limits of your equipment."

What Victoria didn't bring from the naval hospital in D.C. she'd managed to scrounge up in the past few months. It wasn't a full surgery, by any means, but it was the best they could do. The Russians had locked down every major hospital and now controlled any and all drugs and pharmaceuticals. A prudent move that allowed them to control any mass casualties, and thereby literally stave off any organized resistance's ability to care for their wounded.

She looked up into Tyce's face. It was somber, and his eyes were full of sadness. "Tyce, you need to stop your . . ." She halted before she finished the sentence. She bent down with Tyce and started petting Trigger, who kept pulling his head away.

"I know, I know," Tyce said. He held a jumpy Trigger steady by his collar and changed the topic. "I'm pretty sure he understands as well as we do what happened here." Now wasn't the time or place for her empathy and understanding, as much as he probably needed it.

"Dogs are very perceptive," said Victoria. She tried to pet Trigger, but the dog broke free from Tyce and ran a few feet away. His ears back, he turned and looked at the two, splayed his forelegs, then returned and licked Victoria's hand, his ears back. "He's covered in soot. He's going to need a bath when we get back."

Victoria was an oddity to Tyce. Normally she was a very volatile and outspoken woman. Angry and loud at the drop of a hat. Yet he'd also experienced a deeply compassionate side to her. A mood she seemed to reserve for the operating table and the few intimate moments they'd shared without the knowledge of the unit. Any appearance of impropriety would be enough to stir some controversy in the unit, and Tyce just could not afford that. So they remained platonic and aloof, at least publicly. Still, it had happened. And Tyce was not unfeeling or uncaring, and he hoped they would share more time together.

Trigger ran forward, then back to the pair. He nipped Tyce when he held out his hand to pet him again.

"Ow! Damn it, Trigger," Tyce scolded the dog, who immediately dropped flat to the ground, his ears back and his eyes up. He stayed put, glancing sadly from Tyce to Victoria.

"Even Trigger's pissed with me," said Tyce. The last words came like a hiccup from deep in his throat as emotions got the better of him.

Thoughts he did not need right now swept through his mind. They were just more reasons he doubted his fitness to lead his men.

A better man would not so easily succumb to emotion, he thought. *He would remain focused on the mission and not let himself get so easily distracted.*

"Tyce . . ." Victoria reached to put her arm on his shoulder, then held back. "He's just agitated," she said. "He probably recognizes the scent of some of these guys."

"He couldn't possibly. Not even Staff Sergeant Diaz. Not amid all this ash and smoke," Tyce said, reaching out for Trigger once more, but at the mention of Diaz, the dog turned and raced away at top speed.

Tyce and Victoria stood, shaking their head at the dog as he ran off, and the two walked back toward the vehicle column. Everywhere they saw bomb craters and vehicles shredded by shrapnel or reduced to smoking hulks. Some were just metal shells, with only the engine or chassis discernable. They passed a few men searching through the high grass, sometimes calling out when they found a fallen comrade. Some of the fallen troops were found scattered through the field, caught in the open and sliced to bits by the bomb bursts, even though there were several likely spots that could have provided them some cover from the bomb's shrapnel—low ground, rocky outcroppings.

"Why did they run from cover?" asked Victoria.

"I don't know, Victoria. I know those . . . *knew* these men well. Some were experienced war vets, guys I served with in Iraq and Afghanistan. But I guess panic can do strange things to people."

The pair checked another destroyed vehicle and assisted the men in looking through the wreckage. Tyce collected the three dog tags and nodded to the men as they gathered up the remains.

"You all didn't train much to deal with Russian air attack," said Victoria, looking toward the front of the convoy where several vehicles were still burning. They could hear Trigger barking from up near them, and they walked slowly toward the front, surveying the damage as they went.

"Yeah, pretty much. Unless something drove them out of good cover, even in the face of Russian aircraft," said Tyce. His mind started thinking over other possible scenarios, and he glanced up at the hills around them.

"Hey, sir! Over here," came a voice from the lead vehicles. "It's Diaz . . . ah, I mean a fallen angel."

At the same time, several of Victoria's nurses rushed

up to her to let her know a few grievously wounded and unconscious men had been found.

"Shit. This is going to be a long morning," Tyce said, and they parted ways. Tyce headed to the front and Victoria back to check over the wounded.

Once at the front of the former convoy, the soldier pointed Tyce inside the vehicle. Trigger was once again by his side, yapping and nipping at Tyce's pocket. Tyce looked through the broken window and into the front passenger side of the shrapnel-pockmarked SUV. What was inside horrified him. It was Staff Sergeant Diaz. She lay in a heap atop the driver. Her face was a ghastly grey-white and frozen in a death gaze: eyes open and sallow, mouth agape, cheeks rigid. Her right arm was a mess of gore and blood just below the shoulder. Blood had sprayed all over the vehicle, covering the seats, the ceiling, and what was left of the spiderwebbed safety windows. Some of it must have come from the driver, but most was probably from Diaz's arm. Tyce glanced at the driver. He was mostly buried under Diaz, but he could see a giant chunk of shrapnel sticking out of his temple.

Lucky, at least he died quickly, thought Tyce. *Not so for Diaz*. From the looks of things, she probably died from massive blood loss.

"Hey, give me a hand," Tyce said to the soldier. They both tried to wrench the passenger's side door open. A foot-wide bomb crater about ten feet away had blasted what looked like a million steel shards into the SUV, sealing the door. They both gave a Herculean pull, and even Trigger got involved. They tried to shoo him, but he bit on to the door handle and pulled in unison with the men.

The door gave way on the final pull and jerked free

from its hinges. The two men and Trigger fell back in a heap from the door's release, but Tyce jumped back up and crawled into the vehicle to get a look at the woman he'd put in charge of this mission. He was going to personally recover his fallen infantrywoman. An infantrywoman whom Tyce respected as much for her combat skill as for her tenacious leadership.

He knelt over her, but his gaze was drawn to her terrible wound. Sickeningly, the lower three-fourths of her arm looked almost normal, strong and solid with muscle built by gym and hard work. What remained of a tattoo of a row of machine gun bullets crossed above her big bicep. At least, what had been her bicep. Through it was a hole the size of a tennis ball. Skin and sinew on either side of the hole were holding the arm roughly in place, but Tyce could see through it—nothing but shattered bone and flesh. He looked back at Diaz and supported her head in his hand for one last look. Her face was grey, like the ash in a fireplace.

"Damn it, Diaz," Tyce said quietly. "You know Gunny is going to be crushed . . . and probably furious with me."

That's when he noticed her lip quivering. Grunting sounds issued forth from her throat. Then she croaked, "Motherfu—"

"Oh my God!" Tyce exclaimed.

"Get off . . . my fucking leg . . . sir." Her voice was still just a scratching whisper.

Tyce's eyes grew wide in astonishment. He felt like he was looking into the face of the living dead. "Holy . . ." He pulled himself off her leg. Then, at the top of his lungs, he yelled, "Corpsman up! Quickly!"

The response to the battlefield cry for a corpsman in

the Marine Corps or Navy or a medic in the army was the same. Any corpsman or medic would sprint as fast as they could to the man yelling and render immediate aid. It gave the common soldier listening, a grunt, a mix of hope and dread: hope that the corpsman could fix their buddy, but dread that another casualty had been found. Sometimes it was easier to process a dead comrade rather than one who probably wouldn't make it.

In seconds, Victoria was there. She began dragging Tyce out of the vehicle.

"Outta the fucking way," she yelled. Any sense of familiarity between the two was gone. Back again was the Italian ball of fury.

Tyce leapt out of the SUV but remained nearby, watching as Victoria went in through the ripped door and took stock of the badly wounded but apparently still alive Marine Staff Sergeant. Another corpsman arrived, reached through the driver's side window opposite and jabbed an IV in Diaz's good arm. He connected a vein and held up a bag of saline, squeezing it to force the fluid in and replace the lost blood. Victoria sliced apart the remaining skin with medical shears, grabbed a tourniquet, and wrenched it around what remained of Diaz's upper arm, cinching it down tightly. She then tossed Diaz's severed arm out the broken window and ordered someone to help her get Diaz out of the vehicle. There was no saving the limb, but she might be able to save the patient.

"Asher, get me her blood type, now!" Victoria yelled at Tyce. Then, "Purvis, go get more saline and pull all the blood packs we have from the Humvee."

"We only have three bags in the cooler, ma'am."

"I'm aware. Bring it. Then get on the radio and relay back to base that we'll be coming in hot." She glanced at Tyce.

"Tell them an hour and a half," said Tyce, looking at his watch and hastily calculating their time to return to base.

"We have to leave now if we're going to save her and the others," she said to Tyce.

"Understood," said Tyce. The men had already loaded several other possible survivors. Tyce would remain behind and collect up the dead.

An army medic came over. "Ma'am, six is the count. Mostly burns and shrapnel. Some might make it if we hurry."

"Copy. Get saline in all of them, and load them up most A-S-A-fucking-P, you got me?"

"Ma'am!" he yelled as he ran to obey the order, grabbing four troops as he went as stretcher bearers.

Tyce turned to the nearest noncommissioned officer. This NCO was usually the most direct and forceful of the enlisted leaders. "Collapse the perimeter, except for mine and one other vehicle. Have everyone else assist in loading the wounded. Immediately!"

The last part wasn't needed, but with seemingly no resistance in the area, all of Tyce's troops needed to switch roles. Victoria's actions told him that time was now absolutely critical. That, and it had now become more than a little personal to him. Tyce tried to never show favoritism toward any of the troops, but Diaz had proven her worth in the direst of firefights, and he wasn't about to let her die after all the wounds she'd endured in today's attack.

"Hey, sir." Two of Tyce's reconnaissance men jogged over. They were holding a busted, mud-covered rifle.

"Whatcha got?" asked Tyce.

"Sir, over there, in that farm." The Marine pointed with the busted rifle. "The farmer and his son called us over. They could see the whole attack from the upper-story window of their farmhouse. They said they watched the sniper heading up into the hills from his position in the field, a few hours ago or more. They went over once they felt it was safe and found a sniper's hide position. That's where they found the rifle and some gear."

Tyce followed their pointing and saw the two farmers, a boy and his dad, standing at the edge of their farm. They seemed willing to provide info, just not to come over and get involved.

Prudent, thought Tyce. There was no telling if the sniper might seek retribution once Tyce and his unit left. As Tyce glanced at the hills, he could feel a prickling on the back of his neck as the hair stood up. It was very likely they were still being observed. A good sniper would take hours or even days getting into their positions, and probably hours to get away.

"Okay, we'll stick behind and see what else we can find out. If my guess is right, we had a one-man show. The sniper probably called in the whole air strike, took some shots, including on Staff Sergeant Diaz, then headed out."

"How do you know he was alone, sir?"

"If he wasn't, his buddy would be picking us off right now."

"The rifle is pretty badly damaged, sir. Looks like one of the Russian bombs landed a little too close. Take a look." He held up the rifle.

A three-inch shard of steel stuck out of the rifle's forward stock. The wood was split apart, and the barrel had peeled back and away.

Extremely lucky, Tyce thought. He pulled out some binoculars and looked about where the sniper had been. The sniper would have had perfect visibility down the

long axis of the convoy. Then Tyce spotted the bomb crater.
Or maybe extremely unlucky.

The sniper's position was more than five hundred
meters from the convoy. Normally this wouldn't be in the
line of fire from an air strike.

In any case, the rifle was now useless, but Tyce would
keep it to see if they could glean anything about this sniper.
If there was a proficient enemy sniper operating in their
area, they needed to know absolutely everything about
him. Tyce had fought sniper threats before in both Iraq and
Afghanistan. New units in combat were said to be taking
a "sniper lesson." It took great skill, battlefield intelligence,
and diligence. And woe to the unit that ignored a sniper
attack. The ones who tried to convince themselves that it
was just a onetime thing succumbed to the sniper's lesson
again and again. Most snipers were more than glad to
oblige a new unit's laziness.

Tyce watched Victoria race alongside Diaz as two
stretcher bearers carried her quickly to the ambulance.
Once they were rolling in the vehicle, Victoria had medical
shears in one hand and was snipping away at flesh; in her
other hand she had a set of clamps and was looking for
nerves and veins she'd have to tie up or cauterize. All of this
was going to happen while driving eighty miles per hour
down the paved but bumpy back roads to the 150th base
of operations at the Omni Homestead Resort just across
the border in Virginia.

Tyce helped another stretcher crew, then slammed the
back hatch of the medical Humvee shut. The others were
quickly loaded and raced away, with their escorts taking
positions at the front and the rear. Tyce watched them head
off. Then he turned to the remaining men, some of whom

were still keeping an eye on their perimeter. He called them all in to give them a hasty game plan: look around, find what you can. If they were lucky, they'd find some trace of the sniper.

"After all, a neutered sniper is now just another infantryman," Tyce said. "Better to get him now, before he gets ahold of another rifle."

His words seemed to encourage the men, lifting their spirits a bit and putting them back on the offensive. They needed it after witnessing what amounted to a smoldering catastrophe for the unit.

Nearby, up on an east-facing slope on the adjacent mountain, the sniper watched through a pair of heavy, long-range binoculars from the edge of a clearing. She nursed her still-numb left arm. Propping the binoculars up on her knee, she watched the leader of the unit. He and some men scoured the area, picking over her sniper position. Regrettably, they'd found her rifle.

Hmmm . . . she thought. *Either you are combat experienced and know I was alone, or you are exceedingly stupid. I wonder which one. No worries, I'll find out.*

She kept her binos trained on him. One of his men pulled her drag bag out of the weeds. She'd dumped all that wasn't necessary to get away, but now felt a deep sense of resentment at losing her kit and especially her rifle. Even if it was just a busted piece of junk, leaving it behind was contrary to her training. She scanned over the still-smoldering wreckage of the man's convoy, raising her spirits by admiring her handiwork.

Her lip curled in a sneer. *It was worth it*, she thought.

She massaged her arm; a prickly sensation was returning. She put the binoculars back on the leader and began her sniper's breathing regimen, consciously steadying her hand and body. Through her one blue and one brown eye, she fixated on him. She placed the binoculars' crosshair reticle on the man's forehead, just like she would her rifle scope.

"Bang!" she whispered.

CHAPTER 4

Russian Pentagon
Washington, D.C.

The Russians' morning ops-intel briefing was in full swing when a stir behind Kolikoff at the back of the room made everyone pivot to the rear. Four black-clad Russian special forces soldiers were trying to force their way in, while two of Kolikoff's administrative personnel fought a losing battle to bar their entrance.

One of the clerks held up his hand to try to physically stop the men. He'd been instructed by Kolikoff personally to prevent any intrusion into these operational planning meetings. To the shock of the gathered staff, the young soldier's obedience to orders gained him a swift AK-14 muzzle jab to the ribs. He crumpled to the floor in pain, and the men stepped over him, taking up positions at the four corners of the room. Kolikoff had been too slow to intervene—he knew who they were. The special body-guard of the Eastern U.S. district military commander, General Grigor Tympkin himself.

Kolikoff waved the remaining man to stand aside as Tympkin entered and surveyed the room.

"Ah." Tympkin beamed at the small crowd of army and air force officers. "Look at all these great minds working together. I take great faith knowing you gentlemen are inside the brains of our liberation operations. Planning our path to victory, eh men?"

Tympkin was constantly smiles and niceties in public, but in private, Kolikoff knew him to be a completely different beast.

The room snapped to attention, and Kolikoff gave the appropriate greeting. "Good morning, General. Russian Forces Staff Directorate for Occupation Operations reports all men accounted for. The situation continues as briefed."

"Does it?" Tympkin said, then waved his hand for the men to relax. "Very well, very well. One correction, though, Major General Kolikoff. We are to replace the term 'occupation.' From now on, you and your men are the American Liberation, Operations Directorate. Though you will still work directly for me and the Eastern Army."

Kolikoff wasn't surprised. He'd half expected the generals to start rearranging things after the initial invasion was successful. When a fight was going poorly and no reinforcements were forthcoming, the generals renamed and rearranged the pieces they owned. "Understood, General. We will make the change."

"Good. Now, General Kolikoff, release your men for a short break. I need to speak to you privately, and they look like they could use a hot coffee. Or one of those doughnuts outside the Pentagon mezzanine. I see we have brought several kiosks back online. Surely they are accepting the new American ruble we are paying the troops with these days. We need to show the capital that everything is returning to normal."

Kolikoff didn't have to give the order; the room was glad for a break. The three majors scooted out first, with the rest quickly following behind. On his way out, the stricken clerk's comrade collected up his buddy, who was still clutching his ribs.

Tympkin walked to the front of the room, studied the large map of the United States, and was silent for a moment. Seemingly unconsciously, he clasped and unclasped his hand rapidly, Kolikoff noticed. It was a worrisome tic Kolikoff had not seen before today.

"Viktor, I just got off the satellite radio with the 8th Guards commander. They are completely and utterly bogged down against the American 10th Mountain Division in New York. I cannot peel even a platoon away from them for other areas needing . . . pacification in our area of operations on the East Coast." Tympkin poked his finger at West Virginia, then ran it up and down the Allegheny Mountain Range a few times. "And this sideshow of circus freaks continues to be a giant fucking pain in my ass." His volume increased near the end, and he turned and glared at Kolikoff. "What does your computer tell us we should do?"

It seemed an easy way to enter into a conversation, but Kolikoff knew whenever Tympkin posed a question, there were usually several layers beneath the surface. Kolikoff had always known Tympkin was a very cold and calculating man, but seeing a glimpse of his raw rage was unusual. It was distinctly possible that Tympkin was suffering the ill effects of sending back poor reports to Moscow after many months of triumph. Kolikoff tried to put this notion out of his mind. Whatever Tympkin was, Kolikoff's fate was inextricably tied to his.

Kolikoff chose to answer cautiously. "Sir, there is no doubt about it. We must finish the 10th off quickly. If not, we risk much more, and we lose our foothold in the north. We have been working on this problem for some days now."

"Your SPETS-VTOR computer calculated their Fort Drum would be pacified sixty days after the initial invasion phase. We are now ten days past that and supposed to be beginning phase three, and there seems to be no end in sight."

When Tympkin was miffed about missed timetables, he enjoyed ridiculing Kolikoff and his computer. Kolikoff seemed to be quickly becoming Tympkin's favorite whipping boy, but he was confident the computer data was solid. It had paid off time and again. After all, the computer had accurately predicted the best infiltration routes for their special forces, the best targets to sabotage, and the best invasion corridors for their ships and planes. But Kolikoff had decided Tympkin liked loyal dogs more than he liked perfect plans.

Probably the prime reason he keeps me around, thought Kolikoff. He'd personally saved Kolikoff from a firing squad, so Kolikoff both owed and feared his boss. *Which is exactly the way he likes it*, he thought.

Kolikoff answered slowly and deliberately, "The 82nd Airborne should have cracked by now. They are, after all, only the last remnants of the unit: clerks, mailmen, warehouse personnel. The best part of their unit is deployed, stuck in the Middle East. What is left will not last long. When they are defeated, which we calculate will be within the next three months, we can free up the 58th to go support the battles in the North."

"So you're saying things are not as dire in the South as they seem?" Tympkin asked.

"No, sir," said Kolikoff.

"And in the North?"

"It is . . . more dire."

"Is that you speaking, or the computer?" Tympkin was getting annoyed again.

"The computer, sir," Kolikoff answered quickly. Maybe too quickly. It sounded like he was dodging any blame.

"Then you say the southern commander, the commander of the 58th, lies? He says he is making great headway against the 82nd Airborne Division in North Carolina."

"There remains the risk of the enemy 101st Airborne Division linking up—"

"Not my problem," Tympkin interrupted. "Central Army will have to deal with them, and he has all the forces he needs. Besides, 101st is just another airborne unit without their planes. Light infantry on the ground against our motorized rifle brigades will eventually lose. No, the critical battle is here"—he stabbed at Fort Drum—"and, as I've already said, our weakness is here." Tympkin pointed back to the Alleghenies, and his tone became very serious. "Any attempt we make to move forces across the region is spied upon. Every action is reported to U.S. conventional units and coordinated by their vice president. Our supplies and logistics cannot cross the region. How the whole East Coast is split in half by this region of inbred, nose-picking hillbillies remains a perpetual thorn up my ass, and I have shit left for forces to deal with them."

He pointed to major roads that crossed north and south. "Did you know we lost another convoy of food last week? And I'm not talking about a couple of oranges or a few boxes of damn Chex Mix. This was a full supply column. Picked apart and picked clean by these rebels." He took a moment to deliberately calm himself. "What does your SPETS-VTOR think of reducing this pocket of resistance?"

"We must . . . expand our activities in the middle for certain, Comrade General. Gain freedom of movement from Baltimore to D.C. and down to Norfolk and Atlanta. The middle is, as you say, the key to all that. But the threat from the American Center is minimal."

"Yes, agreed. Farther west from there is Central Army's responsibility, and not mine. But expand activities, you say? How? With what forces? I have committed all my forces everywhere else in my third of the U.S. Even your SPETS-VTOR did not predict this level of disruption outside the major population centers."

"I don't know, General. I guess . . . I guess I would need to tweak the variables in the SPETS-VTOR computer to see if there was another solution," said Kolikoff.

Suddenly Tympkin smiled, as if the answer had come to him. "No need, Viktor. I have a solution already. Three solutions, actually." He held up three fingers and winked.

The hasty turn of mood was enough to make Kolikoff wonder if Tympkin might have a latent and significant personality disorder. Then again, he'd once watched Tympkin throw a man out of a helicopter at several thousand feet in the air. Kolikoff had little doubt that he worked for one of the world's scariest and most-enabled megalomaniacs.

What conniving is he up to in his spare time, and how can I steer clear of it? he thought to himself.

"With a little help from your computer, the first and second solutions will clear the way. Then the third will mean we can crush the 10th Mountain and turn our attention to the growing problem in the southern states." Tympkin didn't explain further, instead turning toward the back of the room and holding wide his arms in a welcoming gesture. "Now, here are solutions one and two. My secret weapons."

Kolikoff had been so focused on his boss and the cryptic discussion that he had not noticed two shadowy figures who had edged in behind them. He turned and saw a woman and a man, both dressed in all-black camouflage uniforms. He recognized the male as Captain Shenkov, the highly trained Spetsnaz officer Tympkin used to solve tough and focused tactical problems. The woman was unfamiliar to him.

"General Kolikoff, you already remember the *wolf*, our Captain Christov Shenkov. But I'd like you to meet Major Stazia Van Andjörssen, code name Panther. I believe her skills will be more than adequate for the mission I have for you. What's more, she has already been operating in the Allegheny region."

The female gave a curt nod and stepped forward to salute. Kolikoff noticed she was quite pretty. He also noticed her eyes were two different colors.

Gorgeous, was his first impression, *but there is something sinister behind those eyes*. He found himself staring at her. The eyes stared back, unblinking. Kolikoff looked away.

"Stazia is one of our most polished products from the illustrious Directorate S. Her training with the SVR has been extensive," he said, referring to the Russian foreign intelligence services. "Stazia, list some of your skills for General Kolikoff, please."

"Yes, Comrade General." She came to attention. "I am rated category five in demolitions, two-tier in sabotage, and I'm a black belt in Systema," she said. That impressed Kolikoff. Systema was the Russian special service's secret martial arts program, dating back to the Cossacks. "And I am a fully trained sniper. But my main skills are infiltration and subversion."

"Tell him where you have been these past six years, Stazia."

"I have been here."

"Here?" said General Kolikoff, a little puzzled. "What is 'here?'"

"Here with the United States Navy."

"With the U.S. Navy?"

"*In* the U.S. Navy, actually."

Seeing that Kolikoff was thoroughly impressed and appropriately confused, Tympkin grinned and dismissed both special operators from the room.

Once they were gone, he queried Kolikoff, "You are curious about that one, no?" He smiled wickedly. "Our ace in the hole. Or one of them, I should say. Panther has been reporting on and sabotaging Naval forces from inside the U.S. Navy for quite some time. Born to a Finnish American mother and one of our deep cover agents stationed in South Africa. Her mom was the type, you know, bleeding heart trying to do good the world round. It was a cinch for her father to close the deal. I heard her mother never even knew he was an agent. With permission from her father, Stazia was turned very early in life by our SVR intelligence agency and given premier training in preparation for deep cover operations. She has been a sleeper agent for us, and so much more. She is irreplaceable. You will focus her and Christov on our West Virginia problems."

"What exactly will . . . *Panther* be doing for us?"

"She has already begun, Viktor. She ran a successful test operation in West Virginia aimed directly at an insurgent band. She personally wiped out about a company of their men."

"Sir, I already have tasked several special forces units to find and kill the American insurgents—"

"No, Viktor. She already found them. She will infiltrate directly into the enemy's organization. She will be your eyes and ears on the ground."

Kolikoff was disturbed for being kept in the dark, but eager to get to work. "I can use both agents as I see fit?"

"Yes, they are at your disposal. Use them wisely, especially Panther. By the way, her code name is actually named after the panther chameleon, a cold-blooded reptile evoking the careful, quiet, and adaptable hunter of the forest. It's very appropriate. Don't you think? She is a different breed, Viktor. Put her to good use."

"And Shenkov?"

"He is now your special action man. When Panther finds the enemy's lairs, you will use Shenkov to root them out. He can be merciless, I assure you." Tympkin patted Kolikoff on the shoulder and prepared to leave. "Now, put some of the SPETS-VTOR computing power behind those two and get to work. You have seven days to crush or subdue the enemy network in West Virginia."

Kolikoff gulped. "Seven days, Comrade General?"

"Yes. Seven. We will act decisively. Is there a problem?"

"No . . . sir," said Kolikoff, his eyes still wide with shock. "You mentioned a third solution?"

"I did. The third solution is already in motion, but don't you worry about that. It will solve many problems for us, later. Leave that part to me." Tympkin didn't seem interested in alleviating any of his subordinate's shock. He turned and left the room, his four personal guards in tow.

Kolikoff looked around the empty room. This third solution didn't sound good to him. Whatever it was, Tympkin's tone and hidden implications made it sound more malevolent than the other two. But right now, the thought of a deep spy, one who had actually enlisted in the U.S. Navy, made his stomach churn.

Majors Pavel, Drugov, and Quico entered the room cautiously and sat in the back, chomping unabashedly on tacos from the new kiosk while watched their boss pacing the room.

Infiltrators and spies . . . Kolikoff thought, then muttered an old phrase he'd been forced to memorize in secondary school many years before: "Give me an enemy at the gates, for he is known and carries his banner openly. But the traitor moves amongst those within the gate, through alleys and with sly whispers . . ." He raised his voice and wagged his finger in the air toward the majors as he finished what he remembered of the phrase, shocking the three into silence mid-bite.

"Meet me in the SPETS-VTOR operators' room in ten minutes," Kolikoff said. "We have a new mission." Kolikoff spat on the floor like he'd bitten into a chunk of something sour and pushed past the three men to leave the Pentagon and get some fresh air.

United States Federal "ADX Supermax" Penitentiary Florence, Colorado

Six truck drivers wearing parkas and heavy denim Carhartt jackets stomped their feet on the snow-covered cement and slapped their hands against their arms in an attempt to ward off the biting cold. Giant halogen floodlights bathed them and everything around in a brilliant harsh blue light. The men, their eighteen-wheeler semis, the massive ADX Florence supermax federal penitentiary's loading dock, and a Brink's armored truck stood out in stark contrast to the black night. The ADX prison facility was well known as America's strongest prison. It held high-profile convicts who posed too great a national security risk or had been designated too dangerous for an ordinary maximum-security prison. In short, the worst of the worst.

The steadily falling sleet left a thin, icy film on the big rigs' windshields, and for the third time that morning the men deliberated about who would clear it off. They'd been waiting for over an hour. No one knew when they would leave or even why the Russians had contracted them for the trip. The few things the Russians had told them: be prepared to go at a moment's notice, be prepared to go anywhere we tell you, and don't ask any questions. They were getting paid, and that was good enough.

"Rock, paper, scissors?" said one. They all gathered around and played the game.

The two losers grumbled openly but dutifully climbed up and went to work chiseling the frosted glass with heavy-duty scrapers. The remaining four huddled together and wondered what was coming next.

One man lit up a cigarette, inhaled deeply, and immediately drew greedy stares from the rest. After the Russian takeover, cigarettes, like everything else, had become an exceedingly scarce commodity.

"Hear 'bout them resistance fighters out east?" said the man with the cigarettes, jiggling the pack and staring inside. The last three stared back at him. He pondered saving them for himself, but after a moment's considera-tion, he offered them up to the others. He figured it far better to share them with a few Americans he'd just met that morning rather than lose them to the two Russians who'd been riding beside him in his truck's cab.

"Yeah," answered a man named Clark. He savored a

long drag and hissed the smoke out between his teeth. "It's not going to be enough." The others stared at him. Clark seemed to realize good conversation was the likely price of the free cigarette, so he continued, "I hired onto another Russian troop convoy from Denver airport last week. Watched them offload. They kept coming in. Must've been four or five thousand men. All soldiers, you know, fighting types headed up into the mountains. Headed to Colorado Springs, Calumet, and the like. I hear there are still some big holdouts up there, too."

News was as scarce as cigarettes, but traded more freely. All the other news they heard was strictly controlled, so, like during World War I and World War II, a good chat was the best way to get real news. If one didn't mind the occasional inaccuracy or embellishment.

"Air Force Academy kids?"

"Some," said Clark. "Also regular air force guys from down at Peterson."

"What about the army guys in Fort Carson?"

"I heard some Russian paratroopers rooted them out," said another.

"Most of them. A few army units went head-to-head with the Russians. They had us haul out a shit ton of wrecked gear at Fort Carson, and corpses . . ." said Clark.

"Soldiers? Ours?"

"Yeah. Ours and theirs. Mostly ours. Survivors went up into the mountains. Not sure how many were left," said Clark.

Everyone fell silent for a moment, lost in thought. Then the third man started, "Any idea where we're going next? Or what we're haulin' . . ." but he trailed off quickly as the prison's giant steel doors burst open and a swarm of Russian soldiers spilled out.

The squad of soldiers had their AK-47s up and at the ready, pointed in all directions, including at the truckers. Another squad emerged from behind the first, this group led by a man with strangely shaped glasses and black leather gloves. He escorted three men wearing orange prison jumpsuits. They put the men into an armored car. Then the Russian officer waved his pistol at the drivers and barked, "Get in and prepare to move trucks!"

The men quickly rubbed the lit tips of their cigarettes against snow-caked boots, stuck the remainder of the smokes into their pockets for later, and mounted up. Military escort vehicles slid to the front and back of the line of trucks. In minutes, Clark and the rest of the small convoy were on their way out past the three-strand barbed wire fence, through a sliding steel gate, over retractable vehicle barricades, and on toward Denver.

CHAPTER 5

Tucker County Courthouse
Parsons, West Virginia

Tyce and Gunny Dixon trooped up the wide, wooden stairs leading to Mayor Susanna Holly's office in the Tucker County Courthouse. Visiting Mayor Holly was definitely not the highlight of Tyce's weekly tour around the region. In fact, this week's tour couldn't have come at a worse time, what with everything that had happened that morning, but it had to be done. He usually checked in with police stations and fire departments, as well as several prominent citizens and leaders of the mountain counties. As the only representative of the former federal government in this neck of the woods, Tyce found that staying in touch with everyone kept him informed with goings-on as much as it gave his men a purpose for continuing to fight. A certitude that what they were doing was right and maybe reassured an uneasy populace.

With no intelligence coming down from a higher headquarters, his unit was running blind. Any and all local tidbits helped them stay ahead of the Russians. Mayor Holly was one of the only elected officials who had not run off into the hills or simply disappeared, like many leaders in the Russian occupation zones. His visits to the mayor often left him wondering how much she was actually collecting information on him, but she was the mayor, and she represented the people. And he led the last remaining fighting group in her county and pretty much her whole state, and as such, he needed her help. So . . . he sucked it up and tried to get through the meeting with a minimum amount of friction.

They spotted the sheriff, who looked like he'd been expecting them. A fat man with a big dip of tobacco stuck in his jaw. He opened the mayor's door and, with an awkward sort of grin, ushered them in.

"Did you and your boys forget to take off your muddy boots in the corridor again, Colonel?" said Mayor Susanna Holly before even turning around in her old wooden swivel chair. To Tyce, her syrupy sweet Southern drawl always seemed to mask a myriad of concealed motives.

"We . . . uh, yes, I guess we were in such a hurry we forgot," Tyce said.

Mayor Holly pivoted around in her chair to face Tyce. Well into her forties, she cut quite a dignified figure. Shortish and lithe, with flaming red hair and bright blue eyes. She had all the grace and charm of a Southern belle, but behind it all was a cunning that left no one wondering how she'd risen in the ranks of her town's politics. She was always well made up and looked the part of a professional politician, including a seemingly unending supply of designer suits perfectly tailored to show off her thin but tightly muscled body. Today it was a silvery pants-and-jacket combination with a wide-collared white blouse. Her perfect appearance always left Tyce feeling scuzzy about his own field-worn looks as a leader, yet also wondering how in the world she could possibly be getting dry cleaning done during a Russian occupation.

"Good morning, Colonel." She nodded to Tyce. "And

good morning, Gunny." She nodded to Tyce's right-hand man and the senior enlisted noncommissioned officer for the 150th, Gunnery Sergeant Trey Dixon. Tyce rarely went anywhere without Gunny. He was the eyes and ears of the unit and usually had a good idea of what issues might be most detrimental to morale. He was younger than Tyce by several years, but they'd served together in combat, and Tyce and Gunny had an implicit trust of one another.

"I see we do not have the prestigious Miss Doctor with us today?" she continued.

"Commander Remington is attending to, ah, some medical matters for the unit," Tyce said. He never brought Victoria to the meetings. She was usually too busy, and the two women—Victoria and Susannah—were like oil and water.

"Yes." She stared straight through Tyce with her penetrating blue eyes. "I hear you all took quite a sock in the mouth."

"Yes, unfortunately we were hit pretty hard." Tyce didn't need Mayor Holly reminding him of his failures, so he decided to skip straight to the point. "Ma'am, as you already know, this is not going to be a short occupation. If we want to get rid of the Russians, it's all hands on deck."

"I resent the implication, Colonel," she said dryly.

Gunny Dixon, who was perpetually at odds with Mayor Holly's wit, was quick to butt in, "I got nothing wrong with reminding the Honorable Mayor Holly that we're the ones doing all the fighting."

"And the dying," Mayor Holly said. Her face was impassive. She was a master of picking apart others' defenses. Neither man had a response, which was probably her plan, so she continued, "I am deeply sorry to hear about your misfortunes, but as your military textbooks have no doubt taught you, fortunes in war change from day to day." She gave a fleeting sorrowful look but quickly moved on, "To that point, today I may be the bearer of some of those changing fortunes. It seems a few friends of mine have recently come into possession of some extra materials. Some Russian groceries that were . . . let's just say *lost* up in the mountains."

Tyce and Gunny looked surprised. It was rare that she offered them something for nothing, but feeding the 150th was a chore in and of itself. Any and all supplies were welcome.

"It's a considerable amount, perhaps enough to feed your men for some months to come. Loads of dry goods, and even some fresh fruit and vegetables from Florida. You can pick it up from the sheriff and take it back down south to your valley when you're ready. Bring several supply trucks."

Tyce waited for the ask, but she said nothing further. "Well, thank you Mayor Holly. It's a very welcome thing. We've been low on everything for some time now."

"No trouble at all, darlings. Bye now," she said with her usual sweet smile.

Tyce and Gunny stood and bade her farewell. The sheriff was waiting for them outside the door. He handed each a broom and a dustpan to sweep up the mud cakes they'd left behind.

As they were about to go, Mayor Holly's voice called out from inside her office, "Colonel, if it isn't too much trouble, could you ask your man Mr. Blue to stop in sometime in the next two days? Thank you."

"Sure can do, ma'am. What's up?" Tyce said.

"I have need of his mountain man skills, if you don't mind sharing him for a day or two."

"I'll ask him to drop in," Tyce said. Gunny and Tyce looked at each other, shrugged, and headed out to the waiting Humvees.

"What's that all about?" Gunny asked, once they were in their vehicle.

"No idea, but a month's worth of fresh chow is worth the big guy stopping by to shoot the breeze with our fair Mayor. The men have been eating stale MREs, and the locals don't seem to appreciate us hunting the forests clean."

"Fresh fruit . . ." Gunny sighed. "Think about it, sir. Morale will go through the roof."

"Yeah, it can't do any harm." Tyce put on his helmet and gave a thumbs-up to the top turret gunner and the driver, and they sped off south toward the Omni Homestead Resort—their newest base.

Denver, Colorado

Other than their convoy, the streets of Denver were still mostly deserted. Fuel was in short supply, and anyone out driving had to go through numerous checkpoints and random roadblocks. The Russians made a big show of telling the citizens of Denver that they were free to move about, but few Coloradans had anywhere to go, and paying jobs were scarce. Most folks had been holed up in their houses out of fear since the Russian occupation began.

Their convoy passed a large fleet of armored trucks speeding in the opposite direction and slowed as they passed a car engulfed in flames, a group of Russian soldiers standing nearby. Clark shuddered when he spotted several corpses sprawled out on the asphalt.

As daylight rose and the convoy made its way into the

center of the city, they saw a few brave souls venturing out to join a Russian food distribution line. When they spotted Clark's trucks with its military escorts, some ducked into backstreets and alleys.

They traveled past the gold-domed capitol building, which was flying both the Russian and American flags, past the boarded-up Denver Art Museum, and then pulled through iron gates and into a small alleyway behind a big two-story concrete masonry building. The Russian soldiers signaled for the truckers to dismount, and the leaders met a small group of other Russians who emerged from the building. The truckers were left on their own and again clustered around the big man named Clark. They each carefully fished out what remained of their cigarettes. Clark produced a lighter and passed it around.

"What is this place?" asked one.

"It says U.S. Mint on the front," said Clark.

The men smoked quietly for a minute, pondering the implications of their stop and enjoying the remainder of the only tobacco they'd had for days.

"Did you guys catch who they pulled from the ADX?" Clark asked.

"No. Who was it?"

"I don't know. But I don't like the implications of what we're doing. First the ADX, then here. You know, there's some really sick bastards there," said Clark.

"Do you think it was mass murderers or something?"

"No idea," said Clark between drags, "but I'm not sure I like any of this."

"Well, I for one need the pay," said one. "I have a family, and we gotta eat more than what the food lines are giving."

"What should we do?" said another.

"I don't know, but I'm not sticking around to find out," said Clark.

Just then, the doors to the Mint opened, and the soldiers came out.

The truckers were given the command to load up, and several forklift operators began ferrying large, canvas-covered crates into the backs of their trucks. When they were done loading, forklifts included, the Russian soldiers jumped back into the trucks, and the convoy headed down the 16th Street Mall and then to Denver's Union Station, where a large Amtrak train was waiting.

The truckers dismounted and gathered together, watching as the prisoners were loaded and the forklifts went to work.

"What's next?" the men asked Clark.

"I don't know. But the soldiers in my truck had a mood change on the way over here," said Clark.

"Yeah? What do you think?"

"I really don't like the looks of that guy," said Clark, pointing to the Russian officer wearing black leather gloves and octagonal glasses. "I'm not sticking around."

"They'll stop you. Unless you're abandoning your truck."

"First chance I get."

CHAPTER 6

Omni Homestead Resort
Virginia

"Lieutenant Colonel Asher?"

A Marine Sergeant poked his head into the 150th's makeshift vehicle maintenance bay in what was usually a posh summer ballroom. Not immediately seeing his commander but spotting two soldiers and a Marine gathered around a Humvee, one side up on jacks, he stepped in and gingerly closed the antique cut-glass double French doors behind him and headed toward the vehicle.

"Colonel Asher . . . sir, you in here?"

"What's up, Sergeant B?" came a muffled voice from underneath the Humvee. Two maintenance sleds rolled out from under and across the ornate patterned ballroom floor. The man recognized the grease-and-oil-covered figure as his boss.

"Hey, sir, Staff Sergeant Adams sent me down. He says you're needed up in the CP." The command post, or CP, was the nerve center of any tactical unit. It held the radios, the maps, and a small staff of headquarters personnel who manned it all—including this messenger, Sergeant Berringer. Most were either radio operators or intelligence specialists. Berringer was the latter, and because of that, Tyce always liked getting his opinion on reconnaissance information and larger matters.

"Okay, let me clean up. How urgent?"

"He said ASAP, sir. It's a landline call from somewhere far."

Tyce had been taking his time putting on his prosthetic leg, but at the news from Berringer, he picked up his pace.

He tried not to sound too animated as he asked, "Who do you think it is, Devil Dog?" He used the Marine Corps nickname meaning brother warrior.

"Sir, I try not to listen in on that kind of stuff."

"Yeah, Berringer." Tyce rolled his eyes. "Talk me on target, Marine."

They both knew Berringer had the biggest ears in Tyce's unit. A regiment on paper, it was only a fraction of the real combat formation officially referred to as the 150th West Virginia Cavalry regiment. It was a proud unit with a history as old as the nation. It had collected battle streamers from the American Revolution, for driving Confederate troops out of West Virginia as a part of the Union in the Civil War, and in modern day was reorganized as a RSTA unit: Reconnaissance, Surveillance, and Target Acquisition.

"Well, sir, I didn't take the call. But I'd imagine since they grabbed Sergeant René from second platoon, they were talking to someone in French."

"Huh?" said Tyce, dropping a socket wrench into a standing toolbox and wiping his hands on a grease rag. "Someone from France?"

"Doubt it, sir," said Berringer. "It's past twenty-two hundred hours across the pond. My bet is Canada."

"Got it. The French-speaking part of Canada."

"Sir . . ." said Berringer, pointing behind Tyce. A pool of oil was steadily expanding out from where Tyce and Gunny Dixon had just been working on the vehicle.

"Shit!" Tyce sighed heavily, then looked at Gunny, who just shrugged and shook his head.

"Berringer," said Gunny, then pointed upward, giving him the silent order to get back to his post in the hotel's tower. Gunny didn't mind Tyce chatting up the men. They were glad to be in touch with their leader and more thankful he didn't mind getting himself dirty. He just didn't want them to start asking favors from the CO. Even the best troops sometimes got too familiar with the boss and started asking him for things.

"Sir, you go do your thing. Just remember, there's a reason we don't let you officers screw around with the vehicles."

Tyce frowned at him and was about to say something, then decided not to take Gunny's bait and just shook his head, mouthing the words "screw you." But he was glad to see the Russian invasion hadn't dampened the usual good-natured locker-room banter.

"A complaining Marine is a happy Marine, Gunny."

"Yeah, it's once they stop complaining that I know shit's gone to hell in a handbasket," Gunny said.

"Roger that. You just let me know when that is. Meanwhile," said Tyce, pointing at the growing oil slick with a smirk, "clean this shit up. I expect more from a Gunnery Sergeant of Marines."

"Me and the boys'll close her up. You go do officer shit for a while, sir."

* * *

Tyce had spent the morning patrolling with one of his units and the better part of the afternoon with his maintenance section, trapped under a few of the broken Humvees, trying to find out what he needed to somehow requisition once the opportunity presented itself. He'd found that his prosthetic leg bothered him less the more exercise he got and the busier he stayed. All this static sitting in a firm base really stiffened up his war injuries. Staying still for too long also gave him a more pronounced limp. This and the scar across his cheek embarrassed him to no end in front of the men. Both were earned in combat, but to Tyce, they were just more reminders of his physical limitations as their commander.

Two months ago, Tyce had led the troops in defeating a contingent of Russian forces, temporarily seizing Yeager Airport in Charlestown in a successful gambit to evacuate the vice president and what remained of the Cabinet of the United States to Canada. The victory had been short lived. Funerals for fallen soldiers and Marines had followed. Somber affairs with readings from Biblical verse, Thoric scripture, and a Buddhist rite ceremony. Tyce had learned a lot more about the diversity of his troops, but also had been struck by the realization that everyone and everything under his command was worn out or breaking down in some form or fashion.

Tyce could hear the sounds from the radio room and took a second to compose himself, catch his breath, and take a quick sip out of his resort-wear stainless steel coffee mug. He'd been careful to have his adjutant keep a ledger of what was "borrowed" from the hotel's gift shop.

Tyce walked in. "Who is it?"

"Sir, it's big-time. It's the Governor-General of Canada," said Adams.

"Holy . . ." Tyce was so taken aback, he almost broke his own rule to try to limit his profanity. He went to the phone and picked it up. "This is Colonel Asher."

They had a fairly old and rudimentary encryption set up to try to stop the Russians from listening in on the phone lines and satellites they now owned: a piece of machinery that they'd grabbed from another unit's devastated HQ. Canada had the same devices. Tyce just hoped the Russians didn't. It made the calls sound high-pitched and tinny, like the other party was talking from inside a can.

"Can you hear me, Colonel Asher? This is the Governor-General of Canada. I am standing here with your vice president. We wanted you to know that what we're about to tell you is of the utmost importance to both of our governments. Do I have your attention?"

"You do, uh, sir." Tyce was at a loss as to what one was supposed to call the Governor-General of Canada.

"Good. I'll put him on, but know that Canada is here to support the United States."

Tyce waited a moment, then the vice president came on. "Colonel Asher. We have gotten word from a man in Colorado that the Russians have hijacked a train and are headed to your vicinity."

"Yes, yes, Mr. Vice President." Tyce couldn't figure out what it had to do with him.

"On board are some very dangerous chemicals."

For some reason, Tyce thought of bleach and drain cleaner. "Yes, Mr. Vice President. What is this all about?"

"Have you heard of methylphosphonyl difluoride?"

"No, Mr. Vice President."

"Well, frankly, neither had I. But we own a shit ton of

the stuff. It's supposed to have all been destroyed, but I now know we were still in the process of getting rid of it all when the Russians hijacked some."

"I'm following."

"Good. Now here's the tricky part. All you need is some sodium fluoride and it becomes sarin or soman."

"The toothpaste stuff?" Tyce said.

"Basically, and some other chemical compounds I can't even pronounce. You've probably heard of sarin nerve gas, but soman gas is just as lethal . . ." The VP paused. "Yeah, I'm being told here by the Canadian specialist that soman can be even worse, you copy?"

"So the Russians are bringing nerve gas through West Virginia."

Tyce looked around the room. The men were only hearing one side of the conversation, but it was shocking enough to keep everyone quietly focused on his every word.

"It may be. We're not one hundred percent sure just yet. We wanted to reach out to you, though, because we're giving you a special mission. You're the most organized force I have in the mountains. We need you to intercept—that means stop with everything in your power—that train. I am counting on you to use your best judgment. This stuff can cause a *lot* of deaths. Excruciating and painful deaths."

Before he could ask, the VP voiced Tyce's next question. "You're wondering why they're using a train and not just flying or trucking the stuff. Might be the fear of Canadian air interdiction, might be they just don't trust American truckers. We're not sure of that, either. But they seem to have their reasons. Do you understand the mission?"

"Intercept a Russian chemical train."

"Add, 'don't fuck it up,' and that's it. What questions do you have for me?"

Tyce's began rattling off concerns at a rapid pace. "I guess, when and where? This just sounds so unusual to me. I should also say I'm not set up for any of this kind of thing. Why are they coming through here? What do you want me to do with the stuff once I get it, if I can even get my hands on it? Where are they going with it and what do they intend to do with it?"

"Colonel, I hear all that, and you and I have got some history. All I can say is I don't have all the answers just yet. We're still developing what we can. We'll let you know more as soon as *we* know more, but I need you and your men, Lieutenant Colonel. Whatever the Russians are up to, it simply reeks of evil intent. You must not fail. Do you understand?"

Tyce's voice was slow and cautious. "I . . . I understand, Mr. Vice President."

"Good. I didn't want to have to make it an order, and it sounds like you get the gravity of this thing, as I need you to. I'll be in touch very shortly." And the VP hung up.

"You just got handed a whopper," said Sergeant Berringer.

"*We* just got handed a whopper," said Tyce, staring off into space and lost in thought about the possible ramifications of his newest, oddest assignment.

"With cheese," said a feeble voice from the corner of the high tower's communication room. It was retired Brigadier General Lawton Custis, the unit's resident Sun-Tzu and Patton all rolled into one. He had attached himself to their unit after he and his close friend Bill Degata fled Virginia. Lawton had been blinded by a tactical nuclear blast that demolished his town of Danville and everyone in it. He had no home or job, but he did have a head full of knowledge of history's famous battles from Marathon to Waterloo in addition to his own practical experiences leading Airborne Rangers in the Gulf War and the first half of America's wars in Iraq and Afghanistan.

Tyce hadn't seen General Custis for a few days. He'd told Tyce after their last battle that he felt his age creeping up on him and was going to ask Bill to help him scrounge up some books, but Tyce and Victoria suspected there was something more. Tyce thought he might be struggling with losing his wife and home. Most of the men had no idea what was happening to their hometowns, but General Custis had watched it all go up in flames. Literally. He'd stared directly into the nuclear blast, and it had been the last thing he'd ever seen.

Tyce couldn't figure out which was worse: not knowing or seeing your town turn into a fireball. Regardless, Tyce felt like the 150th was the beneficiary. The General gave sage advice, which Tyce listened to and learned from. It seemed Custis also enjoyed doing something, even if that just mean helping Tyce navigate the same tricky terrain trodden by warriors of a thousand years ago. He sat down with the general and talked while Sergeant Berringer brewed up a fresh pot of coffee.

Chapter 7

Russian Pentagon
Washington, D.C.

"Here," said General Kolikoff, looking at a map of western Virginia. He pointed to Hot Springs, Virginia. "There's a hotel there"—he looked closely at the map—"looks like it's called the . . . Omni Resort Hotel."

Kolikoff and his staff had spread out an array of maps and printouts produced by the SPETS-VTOR computer. It had been a real feat, plugging in all the variables for the mountain state of West Virginia and every known or suspected American insurgent movement, suspicious radio call, or attack on a Russian unit.

The reams of data were indecipherable junk to most, but Kolikoff and his majors had become more attuned to the summations the SPETS-VTOR produced. The other various military staff officers who had taken up residence in the Russian-occupied Pentagon thought Kolikoff's process looked more like fortune-telling than the intelligence analysis his staff was supposed to be producing. They began calling Kolikoff "Rasputin" and his staff "the mystics," but since his calculations were often correct, they never said anything to their faces—and certainly not around General Tympkin.

"Sir, satellite and phone signal concentrations are not showing those areas as prime hotspots," said Major Quico.

"I know," said Kolikoff. "But I'm more convinced that the SPETS-VTOR computer is indicating something else unique at those spots, besides the most obvious calculations we see elsewhere. Something over here, and over here." He pointed to several different concentration of red dots on the map in the western mountains of Virginia. "This George Washington Forest is the perfect place to hide a small unit. The SPETS-VTOR sees some possibilities in that data, and it provides lots of covered routes in and out. Perfect for a band of scared, remnant soldiers and their mountain men buddies. They would remain unnoticed, even from our aircraft. The second spot is here, at Hot Springs, Virginia, by that big hotel."

"Would they really be living in a hotel, sir? It's not well camouflaged, and not easily defended. Not like a good spot deep in the woods," said Drugov.

"Unsure, but it certainly makes some sense, and the SPETS-VTOR calculates it as a possible location. It would give the Yankees a good place to rest, and there's probably food stocks there for hotel guests. The third spot is here at Goshen, Virginia. There are lots of old Boy Scout camps there. They'd be able to make use of their facilities, it's heavily wooded, and no one ever goes up there."

Major Pavel pushed Quico out of the way and, to the general's annoyance, crowded right up next to him. "Comrade General, these other printouts suggest something is being planned near Charleston. The SPETS-VTOR has analyzed radio and phone intercepts." He circled his finger around the capitol of West Virginia.

"I'm aware of that, Pavel," said the general, rolling his eyes. "But it's the capital. There's always going to be something happening there. There is often a lot of intelligence data near the big cities. Some of this will be insurgent activity. Just not the enemy 150th that we need to find and kill right now."

Pavel sat back down in his chair and grimaced. The General sat forward and pulled out a notebook emblazoned with the Russian Air Force logo and held it up. "Look, something about the dates and times we've gotten from our air force spot reports make me think there's more to the SPETS-VTOR data along the border." He pointed back to the same few spots on the map.

"Can we task a UAV to go look at them?" asked Major Drugov.

"We could, but sending unmanned air vehicles over suspected enemy targets will make them jumpy. We'd need multiple passes at all these locations because they'd be camouflaged in the woods or in this hotel. They'll spook and run. The enemy is watching the skies now, Drugov."

"A satellite, then?" asked Quico.

"It'd be a good idea, but everything of that magnitude is being used by our army commanders fighting in New York State and in the Carolinas or out West," said Kolikoff.

"What about getting the air force to do a moving target indicator sweep?" said Drugov hopefully.

"I thought our air force's moving target detection stuff was unreliable up in the mountains. They'd need some holes in the woods or some valleys to look into," said Pavel.

"Yes, you're right. Unless . . ." Kolikoff trailed off wearily. He was tired of his majors' speculations and the guesswork that went into intelligence analysis. He thought a minute more, then made a decision. "Okay, it's time to start a fishing expedition. We don't need to cast the net widely. The SPETS-VTOR has given us several locations, and I want to drop some hooks. We investigate these three locations: Washington Forest, Hot Springs, and Goshen. Call the air force and have them conduct moving target indicator sweeps of all three. My instincts tell me we're close."

"Something drastic, sir?" asked Pavel.

"Yes. I trust the SPETS-VTOR data on this, and I trust my gut. Call in the two Spetsnaz officers, Shenkov and, uh . . . that other one, Stazia Van Andjörssen. We must act now if we are to make Tympkin's time line. Time to let loose the dogs of war."

Omni Homestead Resort
Virginia

Gunny Dixon bent down by the Omni Resort's pool and slapped the water a few times to catch his boss's attention. Tyce had taken to swimming laps in the Olympic-length pool heated by hot springs very early every morning. It not only helped him wake up, it also kept the stiffness from his wounds to a minimum. Someone had tried to find the hotel pool staff, but to no avail. So Gunny designated a few of the troops "pool experts," and they reopened it for the troop's off-duty recreation and exercise. Thanks to these new experts, the troops reeked of chlorine all day and Tyce's cheek scar became more pronounced from the excessive chlorine, but at least everyone was getting exercise.

One of the mechanics had found a heavy-duty 3D printer. After adding in some stainless steel screws and bolts, plus a modicum of engineering, the men had presented Tyce with a swim leg. The thing had black, half-moon and curved plates of lightweight but durable black plastic. It looked like a lobster's tail as it extended behind him, pushing water then snapping back, but Tyce loved it— less for its function than for the men who had taken the time to make it for him.

"Sir, we have another request mast," said Gunny.

"Damn, what's wrong now, Gunny?" A 'request mast' was the right of every Marine to relate a grievance directly to their commander, but sometimes, it could be a pain in Tyce's ass.

Tyce pulled himself up at the side of the pool, undid the lobster tail, and grabbed his prosthetic leg. He buckled it on in one practiced motion. He tried not to look at anyone when he pulled the leg on or off. He was still too self-conscious. He hated more when someone offered to help him. Somewhere inside, he knew they were doing it because they respected him, but it still turned him beet red out of embarrassment and frustration.

"I know you're gonna be pissed, but it's not just one Marine. It's a platoon."

"A whole *platoon* wants to request mast?" Tyce could stomach a few disgruntled men, but this had been picking up steadily, and a whole platoon that was angry enough at their own bosses to ask to bypass them and talk directly to Tyce was more than unusual.

"First, another batch of mail came in last night. The units handed it all out this morning."

"Damn it, Gunny."

Tyce bristled. He awkwardly pulled himself up to a standing position. He had to do a clumsy squat, which he'd adapted in physical therapy, but it got him to his feet without anyone's assistance. Once he was eye level, he leaned in and gave Gunny a sharp look. "I thought I left standing orders to be informed when mail came in."

Gunnery Sergeant Dixon stood his ground, clenching and unclenching his jaw. "I know, sir. But you also gave me *specific* guidance that if I couldn't find you within a few hours of its arrival to distribute it. You said, and I quote, 'Gunny, don't ever let the mail sit more than two hours. Two fucking hours. Anything more, and we ruin morale.' But then you went on that damn scouting mission yesterday morning playing *Private* Asher when you were needed back here doing officer stuff."

Gunny was right, and Tyce knew it. He had been out patrolling with every unit in the 150th practically every day. They'd been fighting and hiding from Russians for many months, and he felt he had to show the men that he shared the dangers, but that also meant he sometimes shirked his duties as an officer. He stared at Gunny a moment, then sighed. "Yeah, you're right, Gunny." He put out his hand, and Gunny shook it. "I'm sorry I got on you. So what's the issue?"

He'd learned in his short career that admitting fault immediately was the only way to prevent the bad blood born of the close quarters required of fighting men. There was no loss of manliness in admitting when you were wrong, and it gave the troops a chance to live up to their own failures. A fighting organization had to remain honest. Many did not and succumbed to cults of personality in which no one confronted the boss when they made a bad decision, and then no one in the unit took ownership of their own failures.

Gunny softened his mood, too. "You have several squads, that amount to about a platoon's worth, who have finally heard back from their spouses. The scuttlebutt among the enlisted is that some of the men's wives are practically starving. They have no pay and are having to beg from neighbors."

"Damn," said Tyce, shaking his head. He picked up a towel and started to dry off. "I don't have an answer, Gunny."

"I know . . . and neither do I, sir. Our biggest dilemma is that we are perpetually getting smaller in numbers, and our enemy is bringing fresh troops ashore by the day. What we don't lose in combat, we lose through men just wanting to go back home for a visit. Patriotism isn't enough."

Tyce pulled on his cammie pants. "Yeah. Though I'm not sure I agree with that last part, Gunny. There's plenty enough patriotism and courage to go around here in the 150th. In fact, it's probably harder to jump ship for a while, turning your back on your buddy and then going home to face a family who is scared to death and never really knows when you might die."

"We live in a blackout, sir. Not enough comms with the outside world or even other organized resistance to know if we're doing what's right. Just where the Russians would want us. Far easier to understand defending your homestead than it is sticking around a rapidly deteriorating military unit."

"Yes, but we can't let the Russians know that. Remember in Iraq when the enemy kept us guessing? We never fully understood their shadow-government structure, or even their own remnant military who fought us from the shadows. I'm not sure we'll know the larger picture of all this until the war is over."

"It was the same for our grandparents in World War II. My great uncle said the only time he ever saw a map was when they prepared for the Iwo Jima landing. Even then, he said he didn't understand at all what the symbols on the map meant."

"He had a shitty officer. That's something we've fixed in the 150th. You know that. Our weekly briefing to the commanders and NCOs gives them the straight picture. I even have the intel folks giving them what news we know around the world. I even told them France and Germany issued Russia an ultimatum—that should give them hope."

"What about all the other countries?" Gunny shook his head. "And anyway, knowing what's happening on the world stage doesn't tell them what's happening in their homes. With their families, their buddies, and their neighbors. There's a greater comfort in those things than their boss standing up in a conference room and telling them that the French are promising to avenge us someday."

Tyce scratched absently at his prosthetic leg. Victoria said it was called phantom limb syndrome when a person could still feel pain, itching, heat, and cold in the lost limb. The body might give, but the mind and heart didn't let go so easily.

"Jesus, Gunny, there's only so much we can do. What *can* we do? Desertions are going to keep going up."

"I don't know, sir. I have no clue what will cure this other than sending kids back home to check on loved ones and giving them enough time and resources to do it."

"A leave chit I can do, but if it's transportation or money you're talking about, we're running into a kind of bad area there."

"Hell of a way to run a war," Gunny said, and they both walked off to the hotel command center to see what new chaos the morning would bring.

CHAPTER 8

Omni Homestead Resort
Virginia

Captain Shenkov and three other Spetsnaz men crouched behind a fallen tree. The soldiers had their rifles in the crook of their shoulders and were scanning for signs of the Americans. Shenkov stared through his binoculars intently at the main tower of the Omni Homestead hotel. There was no activity to be seen, but it was still dark, predawn. His intelligence from Kolikoff suggested that besides an occasional patrol, the American partisans didn't really get active until about six every morning.

Sleeping in, my little bunnies? thought Shenkov. *The good life has made you complacent, hasn't it?*

"Wolf actual, Wolf actual, guns six and seven are placed and ready," came a whisper over the radio set, slightly audible in the otherwise still forest.

Shenkov held out his hand to the radioman for the receiver, but his eyes remained fixed through the binoculars at the tower, "This is Wolf, I acknowledge. Teams Anna and Boris commence attack now," said Shenkov. He loved that his call sign was short for steppe wolf, one of Russia's most skilled nomadic hunters.

He pulled his AK-19 off the log, checked it over, and stood cautiously. Glancing back, he made a lifting gesture with his hand. Behind him, the forest came alive as forty-five camouflaged men stood slowly, almost in unison. Once they were up, Shenkov set off, and they all proceeded toward the Omni.

After about one hundred and fifty meters, they reached an open area, and Shenkov ordered his men to take a knee as he grabbed the radio. "Anna and Boris, this is Wolf. I am in range. Give status."

"Anna is up," came Team A's response.

"Boris is up," came Team B's.

"Machine guns are now all up and ready."

"Okay, I shall lead the attack. Stick to your attack zones, and do not fire into someone else's zone. Attack now." Without looking back, Shenkov personally began the attack on the Omni. As soon as he broke free from the woods, machine guns positioned at key locations commenced fire, and all hell broke loose.

In the periphery, Shenkov could see teams Boris and Anna running toward the hotel, rifles up, a few of them firing, laying down an additional base of fire at the many hotel windows where they perceived movement or a threat. Shenkov himself was the first to the hotel. He glanced back briefly to see the men closing the short open area between the woods and their respective assault positions. Once they made it up to the hotel's brick wall, they stacked in groups of six and raced alongside the wall for protection. The machine guns were still going. Shattered glass and debris from upper-story windows rained down on them. Shenkov didn't let up. He led his group directly to the front entrance of the tower, pulled the pins on two grenades, kicked the doors in with a violent bang, and tossed them inside, waited for the explosions, then was the first to enter. The men followed directly behind.

A mile away, Tyce stared through his own binos at the Omni Hotel. They hadn't been really certain from which direction the Russians were going to come, so they'd picked a good spot with a lot of concealment on an embankment surrounded by woods. It worked, although at one point a long line of about sixty creeping Russians had gotten really close.

Hold your breath, Tyce thought at his men, but thankfully they were too well hidden, and there were too few of them to be noticed.

"Fuck," cursed Gunny quietly once they were past. "Let's not do that again."

"No, let's not," said Tyce. "Did we get any word on the main body?"

"Yes, sir. They all made it safely to the new location."

The voice of their newest addition piped up, "Maybe now you can finally tell me where that is," said Stacey, poking her head up from her own camouflaged position. "Now that we know my intel sources are solid," she added with a slight twist of her lips. The camouflage paint on her cheeks and neck did little to diminish her natural beauty or, of course, her alluring bicolored eyes.

Tyce was thankful when Stacey and two other sailors from Norfolk naval base had arrived and offered her services, including news of a Russian attack. The 150th had been lacking a decent intelligence officer. With attrition and desertion in his ranks Tyce had welcomed the occasional military refugee, mostly remnants from other units that had been destroyed or disbanded. They brought news of the larger fight and sometimes critical intelligence about the Russians. They'd set up a procedure to check them out and bring them into the fold but found some were just deserters from other units. Often they ate some food, got some rest, then drifted off after a few days.

"Well, I don't think I even know," said Tyce. "Our lead LAV scouts got some last-minute details from some locals and switched it last night while everyone was busy trying to squeeze out of here in every vehicle we could get running."

"And on foot," Gunny reminded him. "We'll have to wait until we get another radio call. Noon today is the scheduled time. We'll listen in, and hopefully all the lost sheep will, too. We barely avoided a panicked exodus. I don't think my pulse has returned to normal."

"Yeah. It's going to be a full day before we can hope to have everyone back together. I just hope the escape routes were diverse enough to throw off any airborne surveillance. Honestly, I was more worried in the hours it took to skedaddle than I have been in a long while."

"Nothing to worry about now, chief," said Stacey. The newcomer seemed completely composed. She stood and came over to Tyce, smiling broadly. "We live to fight another day." She set her carbine against the log and took a long sip from her canteen.

"Hopefully. Either way, any chance we have is due in large part to your timely tip, Petty Officer Van Andersson."

"It's my job . . . sir," she said, gently brushing some leaves off his shoulder. "It may be war, but we intel types still have our sources. I'm just glad we found your unit in time to warn you."

Gunny walked over to the other two cautiously, still glancing back at the ongoing activities down at the resort.

Occasionally they heard the report from a Russian rifle; they seemed to be searching all the rooms. Gunny pulled the magazine out of his rifle, checked it for the third time that morning, then popped it back in. "Right about now, they know they've missed us entirely."

"Yeah," said Tyce, "and it's only a matter of time before they start combing the area."

"I'd like to be more than one step ahead. This feels like we cut it a little close." Tyce gave a signal, and they gathered their rifles and radios and hiked over the mountain to the civilian Jeep Wrangler they'd stashed for their own getaway.

CHAPTER 9

Russian Pentagon
Washington, D.C.

"I don't understand the report, Captain Shenkov," said General Kolikoff sternly into the satellite radio handset. One of the majors turned a computer monitor toward Kolikoff, showing him the live UAV feed over the Omni Homestead.

There was a delay, then the radio emitted a pinging sound, and Shenkov's voice came in slightly garbled by the encryption devices that scrambled their signals. "They have been gone only a few hours . . . maybe less. Hard to tell. All the resort personnel are gone, too. We've interviewed some locals, but most are not talking."

Kolikoff watched his three majors crowding around the UAV screen. They could see Captain Shenkov's vehicles parked at the hotel and were watching some of his men milling around like it was a football game.

Only thing we're missing is popcorn, thought Kolikoff.

UAVs back in headquarters were dangerous. Staff personnel stayed glued to it, expectant, wanting to see some kind of action. It was rare to have a UAV up when and where you actually needed it, and when it did catch a firefight, it didn't tell the whole picture. Kolikoff much preferred to talk to someone on the ground.

"Listen, Shenkov, I need you to take the time to send me a solid report. How did this go so badly? The SPETS-VTOR calculated a seventy percent certainty that the signals in that location were coming from a large insurgent base of operations. How could they vanish so quickly?"

Kolikoff watched the majors staring transfixed, like moths, at the screen. *Damn machines can outthink half my officers. Hell of a way to run a war.*

Fort Morgan, Colorado

"Major Uintergrin, sir . . ."

The major had piles of paperwork spread neatly in front of him across the foldout desk. Uintergrin's roomette compartment was quite comfortable, by Russian standards. He carefully screwed the cap back onto his fountain pen and slowly turned toward the door to see one of his chemical soldiers standing there looking quite agitated.

"Yes. What is it?"

"Sir, we didn't want to wake the colonel. That is, we know you've given specific orders to inform you first, err . . . not to disturb him of any . . . well, issues."

"Yes."

"Well, sir . . ." the kid stammered.

Uintergrin could now see two other soldiers behind the first, both dancing nervously on their feet. He smiled a bit. He liked the fear factor. Served to keep the men in line, and insured he received any reports before his idiot Colonel.

"Out with it, man," Uintergrin barked.

"Sir, we've detected a . . . a . . . leak."

"Son of a . . ." Uintergrin stood quickly, tossing his papers onto his otherwise meticulously organized desk and grabbing his cap. "Show me this instant."

Uintergrin followed the three soldiers back through the train past the dining car—which was full of Russian soldiers having a smoke, all of whom stiffened and moved aside as he approached—through the passenger cars, all stuffed to the brim with soldiers in various stages of undress, laughing, and playing cards. Their chatter stopped as he entered a car and turned to murmurs once he'd gone. He and the three soldiers passed the observation car, too, where several soldiers had the entrance barred and locked. On spotting Uintergrin through the glass window, they unlocked the metal door.

The guard chief saluted him snappily and began to give a report: "Sergeant of the guard reports the guests are—"

"Not now," said Uintergrin, pushing past them and to the back of the car. There, he and the chemical soldier donned orange hazmat suits over their uniforms and carefully inspected each other for leaks before opening the door. They closed and locked the observation car behind them. Here, the cold air rushed freely through the passageway to the baggage compartment as the train rushed forward at almost sixty miles per hour, chilling the men even in their rubber suits. The synthetic, flexible fabric that usually kept the heat in between cars had been stripped away, making a kind of open-air breezeway between the observation car and what had once been the baggage compartment.

Uintergrin led the way and knocked vigorously on the next car. There was no window to this car, only a large steel door with a heavy bar lock. After a few moments, the big steel door slid open, and another chemical soldier, likewise dressed in a hazmat suit, ushered them in. He slammed the door behind them and without a word led them through a portable military decontamination chamber, then to the rear of the compartment, where plastic barrels and several steel crates were stacked and held securely to the floor with metal straps. The soldier held an electronic chemical "sniffer" up to one of the crates. The machine registered green, but as they approached more closely, the lights turned yellow. He placed it next to a steel crate. The lights turned red, and a beeping alarm, barely audible to the men in the suits, went off.

Major Uintergrin nodded and ushered the men to follow him out. They closed the door, hosed themselves off, and changed out of the suits, then went into the observation car.

"What do we do, sir?"

"Toss the box," said Uintergrin.

"Just throw it over, out into the countryside?"

"Yes. We have plenty of the pralidoxime chloride. More than enough for us."

"What about the men of the 8th Guards? They will be in the sludge zone fighting the 10th Mountain men when we release the chemicals. Without a robust supply of the antidote, they will be killed along with the enemy."

"They will be fine. We should still have enough, as long as we don't have any more leaks."

"Leaks . . . leaks from what? Antidote for what?" came a voice in broken Russian. A man who had been sitting reading a book in one of the observation car's lounge seats—Mike, his name was—stood up and came over to Uintergrin and the men.

"None of your business," snapped Uintergrin, "Remain

calm and relax until we reach New York. You have nothing to do with this."

"I might not, but I know that the kid you brought with me from the ADX has something to do with the reason you keep putting on those chemical suits when you go back there."

"Mr. Mike, none of that is your concern. You just stay comfy and stay out of the way until we reach New York."

"You know, there was a time when your country needed me, very badly—the intelligence I supplied to you from deep inside the FBI shaped Russian operations globally for almost a decade. I was an important man in your country."

"And now? Now what? Now you are nothing to me. My government has agreed to get you out of jail and out of the country. I suppose we owe you that, but you have nothing to do with my other missions, and you will stay out of the way."

"I had a direct line to the Chairman—"

"And now you have a direct line to me. Each time you try my patience, I grow less interested in ferrying around a traitor."

The man bristled at the accusation. "I will bring this up with your colonel—"

"You will shut your fat trap," snapped Uintergrin. "And if you don't . . . you might just get lost on the way. I really don't think my government would miss you. Your usefulness to us has come and gone. Feel free to bring anything up to the colonel you like. I am sure you'll find out that he does nothing without my say-so, anyhow."

Uintergrin realized he'd said too much. The soldiers in the compartment were very familiar with the broken relationship between their colonel and Major Uintergrin, but they'd never heard it directly from the man himself. Still, if it was open insubordination, there was very little they would do about it except gossip. They'd all watched the two men interact, and they knew Uintergrin was really the one who wielded the power.

"Now," Uintergrin continued, more calmly, "I suggest you go back to reading your Lenin or Trotsky or whatever is making you dream of the halcyon days of the Soviet Union. I have much more pressing issues to deal with."

Uintergrin pushed Mike back and strode confidently from the car and back to his quarters.

At just past eight the next morning, the train left Colorado and entered Kansas, and Colonel Karataev stepped into Uintergrin's compartment. He was wearing a pajama top and sweatpants and sipping coffee from a Styrofoam cup.

He entered and looked over Uintergrin's shoulder. "Are all those chemical equations for the mixtures?"

"No," said Uintergrin without looking up.

"Ah, okay." The Colonel fell silent and watched Uintergrin scribbling on several charts. Uintergrin circled an Upstate New York rail depot on a map and measured the distance to another point with a ruler.

"I heard some commotion last night outside my quarters. Anything we need to worry about?"

"No."

"Okay, sounds good," said the colonel, continuing to try to engage in small talk. "The boys found some more movies. Even some old war pics. Have you heard of *The Good Soldier*, or something?"

"No," said Uintergrin.

The colonel could see his major was busy. "Well, I'll be in my quarters if you need me," said the colonel, drinking his coffee.

"Okay," said Uintergrin, not once turning around to acknowledge his superior.

Tucker County High School
West Virginia

Victoria opened the exam room door and handed First Sergeant Hull a small prescription slip for a pharmacy in Elkins, West Virginia, she had made a deal with.

"Mostly don't scratch at the area," she said. Then, realizing there were people walking past, she quickly added, "Shingles are totally normal, First Sergeant, even at your young age."

She didn't need to mention it, but she also knew that even with a war going on, people would talk. Especially in such a small unit, and especially overhearing people's private medical diagnoses. There were no secrets that stayed secret long in a tight unit. Just that morning she had to tell two of her medical personnel to stop gabbing about some barracks romance that had developed.

"Thanks, ma'am. No way to get this from your pharmacy, or whatever we're calling it?"

"Nope. Not until I restock somehow," said Victoria.

The 150th had taken over the Tucker County High School as their new base of operations. The school was perfect: the classrooms became barracks; the principal's office was both Tyce's headquarters and Victoria's medical facility; the gym was an excellent unit exercise area. For the most part they were invisible from Russian aircraft, and the school's remote location allowed them the ability to send out patrols freely and remain unnoticed.

"But they have our requests for medicine, and they'll work with us, though it's slow. They have to hide any *missing* medicine from the Russians. By the way, are you any relation to the old navy admiral?"

"Matter of fact, yes," said First Sergeant Hull. "I'm the dark sheep, the only guy in the family not to go into the navy. I owe you a family story next visit." Hull thanked her and walked off.

Victoria saw Petty Officer Stacey Van Andersson outside her office talking to Mr. Blue.

Blue was remarking on some kind of sniper rifle, his specialty. "So you want to shoot the Weatherby Mark V?"

"No, I prefer something bigger than yours. What I'd really like to fire is the Barrett .50 cal. That one makes really big holes in things." Stacey giggled, but Blue didn't seem to get the joke and remained impassive.

"Oh, I guess I'd rather have something that was accurate," he said.

Stacey just stared at him. Blue didn't have anything further to offer—he rarely had this much to say—so he nodded uncomfortably to both women and walked away.

Victoria hadn't wanted to interrupt, but the conversation between the unlikely match seemed to be over. She touched Stacey on the shoulder before she could walk away.

"Hey, sailor, welcome aboard by the way. I heard we had some new personnel arrive. You been avoiding the only other Naval personnel in the unit?" Victoria asked Stacey cheerily.

Stacey turned, a look of anger briefly flashing across her face, but it quickly passed. "No. I've been busy merging minds with the headquarters intelligence people and didn't want to bother the administrative and medical peeps."

If there was an insult there, Victoria didn't pause to address it. "Got it. Well, why don't you come in?" She stepped back and motioned for Stacey to come into her exam room.

"Um, I actually have to leave the comp—"

"I insist," Victoria interrupted. Then, seeing Stacey looking for another way out of the situation, she added, "If I have to make it an order, Petty Officer, I'm glad to." She gave the other woman a pleasant but authoritative smile.

Stacey entered the exam room stiffly and sat down hard on the school nurse's exam table. For the most part, the room was laid out exactly as Victoria was used to in a naval hospital and had come with a ready stock of the things she needed for the usual bumps and bruises, of which the troops had gotten plenty over the past few days in their new hideout.

Victoria closed the door and turned to face Stacey. "So, you doin' okay?" she asked, crossing her arms under her chest.

Victoria had been performing double duty as the battalion surgeon and counselor to the troops. Without an actual therapist with the unit, many of the small emotional issues the troops faced would otherwise go unanswered, and sometimes get worse—a legitimate problem, and the unit suddenly finding itself in more intimate quarters twenty-four seven added a lot of hair-raising new stresses.

"Yes. I'm fine," Stacey answered curtly.

"Good." Victoria could see Stacey was going to remain a closed case throughout the exam. She was used to it.

"When was your last breast exam?"

The question was blunt and instantly made things clinical, but Victoria also knew a certain sterile matter-of-factness was actually the only way to get some people to open up about their problems, both medical and psychological. Victoria needed to manage the care of the whole of the 150th. She also had an obligation to keep Tyce informed of the troops' stress levels. It was something she'd done for her other military commanders over the years. She might be oathbound to hide the truly personal medical matters, but at least she could provide a temperature gauge for the unit. After all, Tyce needed to use all the tools he could to know when the constant high levels of stress in the unit were about to head through the roof, as Victoria sometimes described it to him. He couldn't always do anything about it, but sometimes he shifted a worn-out platoon or company out of the patrolling and guard rotations and into training status. The little breathers seemed to help immensely.

"About a year ago."

"Okay. I need you to keep them up, sound good?" said Victoria, pulling on Stacey's wrist and checking her pulse.

Stacey bristled and pulled back her arm. "Look, if you medical types haven't noticed, we're in a war. I don't have the ti—"

"So first of all, Petty Officer, it's *ma'am*," Victoria interrupted sharply. Now it was her turn to become gruff. "Second of all, we all have to take care of ourselves. Or, just like our rifles and machine guns, we'll fail at the worst of times. It's called Prev-Med. We've been practicing it for years."

"Yes, ma'am, but there's a time and a place."

"You're right. There is." Victoria nodded. Then, leaning

over, she grabbed a pair of purple nitrile gloves from a drawer and pulled them on. "And now is the time."

"I get it . . . ma'am," said Stacey, her eyes narrowing a bit. "I'll make sure to let you know if I have any health issues."

"Good. Now, let me get a quick look at your eyes, ears, and throat." Victoria pulled an exam scope and rolled the chair over to look into Stacey's ears. She pulled down her lobe, then tried the small talk again. "Did you catch the basketball game between the army and Marines yesterday?"

"I *played* in the basketball game for the Marines yesterday . . . ma'am."

Victoria pivoted Stacey's head and peered into her other ear. "Oh, good. I'm glad you're staying fit."

"Yes. Yes, I am. I don't mind saying it's good to be around some athletic boys," Stacey said. Then she added with a small smirk, "Do you happen to know if the colonel is seeing anyone?"

Victoria remained expressionless. "Can you tilt your head back, please?"

Stacey complied, still smiling, and Victoria pushed the scope first into one nostril, then the other—both times perhaps a little more roughly than was necessary. Victoria pulled Stacey's chin downward and used a wooden tongue depressor and the scope to examine her throat.

Victoria sat back. "Hmmm . . . who did your tonsillectomy?"

"Uh, what?" Stacey said quickly. "It was done overseas. Why?"

"Well, frankly, they left a mess." Victoria pulled back and prepared to check Stacey's eyes.

"Oh," Stacey said dryly.

"There's a lot of scarring there. You must've bled a lot.

Any long-term complications? Do you have any troubles breathing?"

"No." It was clear Stacey was a woman who guarded her secrets closely and was not going to open up, or even warm up, anytime soon.

"Okay." Victoria held up a penlight. "Stare at the light, please. Follow it with your eyes." Victoria moved the pen, first checking Stacey's blue eye. "You have very unusual eyes."

"Yes," said Stacey. Then she adding toyingly, "The boys seem to admire them. All *kinds* of boys. You know what I mean?"

Victoria now shined the light into the brown eye and began moving the pen back and forth again. She stopped suddenly, pulled back, and narrowed her eyes at Stacey. Then she held the scope up and pointed the penlight directly into the blue eye, then back to the brown.

"Petty Officer Von An . . . um . . ."

"*Van* Andersson," Stacey corrected in a blasé tone.

"Yes." Victoria wheeled the chair back, a hint of genuine concern coming over her face. "When were you first diagnosed with polycoria?"

"Poly *what*?" Stacey said in shock. "I have heterochromia. Had it since birth."

"No, I said polycoria," Victoria chided. It was never easy to give bad news to a patient, even one as petulant as Stacey. Victoria went with her usual pattern: just drop the hammer. "I'm guessing this is the first time, then. It's a condition where you have more than one pupil in a single iris."

"I . . . I . . . what?" Stacey stammered.

"People with heterochromatic eyes—as much as the *boys*

might admire them—are much more prone to polycoria than others."

"What does that even mean?" Stacey said, trying to regain her composure.

"It means you have a pathological condition of the eye. One where your brown eye has begun to develop a second pupillary opening. If we don't correct it, it will get worse."

"Worse how?"

Stacey sounded almost angry, but Victoria had seen all sorts of reactions and continued. "At first, and possibly even now, I'd imagine, you develop some sensitivity to light. At least in your brown eye. Eventually, if we do nothing, you will lose all sight in that eye."

"I . . . well, how long does that take?"

"Years, maybe decades. There's really is no time line to polycoria, but it's best to correct it early in life. While at least some of the pupil can still be saved."

Stacey was silent a moment, and Victoria let her consider the ramifications.

"Do you . . . I mean, what does the operation entail?" Stacey asked.

"It's very complicated." Victoria pulled off the exam gloves and took out a patient form. She filled out the information from the exam, then handed the clipboard over to Stacey to fill in her personal data. "We're absolutely not equipped for that kind of thing here. You'd have to go to a much bigger hospital. One with specialists. If we weren't at war, I could recommend a few. Lord knows where all eye surgeons have gotten themselves off, too, though."

"So what should I do?"

"For now"—Victoria took the clipboard back, stood, and opened the door—"nothing. Keep me informed, and

I'll track its progress. Or retrogression, as the case may be. I'll see if I can contact someone I know back in D.C. when the time is right."

"Fine," said Stacey, and she walked out, shutting the door hard behind her.

CHAPTER 10

Tucker County High School
West Virginia

The school's speaker system crackled to life. "Iron Horse six, Iron Horse six, you're needed in the radio room."

Tyce looked up at the speaker, then back to Staff Sergeant Diaz. Her face was still grey and sunken. Now lying on the makeshift hospital bed hooked up to the tubes, machines, and wires Victoria had scrounged up with some help from the hospital in Elkins, she was thin and already looked like she'd lost a great deal of weight.

"Commander Remington says you're in line for one of those prosthetic limbs," said Tyce.

"Now ya gotta learn to shoot with your left arm," said Wynand, the unit's country boy and certified scrounger. Through rumors and innuendos, most of the troops had come to believe he was a smuggler, moonshiner, or petty thief before the war began. His comment earned him a nasty look from Diaz.

"What if we get you one of those claw thingies," suggested Gunny smiling and holding up spread fingers like an eagle's claw. His comment was the last straw. Diaz had had enough of the teasing, and she socked Gunny in his groin with the back of her hand—hard. It achieved the desired effect: Gunny doubled over, and the other two men's faces cringed in sympathetic pain. In the process, though, Diaz's wires came loose, and one of Victoria's machines started beeping loudly.

"Hey!" said Victoria from across the room. She hopped up from her desk and hustled over. She glared at Tyce, who was still chuckling at his friend's misfortune but was obviously glad to see Diaz was regaining her strength . . . and her temper. "I'd say visiting hours are just about over. *Che palle!*" She barked in Italian slang for them to stop being a pain.

"Agreed to whatever that means," said Gunny, regaining his composure enough to poke fun at Victoria's hand-me-down Italian. "And it sounds like you're needed topside, too, sir."

"All right. Well, you just listen to the doctor's orders, Diaz. That's an order."

"I got it, sir. It's all gonna be fine. Honestly, you jerks are more worried about it than I am. Did you ever find the piece of shrapnel that got my arm? I kinda wanna save it," she said, her thick Bronx accent coming out.

The other three got serious expressions on their faces. They still hadn't told her her injury had been from a sniper, and not the bomb that burst near her SUV. They had left her thinking she'd lost her arm to shrapnel. Better a nameless, faceless piece of metal than a sniper against whom Diaz would most certainly seek revenge—and they knew her well enough to know she'd be on this crusade in a heartbeat. No, they'd tell her later. For now, they needed their best machine gunner to heal up and get back to what she did best: leading heavy gunners.

"Uh, no. We weren't looking for that kind of thing, Diaz. Maybe ask Commander Remington if she pulled anything out of your arm," Gunny lied.

"Oh . . . too bad. I wanted to make a necklace outta it, a good luck charm." Her mood brightened, though she still looked weak from the blood loss and injury. "You know, if I own the piece of steel that has my name on it, at least I know there ain't another one."

Everyone giggled, glad she was at least able to joke around a little.

"I'll see what the boys can find. We left the vehicles there, but we've been in touch with the farmer nearby," Tyce lied.

Victoria frowned at both Tyce and Gunny and started pushing them both toward the door. Once they were away from Diaz, Victoria pulled Tyce aside.

Gunny noticed, but it looked like important boss talk so he nodded and said, "Sir, I'll meet you in radio. I'll let them know you're on your way." Then he left.

"Thanks, Gunny." Tyce he turned to Victoria. "What is it?"

"It's the general." Victoria pulled him farther away from the patient beds so even her nurses couldn't hear. "Look, I know you like having him around, getting his advice and all, but he's getting sicker by the day."

"I know. I've heard him coughing a lot more. But what can we do? He's been irradiated. I have no idea what you're supposed to do for radiation exposure."

"I know, but I've seen him about twice a week for nausea and vomiting."

"Is it getting that much worse?"

"Yes. And without the right kind of treatment, I don't think he'll make it to the end of the year. He'll die a very slow and painful death, his organs failing one by one."

"What do we do?"

"Well . . . there are a few things. They are by no means a

guarantee. I have been giving him table salt, for the iodide, to see if we could save his thyroid. It doesn't look like it's working. I need a medicine called Prussian blue." Victoria looked less than hopeful. "Then we need to put him on a cocktail of bisphosphonates, vitamin D, and calcitonin."

"Um, how do we do that?"

"We need to send someone out to get that medicine. They only have those at the big hospitals."

"Well, Victoria, with this thing being handed down from the vice president, I don't have anyone to spare for a mission like this. What happens if it doesn't work? Or they get captured?"

"If it doesn't work, we have to get an endocrine surgeon. Pull his thyroid out. And if that doesn't work, bone marrow transplant."

"Victoria . . ." Tyce would do almost anything for his men, including the general, but he didn't have the resources or the time to spare. "Look, none of my men would even have the slightest idea how to find that stuff, let alone whether it was even the right amount or whatever once they did. I'd bet even rooting around for that stuff would bring down significant heat. I'm sure the Russians have all that under lock and key, with a notice to tell *comradski* 'whoever' if we go looking for it."

"Yeah . . ." Victoria gave a hint of a smile. "I might have an idea, though. And it involves the general and I going out and getting access to the WVU hospital in Morgantown."

"What?" said Tyce incredulously. "It's an occupied town. Don't you remember, they captured it along with the airpor—"

"Just shut up for a minute. Look, I can use his sickness

and my credentials to gain access. Maybe track down a specialist to check over the general and pick up Diaz that prosthetic limb she needs. Then head over to the special meds department and pick up a bundle of the additional meds we need, including Prussian blue. *Figurati*, it's done."

"*Figu*-what? Look, how do we even know the general is up to the task?"

"Let's go ask him. But he's a warrior. He needs to get out for some air."

Tyce looked at Victoria dubiously as they went back to Diaz, who smiled as the two came back. She must've picked up part of their conversation about someone going on a special mission, and she seemed eager to sell herself for whatever got her out of the hospital the quickest. "Hey, look, Doc, I really think I need to be up and about more. You know, start training my left arm to be as good as my right was." She flexed her left arm in a curling motion. "Least I know bicep and tricep day in the gym is gonna be a whole lot easier." She laughed. Then, sensing Tyce was not happy with Victoria, she glanced between them. "What's up, you two?"

Just then, Stacey stepped into the room. Spotting Tyce, she walked over.

"Hey, *there* you are," she said, a little sugar apparent in her voice as she wagged her finger at him. "They sent me down to get you. You're needed in the radio room." Then she looked Diaz over. "What happened to you?" She pointed at Diaz's arm.

"Russian bomb. My arm got blown off over in Union Valley in that last mission."

"Hmm."

"Okay, I gotta go," Tyce said, nodding to Victoria.

"Present me with a plan, and as long as it works for everyone and there's minimal risk, I'll sign off on it. I'll tell you right now, though, you're taking someone else with you."

"We can fend for ourselves. But who did you have in mind?"

Tyce thought for a moment. "Bill, for one. To help with the general. And Wynand."

Diaz started, "That piece of sh—"

Tyce held up his hand to silence the debate, "Look, he knows the territory. He can shoot, and he's quick on his feet. Resourceful. And he can get you guys out of a jam."

Diaz blurted out, "That hick gets to go, but I'm stuck strapped to this bed?"

"Last I checked," Tyce said, "it isn't a discussion that involved you, Staff Sergeant. The good doctor here is not a gunslinger, and until you get healed up, you aren't gonna be slinging much lead, either." Tyce turned to Victoria. "He goes, and that's final. *Capisce*?"

Tyce left, and Victoria tried to explain to Diaz what was happening without raising her blood pressure. She didn't have the faintest clue how to run a mission like this, and she was planning to ask Diaz for some tips. She knew she could be trusted to give her some good but tough advice on how to deal with the boys.

Stacey was waiting for Tyce in the corridor and fell in next to him. "What was that all about? Are we seriously so hard up that we have to get that Spanglish girl's opinion on some mission?"

"Huh!" Tyce exclaimed, but he didn't have time to dig into the comment, "Let's get up to the radio room." Tyce had only known Stacey a short while and was surprised to hear such vitriol. He eyed her as they walked. "But, for the record, even in her condition I bet she'd whip most Russian Spetsnaz."

Stacey twisted up one side of her mouth. "I wouldn't be so sure about that."

Victoria waited until almost one in the morning, then poked her head out of the women's sleeping area. In the command post, the voices of two Marines on radio watch drifted out into the deserted corridor. Wearing her uniform but barefoot, she tiptoed past, boots in one hand, miniature bottles of scotch in the other. She could see the light still on in Tyce's room. She opened the door and peeked in. "What's up, *compagno*?"

A few hours later, Victoria's watch beeped, and she turned and pivoted out of bed. Tyce didn't move and appeared to be sleeping. She got up and looked at herself in his long, locker-style mirror. She tilted her chin up, made frowny faces, and grunted.

"What the hell are you doing?" Tyce said. One sleep deprived eye squinted at her, the other remained shut.

"Wondering how easy it is to be you. I figure if I just frown a bunch, grumble, and grimace at people, I could run this regiment, *niente di grave*. Simple."

"Is that right?" Tyce didn't understand the Italian, but he knew when he was being made fun of.

Victoria walked over and pulled Tyce's swim leg off the wall, where it was hanging suspended from a captured Russian RPG-7, a rocket-propelled grenade launcher. The launcher still had the high-explosives warhead attached. Tyce didn't really have a deep affinity for firearms like some of the gun-nut troopers, but he respected firearms, and especially the Russian RPG. Lord knew he'd had enough of them fired at him in both Iraq and Afghanistan.

She contemplated the thing a moment. "Isn't this thing dangerous to have inside a school?" She put her hands on her hips and looked back at Tyce, who was scratching at the scar on his cheek.

It was an old wound now, but it still itched. The cold, damp mountain air was making all his old wounds act up. This one was from an insurgent's razor-sharp knife across the cheek—the same man who dragged him down to the floor in a vicious hand-to-hand fight. By doing, so the insurgent had inadvertently saved Tyce's life. As the man slashed at his face, Tyce quickly rolled him so the man would absorb the majority of a grenade's blast. Tyce got a scar across his cheek and had his leg blown off.

"You know, hon—"

He stopped short, interrupting himself too late. He noticed Victoria narrow her eyes at him. Tyce saw it as a sweet term, but clearly their relationship hadn't advanced enough to include the use of cute diminutives.

"I ain't your fuckin' honey, honey," she said. But then, realizing her quick temper had probably killed the mood, she flapped Tyce's lobster-tail leg at him. "And if you can't behave yourself, I'm going to boil this thing up in butter."

"Victoria." Tyce smiled. "You're such a snob."

"Well, what do you expect? I come from a good family." The comment hung there a moment, the implication being Tyce did not. She tried to recover. "And family is important to me."

Tyce didn't respond. Victoria's Connecticut pedigree seemed to impress some, but Tyce was a little bit too much of a country boy to care about good breeding and cultured upbringing. In spite of her family, Tyce knew there was something about Victoria that just seemed to revel in first-rate verbal sparring.

A New Englander's attitude coupled with an Italian's temperament, thought Tyce, *and at times, such a firecracker.*

"You know what's interesting, Tyce?" Victoria said, moving back and sitting on the edge of the bed. They'd been seeing each other secretly for several months, and he thought by now he'd be used to her switching from antagonizing to affection at the drop of a hat. He wasn't. She reached up and traced his scar with her fingertip. "You never really talk about *your* home."

"That's right," he said smiling. "As far as you know, I'm married and have three kids."

She slapped him on the shoulder but was quick to point out, "You've never worn a ring. Or said you missed someone. *Cretino!*"

"You never asked," he said, and though he saw it coming, he didn't duck in time before a pillow came smacking down on his head. He pulled the pillow aside and glanced around it to see if it was safe. Victoria was still sitting there, her arms under her breasts and squinting one eye at him.

"If you're married, I'll fucking shoot you with that rocket."

Tyce laughed. "I suspect you would."

She flashed an impish smile. "Okay, it's time for twenty questions."

"Oh, crap. Hon—uh, Victoria, I have to get some sleep. I have shit to do tomorrow."

"Oh, and I don't?"

It never worked when he tried to call her bluff. She could out-argue him any day of the week. "Like what?"

"Don't get me started, *tipo*. For starters, tomorrow is sick call." She rolled her eyes. "I mean, for a supposedly tough, battle-hardened group of grunts, I sure have to nurse a lot of boo-boos and owies."

Tyce sighed. It was clear he wasn't getting out of this. It was time for the Q & A he had figured was going to happen someday, "Okay, shoot. What are we gonna talk about at three a.m.?"

She looked pensive. "How come you always clam up when I mention the war in Afghanistan and Iraq? You know I was there, too, with a lot of other tough ladies. Or is it just a Marine thing, and I'm too *navy* for you to share? I've seen it all. You know I spent a hell of a lot of time stitching up you Marines."

Tyce sighed again. So it was to going to be *that* kind of conversation. "Look, Victoria, what do you want to know? War is hell. I fought, I led men, I lost my leg. But it's all duty, and I believe in us. This. America." He gestured vaguely around him.

She rubbed her finger on his scar again, "I know, I know. But sometimes you seem so sad. So distant. I know there's other things troubling you."

"War." he said bluntly, "Then I . . . we . . . most of us come home, and our peace is shattered. Our government, our country, all turned upside down."

"Those aren't real answers." She looked into his eyes. "You don't have anything that scares you anymore, do you?" Her own pretty, deep-blue eyes remained fixed on his, awaiting an answer and ready to judge its truth.

"Sure I do."

"Like what."

"Like . . . like . . . I don't know. What scares you?"

"*Non c'è modo*, I asked you first."

Tyce couldn't escape her gaze, and what's more, he

liked it. He respected her opinion. So he answered, "There's probably too many to list, but I keep . . . I . . ." She leaned in and kissed him gently on the cheek, as if to say, *You're safe, you can tell me.* "I keep thinking I'll lose my leg in combat."

She looked puzzled and backed away. "What. The other one?"

"No, no . . ." Now he was embarrassed. "The one I already lost."

"I don't follow. You already lost it, so . . . *che cosa*?"

"I know, it's stupid." He tried to look away from her. "It's irrational."

"What the hell? Why would you be worried about that. That's so silly."

When she said it, Tyce knew it did sound rather silly. He knew it was foolish, yet something about his leg coming off in the middle of a battle terrified him. But he didn't want to talk about it anymore and tried to change the subject. "So what are you afraid of?"

"No, no. I'm sorry. I didn't mean to downplay your fear. It's just that, well"—she puffed her chest out and made the frowny face again, deepening her voice in imitation— "you're Colonel Tyce Asher."

"What's that supposed to mean?" he asked, scratching at the scar again.

"It means your men will follow you anywhere. Losing your prosthetic won't matter a hoot to those guys. They follow you because you kick ass." She bounced once on the bed lightheartedly.

"Well . . . I don't about that, but . . ." Tyce was still looking for a way to be done with this conversation. "You haven't answered *my* question, though."

Right as Tyce said this, someone knocked on the door. Tyce sprang up and threw on his camouflage pants while saying, "Yeah, what is it?"

A voice came through the door, "Colonel Asher. It's four a.m. You told me to come get you before your discussion with the leaders this morning."

Victoria dashed over behind the lockers. She was still only half clothed, and she knew the last thing that either of them needed was for one of the troops to find them together.

"Okay," yelled Tyce. "I'm coming now." He pulled on his T-shirt and camouflage button-up and was headed for the door when he turned and ran over to Victoria, kissing her quickly. "We'll talk more . . . we'll finish this later, promise." And he left.

Victoria collected her uniform and started to put it on. She needed to prepare for the very same meeting. She sat on the bed, tugging her boots on. "Leading," Victoria said in quiet answer to Tyce's disappearing form. "Leading men into battle."

CHAPTER 11

Tucker County High School
West Virginia

"Where, or better yet, *how*, do we intercept this train, sir?" Gunny asked, staring at the school's over-sized roll-down wall map of the U.S. "I mean, what the hell are we supposed to even do with it once we find it?"

The teachers' conference room was a pretty good command post. It had maps, office supplies, and plenty of reference material in the adjacent school library. Tyce had enjoyed their stay at the Omni Hotel, but now it finally felt like they had some practical resources and a tangible purpose to boot.

"Can't we just blast the thing?"

"Probably not a good idea," said the general from a corner, where he sat in a wheelchair with a blanket across his lap. Not walking much anymore, he was wheeled around by his friend Bill Degata. The general's eyes were watery, his voice was hoarse, and he looked frailer with each passing day. "Do you have any clue what's going to spill out and infect the water, the people, the crops? You might just be headed into a disaster worse than Union Carbide."

When no one responded to the general's reference, he

added, "Bhopal, India . . . 1982. Sixteen thousand killed, over five hundred thousand injured . . . Worst chemical spill in history."

"Ugh," said Gunny.

"How exactly is this our fight?" asked Captain Ned Blake. "I mean, shouldn't there be some kind of national task force? We're not equipped to secure chemical weapons."

"There is one," said the general. "It's called CBRNE, or more often NBC. Short for Nuclear, Biological, and Chemical response forces. Mostly National Guard, and even some Marine units in D.C."

"How is that any help? Because I swear, you ain't getting me in one of those biohazard hazmat suits," said Gunny.

Tyce shook his head at Gunny. "Whoever goes near that train brings suits. Every soldier, sailor, and Marine has one issued, and I'll want all that and gas masks on the gear list. We're not NBC guys, but we have good gear."

The general interjected, "It'd be better to get some NBC specialists. The training facility for the NBC national response force is right over near Charleston. What if you grabbed one or two of their specialists? You'd at least be on par with whatever knowledge the Russians have about this stuff."

Tyce looked at Gunny, the general, and then Ned.

"Oh no, sir," said Ned. "I can already tell where this is going. I know you like using me and my men for all kinda snoopy-poopy missions, but—" Ned stopped short and stared at the gathered leadership team of the 150th. They all stared back at him, and he sighed at their expressions, especially Tyce's set jaw and steel gaze. He had a "let's just get it done" look that the troops had come to understand meant the decision was made. "I'll get a squad together. When do I launch?"

"We gotta jump on this thing ASAP. According to the VP, we're the only organized unit that can even come close to dealing with it. Get out of here within the hour. Find and wake those NBC guys. Shouldn't be hard to find, since they're part of the West Virginia National Guard. One of the admin bubbas can probably track down their addresses. Then bring them back, and we can have them figure this whole thing out for us."

Ned and First Sergeant Hull didn't wait; they knew they could ask questions later. They grabbed their helmets and gloves off the table and went to organize their men.

"Well, that solves half our problem," said Tyce, "but we still are no closer to finding the train."

"Maybe you need to think like a Russian chemical officer. I can't imagine they'd put anyone on the case who wasn't trained to deal with this kind of thing."

The general often prodded Tyce and the others to think about their tactical problems. Tyce thought it meant he had all the answers. He didn't. But he did have a vast wealth of historic knowledge. Enough to get everyone thinking about the things they needed to focus on and usually adding some historic context that affirmed their decisions.

"Well, since I don't speak Russian and I know bupkiss about NBC," Gunny said sarcastically.

"Not sure you need either one of those, Gunnery Sergeant Dixon," said the general. For a minute, he sounded like his old self, the old army paratrooper and one-star general dealing with a doubter before a big mission. It was enough to get the Gunny to stiffen up a bit. "If you were carrying a chemical weapon across the United States, what would you worry about?"

"Insurgents. Us," said Gunny.

"Surely, but what I mean is do you cross through major towns? Cities, like Chicago."

"Not during the daytime," said Tyce. "Any kind of misstep, and you'd be accountable for a huge humanitarian disaster."

"Truly. And I am certain that's not their intent. They aim to use it just as the vice president said they would, on some U.S. military unit. Shorten the war."

"Could they be taking it out here to use on us?" asked Gunny, his eyes widening at the sudden realization.

"Doubt it," said Tyce. "Too tricky to use in the mountains, and we're just a small unit. Not a likely target when there are still big U.S. Army and other units fighting them. So for that, you'd stick to backwoods tracks."

"Yes. I am sure you would," said the general.

"You'd only travel at night," said Tyce, starting to get into the role of a Russian with a bunch of chemicals at his disposal. "You'd send reconnaissance ahead during the day. You'd use a civilian, unmarked train. Anything else, like big cargo or box cars, even bulk tanker cars, and people would think you were someone trying to smuggle food or fuel across the U.S. No one's moving much cargo these days, so you'd probably get overwhelmed by locals looking to help themselves."

"Now you're thinking," said the general.

"So if they came from somewhere out near California, went to Dugway through Utah and then to Denver"—Tyce picked up a wooden yardstick and traced the route slowly, pointing out the locations on the wall-sized map. The old school maps showed most of the major rail lines—"you're pretty much already stuck on the northern routes. Except maybe once you get farther east. I mean, just look at the northern routes. You'd be stuck going through Iowa, and from there you're locked into going through Chicago. You wouldn't want to do that."

"Ah, yes. All rail does lead east, then north and south," said the general, "So is there a southern route that goes somewhere off the beaten path?"

"Hmm. Well, there aren't that many crossover spots to go from the northern rail lines to the middle or southern rail lines," said Tyce as he and the others stepped in closer to examine the small train tracks that crisscrossed the map.

"Makes your job easier, doesn't it, Colonel Asher?"

"Yes." Tyce leaned the yardstick against his chin and drummed on it, contemplating the map. He pulled back and pointed with the stick. "Right here in Nebraska, you can cut through into Kansas and into Missouri on the Union Pacific lines."

"But we don't even know how far he's gotten," said Gunny, a little nervous that more doubt would provoke the general again.

"Well, I guess that's the question," said Tyce, looking up doubtfully.

"And that's the easiest thing you have to worry about," said the general. "That part is all just a question of mathematics, my boy."

Tyce looked at Gunny, who said, "Don't look at me, sir. You officers are supposed to be the ones with all the fancy college degrees and all."

Tyce pulled out a pencil and a notepad. "Let's see. Traveling at . . . I'm guessing fifty-five, maybe sixty-five miles per hour. Going eight, maybe nine hours a night, then stopping only in the middle of nowhere. Hmmm . . ."

he wrote out the arithmetic. "That's about four hundred eighty miles a day."

"Now add those calculations to their last known point," said the general.

"The vice president said the last spot anyone saw them last was two days ago in Denver. That puts them about . . . here." Tyce picked up the yardstick and put the tip on Louisville, Kentucky.

"Holy shit," said Gunny. "That's closer than I thought."

"Yeah. That's if you are avoiding Chicago and not taking the other populated routes. Pretty much all of Illinois, Indiana, and most of Ohio. Those are so full of American industry, and densely populated, as well. No chance you'd get through on any side tracks. You'd be lucky if there weren't a bunch of long trains still blocking the tracks, too, stuck there since the war began."

"Probably all picked clean by now," Gunny added.

"Exactly what our Russian train is trying to avoid," said Tyce.

"All of the United States is still divided up by the old rail networks," said the general. "What you've just figured out are the old Union Pacific to BNSF routes. Now your Russian chemical train—theoretically, at least—is entering the zone in which you find the Norfolk Southern routes." He was looking up in the air now, his sightless eyes staring into nothingness, but his knowledge was deep from years of school learning and thinking.

Damn, he's like a living Google, thought Tyce, suddenly wishing he'd paid better attention in high school.

"I guess I can see why the VP called us. We're pretty much the only thing in its path if they want to avoid all of America's rust belt and slip a train from the West Coast to the East Coast, then up the East Coast to New York."

"That is, if our math on the back of a napkin is even close. There's a huge gap in there for error," Gunny said. "Besides, why didn't the VP just tell us we were the only unit in its path?"

"If he knew, he would have. I'll bet he's half guessing too. Maybe even turning out other forces to our north and south to look for the train, too. Maybe the Canadians still have a satellite up. They used to have access, and might still have some back door. Who knows? But at least we can get the NBC guy and find out what to do."

"Yeah. Unless it's a huge waste of time and the train has already passed us," said Gunny. The general glanced in his direction, his white, sightless eyes giving Gunny the creeps.

"That math is inaccurate, but very close," interrupted a voice from the corner of the room. It was Stacey. She was behind a laptop and holding up her own notepad of scribbled notes. Everyone had pretty much forgotten she was there, but as one of the newly acquired intelligence chiefs for Tyce's unit, her early warning of an impending Russian attack had earned her a place in the headquarters. "I redid the math, and my numbers put the train east of Charleston, West Virginia. Tomorrow night."

"Holy shit," said Tyce. He went over and peered at Stacey's math. "I think she's right."

"So what are your orders, sir?" said Gunny. Like most senior enlisted men, he was glad to be a part of the figuring, but he recognized when the talk was over and the officers needed to just assign a mission.

Tyce looked around the room and at the disarray of maps and notes on the command post's central table. He came over and stared at the map for a second longer. "We ambush. Tomorrow night." He pointed to a spot on the map with the yardstick. "Look, there's a natural choke point here right at Huntington. One side of the train is against the Ohio River. If they have a force in front of them controlling the tracks or something, they can't switch tracks in this spot. Nowhere else to go."

"Hit the engine, sir? Cripple them?" said Gunny.

"Then pick them off as they come out. Avoid hitting any of the cars that might have the chemicals."

"Keep the ambush away from population centers if you can. Remember Bhopal," said the general.

"Right. Gunny, go tell Ned to wait up. We'll take his company and my 4th LAR guys."

Gunny sprinted off to tell Ned to prepare a larger force. The general, who till now had been really enjoying being back in the thick of things, gave in to a fit of rough coughing. Bill wheeled him out and back to the battalion aid station.

In the suddenly still room, Tyce sat for a moment, thinking about the steps that they needed to go through to prepare for the ambush.

Trigger had been lying nearby, and when the meeting broke up, he stood, his tail wagging hopefully. He trotted over and bumped purposefully against Tyce's leg. Tyce patted him on the head and focused on jotting down some notes. Equally as absently, he reached into his pocket, pulling out some stale gummy bears, Trigger's favorite treat. Trigger eagerly chewed on them, shaking slobber from his chin and onto the floor. Tyce stood and hurried off to his office to write up some orders. Trigger began to follow, then stopped to stare at the last person left in the room. Stacey was still there, silently listening and observing everyone's departure.

"What are you looking at, dog?" she said.

Trigger's tail halted mid-wag. He let out a low growl

and bared his teeth. Stacey kept her eyes on him, then picked up the yardstick. "Try it, dog, and I'll split your stupid muzzle in half."

Trigger didn't move. He just stared steadily at Stacey.

"Whatever, you stupid fleabag. I have places to be." She stood up slowly, keeping the yardstick trained on Trigger as she backed out the door.

CHAPTER 12

Russian Pentagon
Washington, D.C.

Pavel knocked on the open door to General Kolikoff's office and looked inside. The general sat in what was once a U.S. Army strategic planner's office. Maps and cross sections of tanks and fighting vehicles covered the wall. He was lost in concentration, staring at his SPETS-VTOR computer terminal, and didn't hear Pavel.

"General, it's time. Wolf and Panther have both arrived."

Kolikoff looked up, still lost in thought. "Ah, okay. How does she move around so quickly?," he said absently. Then he seemed to come alert. "Wait, what time is it?"

"It's time for your early meeting, sir. Both the Spetsnaz officers have arrived and are waiting in the Iron Room. They only have an hour before they have to leave again."

"Crap." Kolikoff glanced at his watch. He had spent the better part of the night tinkering with the West Virginia intelligence data and entering it into the SPETS-VTOR, so far with no discernable results. He grabbed a swig of his cold coffee, his fourth cup of the morning, and took a stack of folders, then raced off down the eerily empty Pentagon hallways and into the Iron Room.

When Kolikoff entered from the rear of the room, he

could see it was still a hive of activity. The 10th Mountain division had gotten ahold of a fresh stock of weapons and supplies and had managed to fend off two major offensives, and all the Russian intelligence services were trying to sort out how they'd gotten ahold of the weapons.

We should be focused on the enemy 10th Mountain in New York, not this West Virginia sideshow, thought Kolikoff. But General Tympkin ordered him to get rid of the 150th cavalry, and so far, nothing was working. *Maybe the Spetsnaz have some useful information.*

One of the staff held the door open for him to an antechamber off the main room that they were using as a hybrid command center for intelligence and special operations. Kolikoff walked in to see Captain Shenkov and two of his men lost in their own chatter, dressed in dirty field gear and uniforms and still armed. They'd been busy trying to track down every lead on the enemy 150th's whereabouts, including shaking down everyone in a ten-mile radius of the Omni, but to no avail. Shenkov had his muddy boots up on the desk. He started laughing at a crude joke one of his men cracked. Stazia sat at the opposite side of the room from Shenkov with her back turned and was typing on one of the SPETS-VTOR terminals. She looked like she could have been one of the Pentagon's former occupants just going about routine navy paperwork.

Maybe she even worked here, thought Kolikoff, and a chill went up his spine. He made a mental note to try to find a file on her.

Kolikoff walked around the room. He pulled the keyboard roughly away from Stazia and unplugged it from the computer. "Need to know only, agent Panther," he said. Then he walked over to his seat at the head of the table and started arranging his files. Without looking at Shenkov, he snapped his fingers and pointed downward. Shenkov and his men went silent, and Shenkov dropped his boots off the desk. He began to wipe some of the mud away, but it mostly just smeared across the desk's surface.

Kolikoff folded his hands on the table and looked up. "What good information do you have on your target?"

Shenkov was the first to speak up. "Not *good* news, but I do have something we've learned from the hunt."

"Yes, what is it?" Kolikoff had been spending twenty-hour days in his office, and his usually glum mood had grown even more so in the past days.

"We know the 150th Cavalry unit has moved back into West Virginia. Our sources place them somewhere in the northeast. We conducted an interrogation of some locals, and we believe they are operating out of a school. Maybe a high—"

"False!" interrupted Stazia.

Kolikoff shifted his gaze over to Stazia, but it was hard to maintain eye contact with her. "You have something for us?"

"Yes. They are in, or near, the capitol of West Virginia."

"Not according to my sources," said Shenkov.

Kolikoff quickly flipped through his SPETS-VTOR printouts and pulled out some data. "We did have some intelligence about schools. The computer placed a fairly high probability that the 150th would avoid big towns and gave a sixty-six percent chance they'd use a university or a school as a firm base. The only higher probability was that'd they'd use a coal mine or a mining shaft of some sort as a base of operations." Kolikoff paused for a second. "The data seems pretty good, Staz—er, Major Andjörssen. Why do you suggest otherwise?"

Shenkov interrupted before she could answer. "General, I am growing tired of SVR's input on tactical field problems. The SVR needs to go back to stealing computer data tapes and sleeping with politicians."

Stazia's face twisted into a snarl, but quickly faded as she gained control of her anger and said, "They will ambush General Tympkin's train tonight."

"What train?" said Kolikoff and Shenkov, almost in unison.

"General Tympkin has a train entering West Virginia tonight. It carries a top-secret cargo." She seemed to enjoy the fact that she knew something even Kolikoff didn't. "I just assumed you knew," she said, again the corner of her mouth curled up slightly. Shenkov looked so angry that she suspected that if she had been male, he most certainly would have gotten up and hit her.

Now it made sense, Kolikoff thought. *The reason for Tympkin's order to hurry it up, and why he only gave me seven days to pin down the 150th.*

"How the hell could you know this information?" said Shenkov.

"As you mentioned, the SVR is quite capable of gathering intelligence, and all of it without having to drop our panties. Or maybe worse . . . attack the wrong objective," she said.

Kolikoff didn't have time for what seemed to be a dangerous rivalry between his two top special forces agents. In any case, none of this intelligence, even if correct, changed the fact that he had less than forty-eight hours to stop the 150th. At least now he understood his objective better, though know there was the mystery of what Tympkin's train was all about. "Do we know where they will spring their ambush from?" Kolikoff said, holding a hand up to Shenkov, who had risen from his chair.

"Yes," Stazia responded. "Near Charleston and west of Huntington. Right on the tracks where it joins the river."

"At what time will they ambush?" asked Kolikoff. He again motioned for Shenkov to sit.

"Early evening. Sometime after dark. That's the limit of my intelligence," said Stazia.

Shenkov sat back down slowly but still looked unhinged. It was hard for Kolikoff to blame him. He was a field soldier and had clearly never spent much time around a headquarters. Fits of adrenaline were quite literally in his blood; as a member of the Russian Spetsgruppa V, known as Vympel, the elite of the elite, aggression had been rewarded and encouraged all his career.

No matter, thought Kolikoff. *We need all kinds if we're going to smash this band of hillbillies.*

"Okay. Both of you listen up." Kolikoff checked his watch. "At zero eight hundred hours. We will send you both as an intercept force. I want you to hit them so hard that they cannot interfere with the train and it gets through damned West Virginia. I will get you what air support I can muster."

"We couldn't possibly make it there in time," said Shenkov. "I wasted many hours even coming out of the hills to be here for this meeting."

"Shenkov, don't be thick. I will have you airlifted," said Kolikoff.

"My men?" he asked.

"The beauty of vertical lift, Comrade Shenkov. We'll have them picked up en route. Radio ahead and have them prepare. They can leave their gear and vehicles in a safe

spot. Take only what is necessary for an overnight ambush."
He turned to Stazia, who seemed more than a little pleased
to see Shenkov belittled by their boss. "Major, Captain
Shenkov will be the on-scene commander. That means, for
the purposes of this mission, you will fall under his authority. You are to be a support element and will provide some
sniping and overwatch."

Stazia whipped her head to look at Kolikoff, her blue
and brown eyes flashing her annoyance and her smile van-
ishing.

Kolikoff saw her expression and fired back, "Are my
instructions clear? You will be Shenkov's eyes and ears. I
expect you to provide him timely intelligence and target
acquisition. Acknowledge the order, Major."

This general knows what he's doing, Stazia thought. Her
mood dropped off, and she said in a dutiful tone, "I acknowledge and will obey, Comrade General." She straight-
ened up and saluted him.

Kolikoff nodded, then went over to one of the big gear
boxes piled up in the corner of the room. He returned with
six smallish devices. "These just arrived. They are the new
dual-purpose satellite comms devices and ID beacons.
With an unrestricted line of sight to the sky, we'll know
your position, and you can communicate just like texting
on a cell phone. I need you to take them and use them."
Both officers picked up a device from the table and looked
at it suspiciously. "Don't worry, the enemy sensors cannot
see them. They are specially coded to communicate with
our satellites and for your night vision devices so that our
aircraft can distinguish you from the enemy, and you from
one another." Kolikoff turned to face Shenkov. "Now, you.
Acknowledge the orders, Captain."

Shenkov stood and saluted crisply. "Acknowledged. We will succeed, Comrade General."

"Good." Kolikoff sighed. He hated to bully subordinates, but he had been at this game a lot longer than these kids, and though they were both clearly quite competent in their own domains, he knew a few tricks they had yet to learn. "We have no time to waste. Get moving. I'll expect to hear the tactical satellite radio nets alive with the two of you cross talking to accomplish this mission."

They both turned to leave, but Kolikoff stopped Stazia. "Major, what do you need to be successful? What plans to get to the objective?"

"None, Comrade General. I will drive there myself."

"How will you make it?"

"The same way I came here—completely incognito, and in my own way." Seeing a look of doubt cross the general's face, she added, "Do not worry, General, I will be at the objective early and ready for action."

The general nodded and went back to his SPETS-VTOR as Stazia made her way out. *Yes, I suspect you will*, Kolikoff thought, *and when you return, I will have to find out how you know what you know.* He thumbed his chin. *And remember to keep you as far away from my SPETS-VTOR as possible.*

CHAPTER 13

Outside Huntington, West Virginia

Tyce looked over the terrain through his binoculars. It was a near-perfect ambush position. Practically textbook. Ned's men were still finalizing their positions but were mostly arrayed in a tight fighting line below the ridge of a low hill, overlooking the river and facing due south. They could see the train tracks in full view while still remaining in the relatively dense wood line.

The train's full length will be in view. I guess, depending on their speed, we'll have plenty of time to pick our targets. There's direct fire dominance and good protection from observation. There's even some overhead protection, Tyce thought, evaluating the spot's strengths point by point. The woods were still barren from winter but provided thick cover. The men had set up deep enough to be partially obscured, but not so deep as to block their own fire, about five, maybe six meters in.

He looked up at the sky with some uncertainty. He never thought he'd live to see a day when he couldn't trust the sky. All his career, he'd fought under the auspices of U.S. aviation dominance. Not so anymore. He had seen precious few U.S. aircraft since the war began, and basically none in support of his operations. Most of what he had seen or his men had reported was moving extremely fast, and extremely low. Some of these phantom sightings were presumed to be remnants of the U.S. Air Force, but he would be getting no help from them tonight.

Well, since the Russians won't be expecting us—he lowered his binoculars to once again survey the terrain—*even after we attack, I doubt they can get any air response forces here in less than a few hours. I don't intend to stick around long enough to find out.*

Tyce reached down to pet Trigger, who had come panting up beside him. A second later, a Marine NCO came up behind Trigger and said, "He always knows how to find you, sir." Tyce waited and let the man catch his breath. Then the NCO finished, "That NBC guy just arrived. He wants to talk to you."

"Okay," said Tyce, shouldering his rifle and looking back to the small warehouse and boat repair shop near Ned's positions that they'd turned into a temporary HQ.

"Are you ready, Trigger?"

The dog looked up at him, but his tail wasn't wagging. Trigger had more time in combat than most of the men in the unit. He could smell the stress and feel the adrenaline, and he knew that when all his human buddies were working as fervently as this, things were about to go down. He raced in front of Tyce and the NCO as they wound their way back down the hill, looking into every shadow, his ears twitching forward and back as he listened intently to the forest.

A new unit from the 150th, Tyce's own Marine 4th Light Armored Reconnaissance, had arrived; their lieutenant and his men were awaiting a briefing directly from Tyce. Ned's forces had been the first here and, as the primary ambush force, had chosen the terrain. The LAR guys were there to support Ned but had stopped to fill up their LAV-25s, which looked a lot like tanks with wheels and had formidable 25mm cannons on their turrets.

"How are your pigs, Lieutenant Bryce?" asked Tyce.

"LAVs are topped off for fuel, sir, and we have four uploads. Two HE and AT apiece," said the young, fair-haired kid from Nebraska. The HE stood for high explosive and the AT stood for anti-tank. The gunners in the unit were trained to know when to use high explosives and when to use anti-tank against their enemy: ATs for enemy armor, and HEs for soft-skinned vehicles or people, as the need arose.

"Okay, look." Tyce had drawn a simplified map of the battle plan on a chalkboard in the repair shop's office. "The river valley narrows and squeezes the train tracks up close to the edge of the Ohio River and the steep hills on the south side." He used his Marine Corps K-BAR combat knife as a pointer to direct their attention to each spot. "The range isn't optimal—about five hundred meters. Close to maximum range for most small arms, but well within killing range for machine guns and your own 25 mike-mike. You will set up two LAVs on either side of Captain Blake's forces and provide fire support as he directs. Questions?"

"Sir, did we plant any explosives on the tracks to stop the train?"

"We didn't. We got here just about forty-five minutes before you did. But a few well-placed rockets on the engine will halt the train just fine. Get with Captain Ned Blake and see if he can use you to help kick off the ambush, too. I'm pretty sure you could make mincemeat of that train if you need too."

"Ah, I'd rather you didn't," said a voice from the sidelines. An army chief warrant officer stepped up to the chalkboard. It was the NBC specialist Tyce was expecting. "If that train is carrying what you all said it was carrying, one round through any of their containment vessels will expose the whole area to one of the worst chemical disasters this country has ever seen."

Tyce nodded. "We'll get the word out to everyone ASAP. We can still aim to cripple the engine and then take under fire any troops that disembark into the open. If they fire from inside the cars, they won't be very effective against us in the dug-in positions. Then we'll keep them pinned and maneuver over there to take them out with our small arms." Seeing the chief was dissatisfied, Tyce quickly added, "Ned's men are precision marksmen. I've seen them in action. If I tell them not to hit the cars, they won't hit the cars. Lieutenant Bryce's LAV gunners can reach out and hit a moving car at one thousand four hundred meters with their stabilized 25mm chain gun. Don't worry."

"Uh, so what happens if we hit one of the chemical drums?" Lieutenant Bryce asked.

"Best case, everyone in everyone in this valley, including us and every town downwind for sixty or so miles, dies," said the chief. "Worst case, the Ohio River from here to Cincinnati and on to St. Louis remains poisoned for the next ten years and kills about a hundred thousand people through terribly painful deaths."

Tyce scowled at Bryce. "So don't hit the cars, Lieutenant."

Owing to the fact that Tyce came up in the ranks in the

same type of unit, he trusted Lieutenant Bryce as much as he trusted Ned, but the lieutenant's dumb question seemed to give the newest addition to the 150th some concerns. Tyce dismissed Bryce and the 4th LAR men and turned to the chief.

He shook the man's hand, "Hey, Lieutenant Colonel Asher. I'm in charge of this lash-up we call the 150th."

"Got it, sir. Chief Warrant Officer William Wheeler."

"Okay, listen, Chief. Once we secure this train, I am going to need your help in identifying and moving those chemicals out of here. Did you bring any gear?"

"Sir, I was only able to grab two NBC suits when your men practically kidnapped me. They didn't tell me much. Your man Sergeant Berringer said it was all top secret, hush-hush. But I'll advise you that moving anything is going to be extremely risky. Especially because we don't know if the Russians rigged it, or what kind of storage containers they're using."

"Are you familiar with the chemicals they might have gotten from Dugway? That's where we understand the Russians stole the chem, or bio, or whatever it is."

"I am. The NBC and chem-weapon field is a pretty tight community. If it's packaged in the standard polyethylene barrels that Dugway uses, we're looking at stuff that needs special chem suits, forklifts, hazmat spill kits. I'd need more than just me and my NBC suit."

Tyce frowned, and his voice deepened "Look, Chief, I have a train full of angry Russians who want to do who knows what the hell with a load of very poisonous shit if we don't stop them. If I coulda picked a beautiful summer day with zero breezes and a truckload of you and your brother chem dudes to help, I woulda ordered that up on a menu. But me and my men are going to stop this train.

That means here, and that means now. I'm not risking the chance that it gets past us and does whatever evil work the Russians have in store for it. We're in a war for our country, and as far as we know, they intend to do exactly what you laid out in your worst-case scenario."

"Got it, sir. Sorry." The chief's mood changed instantly; he was senior and old school enough to recognize Tyce's words as a subtle but professional ass chewing. "I am just used to working with near-perfect conditions, and now I understand better what you and your men have probably been through while my unit and I have mostly been home with our families trying to figure out what hit our beloved U.S. of A. I'm fully onboard, sir. Do you have any of your own gear?"

"I have one company of special ops soldiers, and a platoon of vehicle-mounted recon Marines. Each has the standard-issue Sheridan MOPP suit. That's one thing no kid in the unit forgot on our hasty gear list," Tyce said, referencing the military's version of a biohazard suit.

"Got it, sir. When your men kill the engine and neutralize the Russians, I promise to do my best to advise and assist you on how to get that stuff away from here."

"Good, because my guess is we'll have two hours from when we kick off the ambush before the Russians will get a reactionary force out of Charleston or elsewhere, and I aim to be long gone by the time they show up.

"Do I have your permission to go give some tips to the men?"

"Abso-*frickin*-lutely."

The chief saluted Tyce and raced off to brief the men.

* * *

Stazia looked across the river through her JIM HR, a set of high-speed, special operator thermal binoculars that linked via a data cable to her satellite radio and via a closed Wi-Fi network to her rifle's sight system. Her hide position on the south side of the river offered a perfect view to the north and pretty much a three-sixty-degree arc of observation and fire around her. An industrial zone consisting of an open yard of two- and three-story-high piles of raw coal, warehouses, cranes, and gantries to load river barges skirted the south side of the river. The six-story-high bulk petroleum tower where she had established herself was set back some and wasn't the tallest structure in the yard, nor the closest to the water, but she figured those attributes made it even less likely someone scanning from the northern side of the Ohio would suspect it for a sniper hide position.

Stazia fully anticipated someone would be looking in her direction. Possibly already were, as she'd been observing the men from Tyce's 150th since they'd arrived.

She flicked a zoom switch to get a closer look at the thermal image of someone moving across the American ambush front line. A biggish man, strong and muscled. Stazia watched his broad back, brightly illuminated in orange and red hues as he stopped to check each position.

That has to be the captain, what's his name . . . the special forces officer, she thought.

She'd stolen the JIM HR, highly specialized and accurate military-grade tech, from an SOF unit when she was in Norfolk helping to pave the way for the Russian invasion forces. She had been extremely busy in the forty-eight hours before the invasion, but when she'd tripped a motion sensor in the Navy SEAL compound's armory where the JIM HR had been just lying out in the open, she helped herself. Of course, it was a fully locked and guarded armory, but she'd picked the locks and disabled the cameras in less than five minutes. Tripping the alarm was unfortunate, so when she was done, she just waited for the lackadaisical base response force and triggered her explosives as they entered, killing them all.

Perk of the job, she thought as she fine-tuned the thermal's gain for better resolution.

She couldn't be sure the figure was the special forces captain—the thermal image didn't give quite a perfect definition at that distance—but she knew it wasn't the lieutenant colonel. *No, I'd recognize his gait. He tries to hide that limp. Nothing more than a slight body swivel, but I'd know it if that was him.*

She contemplated that thought for a minute, toying with it in her mind. Was she going to shoot Colonel Asher if he got in her crosshairs tonight? "Possibly," she breathed in a whispered response to her own question. *But I am running the show tonight. We'll see how it goes.*

She went back to scanning the American fighting positions. She pressed a button at each fighting hole to log them as targets in the superexpensive binoculars' microcomputer brain. Once she was finished, she checked the data cable up to her radio and uploaded the positions to the Russian satellites overhead.

She turned briefly to watch as a civilian truck entered the yard behind her. Two men got out and went into a nearby building. If she'd had the time, she'd have killed them both. She preferred no witnesses. Now was not the time, though; she had other matters to attend to, so she'd just have to ensure they didn't see her. Civilians on a battlefield could be such a nuisance.

She pressed the backlight button a few times to check the upload progress while she tugged out her dad's red hammer-and-sickle handkerchief and tied it around her forearm. She checked over her new rifle, a 6.5mm Creedmoor Ruger Precision Rifle, or RPR for short. Everyone turned RPR into Reaper, but Stazia always gave her guns her own nickname. It was a fairly advanced rifle, but its ballistic drop would challenge even her skills. She preferred a rifle with a flat trajectory, but the RPR was plenty deadly for tonight's mission. She lay in a prone position behind the rifle and looked through the specialized but bulky night sights. The definition was not quite as good as her handheld device, but it would do.

She adjusted the cheek pad to her satisfaction, then worked the bolt back and forward a few times. It slid easily, and she liked the way it locked snugly into the chamber. It wasn't her favorite Russian-made Orsis T-5000—she was still mourning the loss of that beauty. She'd undergone the SVR special sniper academy training with the T-5000, and like most snipers, she felt an emotional attachment to precision firearms, which included naming them. She also felt a compelling need to avenge their loss.

Not sure who I'll exact vengeance on, she thought, *but someone is going to pay for the loss of the T-5000. It's okay, Vlad will do the trick.* Vlad. It had a nice medieval ring to it.

A barely audible click came from the binoculars. Stazia pressed the radio's backlight again, and this time a full bar confirmed that the location data for the American units had been sent to the satellite.

"Now, Vlad," she whispered to her rifle, "we just have to wait."

* * *

"Ten minutes to target," the crew chief told Captain Shenkov over the helmet intercom. "The general sent a message reminding you to turn on your locator beacons."

Shenkov nodded to him and signaled for his senior enlisted man to unbuckle and come over to his seat near the open helicopter hatch. Even with the volume knob maxed on the intercom, it was nearly impossible to hear anyone over the rotor noise of the Mi-8 AMTSh-VN special-purpose assault helicopter and the wind roaring as they skimmed at treetop level over the mountainous terrain. Shenkov had ordered that the side hatches remain open, increasing the noise but also ensuring he had as many guns facing outboard as possible. There was a second reason he wanted them left open: the cold air would keep his men on edge. There would be no napping. Soon they would strike a hot LZ.

"Starshina Smirnov." A Russian Starshina was the equivalent of an American sergeant first class. Shenkov cupped his hands over the man's ear so he could be heard. "I want you to break right once we touch down. Grab a few men and pull out your flashlights. Signal Teams Anna and Boris, and direct them toward me. It will be completely dark, so I want to personally vector them into the assault."

"Comrade Captain, should the pilots still light them up with the 12.7mm as we approach?"

"Yes, then drop us in the zone and take off immediately to give us aerial fire support throughout the mission."

"Do we think the lady operative's intelligence is accurate?"

"We'll know once we hit the ground."

"Where will she be during the battle?"

"Who knows? Who cares. Look for her beacon," he said, waving off the Starshina to go inspect the men a final time.

Her damned intel on the Americans better be right, Shenkov thought, *or it will be her final mistake. I've had it with her and all the SVR's bullshit antics and posturing. It's time for action and fighting, not all this crap espionage.*

A small red light above the cockpit door changed from red to green. It was time to attack. He flipped open and checked his mag pouches, pulled out a magazine, and locked it into his rifle right as the sounds of his and four other Mi-8's 12.7mm cannons roared to life. It sounded like fabric ripping all around them, their red fire lighting up the night sky like Roman candles.

"They came from . . . behind," yelled a bloody Marine sergeant as he crashed into Tyce's command post. "They landed—"

The sounds of cannon fire erupted once again, and before the kid could complete his sentence, rounds slammed all around their building.

Boom-boom-boom!

Tyce and others hit the ground, but the newly arrived wounded Marine wasn't so lucky. He was caught in the doorway, and the light from inside cast his silhouette as a perfect target. Ten or twelve of the heavy-caliber bullets blasted the door, the window, and a good portion of the wall to splinters. Tyce looked up. Anything recognizable as his Marine had vanished amid the hailstorm of bullets— as had the wall, and part of the roof.

Through the huge hole in the metal siding, Tyce could see the helicopter that had fired on them. It was only two or three football fields away, holding in a low hover and orbiting in a rapid drift to the west and over the Ohio River.

"Everyone stay low, it's still searching for targets in our area," Tyce yelled, hoping his men weren't too deaf from the rocket attack to hear him. "Okay, men. We're out the back door in groups of four. Grab any maps and radios we need. Then hoof it over to Captain Blake's positions."

"What then, sir?" someone asked.

"Then you get in the line and fight." Tyce said

CHAPTER 14

Outside Huntington, West Virginia

"Get me a radio!" Tyce called out to the small pack of men who had made it out with him from their now-decimated headquarters. Tyce and twenty others were caught in a drainage ditch in the no-man's-land below Ned's hill. They couldn't go back; the helicopters were destroying every building in sight. They couldn't go forward; Ned's positions were awash with gunfire.

One of the men crawled over to Tyce and handed him a tactical radio. The woods were lit up with the constant streams of red and green tracer fire. Tyce could tell which came from Ned's men. Their tracer fire came in clusters, the men fighting from their pre-dug positions but now turned around one eighty degrees to face uphill. The Russian helicopters' attack runs started at the river and made passes directly above Tyce, aimed at what was now Ned's back side. They peppered the hill with 12.7mm cannon as Ned tried to focus up the hill. He was getting hit from two sides.

The noise of the battle was an awful din. The heavy, brass casings from the attacking Russian helicopters fell around Tyce and the men as they swooped over, adding to the chaos and confusion.

"Comanche six, this is Iron Horse six, can you gimme a SIT-REP," Tyce asked, using the military shorthand for "situation report" to communicate quickly and trying to sound as casual and calm as possible.

The voice of First Sergeant Hull came over the radio. "Iron Horse, we're fightin'."

"I copy, what do you need?" It was a dumb question, and Tyce instantly regretted it, as Tyce had little to offer them. But it was born out of many days when he had had the upper hand and could issue an order or two to get someone out of a jam.

Ned's voice came back. "Iron Horse, this is a pretty hairy SIT. I've got what probably amounts to a company of Russians who tried to infiltrate directly to my rear—"

The transmission cut short for a second as two machine guns went off somewhere directly adjacent to Ned, blanking out the radio completely. In an acoustic anomaly, a fraction of a second later, Tyce heard those same guns echoing from off the hill.

"Fortunately, I had sentries and flankers out. We lost them all, down to the man, but we got the company turned around in time." Ned paused as the gunfire picked up again, then said, "It's not very helpful that those helos keep sliding up and down the Ohio, raking my positions. Every time they do, my guys go to ground, and the Russians creep in a little closer."

"I got it Ned. Break, break." Tyce switched to a new conversation. "Lieutenant Bryce, you up on this net?"

"I copy, sir," came Bryce's voice.

"Good. Listen, I'll make it quick. I need you to suppress those helos to get some of the pressure off Captain Blake."

"I can, sir, but that whooshing sound you heard earlier was rockets off one of those helos. They must've spotted one of my LAVs, and they're not responding on the radio. I'm down to three vics."

Only three vehicles left, Tyce thought, shaking his head. Out loud, he said, "Copy. Do what you can, but do it now."

"On it, Iron Horse," said the LAV man, and seconds later Tyce heard the growl of an LAV engine as the big, armored beasts tried to reposition to get better views of the sky.

CHAPTER 15

Outside Morgantown, West Virginia

Wynand slapped the dashboard a few times, then turned to Victoria and Bill. "It's got gas, but there's something wrong with the engine."

"Can you get it started again?" asked Victoria hopefully. She looked outside the window into the dark. A few houses had lights, but otherwise the neighborhood was completely quiet.

"Nah, that's it. We've drained most of the battery, and even if the starter wasn't making that noise, we'd only get maybe another few blocks before it conked out. At least parked here we're out of the way—"

"Of Russian patrols," Bill finished for Wynand.

"So we hoof it," said Victoria as more a statement than a question.

The three exited the Bronco and looked around. They hefted their packs from the Bronco's hatchback. Wynand strapped on his pistol belt, and Victoria looked over her rifle, then went to help the general out of the truck. He swung one leg at a time and stood weakly. Victoria could see him forcing a smile in the darkness.

"Which way?" asked Victoria.

Wynand pointed vaguely west. "Thataway. About four

more miles. Five if we keep to the back roads, like we done."

"Any more bridges to cross? Choke points?" she asked.

"Nope, but we can't cross near the airport. That's sure to be in Russian hands and patrolled heavily."

Bill pulled Victoria aside and whispered, "The general can't make it that far. Especially if we're dodging Russians."

"I can hear you," General Custis said in an overly loud whisper. "Remember: blind guy hearing, it's better than y'all's. Bill, stop making trouble. You guys just get going in the right direction. I'll be fine."

Victoria looked at him, his silver hair glistening white in the moonlight. He appeared gaunt and not up to the task of walking. Bill shrugged and stared off in the direction Wynand had indicated. Victoria made sure the general was moving, then caught up with Bill as they walked slowly through the Morgantown suburb.

"He's made of some tough stuff, miss," Bill said quietly when he sensed her beside him. "He's been through three wars, but I'm not sure how far he can go"

"Two, I thought."

"Three. Iraq for the first go around, then Iraq part deux, then Afghanistan. I'd even say four, if you include this one."

"Well, this is the first one where he was exposed to a nuclear blast."

"Yeah, but you gotta know him like I know him. He's a stubborn old goat, and he'll keep on going until he collapses. Nothin' you can tell him unless we force him."

"So we just go until he collapses?"

"As his official wet nurse . . . I dunno. I just know we should stop soon."

Victoria grimaced, then fell back to walk beside the general, who was following the sound of Wynand's footfalls. Wynand seemed uninterested in the general's plight and walked faster to catch up to Bill, leaving Victoria to guide the general.

"You okay, sir?"

"I'm fine. It's not my legs that hurt, you know. It's this damn stomach. Feel like a nest of hornets decided to take up residence in my intestines."

"Did you take that Maalox I gave you?"

"Yep. Can't you give me something for the diarrhea, though? I don't want to have to stop the crew for another . . . *potty* break." The general grimaced at his own grim joke.

"Sir, you know I can't do that. You gotta keep passing all that stuff out of your system." Victoria glanced at the general as they walked. His face was impassive. He seemed to be focusing on putting one foot in front of the other. "Is there still bleeding? You know, when you—"

"Yes, I know, Doc. No. Not anymore. Just diarrhea. But the sores on my arms are worse."

"How much?"

"Since we started driving, it feels like pressure under my shirt sleeves."

"They must be full of pus again. I'll need to drain them. You need to keep drinking water. Until we can get you the potassium iodide or some Prussian blue, you're going to remain dehydrated."

Victoria shouldered her rifle and gave the general one arm to lean on. She could feel how light he had become. He had probably lost more than seventy pounds since he'd gotten sick, and even though he held on to her tightly, she kept him in tow without much effort.

"I wanted to say thank you. You know, for going the extra mile, I mean."

"Of course. I'd do it for any of the men," she said, trying to sound cheery but professional.

They'd only walked four blocks, and already his feet were dragging. "Well, I'm glad we get to talk a bit, because I agree with one thing you just said, and I need to tell you something." He paused for a minute. He was starting to get out of breath, but seemed gearing up to tell Victoria something that was weighing heavily on him. "I've given it a lot of thought, and I know that I am taking you away from what really matters. And what you just said confirms it in my mind. You see, I am pretty good with strategy and tactics, but matters of the heart are not my forte."

"What are you saying, sir? Because I'm not liking where I think you're going with this."

"I know, but I also know that you need to be with the men. Tyce's men. They'll get into some real situations, and they need your skilled hand. Right now, you're wasting precious hours messing around with my medical concerns when you have a whole troop counting on you. This mission is robbing the boys of the most competent field medic they got."

"This is the mission, General. And I happen to know *you* are very valuable to the unit, too."

"Pretty sure your doctoring is more valuable than my tedious tidbits from ancient history."

"Ha. Tyce calls your advice 'wisdom from Yoda.'" She smiled a moment, but the gravity of the general's words was clear. "They'll be fine. The rest of the medics are a great crew. Some of us deployed together to Afghanistan, and a few were in Iraq. They've got things covered. Besides, what could they get into in just one night?"

The two had already fallen half a block behind Wynand and Bill, shuffling along past blacked-out houses in the seemingly deserted neighborhood.

Parsons, West Virginia

Georgia-Blue Templeton sat on a wooden bench outside the mayor's office nervously thumbing his empty leather holster. He'd taken his own sweet time coming to see her, and then he'd been told to sit and wait. The newly acquired pistol, as well as his favorite Weatherby Mark V rifle, had been taken from him by the sheriff upon his entrance. Even before the Russian invasion, he hadn't been to many places without it by his side. He felt particularly naked being here without it, and without any understanding of why he'd been summoned by the Honorable Susanna Holly.

He'd been in this building, the Tucker County Courthouse, before, but not upstairs on the mayor's floor. In fact, he'd really only been this close to an elected official once in his life. One year when he was young, his parents took him to the office of the mayor of their small town in rural Georgia. His dad had been in the Gulf War and had gotten out of the service before they could present him with a medal. It was forwarded to his town by the U.S. Army, and the mayor had awarded it to him in his office on behalf of the federal government. A living Medal of Honor recipient had been there to personally pin the medal on his dad. He remembered his parents and relatives talking about the man with reverence and respect. Ultimately, the other man seemed just like his father, solemn about most things and quietly confident. Whatever it was that made those men so stoic, Blue hadn't wanted to follow in their footsteps. But he had still listened and absorbed every ounce of his father's teaching on shooting and marksmanship.

The sheriff walked out of the mayor's office, and in passing, Blue he looked over. "You still here? How long ya been waitin'?"

"Ah, since seven," said Blue, rising when he was spoken to by the sheriff. He'd learned precision marksmanship from his father, but his mother had taught him his manners. She was a loving mother, but she kept a wooden spoon nearby and used to crack it on his and his sister's backsides when they strayed too far.

"Seven o'clock?" He looked shocked. "That's nearly two hours ago."

"No, seven this morning."

"Cripes, man, are you simple or something?" The sheriff had seen Blue before and, probably because of his massive size, had always taken him for a bit of an oaf. "Why didn't you say something?" he said, slowing his words down as if he were talking to a dimwit.

"Everyone looked too busy runnin' in and out. I didn't want to bother nobody."

"Jeez, kid." The sheriff stepped back and regarded him for a moment, then tapped his chin. "I'm pretty sure I know what this is about. I'll let her know you're still waiting." He disappeared back inside. When he didn't immediately return, Blue sat again and wondered what could be so important that they'd keep him waiting until the place was nearly deserted.

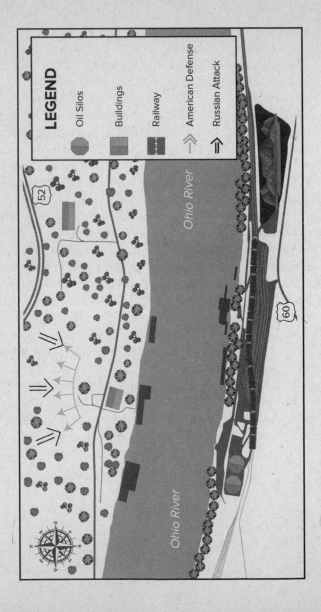

Chapter 16

Outside Huntington, West Virginia

Stazia could plainly see the American machine gunner through her thermal sight. His whole body was clear, as were the red-hot blasts coming from his machine gun as he fired long bursts in the opposite direction from her and up the hill toward Captain Shenkov's attacking force. The sound of the gunfire was loud, and because of the acoustics in the valley, she heard every shot three times as it echoed up and down the river and off the hills behind her. She moved the gunsight off the machine gunner and played it over to the Russian side and Shenkov's troops. They were advancing by the minute, gaining ground in twos and threes and firing from behind the cover of trees and tossing grenades.

A message came over her satellite comms system from the Russian Pentagon reminding her to turn on her beacon. She ignored it and went back to focusing her sights back on the gunner. She placed the crosshairs between his shoulder blades, made a last-second adjustment for distance and elevation, and squeezed the trigger. The sound of the shot was absolutely lost amid the noise from the raging gun battle. There was a millisecond pause as the rifle settled, then she saw the gunner. His back was now as red hot as his gun barrel, which lay unmanned on the lip of his fighting hole. The men to his left and right pulled his lifeless form down into the hole. Then, as one looked him over, the other jumped up to take over the gun. Stazia took aim at him now, this time deciding on a head shot.

"So you need something bloodier to convince you to stay off that gun." She aimed only briefly; then, confident now of her windage and elevation, she squeezed the trigger. The rifle jerked again, then settled, revealing to her that the second man had fallen across the machine gun. A red mist sprayed up in her sight from the man's head. The third man remained down, not even daring to reach toward his fallen comrade.

"Good. That settles that." She looked into the JIM HR at the green left arrow. She followed the arrow, which put her basically on target for another machine gun nest she'd tagged earlier. "Nah, we'll leave the rest of the guns alone for now. Hmmm . . . what next, Vlad?" She switched back and forth from the JIM HR to the RPR sniper rifle's scope but let the JIM HR guide her view directly back to the stored targets.

"Are you ready?" she asked the rifle. The massive gun battle raged across the river from her, lighting up everything around. Target acquisition in this confusion would have been nearly impossible if it weren't for the advanced JIM HR.

"How did those stupid boomers do it in Vietnam?" she asked herself, thinking about the snipers of an earlier era. It crossed her mind that they never would have taken her into their ranks back in those days. "Barely do these days . . ." she muttered to herself as she lined up a new target, this one a U.S. mortar team furiously hurling mortars. Captain Shenkov's men were so close now, the Americans could practically throw them by hand.

Stazia thought she recognized the mortar sergeant.

I remember you, handsome boy, she thought. *Dark hair, a swarthy Latin look. But that ridiculous moustache. Why do men always think a moustache makes them look sexy?*

It was hard to be sure, to even make out any facial features from this far away, but she was a skilled study of the human form. Born blessed with a mastery of reading faces and body language from across the room, as well as with zero empathy to hold her back.

"Fuck him," she said, and she squeezed the trigger. The man had been standing aside the mortar coaching his men, yelling out angles of deflection and generally hastening the younger men in getting accurate mortar fire out as quickly as possible. When he crumpled at the waist, Stazia could see the others pause and look over at their trusted boss. The others looked to be young, green troops, the type who would need encouragement from their leader's example of bravery under fire. Now, they stopped, shocked and unsure, and watched their leader, sitting motionless on a mortar crate, as blood poured from his mouth.

Tyce was pinned in no-man's-land. The incoming Russian gunfire was not aimed at him, but every shot that went even just an inch over Ned's men's heads still rained down the hill at a steep angle, kicking up dirt, rocks, and chunks of grass all around Tyce and his small group huddled in the drainage ditch. Behind them, the helicopters were raking Ned's men with 12.7mm gunfire. As soon as one

helicopter finished a gun-run and was taken under fire by
small fire from the Americans, it raced off upriver, and
another approached from a different angle. It was like a
deadly round-robin: each pass seemed to lay waste to one
of the fighting positions, and the Russians advanced down
the hill even farther.

"We can't stay here!" yelled Tyce, looking at the men's
scared faces, illuminated by white-hot grenade explosions
and tracer fire.

"What do we do, sir?" yelled Sergeant Berringer.

"Grab your shit and follow me. When the next helo starts
to move off, we make a run for that house. Make sure you
have the radios—we're going to direct fire onto those helos.
Now, go!" With a mighty heave, Tyce, ladened with gear,
pulled himself up the bank of the ditch, crawled, then stood
up clumsily and ran toward a lone two-story civilian house
in a field. The men followed. Some were hesitant, but once
they saw they were going to be left alone, the reluctant few
found their courage and their speed.

They raced in disorganized clumps, reaching the house
just as the next Russian helicopter started its terrifying
attack. As Tyce and the men crashed through the front
door, they could hear the upper-story windows smashing
to bits. The helicopter must have caught sight of them. A
hail of bullets blasted through the upper-story floorboards
and tore through the first-floor ceiling above, narrowly
missing them all. Some of the men backpedaled, but it was
unnecessary.

"Upstairs, and throw up an antenna," said Tyce.

"Sir, that's madness," yelled one of the men. "They've
taken out the upper story."

"Nah, lightning won't strike twice. Follow me, we're in

a perfect spot to direct traffic," said Tyce, running up the stairs. The house was situated in the middle of a spacious and formerly beautifully manicured lawn. Uphill were Ned's men, below was the river and the Russian helicopters' most likely spot of approach. At the top of the stairs, Tyce could see that huge chunks of the roof were gone and most of the windows had been turned into gaping holes. To make matters more interesting, a part of the rafters was on fire, and the blaze looked to be spreading fast.

"Christ, sir, are you sure about this spot?" said Sergeant Berringer.

"Yes, now listen to me. You are going to face toward Captain Blake's men. Grab two radiomen and give him spot reports. You don't realize it yet, but here we can see Blake's whole line. You are going to be in a perfect position to advise him if any part of his line is weakening, if the Russians look about to break through one side or the other."

"How do I tell him where they're coming in? It's pitch black, they're all turned around now, and I don't even know his unit's SOP." he said, referring to the unit's standard operating procedures.

"Easy." Tyce made a blade hand and pointed first left, then middle and right. "He knows his own lines, and he knows left, right, center. Start with that, and once he realizes you can see more of the battlefield than he can, you'll figure out the rest. Got it?"

"Got it, sir." Sergeant Berringer seemed fully on board now. He grabbed two radio operators and pulled some night optics from a pack.

Tyce grabbed another two radiomen and positioned himself by the holes that used to be windows. "And we're going to guide the big guns on those LAV-25s onto those fucking helos." Tyce looked out and up to the horizon. He didn't even need optics; the battlefield's massive gunfire and even the burning house they were now occupying illuminated the helicopters perfectly.

CHAPTER 17

Outside Morgantown, West Virginia

The general tripped for the tenth time, but this time was different. This time, he didn't catch himself, and he landed on his knees. Victoria lifted his feeble frame up, but she could tell he was now in great pain.

Bill and Wynand looked back at them from the end of the block, where they were waiting just outside of the light from a streetlamp. When they saw Victoria put the general's arm over her neck and try to help him hobble along, they realized it was worse than before and trotted back.

"He can't keep going like this," Victoria said.

"We can't rest here," said Wynand, looking around at the unwelcoming houses nearby. They had tried to remain unnoticed, sticking to lawns or sidewalks with fences or hedges in case of a patrol, but many of the house's lights had gone out as soon as they passed. People were there, but they certainly didn't want trouble.

"Can't we just leave him at one of these houses, go get the medicine, and come back?" said Bill.

"If you think any of these folks want to get involved in our nonsense, you're an idiot," said Wynand. "They just want to be left alone to suffer in silence."

Victoria gave Wynand one of her enraged looks, though

the effect was probably lost in the darkness. But before they could settle the debate, three pairs of headlights rounded the corner where Bill and Wynand had been standing just a minute before. They all dove into the bushes, Victoria falling in and pulling the general painfully through its needled branches.

They waited, chests heaving, trying to silence their breaths. The general lay motionless, mostly inside the bush and suspended upright by several branches. When the three vehicles had passed, everyone remained silent a few moments longer before Victoria spoke.

"You okay, General?" Victoria whispered out softly, still holding his hand in hers. He grunted, sounding utterly exhausted.

"How far do you figure?" Bill asked from somewhere inside the bush.

"We only made it 'bout a mile," said Wynand.

"We can't go on like this," Victoria said.

"What do you suggest . . . ma'am," Wynand asked sharply.

"On the next block, there looks to be a big building. Looks like a school. Let's get in there and rally up. Think things over a bit. I'm sure things will be a bit clearer when we catch our breath."

"And get me out of this infernal bush," the general croaked out weakly.

Parsons County Courthouse

Finally, the sheriff returned, opened the mayor's door, and beckoned Blue in. "Mayor Holly will see you now," he said, half a smirk on his face. As soon as he let Blue in, he exited and closed the door behind him. Blue heard the *clack* of the lock as the sheriff turned his key and locked the mayor and Blue in together.

The mayor's office was actually in the next room over, but the door was open, and it was brightly lit. A sweet, Southern voice came from within. "Is that lil' ol' Mr. Blue?" she said, "Get on in here. I heard you been waiting outside a rather long spell. Is that true?"

"Yes, ma'am," said Blue as he walked into her office.

Mayor Holly sat at her desk—looking tall, but Blue knew her to be an average-size woman, probably about five foot seven. She had bright red hair and was in her early forties. She was wearing a slick, designer civilian suit, the top of which was a vest that clung to her curves. *She certainly looks dressed to kill*, crossed Blue's mind, though the suit looked out of place even in her own office with the current state of the country, especially since Blue had spent the last few months in the same set of civilian attire. He still wore faded jeans and a simple plaid shirt, now with a few buttons missing from the shirt and tears in the crotch and knees of his jeans.

"Please, do have a seat," the mayor said, gesturing to two couches in front of her desk. Blue sat, sinking deep into the cushions, but as a man of almost no words, he said nothing, and he didn't move an inch once seated.

Mayor Susanna Holly flashed a kittenish smile, then began slowly, as if choosing her words carefully for her specific audience. "Mr. Blue, thank you so much for coming at my behest. Did you bring that rifle of yours?"

Blue nodded.

"You strike me as a man who likes to get right down to business." She stood up and walked around the desk, then sat down on the front edge. She was wearing a short skirt that matched her outfit. "Have you heard what's happening with the governor of the great state of West Virginia?"

Blue shook his head.

"Hmmm . . . I suspect news of what the new government is up to is scarce."

Blue remained motionless.

"Major—that is, Lieutenant Colonel Asher hasn't told you all much about the politics, has he?"

Blue shook his head again.

"Well, I'm gonna explain something, and I'd like you to pay close attention. I think you are the kind of man who believes deeply in this democracy of ours. A government of the people, for the people."

"Mr. Lincoln said 'of the people, *by* the people.'"

"Ah, now. You see, you *are* the right man. And to think the sheriff wasn't certain of your faculties."

"Of my what now, ma'am?"

"Never mind." Then her eyes softened into an odd sort of pleasant look that made Blue a little uncomfortable, and she continued, "You need to know something. While you and the colonel have been fighting the Russians, we folks in the duly elected governments have been trying to do what's best for the people. You do believe in the people, don't you, Mr. Blue?"

"Yes, ma'am."

"Good. I suppose you wouldn't be up in those hills, fighting the good fight, if you didn't. So what would you say if I told you the governor of West Virginia isn't the actual governor, but a Russian plant? One who stole the election. Do you remember the last line of what President Lincoln said?" Blue looked uncertain, so she continued, "That a government 'of the people, by the people, *for* the people, shall not perish from the earth.' That last part is possibly the most important."

Blue felt tense. He had an overly large sense of patriotism and of fair play, and the news of a Russian heist of his government, although possibly inevitable, struck him as just plain wrong.

"Let me explain it a little further." Susanna held up a chart of something Blue didn't recognize. "You see this data here? These are all the edicts and orders coming from the governor's office. Did you know we've pieced them all together, and we've seen something bad? Really bad. The governor is working to run off local leaders and replace them with his own, handpicked, Russian-sympathizing cronies. People who will further ruin our country and perhaps cast us inescapably into the abyss."

Blue looked puzzled but still didn't speak.

"You see, once those people are in place, he can do whatever he wants with the state. And for the most part, the people will obey. Then we'll be no better than a Russian puppet state, and the Russian plan will be complete."

"How does that affect me and the boys of the 150th?" Blue asked.

"Well, I'm glad you asked," she said, her eyes narrowing and a half smile curling up one side of her mouth. "Do you know where the 150th comes from?"

Blue sat and pondered. He thought he knew, but the question seemed too complicated, and the mayor seemed to talk in riddles. "Not really, ma'am."

"They come from the West Virginia National Guard, sweetie." She paused, letting it sink in, but when Blue again said nothing, she went on, "That means he gives the orders. He can recall the 150th at any time of his choosing."

"They don't have to obey him iff'n he gives them an illegal order."

"Ah, you're right. Did you read that somewhere?" she said, leaning in slightly and waved a finger at him, like he was a kid caught stealing a piece of candy.

Blue blushed openly. "Naw, it was in a movie."

"Well, you are right. So here's a question for you: What happens if his order to the 150th, to Colonel Asher, is legal? What happens if he recalls the regiment and tells them to just go home?"

"Well, they'd keep fightin' I reckon'."

"Some might . . . but what about the men who are homesick? The ones who want to check in on their families. Or maybe there are a few who are just plum tuckered out from all the fighting." Susanna sat farther back on her desk in a natural-seeming motion, but as she did so, the slit in her skirt parted, revealing more leg than Blue had seen in a long while.

"Them boys ain't gonna quit, Mrs. Mayor," Blue said with a frown, but at the same time, he thought back to the discussions he'd overheard Tyce and the Gunny having. He knew some men had already deserted, and he knew their surreptitious departures had dampened the combat morale of the remaining men, and affected Tyce quite a great deal.

"First of all, it's *Miss* Holly, but I know what you're thinking." Her cherry-red lips slowly transformed into a devastating smile, like a spider might if it were all but certain of what it had caught in a carefully spun web. "Because I know those boys . . . I mean, *our* boys have a lot of good fight in 'em. They are holding the line against one of the most despicable enemies we've seen since the British tried to wipe us off the face of the map. They'll fight to the end, no one's questioning that." She sounded strong, patriotic, and supportive of the "boys," and it made Blue feel proud to be a part of Tyce's unit. "But you and I both know the unit will slowly break down, one squad, one platoon, and one company at a time. Guess what's worse? I know something that will hasten the demise of the 150th."

Mayor Susanna used big words, but he understood, and her bright blue eyes bored deeply into his as she continued. "What if the governor asked Tyce for a position report? You know, started to make it look like he wanted to be more in charge of all his forces fighting around the state and asked Tyce where he was on a daily basis. Couldn't he easily slip a note to the Russians on his—I mean, all y'all's whereabouts. No one would even know. Just one day, after many men had already departed in desertion, the Russians would show up on your doorstep right when you least expect it."

Blue thought hard about what the mayor had just said. Even if the governor didn't straight-up rat them out to the Russians but just ordered them to disband, or to simply take a break from fighting and take some much-needed leave to check on their families, it would tear the unit apart piece by excruciating piece. Blue had stayed clear of all that kind of leadership stuff, but this talk made sense. Especially the way Mayor Holly described it. He knew enough about morale and discipline, having watched the 150th under the careful direction of its leaders, to know that what she said was true.

"Why don't you tell the colonel about all this?" Blue asked, realizing he was just a small piece of the larger machine and thinking it was odd she would approach him about it.

She seemed prepared for the question. "He can't disobey an order. You know that, honey," she admonished as if it were obvious. "He has to keep the faith with the military system. That means strict obedience to orders. But a civilian, one acting in good faith, could do more. You see, you and I are unrestrained."

As if sensing Blue's inner turmoil, Susanna's voice sweetened once more to calm reason, but now with had a flirty edge. "I have a little mission for you. A secret mission," she said, now in a conspiratorial whisper. "One you mustn't tell our fair colonel about. A mission that demands the utmost secrecy and a man of your . . . shooting talents."

Mayor Holly sat back on the desk farther, placing her hands on her knees. Whether by accident or careful planning, her skirt opened slightly more. Susanna watched closely where Blue's uncontrolled gaze went.

Again, the pretty red lips smiled brightly, this time almost triumphantly. "Do you think you can do a special mission for West Virginia, for the nation? Or maybe," she said, running both hands slowly up the sides of her skirt and over her hips, "could I convince you to find it in your heart to do this little ol' favor just for me, Mr. Blue?" The sound of her hands against the silk and her soft voice made Blue's heart jump in a way he hadn't really felt since head cheerleader Cindy Harper had tricked him into following her inside the band rehearsal room that one day after football practice.

CHAPTER 18

Outside Huntington, West Virginia

Captain Shenkov grabbed the radio out of its operator's hands while the man was trying to take a report. "I said pour fire onto that area. Crush it. The last report said that side of the line is weakening. I personally witnessed your men getting within ten feet of the enemy line on that last push before they fell back. That's where we make our breakthrough, that's where we begin the slaughter, and we do it now!"

He didn't wait for an answer from Team Boris's commander, shoving the radio handset back at the operator and grabbing the other radio handset for the helicopters' radio net. "What the hell was that last pass?" he yelled. "I saw the impacts of your cannon fire, and they're *all* going wide. I need concentrated fire at the point I designated."

This time, the radio came alive. The helicopter pilot sounded stressed, but defensive. "Captain, we cannot attack from a lower angle. There may be electrical wire hazards, and we are already taking heavy small-arms fire on each pass."

"Don't talk to *me* about small-arms fire, you horse's ass. Get your Goddamned noses into it! The enemy lines are breaking." Shenkov threw the radio receiver back at the radioman, striking him in the face. He stood up and gestured for the man to follow, then, without a word, raced off. The small contingent he kept around him as his own personal riflemen and bodyguards followed him back to the front lines.

Stazia had now racked up a dozen American kills. All small unit leaders, all at critical moments of the fighting. She was careful not to keep one zone under fire for too long and instead switched to other parts of the battlefield. If she didn't, eventually someone would figure out that they had a sniper working them over from behind.

"Well, what the fuck is this?" she said. Through her rifle sight, she could see eight or nine figures loosely hunched behind a huge boulder up on the Russian side of the hill. One or two new men arrived every few seconds. It looked like the Russians had found one of the weak points in the lines, partly aided by the fact that Stazia had killed several of the young leaders who had stepped up, heroically, but tragically, to reman machine guns or to rally the men. Each time they did, she had taken out the leader or even their assistant, and the American rally had stalled.

Stazia played with the focus and gain on the JIM HR optic. Yes, she was sure of it. *Aha, finally our Russian Wolf steps out of the shadows. Are you ready, Vlad?* She centered the rifle directly onto the head of the figure she was certain was Captain Shenkov.

She touched the trigger ever so lightly and said, "Bang! You asshole."

* * *

"Captain, it is General Kolikoff on the radio. He demands you make a report personally. I tried to tell him—"

Ping-zing, two bullets ricocheted off the rocks. One of the American units at their flanks had noticed the Russians gathering there, but the slow rate of fire was enough to let Shenkov know it was probably just one or maybe two men firing into the shadows. They had a few moments yet before the Americans would notice he had infiltrated right up next to their lines and was about to bring a whole platoon up.

"Give it to me," he said, taking the radio receiver. "General, can you hear me?"

"I hear you . . ." came a staticky voice. It was weak and barely audible, but Shenkov could make it out. "I need a progress report, immediately. General Tympkin . . ." The rest of the transmission was washed away.

"God damn this," Shenkov said aloud, balancing the radio receiver against his shoulder and ear. He put his rifle on the rock, pulled the magazine, and switched it to a fresh one. No telling how many he'd fired; he'd lost count while getting his boys this close. Inspiring them to advance in the face of sustained enemy fire was a hell of a feat, even for an elite Spetsnaz unit. After all, he knew the enemy was the just-as-elite American special forces. That was what was going to make today's triumph so great, and perhaps the only reason he'd actually stopped to talk to the general. Otherwise, he would have just blown it off until the battle was concluded.

"General, if you can hear me, my report is as follows: we are at the enemy lines, time now. I am assaulting their middle. Their ranks will break any moment. I will call when I am mopping up."

He was about to hand the radio back and commence the final push when the radio came back to life. "I hear—" *Screech*. Static broke the satellite transmission, but it quickly came back—"Do not let"—*squeak*—"with that train." Then the line went dead.

Ten more men had shown up while Shenkov was speaking over the radio. He half turned to face the senior man, his able Starshina Smirnov glad for his arrival. "Refresh your rifle magazines. Grenadiers commence the assault. I want two or three sustained volleys of grenades against that bunker, and that one over there." He pointed to where the bursts of rifle fire silhouetted two adjacent American fighting positions. Tracer fire and the echoes of rifle shots continued. Farther away, machine guns blazed, but for the moment his frontage was very lightly defended.

"Ten more men coming, sir, should we wait for them to make it up here?"

"No, the time is now."

As he said the words, the radioman next to him fell back, his helmeted head crashing into a rock with a thud. At first it looked like he had just misread his footing, but then another man above them and partially behind the rock gave a gasp, dropped his rifle, and clutched at his throat, gurgling loudly.

Stazia switched to the man next to Shenkov and squeezed the trigger again. The rifle let off a report, and the man went down. It looked like it was Starshina Smirnov, but she wasn't certain until she watched with glee as Shenkov dropped down to his knees.

"Now you know someone has your ass. Not so bold now, are you? You asshole." Then she fired again, killing another rifleman whose head was still visible above the rock. Much to her annoyance, Shenkov didn't run or go to ground, but instead brazenly stood, shouldered his rifle, and leaned up and over the boulder to fire off an entire magazine. Then he reloaded and fired another down at the U.S. Army troops.

Her angle on Shenkov and what remained of his assault men was greater than the Americans, so what looked like cover from the Americans at the base of the slope was still well within her view—the second reason she'd chosen this vantage point, that she could see both sides clearly. She also knew in the noise of the battle, no one would ever be the wiser. After all, being under the fire of one sniper is a real situation, but being under fire from multiple sources at the same time is just a battle.

That's when a real sniper can get some work done, she thought. Then aloud, she said, "This is not your fight, you bastard, it's mine. You don't break through the Americans unless I want you to." Another shot, and another Russian went down. Stazia smiled from ear to ear.

CHAPTER 19

Morgantown, West Virginia

Wynand's hand was wrapped up in his jacket. He quietly smashed the glass window of the school, then deftly undid the lock and pushed it up. He looked down below at Bill, who had him boosted up onto his shoulders. "We're in."

"I know," said Bill with clear sarcasm. "I've got glass all over my head. Do you think you can climb in?"

Wynand didn't answer. Instead, he grabbed the sill firmly and uncomfortably jumped from Bill's shoulders, then hoisted himself up and in through the window. Victoria half dragged and half carried the general over to the front stairs. Bill came to help, noisily complaining as he brushed the broken glass out of his hair and rubbed his shoulders.

"Bill, shush," Victoria said as they both put the general's arms over their shoulders and waited for Wynand to come around and unlock the door.

"Do you think he'll make it?" Bill asked matter-of-factly. Whether it was his culture or just his nature, Bill Degata had a way of cutting right to the point.

"I don't know."

"Well, surely you have some sort of diagnosis."

"It's not that easy. Radiation exposure is complicated."

"Wait a minute. You *don't* know, do you? You don't know anything about radiation."

"I . . . I do. I mean. Well, it's not my specialty, but I know the basics."

"So we could have made it all this way just to have the general die once we get to the hospital."

"No."

"Yes. Victoria, you could have saved us a trip. One where we still might get captured. One that probably shortened the general's life even more."

"Stop it, Bill. You're going to upset him."

Bill shifted his body, and the general's now limp head wagged from side to side. "He ain't hearing none of this. He's out cold. Has been for some time."

"Bill . . . it's true I'm not a nuclear medicine doctor, but I know the fundamentals. We learn basic decon in the military."

"Look, if I find out this mission was just your chance to try to prove your worth—or worse, you just want to save the general because your boyfriend Colonel Asher needs him around—I'm going to kill you."

Victoria was rocked back by his harsh words. She'd only known Bill Degata a few months but had never heard him speak like this. Maybe it was exhaustion, or maybe he just loved the general too much to see his life wasted for what might be a frivolous mission. Either way, she wasn't going to let the comment go.

"Look, we'll speak about this more later, but I am risking my life, and you two volunteered, so maybe your perspective will change once you get some sleep."

They saw Wynand's shape through the glass on the door. He pushed the bar and let them both in.

"Hey. There's no heat on, cold as hell, but I found a

windowless janitor's room with a sink and hot water. At least we can turn the light on in there without being seen from outside."

Victoria was always surprised at Wynand's quick thinking and street smarts, but she also knew his past. He'd been a moonshiner, running booze across state lines for many years, committing petty crimes and generally staying one step ahead of the law. True to his nature, he was resourceful—probably the main reason Tyce had recommended he come along. Still, she couldn't shake the feeling that given half an opportunity or a chance for profit, he'd sell them all down the river. He seemed like a man with no loyalties.

He probably wants to steal some medicine and sell it, she thought, then instantly chided herself for her doubt as he led them to a storeroom and kitchen of sorts. Stocked with canned food, pots and pans, and a small, vented gas grill. Maybe it was out of fear, maybe hope that someday the school would reopen, but it spoke volumes of the locals that no one had looted the school. At least it was nice to see that some things remained sacrosanct, even in a bitter insurgency against a Russian occupier.

That is, until we came along and smashed the windows and stole the food, she thought.

She couldn't help that with her Italian upbringing, she often saw the negatives in people and circumstances. While many were eternal optimists, she was a decidedly glass-half-empty person.

Wynand popped open a can of corn and another of string beans and started the propane grill. In minutes, he had them both simmering. Both Victoria and Bill heard their stomachs rumble. They had skipped breakfast because they were too busy getting ready and, once on the road, none had had time to eat the rations they'd packed. Hunger and fatigue were settling in and, as Victoria laid the general out on the janitor's cot, she began to feel the effects of the stress.

"Do you think we can make it by foot?" she asked Wynand.

"No," he said, not looking up from stirring the beans.

"I think we need to talk about whether we should even be on this mission right now," Bill said, his metal folding chair creaking as he stood up. "I think the lady doctor has been having us along for a pointless ride."

Victoria bristled at the comment, but she had developed a thick skin. She'd had to. She was smart and she was beautiful, and so she'd been verbally assaulted all her life. Whether it was other doctors assuming she was an idiot because of her appearance, or would-be boyfriends who assumed she was a nerd because she was a doctor. She held back her famous temper and instinct to lash out. For the moment.

"Bill, you of all people know how strong the general is. You've known him longer than the rest of us—"

"So I have more reason not to trust people who might not have his best interests at heart," Bill interrupted.

Wynand stopped stirring the food and held up his hands to silence the other two.

Outside in the hallway, they distinctly heard the sounds of several sets of footsteps—quiet footsteps that were closing in on the doorway to the room. No one breathed a word or moved a muscle. Just outside the door, the footsteps stopped.

* * *

Blue looked back up at the mayor's window before he entered the sheriff's squad car. He couldn't help but feel manipulated, but it wasn't really manipulation if he agreed with the outcome. Was it? He just wished there was someone smarter than him there who he could ask for advice. The sheriff was silent as they started off for the capitol of West Virginia in Charleston.

The words "the ends don't justify the means," kept running through his head—or was it "the ends *justify* the means"? What was it his teacher had said all those years ago? Damned if he could remember. Snippets of learning came and went with Blue and, though he had tried to pay attention in school, he'd only been given Bs and Cs because well-meaning teachers thought his position as offensive tackle on the high school team was worth a little extra credit. He'd certainly had a glow about him in school, and though he was as honest as the day was long, he knew he got away with more than other kids. He also knew it was partially because of his openness, his no-nonsense honesty, that people seemed to love him all the more.

He didn't understand people at all. So many people seemed to be so clever that he'd always found it best just to be quiet and listen. Eventually, the best decisions and most intelligent people seemed to step up and make things right—one of the reasons he was finding it so easy to be among the military men and women. Though they still succumbed to what he thought of as locker-room politics, they always came together and listened to their leaders when they needed to. Just like his football team.

But he had tried so hard to take his studies seriously. He knew it was all really important. He knew it because his mother would gush when he got a good grade, yet barely attended any of his games. His father, on the other hand, never made a single game. He worked most days until well past midnight. But when he heard of a good grade, he sometimes left Blue a note in his jacket pocket. It usually just said, "Good work, son," or "Remember, learning keeps the lights burning," or some other such phrase handed down in his family for generations. Though the maxim had apparently never been adhered to in any generation. Blue was just like his father, and his grandfather before them, in knowing that learning was vital, but seemingly never able to make it stick. So, like his father, once he left high school, he went and got a job.

Blue looked his Weatherby over. He pulled the bolt back and checked the chamber just enough to see some of the brass of the preloaded rounds in the dim light. Probably the most important lesson his father had given him was how to shoot. His dad had not only taught him to shoot and hunt at four years old but had counted on him killing several deer every winter after he turned six. Learning might keep the lights burning, but shooting put food on the table and didn't demand hours of study just to memorize some pithy words from a hundred years ago.

The sheriff turned on the high beams, and Blue settled into his seat. The sheriff was clearly not going to speak, and though Blue had a lot of thoughts on his mind, he had no interest in discussing them with the sheriff, a man for whom he had little regard. He often read people based on his own observations and a keenly developed sixth sense of what they stood for. The military men and women he'd been around these past months scored high marks, and his gut told him that, except for one or two, they really cared for their duties to their nation and the defense of its people. His read on the sheriff was altogether the opposite.

CHAPTER 20

Outside Huntington, West Virginia

Captain Shenkov looked around him after dumping four 7.62mm magazines down on the Americans in what amounted to rage shooting—controlled rage shooting. He thought he'd hit two, maybe three of the U.S. soldiers. Hard to tell in the noise, but he could tell someone had redirected additional forces back into the line he had only moments earlier intended to penetrate with extreme violence.

He was not a junior officer. Quite the opposite, he was battle tested and exceptionally well trained. So, as he watched or sensed his men dropping around him and pulled out the third magazine, he already realized he'd lost the advantage. The moment in time was gone. It was simple arithmetic; his penetration force was now outnumbered. There would be no breaking through the enemy lines tonight. He fired on full auto, then dropped in a fourth magazine, remained standing, and poured fire onto the enemy at the origin of some enemy tracer fire or the audible shouts of an enemy leader repositioning his forces back in the line or the fleeting movements of an enemy tossing a dead comrade aside and jumping into his fighting hole. When the enemy got first one, then the other machine gun working again, Shenkov finally took a knee behind the rock and put in his last magazine, panting heavily.

It was a testament to Shenkov's skill that he hadn't been hit. His skill, plus some of the usual battlefield luck. But he also knew from experience that an enemy reoccupying a fighting line remained disoriented for the first few moments. It seemed counter to natural instincts, but when soldiers were moved from a section of the battlefield they'd gotten used to into a new section in the lines, they were often reluctant to shoot, even when being shot at. The risk of shooting one of their own guys and the challenge of orienting themselves quickly on which way was forward and which was back came only after many, many months of combat experience.

The fight had also seemed like hours, and in battlefield time, it had certainly felt so. In actuality, it had only been about two minutes. Time seemed radically extended. Adrenaline was one factor. Greatly heightened senses contributed to an overload of the brain, which many didn't know was one of the primary functions of the adrenaline. It gave the brain the temporary ability to process more than two or three senses simultaneously. The body told the brain that death was all but imminent so all systems needed to cooperate or the living organism called the human body would cease to exist. Millions of years of evolution hadn't quite caught up with the speed of bullets, but it certainly had learned to deal with and speed up trigger responses.

Shenkov felt the adrenaline wear off. He could control it to an extent, like most battlefield veterans, but he couldn't prevent it switching off when his body sensed he was out of danger. That would come with even more years of fighting, he knew. He felt tired, and extremely thirsty. He reached for the canteen on his hip belt but felt only a wet mess. He looked down and noticed two rounds had passed cleanly though. He hadn't registered even being hit.

The volume of fire was steadily picking up around him. The rock they had only momentarily earlier thought of as a rally point to drive a wedge in the American lines was now a shelter rock. The machine guns were raking the top and sides of it. He had to respect these American special forces NCOs; they must be excellent leaders.

Almost as good as mine, he thought. Just then, he realized that, in his low crouching position, he was staring directly into the stony dead face of his own favorite NCO, Starshina Smirnov.

Time to go, he thought, and he slung his rifle over his back and began a low crawl back up the hill, using the rock to shield him from fire.

"Hey, sir," Sergeant Berringer yelled from the back of the building. "They've shifted forces successfully. I think he realized the hole in his lines about the time I did."

"Yeah, but he probably wouldn't have acted on it if you hadn't confirmed it. Good work, Devil Dog. Keep your eyes peeled," Tyce yelled back. He was waiting for the LAV commander, Lieutenant Bryce, to get back to him. He didn't have to wait much longer.

Bryce's voice came over the radio. "In position now, sir."

"Okay." Tyce held up a hand to one of the radio operators who had run over to ask if Tyce had any spare rifle magazines. "By my count, you have about another ten seconds. How many LAVs did you move?"

"I was only able to get mine into position. Red two is caught in a farmer's barbed wire, and the other is still supporting Captain Blake's men by filling in that hole in his lines."

"Okay. Can you see that industrial site on the far side of the river?"

"Yes, sir. I have it clearly in my thermal sights."

"Good. Now, see that gas tower? The one right behind the river barge area. That's about where they are starting their gun-runs."

"Okay, got it, sir. By the way, I see a figure up there—"

Tyce heard the faint sounds of a helicopter's rotor blades and interrupted, "Here he comes, Bryce! Get your gunner on that spot, and wait to fire until I tell you. I want to dust this asshole, but I want you to hit him over the land. If he goes down in the water, it won't have as big an effect on the rest of the helicopters and demoralize the Russian infantry, and we're going to try to hit *three* birds with one stone tonight."

"Copy, sir. Hey! We have him. Just where you said, sir. He's lights out and low to the ground, almost right over the water."

"Copy, I have him now, too." Tyce was using a pair of binoculars, which would normally be useless at night. He'd spent his whole life in Marine reconnaissance, so he'd learned binoculars could still be effective at night as long as you knew how to use the bursts of light and shadow that always accompanied a big firefight.

"So that's where you've been hiding." Stazia lined up on Colonel Tyce Asher. She was certain it was him. "Same strong jawline," she said, zooming in for an even closer. She imagined she could see the faint scar on his cheek he'd earned fighting hand-to-hand in Iraq. He was one of the most experienced combat veterans she'd ever come to know.

All the more reason having him in her sights was so tantalizing. "Hmm, yummy." His helmet was off, and he had a radio handset up to his ear and his carbine balanced in the elbow of his other arm. The building he was in was on fire, and even when she pulled away from the JIM HR she could see his outline against the flickering firelight.

It looked like he was directing something important. Maybe he had spotted the train. She hoped not. The general had said he was going to have it delayed or diverted. Protecting the train was still her primary mission. Her only real mission, even if her personal goal was toying with Shenkov and killing as many Americans as she felt was necessary to end the night's battle in a draw.

Whatever Tyce was doing, he was essentially facing her, while the rest of the battle raged behind him. She held the sight on his forehead and started her breathing cycle: *Odin . . . dva . . .*

Her mind started to race. *Father, is it time to finally kill this fucker?*

She rubbed her fingers gently against the red handkerchief tied to her forward bipod and continued counting: . . . *tri . . . chetyre . . .*

Her trajectory, windage, and elevation were perfect. She'd proven that all night, against both the Americans and some of Shenkov's forces. She'd already heard the general frantically trying to get another status report from Shenkov over their satellite radio, with no response. She took her aim off Tyce and looked back up the hill. Switching targets after counting was a no-no, but she had to look. Shenkov was now out of sight. She'd enjoyed watching him slither in the dirt as he crawled his way out of the predicament she had set up for him.

Her count had almost reached its zenith. She focused quickly back on Tyce.

. . . *pyat'* . . . *shest'*. She held her breath a moment, then squeezed the trigger.

Tyce adjusted his rifle forward in excitement and held the radio tightly to his ear with his other hand. He didn't need the binoculars anymore and had let them dangle around his neck as he watched the Russian Mi-8 attack helicopter approach with his naked eyes. His mind was rapidly calculating its speed and distance, trying to get the timing just right. Its guns and rockets were now blazing, making it plainly visible, though it was at his maximum range. Tyce heard the bullets zipping by and could see the miniature red trails of the rockets, and hear them, too, as they sizzled overhead and smacked into the hill behind him.

"Now, now! Fire now, Bryce!" Tyce yelled into the radio. Then *bang*, he was knocked violently back.

Stazia watched Tyce fall back. The size of the hole in the house's wall was wide enough that she could still see his legs, though the rest of his body had fallen back and out of sight. She held her breath. She heard the *crack-crack* of a loud gun from across the river, then the flat blasts as the shots hit one of Shenkov's helicopters.

"Ah, so that's what you were up to." She pulled her eye off the eyecup and watched the Russian Mi-8 burst into flames and spiral on its rotor blades' axis as it fell rapidly out of the sky and smashed into the field near the house Tyce was in. Two, then three more times the helicopter exploded as fuel and ammo started to cook off. Showers of sparks flew in all directions as rockets and bullets caught fire.

She went back to look at Tyce. After a second more, she saw his legs moving. Then he was back in the window looking stunned, cradling his right arm against his body and pinning it against his knee.

"Ah, good. I still never miss, Colonel," she said, and she made a pouty face and kissed in his direction. "Just one more to go."

CHAPTER 21

Outside Huntington, West Virginia

"Sir . . . sir?"

Tyce could hear the radio handset behind him where it landed after he flung it from his hand. He reached up and felt the leather strap that had once held his binoculars. One of the eyepieces and part of the frame still dangled there, though the most of it had burst into pieces when he'd been shot.

Did I just get shot?

Tyce felt his chest with his good hand. His other hand, the one that was holding the rifle, now buzzed and didn't seem to want to move. He felt a hole in his body armor. The ceramic plate had dissipated the force from the shot that the binoculars' metal housing hadn't, but, like the binoculars, it had also burst into pieces. *As it's supposed to*, Tyce thought. He'd seen many men hit by bullets, and if they were lucky, it was always the same. Their body armor was shattered and useless, but all because the armor had done its job. It was important to protect your front if you'd been hit because a second round didn't need to penetrate the exact same spot. Pretty much any shot to the ceramic plate would now penetrate. The jacket needed to be discarded after one hit.

Holy shit, I got shot! Tyce scrambled back deeper to the safety of the room, making sure to stay concealed behind the wall. It was pretty stupid to stand up in the blown-out window, but he had not counted on anyone firing from the river side of the battlefield. As far as he knew, they still owned everything up to and including the river.

Tyce looked for his rifle and, finding it, instinctively put the buttstock up against his shoulder. Then he crawled over to the radio, snatched the handset, and quickly came back to the safety of the shadow of the wall.

"Bryce, do you copy?"

"Shit, there you are, sir. I have visibility on another helo. They've shifted tactics to try to avoid my LAV's cannon fire, but my other vehicle got unstuck and has a vantage on the point he thinks they are going to approach from."

"Good work. You time this next one and get me another kill."

"You want this one on land, too, sir?"

"Doesn't matter now. Drop him wherever you can best kill him. You're now inside their heads, and Captain Blake has his rear flank free, so he can go back to concentrating on the Russians on the hill." Tyce knew that was only partially true. There was certainly someone operating behind them, but so far, he hadn't heard any reports of a sniper—besides his own experience. Tyce knew better than to poke his head up to look, but he now had to assume they had one or more sharpshooters. Not as deadly as the helicopters' withering round-robin, but he'd need to inform Ned.

Tyce crawled over to Sergeant Berringer, who was still dutifully watching and reporting Russian movements to Ned's radio operator. The man turned toward at Tyce when he came up, a look of battlefield glee across his face. He and the radioman had their helmets off, and they'd drawn a small sketch of the lines as best as they could see them on the floor in front of them.

"Hey sir, there haven't been any fresh Russian attacks for a bit, and Captain Blake hasn't been on the radio in a while. Maybe not a bad thing. I heard First Sergeant Hull on the admin-net yelling for their supply chief to bring up more ammo."

"That's a good thing. If he's able to focus on logistics, it means he's not just fighting from hole to hole anymore."

"Maybe, sir. Unfortunately, the supply sergeant said he was out of ammo." Sergeant Berringer glanced at the dangling leather and remnants of the binoculars still hanging around Tyce's neck. "Everything good on that side, sir? Thought I heard a bang."

"All good, Berringer." Tyce heard the clatter of LAV cannon fire out in the front. Another loud bang and he could hear the whine of a second helicopter plummeting toward earth. Tyce and the men were looking out into the backyard and at barren trees on Ned's hill, but the fireball from the helicopter exploding in the front yard lit up the hillside.

Tyce, still a little stunned, remembered the radio handset and picked it up in time to hear Bryce mid-broadcast: ". . . is down, and Red two reports he thinks he saw the other helos moving back north."

"Copy. Good work, Bryce. Your LAV's saved our asses today. Those helos were making mincemeat and forcing Captain Blake to fight in two directions."

"Good to go, sir," said Bryce over the radio.

Then someone spoke behind Tyce. "Sir." It was one of the other NCOs, a Corporal Kendrick. "We need to get the fuck out of here." He pointed up to the roof. The ceiling was still intact, but through the punctured and shattered ceiling drywall, he could see a bright red glow. The fire was burning though the rafters and would soon reach them—or worse, the house would collapse.

"Copy, we can't do any more from here. Fold up shop and get to Ned's lines immediately. Good work, boys, you all really kicked some ass tonight."

Stazia could see the entire hillside now without her thermal optics. It made it a lot easier to find the one target she'd been looking for.

There you are. It was Captain Blake. He was so well il-luminated in the scope's reticle by the downed helicopter that she didn't even need her count. *Not so special now, are you?*

Bang!

Tyce and the men hastened to grab rifle magazines, water bottles, and radio parts. Tyce looked around once more as they got ready to leave, and none too soon. The room was definitely starting to get hot, and the glow em-anated from up in the attic through the rocket and bullet holes to light every room like a dozen lightbulbs.

"Sir, what about that train?" one of the men asked. "I'm hearing that someones spotted it."

"Holy shit." In all the action, Tyce had nearly forgotten about the train. Since they were the ones ambushed by the Russians, instead of the other way around, he lost track and just assumed that the Russians had probably taken the extra time while the Americans were pinned down to divert or halt it.

"Sir, I'm getting two reports at once. One from Comanche that says Captain Blake is hit, the other from Lieutenant Bryce's men. They just reported that they can see a train now racing by on the other side of the river. He hasn't had time to report it on your tactical net yet."

Tyce was puzzled by the first radio call, but he didn't have time to figure out what they meant, and any second the building would collapse around them. He had practically just spoken to Captain Blake, so he was sure it was an erroneous report. More important, the train might be speeding by. The entire reason for their mission might slip though his fingers if he didn't act now.

Tyce knew he had seconds to act. He yanked the ruck-sack radio set off his back and called Bryce. "Dragoons, Dragoons, interrogative: Do you tally the train?" He was unable to conceal his emotions on the radio. His chest was pounding from pain and adrenaline. He was almost certain he'd actually heard a few of his ribs breaking from the impact of the bullet.

"That's affirm, sir. Was just about to tell you," said Bryce. "What do you want me to do?"

There was absolutely zero possibility that anyone other than the LAVs could do anything about the train over six hundred meters away and already speeding off into the distance.

"Can you see the engine?"

"Engine's already past, sir."

Tyce remembered the NBC Chief Warrant Officer Wheeler's words—then immediately chose to ignore them. He had to make a decision. "Fire," he said.

They had been thoroughly surprised, ambushed, and

had taken casualties, but Tyce couldn't forget their primary and stated purpose. And that was to stop the train and seize their cargo. Since that was nearly impossible now, they had to slow it down, even if it meant causing the nightmare scenario of a gas or chemical leak. He had to at least try to delay the Russians from reaching their goal, whatever that ultimately was.

"Pick a car and hit him with a burst. No more than a burst. Aim for the rail wheels if you can."

"Copy, sir," came the response, but Tyce could already hear the *thump-thump-thump* of an LAV firing. He knew he'd possibly just signed a death warrant for hundreds, possibly thousands of civilians—anyone who was anywhere near the speeding train, as well as those up the tracks on the way to the train's destination.

"Holy hell. What have I done?" Tyce whispered to himself.

One of the radio operators held out a radio handset. "Sir, Captain Blake is confirmed dead. Shot."

Tyce shook his head at the man, shoving him hard toward the exit. No time to deal with that now. They needed to get out of the building—fast. He took three deep but labored breaths, then sprinted out into the field with the last of his three men, with the additional sensation that there was now a sniper's crosshairs square on his back. Behind him, they all heard a crack, and the sounds of wood ripped asunder. He felt the blast of hot air at his back as the house collapsed in on itself.

CHAPTER 22

Outside Huntington, West Virginia

Tyce made it up to the top of the hill and into the open pasture there just in time to see one of the SF platoon's leaders, Lieutenant Shmalcs, in the middle of issuing orders to a pack of NCOs. "Then I want you to spread load the rest of the ammo out to the squads."

Tyce had already been over to visit Ned's departed remains and say a few words to wish his friend a safe journey. His duty now was to the living, and it wasn't going to be any easier. But he had choked back emotions for so long that he was able to remain stoic. He listened to the hasty field briefing without interrupting.

One of the sergeants spoke up. "What about the dead men's ammo, can we grab that, too?"

"Goes without saying, troop. Grab it and move on. They won't be needing it in Valhalla," said Lieutenant Shmalcs.

The men had been kneeling around their lieutenant, all of them looking completely fatigued by combat. Tyce was encouraged just by their faces and the fact that after such a hellish battle, they all seemed ready for more. Some were reloading magazines, some sucked down MRE rations from foil packets or drank water as they'd listened, but all, as if of one mind, stood and trooped off to carry out the instructions. It was impressive to see, and Tyce was in awe of their esprit de corps—especially because he was certain by now everyone had gotten word that they'd lost their popular commander.

"How'd we do, Lieutenant?" Tyce said the words, even though they sounded stupid. He was pretty sure he knew how they did: a Pyrrhic victory. Tyce had been actually afraid to ask him that. He hated voicing objective questions, such as requesting casualty counts from his subordinates during a firefight, and the like. It made him sound callous, out of touch with the men directly in the battle and just plain administrative. Unfortunately, it was all part of leadership. He couldn't make decisions without knowing how his units were faring.

Shmalcs turned, brightening at the sight of the colonel. "Hey, sir. helluva a fight. More intense than I think I've ever been in, and that includes actions on my deployment in Syria against ISIS." Tyce knew of Shmalcs as a real warrior type but had forgotten he'd been deployed into combat once before. The lieutenant continued, "But we did good, sir. We hit them so hard, they retreated. The last command we got from Captain Blake was to pursue without mercy. The men went on a rampage. By the time I made it up here, the last Russian helicopter was already on the horizon, but the NCOs from my platoon got a good piece of them as they were trying to skedaddle. Killed about five as they were loading onto their helo. One of my men even capped a guy as they were lifting off. They said it was sick watching him fall off the bird at about two hundred feet." Tyce could tell Shmalcs was probably masking the loss of his captain with some bravado, but the pride in his men was genuine.

Tyce squared up on Lieutenant Shmalcs and switched

from a friendly tone to pure business. The next order was going to be hard, but he knew it had to be done immediately. "Okay. I have an order for you. You're now in command of your company. Company C, the Comanches of the 19th Special Forces, are now yours. At least until I can get in touch with your battalion. Turn your platoon over to your platoon sergeant and assume command."

The man nodded. It was clear he had already thought about it. He was the next most senior officer in Comanches.

"Your second order is to get your men back safely to base. Once you have everyone back and you are on top of things, come give me a solid report on what we need to do to get Comanche back on their feet and back into the action. We'll hold a ceremony to honor your boss and all our fallen heroes when we can catch a breather. You copy?"

Lieutenant Shmalcs looked neither eager nor downtrodden at the orders; he was now all business. "I copy, sir. Comanche will get the job done."

And there it was. Tyce had now personally witnessed a man becoming a little more callous to the happenings of a battlefield. *Therein lies the nickname*, he thought. They called a grunt a grunt because after enough scar tissue built up, all it ever really came down to was enduring, grunting, and moving on to fight another day. *Will society be able to deprogram them all when it's over?* he wondered. The population at large were probably going to need just as much mental care as his men. Probably more. At least the men had their compatriots to fall back on, to commiserate with.

First Sergeant Hull walked into the pasture and hastened over to them. "The guys said I could find you here. Without your Gunny here, I didn't have anyone to report casualty figures to on the radio." The mood among the men changed instantly. While there was a certain warrior's bravado in describing a battle, getting the casualty counts was like the specter of death sweeping his scythe.

Hull pulled out a notepad and went through the tally. "Fifty-six wounded."

Tyce's jaw clenched. He had known the figures would be high. As Shmalcs had said, it had been a helluva fight, but that number was almost half of Comanche company.

Hull continued. "Twenty-six fallen angels"—the euphemism didn't do much to blunt the blow—"and still counting." Hull closed his notebook and looked up to both officers.

Inwardly, Tyce was greatly disturbed by the high numbers and the loss of Ned Blake. It basically meant the whole SF company was now combat ineffective. Almost three-quarters of their men killed or wounded, and they'd lost their leader. In any normal outfit even going back to World War II, those figures would be enough to pull the unit for rest and refit, and to try to get them replacements. He didn't really have either to give them.

He owned the numbers, though. Just like he owned the failure that had become of their mission. No one besides him had probably reconciled it that way yet, but he knew they would soon enough. He had been the one who had hastened them into combat with very little planning. It was a gamble, he had known it would be, but the battlefield calculus had never included being ambushed. He just hadn't seen that coming.

The Russians had somehow gotten inside his operational loop. He had a lot to reconcile, but it was now clear to him that either the Russians were in his radio nets, or he had a mole.

The last possibility disturbed him the most.

An NCO hurried up to the three men clustered at the edge of the bald hilltop. "There you are, sir. That chief warrant officer from the NBC group was looking for you. He says one of his chemical alarms is going off. He said everyone still back in the valley needs to put their chem suits on immediately. I told everyone I could see as I ran up here."

Tyce was already feeling the lowest he'd felt in a long while and hadn't realized he could sink lower. This latest report crushed his spirits far beyond despair. He nodded to the man and walked off to help Shmalcs and Bryce get their men back to the command post.

Major Uintergrin had heard the alarms they'd rigged up go off all over the train and was calmly putting on his specialty NBC suit. He hadn't heard the incoming gunfire directed at them, but he had seen a house on fire across the river as the train had raced along and could still hear the squealing of something metal toward the back part of the train. He pulled on the rubber gloves, then his overpants and top.

A man dressed in one of the disposable chem-bio suits issued to the soldiers clumsily saluted. Then a muffled voice came from behind his mask. "Sir, we have a leak."

Uintergrin held his special face mask and hood in his hands as he stared at the man. He contemplated chewing him out for stating the obvious and coming into the forward cars in his chem-bio suit, but he decided against it. This man was stationed in the prisoner car in front of the chemical car and would likely not have been exposed since the train was still moving, although they'd slowed considerably. He pulled on the mask and hood, letting his anger and impatience subside. Then he responded loudly through the plastic. "Follow me."

He led the man through the compartments toward the back of the train to a car they had rigged up as their chemical chamber. As they proceeded past the prisoner car, he saw the trio of "guests" kicked back on a couch watching TV. They were an unlikely mix, but he was glad to see they were all wearing NBC suits. The one he called the traitor looked as if he wanted to get up and talk to him, but fortunately the guards had followed protocol, and four men stood over them, their rifles at the ready. They might be guests of the general, but the men also knew Uintergrin had emphasized the other two cargoes as more valuable.

When Uintergrin made it to the chemical car's airlock, the first thing he noticed was the containment door was wide open, and outside air was rushing into the car as the train sped along. His spotted his two chemical officers inside. Both were working frantically to move a chemical barrel by hand. The barrel was very obviously split, and its contents were sloshing all over the men and the floor.

When they saw the major approaching, they stopped and put the barrel down like two chastened dogs caught leaving a mess on the carpet.

"Give me a report," Uintergrin yelled. He had to shout to be heard over the suit's synthetic barrier and the noise of air rushing in through the train's open side hatches.

The men were some of Uintergrin's own, handpicked and well trained. They were very familiar with communicating while in their suits and stepped almost right up to Uintergrin's face so they could be understood.

One began, "We have two barrels hit. Looks like shrapnel from American gunfire. The contents are completely compromised."

"Were they A or B barrels?"

"Both A barrels, sir."

"Thank God for small miracles," said Uintergrin.

"But we have four casualties. Some of the guards got a report from the engineer that the last car's wheels were damaged."

"What happened?"

"They came into the room without suits to try to assess the extent of the damage. We warned them, but they said they had specific orders from you to keep the train rolling through a possible American ambush—'as fast as possible, and no matter what.'" The man pointed to a corner near the open side door. Two men were curled up against the open doorframe. Their faces were dark blue, and their bulging eyes were stained bright red from burst blood vessels.

"Yes, those were my orders," Uintergrin said. "What about the damaged car?"

"We're treating it as exposed. We believe the other two men stationed there must've been badly exposed also. They came through while we were busy here, and we think they managed to disconnect the jammed emergency brake on the last railcar, but they have yet to come back forward. We assumed they died back there, but we were too busy trying to detect the leaks and get them sealed."

"Why did you not seal the barrels with the specialty tape?"

They both shook their heads. "We've been trying, sir. The barrel sides are slick. They're too wet now for the tape to adhere."

The other said, "The tape is only supposed to be used

on an aerosol leak, and these barrels were cracked too low down the sides. They were leaking liquid."

The first continued, "We called to the men off watch to hasten the full cleanup kits, but they haven't arrived from the storage section up front yet. We were waiting for you to see what protocol you wanted to employ."

Both men held up their wet gloves and pointed to a multitude of pieces of repair tape they'd stuck all across the barrels in their attempts to seal the barrel's contents. None of it was containing the liquid.

"Good work. Glad to see *my* men actually doing their duty. Dump them. And the bodies."

The men looked at each other. "Out the hatch, sir?"

"Yes. Both barrels. We can then begin the process of spraying down the remaining barrels with the liquid foam."

"Do you wish for us to wait for a spot outside any American towns or villages? The A barrels alone will still cause many deaths."

"No. Throw it all out. That includes the cleanup materials, too. Besides, if the Americans know enough about our train to shoot at it, then they already know what our cargo is. They can deal with the consequences of their own actions. We have a mission, and we continue without hesitation. Once the cleanup kits arrive, thoroughly wash down the entire compartment."

"We will need to clear the rest of the barrels out to do so. Should we move them back to the treasure car to complete the cleanup?"

Uintergrin thought for a moment. Because the treasure car was behind the chemical car, a large amount of aerosol component A would most likely have spread there. The chemical was persistent, and if not decontaminated properly, protocol dictated that everything in and to the rear of the chemical car be considered completely contaminated.

There's no way we can decontaminate all that stuff. We can sort that out in New York, he thought. "No, decontaminate the barrels one by one and move them forward one car once they are cleaned. Let the prisoners share the danger for a change. They have suckled on the Russian teat for free, and now they can bear some of the burden of our invasion. If your decontaminations are thorough enough, they will be in no grave danger."

"Understood, Comrade Major." Both men saluted sloppily, chemicals flying off their gloves as they did so. Then they hastened to roll the barrels over to the side hatch.

Uintergrin remained long enough to help them roll the first barrel over and out the side. He could see the lights of some village as they sped past, but a bunch of crops or some cattle and farmers really didn't concern him. Then he went to the decon station at the front of the car and began the laborious process of decontaminating his suit.

For now, the back of the train will remain thoroughly contaminated. But as long as we keep moving, the front cars will remain free from contamination. The air will sweep the airborne particles out as the men clean up, he thought.

They would go through the correct procedures of washing down, but everyone in the rear three cars would have to remain in their NBC suits for the remainder of the trip. It would slow things down considerably, but it was a hazard he had considered.

The single saving grace was that only the A-type element had leaked, so the two hadn't mixed. That would have been a complete catastrophe. The B element would have chewed through the disposable suits, and the resulting contamination would kill them all. That protocol was much different and included opening all the train's outer doors and windows. He'd seen it before, and there was very little defense. As it was, there was still enough of both chemicals to do the job General Tympkin wanted accomplished, though only just barely.

As Uintergrin stripped off his suit, he noticed a piece of the barrel leak tape was attached to his suit. He pulled it off with a gloved hand and stuck it into a clear plastic chemical containment bag, finished his washdown, and made his way forward. He waited a moment outside Colonel Karataev's door. The man was either cowering inside and awaiting a report or still sleeping. Uintergrin wasn't sure which was worse. He knocked, and a weak answer came from within.

So he is a coward. Uintergrin slid the door open to see his boss crouched up on the train seat, the window wide open, air blowing hard against him. He must've pulled the window's emergency latch. Uintergrin could see both panes had fallen free. Mostly he noticed the man was still not in his NBC suit.

Too panicked to move, he thought. *The fool studied nothing of the chemical protocol and procedures manuals I gave him.*

"Is it safe?" the colonel yelled over the rushing wind.

"We've had a containment leak," Uintergrin said loudly but calmly.

"How bad is it?" Karataev said. His eyes grew in horror, and he bent his face closer to the window.

"Two barrels cracked. Limited liquid and aerosol leak. We'll move the good barrels to the prisoners' car . . . and the last car is to be considered contaminated."

"Unfortunate. But I heard we lost men. I heard they died horribly from the exposure." He sounded pleading now.

"It's true. We had four patriots who died heroically for Mother Russia. Their names will be noted, and I will ensure the general declares them heroes before the month is out."

"Fine, fine, I will call Tympkin shortly and let him know. But shouldn't we ditch the train and abandon the mission? We are already limping along . . . must be twenty, maybe thirty kilometers an hour. Will you keep the prisoners—I mean the comrades—in their bio-suits? I know I'm in charge of this mission, Uintergrin, but you know I'll support your decision if you think we ought to call this quits." His voice was coming in fits and starts. He added, "Doomed from the start, just as I said," before Uintergrin could speak.

"We have it contained. We can continue the mission."

He saw Karataev's body slump; it was not the news he wanted. It was clear the man wanted to be anywhere but here, and Uintergrin's news sent him further into a panic.

Like a cornered rat, now Karataev lashed out. "Damn it, man. This will not work. How can we continue? I must call Tympkin. We should let him decide. After I give him all the facts, that is." Karataev heaved a few times, like a child in the middle of a crying fit. "He'll see. It's madness to continue. I just need to know when it's safe to leave my cabin. Then we can get some answers."

"Yes, sir. You are, as you said, in charge." Uintergrin watched the man whimpering and gasping a moment more, then moved to leave.

Before he did, he opened the plastic bag and pushed the open end over the door handle, making sure that the still-wet chemical tape covered the handle thoroughly as he turned it and slid the door open.

He looked back at his boss and slid the bag off the

handle. "It's safe now, sir. All the chemicals are contained in the rear of the train, and all the aerosol that leaked will flow behind the train with the wind as we continue to clean the cars. The towns we pass through might not be too glad tomorrow morning for their new presents, but we will remain fine up here. You may make your report to the general when you are ready."

Karataev nodded and was visibly relieved, but remained gulping the cold night air coming through the window.

Once outside the cabin, Uintergrin sealed the bag, careful to only hold it by the outer plastic edges. He walked to a window, released the catch, and lowered it, still holding the bag with his other hand. He meticulously peeled off each finger of the special charcoal-lined black leather gloves he always wore, then tossed them together with the bag out the window. Next, he hurried over to one of the nearby portable decon stations and fastidiously washed his hands and arms with the chemical reacting foam. If he'd been fast and careful enough, any limited exposure to his skin shouldn't cause any problems. His boss, he believed, would not be as lucky.

CHAPTER 23

Tucker County High School
West Virginia

"This is the worst possible scenario, Colonel Asher," said the vice president. "I'm still not clear how you let them get by you. Where does your intel section place the train now?"

Tyce had his head down as he listened to the vice president on speakerphone, but the question brought him out of his own thoughts. He looked over toward the intel section and caught Stacey staring at him. She looked away when he caught her gaze, but she seemed to be paying close attention.

Her hair was still pulled back and her cheeks were rosy, fresh from some reconnaissance mission she had been explaining to Tyce just as the VP called. She seemed to like working alone, like most intel types, and Tyce appreciated her autonomy in getting her job done, especially given how busy his command post always was. She glanced at a note one of her men handed her and cleared her throat in a melodic way, almost like an opera star trying to find the right pitch, and spoke.

"It looks like—and this is considering the time it took for you all to get back and factoring the train's current speeds that we gleaned from the hasty debriefs—they are somewhere on our side of White Sulfur Springs, soon to be headed into Virginia. In another four or five hours, they will be in a position to either turn north or south in the Shenandoah Valley."

"Your old stomping ground, Colonel," said the vice president. "Too bad you don't still occupy that piece of ground. Do you think they'll use the big rail lines?"

Stacey answered for Tyce. "They won't . . . sir. They'll carefully keep to the backwoods rail lines. Getting caught in a city along the coast or anywhere near the suburban sprawl around D.C. or Richmond and Norfolk would kill their momentum."

"Got it, thank you. Good analysis. Our team up here is nodding, they agree. Is that the new intel officer you were telling me about, Colonel Asher?"

"It is, sir. She's proven invaluable. She also just got back from a mission conducting some local reconnaissance. But if I could also mention, we think we slowed them down at least some. The men said they could hear one of their cars had a jammed wheel or something after the parting shots I mentioned at the beginning of the call."

"What's to say we didn't hit any of their cargo?" The VP's voice sounded worried.

"We did, Mr. Vice President, but after the Russians took a chunk out of us, I personally felt we need to do something to accomplish our stated mission. I take full responsibility for any fallout."

The room went so quiet for a moment you could hear the radios hum, but the vice president spoke first. "Okay, good work, Lieutenant Colonel Asher. I know those decisions on the ground are terrible, but I want you to know, and I need all of those in the room listening to know, that I support you one hundred percent."

"Thank you, Mr. Vice President." Tyce had been holding back, but up until that very moment, he had guessed there was a fifty-fifty chance of him getting relieved on the spot. He clutched his chest where the bullet and the binoculars had crashed against him. He had yet to go get it checked out, and it hurt, badly. "Our new chemical officer remained behind to gather some of his folks and assess the damage. We should get a report tomorrow."

"Okay, boss man," said the vice president. His tone was more upbeat now that he knew where things stood. "We don't have the time for you to wait for that report. You and your team are still the best force I have in the region, and before you go off to formulate a new plan, I have some more intel updates for you. News that may change some of your strategizing."

Tyce looked around the room. Everyone had a pencil and paper out or was listening intently. "Okay, sir, go ahead. We're all ears."

"I'll make my acting director of the CIA available to you all afterward for your intel section for any additional details, but I want you to hear it all from me first so you know the gravity of your ongoing assignment. We've identified the prisoners that the Russians sprang from ADX Florence—that's the supermax prison in Colorado—and you're not going to like it. First one is former FBI agent Michael Hanson."

A few exclamations went up around the room, especially from Stacey and her intel section.

"I take it from the noise most of your folks know who that is. The very same FBI senior agent in charge of counterespionage. Career man, worked for the agency for nearly thirty years, all the while feeding information over to Mother Russia. He was so good at his job, they say he single-handedly set our intel apparatus back twenty years. We were picking up the pieces on that disaster for a decade. He was directly responsible for the deaths of ten of our agents and likely more, if you include partnered nations' agents. Most won't divulge this, but we had to give up details on everyone he'd touched in thirty years to every one of our partners. Huge egg on our faces. He also helped many, many other operators infiltrate the U.S. before we caught him. No reason to explain why the Russians want him back; it's pretty clear he is quite a prize for them, and springing him shows just how far they'll go to take care of their own. Likely there are more of his sleeper agents out there."

"Who ever said no one likes a traitor?" Gunny whispered jokingly to Tyce, who waved him to be silent.

"Your number two man is one Professor Doshkar Kozinski." The room again broke out in a rumble of voices, this time more so than before. "Ah, so you all remember the so-called Omni-bomber. PhDs in chemistry and physics from Harvard. Worked at Aberdeen Proving Ground in the army labs for ten years as the absolute darling of the chem-bio defense world. Girls loved the pictures of him with his Einstein hair and boyish good looks. Put us on the map for modern chem-defense in countering other nations' chem and bio. Seemed like an all-American. That is, until something clicked, and he unleashed the deadliest series of ricin attacks our country has ever known. For months we struggled to find out who could be behind it all, and he covered his tracks so well, even to this day there's doubt among the public that it was him. All we know is the attacks stopped once we locked his ass up."

"There's still that geeky haircut named after him," said Gunny.

"We got the right guy," someone else said.

"I didn't order from Amazon for a year," said Sergeant Berringer.

"Who did?" said Gunny. "I mean, who suspects an Amazon package? We get them so regularly, you never even stop opening it long enough to think if you even ordered something."

Tyce shushed them all; he was growing impatient.

"We believe he is on board to help with the chemicals. Exactly how—we have some guesses. We think that having a known criminal and serial chem-bio terrorist gives them the perfect fall guy. They understand the international ramifications of using chemicals against us and may have concocted some kind of scenario where they pin the attack back on the professor."

"Fucking genius," said Gunny. "They slime us with our own chem, then point the finger at this joker, and they're off scot-fucking-free. Bet they even arrest his ass after the fact. Then they own the whole show, up to and including taking credit for his capture, all while avoiding any fallout. Very Soviet of them." He chortled and glanced at Stacey, who grimaced back but kept her gaze fixated on Tyce.

"Possibly," said Tyce. It sounded far-fetched, but it did clearly give the Russians both a method and a means. It was the motive that still wasn't clear; but then again, things were rarely clear on a battlefield. The enemy was a thinking, living being, an opposing will, and that usually left motive difficult to discern. "They'd only use it in a spot where they were stuck. I don't see the big picture, Mr. Vice President, I'm too focused on my own battles. Do you all have some ideas?" Right at that moment, Tyce realized just how much he needed General Custis. The general always seemed to see the big picture so well.

"We do. We believe they might use it to target the 82nd Airborne division down at Bragg or up north against the 10th Mountains Division at Fort Drum."

"Jeez, that doesn't bode well. If they're North Carolina bound, we don't have much time to waste."

"Exactly," the vice president said. "You get about an extra twelve hours if it's New York. In any case, I can't stress again how time is absolutely of the essence right now."

The room was stunned into silence, with everyone lost in their own reflections on the implications of either target. "All right," continued the vice president. "Our last man is still a bit of a mystery. He is Jean-Jacques DelaCroix."

The room stayed silent.

"Yes, we had the same reaction: Who the hell is Jean-Jacques DelaCroix? No one seems to pay attention to the uber white-collar criminals, even though he's possibly the worst and has had the widest-ranging effect of all of them. Jean-Jacques is a computer hacker. In fact, unlike the others, most of you have probably unknowingly been touched by his wizard powers at one time or another. One of the world's best. He broke into eBay's payment system and set up a funnel site that stole pennies from every purchase made, then converted it into untraceable Bitcoin. Flush with cash and confident in his abilities, he crashed Wall Street . . . six times. Each time, he made it look like foreign interference from—ironically—Russia and China. Worst fact: our NSA believed every crash *was* attributable to foreign governments and started to do the same things back to them."

A few comments broke out in the room.

"Yeah, you probably never heard that before." There was some commotion on the other side of the phone, then the VP continued, "I'm being told it might be best you disregard that little tidbit. Besides the numerous worms, viruses, and hacks, he sent through the web of which you were all probably unwitting recipients, he is probably best known for dumping millions of bits of U.S. classified data, then letting his friend Julian Strange take all the blame. You've heard of Julian, but the real mastermind, the one who stole all the data, was Jean-Jacques. He did it to conceal his sixth and final Wall Street hack, but that was actually the sole reason we caught him. Otherwise, he'd still be at large counting his billions. What the Russians want with him is anybody's guess."

Tyce waited to see if there was more, then looked around the room to see if there were any questions. There were none, so he spoke up. "So what does this mean for our mission, Mr. Vice President?"

"In short, it means you must get that train. Can you please clear the room down to just your inner circle? We have some sensitive future operations to discuss."

"Sure." Tyce would prefer if all his decision makers remained, but he dismissed everyone but Gunny and Stacey. If Victoria or even Blue had been there, he would have kept them, too, but Victoria had yet to report in, and no one knew what had happened to Blue after he was summoned to the mayor's office. Tyce looked at his watch; it was almost midnight. The clock was ticking, and though the purview of officers was supposed to be planning, he really felt they needed to get on the road and back into the fight.

A terrible, sweaty feeling had been creeping over him throughout the whole briefing. His insides were screaming for him to jump into action. Things seemed to be slipping away from him on the battlefield. He also knew that overly hasty action was exactly what killed Ned and so many of Ned's men. If Victoria were there, she would have understood his predicament. Tyce was now personally feeling the loss, death and sickness of much of his inner circle

Tyce indicated that the room was clear, and the VP continued, "A chemical attack on our troops would take out a unit and also serve to kill the morale of the other units still fighting. Including yours. It would make it clear that we have no other resources to protect you. Because, speaking frankly and mano a mano, Colonel Asher, we have no more tricks up our sleeves. The Russians would only need to hint at using chem again and the rumor mill in all the units still fighting and among the troops would account for the highest desertion rates we've ever seen."

"We're sure they won't use it against civilians?" Tyce asked.

"Even with the professor as a scapegoat, politically they couldn't justify an attack on civilians. The Canadian military has come to the same conclusions, you may like to know, and they have grave concerns if their ultimate target is Fort Drum."

"*Only* if it's Fort Drum?" Gunny scoffed, only somewhat under his breath.

Enlisted men, especially senior enlisted men, had a knack for snide and offhanded remarks. There was a certain leeway given to them by their officers. Having a group of mid-level leaders who spoke their mind and voiced doubt had come in handy through most of the Marine Corps' almost 250 years of existence, and Tyce certainly appreciated the men who spoke freely. It was when they held their tongues that he got really worried. Often, that meant they didn't believe in the mission or, worse, in their leader.

The VP was still going. "A full-fledged chem attack, enough to kill or sicken the men of the 10th Mountain, would decimate the entire region. The men up there are fighting from towns, houses, in the forests, and, like you all, up in the mountains. The Russians would need to spread those chemicals very broadly over northern New York State, and the analysis from our Canuck buddies is that Lake Ontario would be rendered a dead sea within the month. With the Russian invasion, world food supplies have become scarce, expensive, and harder to move around. The Russians have, as of yet, not blockaded commerce at the mouth of the Gulf of Saint Lawrence, but they have been using aircraft to stop anything coming across the lakes from Canada. Canada is counting on those lakes for a meager fish supply, as are we."

"So why doesn't Canada intervene?" asked Tyce, "I mean direct military intervention. Shouldn't Canada be right at our side in this? They need to demonstrate that they are truly our allies."

"I can't tell you everything, Tyce, but I can tell you they are doing their part. Just as Mexico is. I . . . that is, what remains of my cabinet all believe, as does their government, that it's best for Canada to try to appear neutral, at least for the time being. Until we get a better idea of where they can really help. We don't want a third army trooping around on our soil looking for Russians. We know for a fact, from intercepted . . ." The VP trailed off again when someone in the background stopped him again, then restarted. "Some *sources* suggest that they'd love for Canada to get directly involved. It would possibly turn a lot of Americans toward the Russian side, or at least muddy the waters on who is the invader. Can you imagine if the Canadians killed Americans? You know, if some civilians got caught up in the cross fire. Still, we're talking about things months in the future, and possibly not until next spring."

"If we even make it that long," Tyce muttered. It was all news to Tyce, but he knew next to nothing about the big picture.

"Come again? Didn't hear that last question, Colonel."

"Uh." Tyce realized too late that he'd spoken out loud. Gunny gave him a reproachful look that seemed to say comments like his were better left to the enlisted men. "I was just wondering how long?"

"Just get eyes on that train and tell me which way it's heading. If it goes north, I may be able to get you some additional support. I trust you to get the job done. The nation—or perhaps I should say two nations—are counting on you."

Tyce rubbed his bruised and possibly broken ribs. He could feel several of the bones there clicking as he breathed, each time sending sharp waves of pain across his chest. "Got it, Mr. Vice President. You can count on the 150th," he said. He knew he wasn't able to muster up anything near the bravado he imagined the vice president needed to hear.

CHAPTER 24

Russian Pentagon
Washington, D.C.

General Kolikoff looked Captain Shenkov up and down. Shenkov hadn't said a word since the general had put him at attention and told him to wait for General Tympkin to arrive. He was a battle-hardened warrior, but Kolikoff felt he deserved no more leeway after his latest fiasco than any other officer under his command.

Kolikoff jumped in his seat a bit as two black-clad men entered his makeshift office and looked the room over before opening the door and admitting General Tympkin. Tympkin wasted no time. He came around and shooed Kolikoff out from behind his own desk, then sat down and indicated for both men to sit in front of him. It was an uncomfortable position, to be sitting adjacent to his captain, but Kolikoff knew it was coming. He was just as much if not more to blame for the failed ambush.

"We are missing one. Where is Agent Panther?"

"Major Stazia Van Andjörssen is still out on the battle-field. Her last report stated she had killed more than twenty U.S. soldiers, but even with all the American units' locations tagged and sent by satellite to Captain Shenkov, the . . . uh . . . attack failed." Kolikoff was good at shifting blame, but there was no way to avoid this one. He hoped to sound contrite. It was a cowardly act, but he had seen just how willing Tympkin was to rid himself of a recalcitrant or failing subordinate, and tonight he intended that wouldn't happen to him.

"I take full responsibility, Comrade General," Shenkov barked out, standing and saluting. Kolikoff was as much surprised at the outburst and acceptance of blame as he was the reaction of the two black-clad guards. Both leveled their AKs at Kolikoff and Shenkov and seemed very nearly about to pull the triggers.

"Now, you see"—Tympkin held up a hand of restraint—"that is the kind of accountability I like," he said while staring at Kolikoff. "Now, for the first part of this conversation, I will speak, and you will listen. Am I clear?"

Both men nodded assent.

"Good. My train has been disabled but is continuing on to its destination and will fulfill its mission. You two have only one assignment now. Get my train to New York. Nothing else matters. Am I clear?"

Both men nodded, but to Kolikoff's further annoyance, Shenkov decided to speak. "General. Why do we not just load up everything onto a transport aircraft and be done with this train nonsense?"

"Ah, I am surprised no one else has had the balls to ask that question. There are three reasons. First, part of my special cargo is too heavy to send by one aircraft. Second, the chemicals are volatile. The third reason . . . one of my guests is afraid to fly."

Kolikoff and Shenkov both looked at each other in surprise.

"Yes, and I need that man as much as I need my cargo."

"Ah, so one of them is a chemist." Shenkov nodded his head.

"No. One of them is an economist," Tympkin said, "and he and my special cargo are more important than all the chemicals, guns, and riflemen under my command. Now get in touch with my train, and get to work."

Both men jumped to attention as Tympkin walked out of the room, leaving them to figure out exactly how to tackle the order.

Morgantown, West Virginia

Victoria and Bill had been so busy arguing that they hadn't heard the footsteps until it was too late. The door opened quietly, and an old woman and two kids had poked their faces in. The mood changed immediately, and Victoria and the men had simmered down, made introductions, and after hearing their story, offered up their cooked food. Victoria looked around at the new faces. All three gobbled down the corn and beans they had earlier hoped to make a meal out of.

"Mrs. Gess," Victoria started.

"It's *Geis*. Mable Geis, and this is Jan, and the little one there is August."

Both kids looked up, but only briefly before diving back into the bowl of mixed vegetables. Victoria stared at both children while they ate. Something struck her as not quite right, and even under the circumstances, she could not deny her curiosity as a doctor.

"Where do you live?" she asked.

"We are right next door. We saw you breaking into the school and needed to come over to warn you."

Wynand gave a sour look to Bill, who in turn looked at Victoria.

"We appreciate you doing so. What do you know?" Victoria asked.

"There are Russians here . . ." she started, then helped young August to put the fork in his mouth. His skin was pale, and his hand shook. "I'm sorry," Mrs. Geis said, "it's been quite some time since we've had a square meal. The children and I have been too afraid to leave the house. You see, their father—that is, my son in-law—left over six days ago to go out and try to get some food. There were rumors of a Russian food distribution site being set up."

"He hasn't returned?" Victoria asked.

Mrs. Geis seemed reluctant to talk in front of the children. They couldn't be older than four and five years old, but they now seemed engrossed in the food, so she continued, "Well, maybe he's found some and just hasn't been able to return. At least, that is what we have been praying every night." She rubbed the girl's back and helped the boy put the fork back to his mouth again.

"And their mother?"

"Do we have the time for this?" Wynand exclaimed.

Victoria waved him off angrily. She was exhausted and at her wit's end, and Bill's doubt in the mission had pushed her well beyond her limits.

"She . . . she finally had enough of the hunger, and yesterday she went out and flagged down a Russian patrol. She said it was better to throw herself on their mercy than to slowly starve to death. She'd learned the Russian word for emergency. She ran out into the street yelling— *Avariynyy! Avariynyy! Avariynyy!*" Mrs. Geis paused, swallowing. "We watched from the window as they picked her up . . . and then they, um, drove off." Mrs. Geis spoke the last words reluctantly, and only after petting the youngest on the head.

"Ah . . ." Victoria got the gist. A young woman, desperate to feed her children. Mrs. Geis painted the picture of one of the very ugliest of truths in a war. A truth America had not been witnessed on its own soil for over a hundred and fifty years.

"Commander Remington," Wynand interrupted abruptly, "may I have a word with you? In private." He pointed to the hallway.

Victoria touched Mrs. Geis on the shoulder and followed Wynand out into the hallway. Bill Degata followed them both and shut the door behind them.

"Just what the fuck are you doing?" Wynand said.

"I'm doing my fucking job." she hissed.

"Your job entails getting caught up in some local bull-shit?"

"I have an oath," she growled.

"Last time I checked, your oath says 'do no harm,' not 'spend hours dealing with some fucked-up family and their fucked-up problems.' You do know that behind every single-mother-fuckin' door on this street there's a similar God-damned story, don't ya?"

Bill interjected, "We're on a mission to get the general some meds, and maybe a prosthetic for Diaz. Nothing else."

"Well, that's interesting," Victoria's snapped, her anger boiling over. "Aren't you the same guy who said just an hour ago that this mission was a farce? Well, which is it, Bill? Or are you just the fair-weather friend of the general?"

"Okay, okay. I've heard enough from you two bickering about the God-damned general," said Wynand. "We're already on that mission, and I for one ain't gonna stop until we get into that hospital and break into their medical supply."

"So why exactly do you want to be in that medical supply room, Wynand?" Victoria was sorry for it, but it just burst out.

"So now *my* motives are in question?" Wynand asked.

The three seemed about to come to blows when the door opened and the general looked out. "Hey . . . you all going to eat these leftover beans?" He looked impossibly weak, but it was likely that their louder-than-intended conversation had stirred him awake, only to find himself in a room full of strangers.

Bill went over, held the general up by the arm, and walked him back to the cot, then fixed him a bowl of the remaining beans and corn.

"This sideshow is over," Wynand said. "We leave within the hour, and we leave the general here. The old woman and the kids can look out for him while we go find some transpo and get that medicine. And that includes anything else they have that needs to be took. 'Cause I *guaran-fuckin-tee* that we need it all. As much as we can carry." After that, Wynand stomped back into the room, slamming the door in Victoria's face.

"And I guaran-fuckin-tee," Victoria said, "that I have come 'for the benefit of the sick,' and that little boy has untreated congenital hypothyroidism. And that is my oath, you *figlio di puttana!*"

Victoria felt betrayed by two people she had trusted, but nothing could make her forswear the duties of the oath she had taken as a doctor. She opened the door and walked back into the storage room, knowing what she had to do.

Victoria went over and held the boy August's cheek in

her hand, looking into his eyes while Mrs. Geis watched. Wynand had already stripped most of his gear from his pack, ostensibly to make room for more medicine when they got to the hospital, and Bill had made a cup of chicken broth for the general, who was lying back on the cot. His knees were skinned, but Mrs. Geis agreed to bandage him up with supplies from Victoria's medical bag once they'd left.

"Did the kids have regular medical checkups?" Victoria asked Mrs. Geis. "I mean before the invasion."

Wynand locked a new magazine into his M4 with a loud *clack*, shouldered the carbine, then brushed against Victoria on his way out the door in a not-so-subtle hint that he was now leaving.

"They did. That all stopped, though, as you said."

Bill rose and pulled on his empty pack, grabbing his rifle. Mrs. Geis turned to him. "Do you have the key?" she asked. Bill held up the key to the Ford Mrs. Geis had loaned them. "Don't worry too much about the car. I mean, if it gets dinged up or something. Until things settle down, we really don't have anywhere we can go. Just remember the Russians own the city. If they see a car driving, they will stop you for sure." Then she added, "God bless you and protect you." She made the sign of the cross, and Victoria did the same.

Victoria bade her and the children well and quickly followed Bill out of the school and through Mrs. Geis's yard and to her garage. The car was there waiting for them, just as she had promised. They all got in silently, and Wynand backed them up with the lights off. Then he drove off toward the center of Russian-occupied Morgantown.

CHAPTER 25

Tucker County High School
West Virginia

After the vice president hung up, Tyce looked at Stacey, then to Gunny. "We have a mole."

Both of their eyes widened in looks of shock and surprise.

"You're kidding, right, boss?" Gunny exclaimed.

Stacey remained silent, but her expression changed to one of genuine worry.

"Wish I were. No other explanation. I just have no idea who, or even how and where to start looking."

"What makes you sure?"

"No other way the Russians could have known about our ambush plans at the Ohio."

"Aerial surveillance, a disloyal local farmer with a cell phone, even satellite intel. They own all our satellites now. What makes you so sure?"

"I guess it's more of a gut feeling. But I want to begin a search," said Tyce.

"Sir, you know a mole hunt can tear a unit apart. It's kind of like yelling sniper on the battlefield. It might just be some doofus with a rifle who got a single shot, but everyone feels that crosshair burning into their brain and goes to ground," said Gunny.

Tyce shook his head. Nothing was working out. He felt like he was failing at even the most rudimentary tasks of being a leader. Shit, he couldn't even protect his units from basic harm, let alone prevent the infiltration from some Russian plant. He sat down and started poring over some of the headquarters' charts left on the command table.

"A mole hunt is very specific," Stacey said, moving over beside him. "There's a full counterintelligence procedure."

"*Jee*-sus." Gunny scratched at his day-old beard growth and stared at the ceiling.

"How long does it take?" Tyce asked Stacey.

"A lot longer than you're thinking," she said. "And I've never honchoed one before."

"Do you know how to do it?" Tyce asked.

"I mean, theoretically, yes. I was in a unit where they— uh, *we* suspected a mole. So I understand how a search is to be executed."

"How did that go?"

"Well . . . we never caught the son of a bitch." The cusswords were uncharacteristic and sounded almost foreign coming from Stacey. Tyce looked at her for a long second, then back to searching for the chart. She was a beautiful creature in an almost delicate way, so foul language sounded out of place with her character.

Whatever. Tyce was used to all forms of locker-room banter, and junior personnel often tried to mimic the speech patterns of their superiors. "Hmmm. Okay. See what you can come up with. I need to get the rest of the 150th refocused back on that train." Tyce turned to Gunny. "Guns, we can't use Comanche on this next mission. With the loss of Captain Blake and so many of their men killed or wounded, they're gonna need some time to recover."

"Probably a good while, I think, sir."

"Yeah." Tyce considered the time they'd need to bury their dead and continue to sort out the wounded. For now, his medical staff and even some of the local hospitals were going to have to suffice, but he was already feeling the effect of Victoria's absence. Having a senior officer in charge of medicine gave the men confidence that they could go into harm's way and, if anything happened, be patched up by the best. That notion was rapidly slipping away. Tyce had yet to go back to the medical section and visit the men. More pressing was getting back on top of that train.

"Gunny, let's use our LAV guys. They are fast and mobile, and we if we get them on the right roads, they could potentially get out ahead of the train and stop it. Can you make them ready within the hour?"

"Absolutely. Lieutenant Bryce is on alert already. If you only want a platoon, he can take one of the other two fresh platoons that weren't with him at the river. But just where are they going?"

"We don't know yet. I'll want your intel section to see what you can come up with"—he pointed to Stacey, who nodded—"but we want Bryce out and looking. He's the best reconnaissance leader we've got."

"Besides you," Stacey said sweetly.

"Got it, boss. Do you plan to go with them?" said Gunny.

"No. I'll take your earlier advice and stay put to try to get our house in order. Otherwise, Bryce might return to find no unit waiting for him when he gets back. Besides, he doesn't need his regimental commander breathing down his neck."

Any more than I already have, Tyce thought. Maybe the men would do better if he just issued the orders and stayed out of their hair. *No, can't think like that.* "You two got your assignments, go make it happen."

"Aye aye, sir," said Stacey with a smile.

"Roger, sir." Gunny grabbed his gear and started to leave. He turned back briefly at the door to see if there was anything further. He noticed Stacey had moved closer to Tyce and was standing right over him as he sat pouring over the diagrams of the 150th. He wrinkled his nose a bit but dashed off to get Bryce and his men ready for their assignment.

CHAPTER 26

Russian Pentagon
Washington, D.C.

General Kolikoff stared at his three majors. None of them stirred. Each was staring at their computer screens pretending not to notice he was glaring at them.

"Well? What do the newest calculations tell us?" the general asked.

"General, do we really think this is a fruitful use of our time?" Captain Shenkov said from the side of the room. "This SPETS-VTOR computer thing. I mean, we could just mount my men back up on helos and head over to reinforce the train. Maybe we could even use the helo to airlift something off the train so it's less vulnerable."

"I've considered it, but I want to see what the computer says, given the newest variables."

Captain Shenkov looked the general and his three majors over. *Useless idiots*, he thought. *We waste time while the enemy concocts plans.* He knew General Kolikoff was a falling star—his meeting with Tympkin had proved that—but he was still a general, and for some reason, Tympkin still trusted him to run his operations. Shenkov walked out to the helicopter pad to inspect his men. Might as well get moving since his time here had been wasted.

* * *

"What news from Agent Panther Chameleon?" General Tympkin stopped in at Kolikoff's office just off the operations room floor.

"I'll ask, General." Kolikoff leaned out of the office and shouted, "What is the latest report from Agent Panther?"

A watch officer spoke up immediately. "Nothing yet, General. We're watching for her device on the satellite feeds. Wolf's device is turned on and giving a location, but Panther's device is turned off."

"Do we at least have a last-known-position report?" asked Kolikoff.

"General, she submitted some notes soon after the actions on the Ohio River. Beacon has been turned off since."

"Hmmm . . . we could use her reconnaissance reports," Kolikoff said to General Tympkin, "but I'll have the men use the SPETS-VTOR to figure out some appropriate next steps."

Stazia had proven valuable before, and it was difficult to disregard her now, but agents and intelligence were like that. The more you tried to attach a leash to them, the more independently they operated. In his experience, trying to direct them was nearly impossible.

Tympkin nodded and leaned forward. He seemed to be about to tell Kolikoff something in confidence, but then Kolikoff's door opened.

"General." Major Pavel nodded to each man and walked in, rather presumptuously. "There is something here in the SPETS-VTOR data that might be of use."

"How's that?"

"Well, it's from some of the old calculations, but it's an

item we haven't done much with. It was an earlier analysis on where the Appalachian hillbillies might set up camp."

"Yes?"

"Well, I cross referenced the SPETS-VTOR analysis of likely headquarters locations with recent radio intercept patterns. As you know, the Americans have, for the most part, stayed off their own military radio networks. But there is a spike around the Tucker County, West Virginia, region."

"And?" said Kolikoff.

"Well, we had been looking at the data from *before* Shenkov's ambush at the Ohio River. The SPETS-VTOR suggested we look at data collected *after* the attack."

"For Christ's sakes, Major, get to the point," said Tympkin hotly.

"Well, sir, there is a distinct spike in activity up around some buildings in the mountains. Google Earth has proven very useful in identifying some of these U.S. buildings." He held up a map printout. "It's near a high school, just like the SPETS-VTOR listed as a probable location. With the new data, there is a seventy-five percent chance it is now one of the enemy's operating bases."

"Hmmm. Send the data over to my computer, Major Pavel," said Kolikoff, who then turned to Tympkin. "This may be the intelligence we need to close in on the enemy mountain forces."

Tympkin flicked his hand at Major Pavel, who saluted and went out. "Okay, go ahead and look at it. I'll wait."

General Kolikoff looked over the intelligence and supposition analysis overlays generated by the SPETS-VTOR, then looked at the Google Earth link Major Pavel had found. The data looked good.

"Let me see if there are any spot reports from any of

our aircraft operating in the region. Even a debrief from some of our reconnaissance aircraft noting vehicle traffic would be useful. We usually have something up in the air twenty-four seven."

Tympkin didn't say anything, but he thought, *This is why I keep Kolikoff around. One of my only quick thinkers. The SPETS-VTOR is nothing without him—and vice versa.*

"I'll check the flight reports near the location of that school and the last-known location of that response force we tailed from the Agent Panther Chameleon's strike near Union, West Virginia," said Kolikoff as he tapped into the Russian attack aviation flight debrief logs. "Just another moment, sir." He dialed a phone number for the operations room floor. A minute after Kolikoff placed the call, Major Drugov was at the door.

"Sir, you have orders?"

"Yes, Major Drugov. Get on the phone over to the 79th Aviation Regiment. We have a location that coincides with airborne detection and signals intelligence. Tomorrow morning, I want to bomb these assholes back into the Stone Age."

Tympkin smiled. "Good work, Kolikoff. I can see why they are calling you Rasputin."

Kolikoff went back to his computer, completely forgetting that Tympkin had been about to tell him something. Tympkin hesitated and, seemingly deciding against sharing, left without saying anything more.

Blue shifted uncomfortably in his seat. It had been a few hours since they'd started driving, and there hadn't been a word between him and the sheriff, but his movement seemed to take the sheriff out of his thoughts and made him remember he had a passenger.

The sheriff spoke very slowly. "Are you up for this?"

Blue thought it a funny question; after all, the sheriff could probably have done this assignment himself. He most likely just didn't have the stomach for it.

"Yep," Blue said.

The sheriff was silent again for a moment, focused on the road, but now he seemed interested in talking. "You know this ain't gonna be like shooting some Russki."

Blue was fairly clear on the ramifications of his actions, just unsure of the motive. He chose not to respond, but the sheriff continued anyway in a chiding sort of tone. "I mean, you are about to kill a U.S. citizen."

Blue remained silent. The sheriff shifted his gun belt over his large stomach and held onto the wheel with one hand, the other going for his coffee cup. He took his gaze off the road a moment and glanced over at Blue to see if there were any emotions visible. Convinced Blue was too simple to understand his actions, the sheriff seemed to perk up like a dog that sniffs a cat and in a brutal way wants to play and see if he can kill it.

"I killed before," Blue said.

"Yeah, but not another American, I reckon."

"No," Blue said.

Sensing he was on to something, the sheriff circled and tried another approach. "I mean, this ain't just an ordinary American, he's an elected official."

"A corrupt official," Blue said, sounding a little like he was reassuring himself.

The sheriff was silent a moment again. Then he said, "Might be, but when you kill him, you kill the thousands of votes from the people. Don't that sink in with you any? Or are ya too dumb to know what all that means?"

Blue flicked his rifle's safety on and off and stared out the window. Seemingly satisfied that he'd broken into Blue's mind, the sheriff turned on the radio. The only station that worked was playing some kind of Euro-techno music—one of the many stations that had cropped up when Russian military DJs had taken over the U.S. radio stations in some vain attempt to calm the masses and still control the national news cycles. It was as jarring to Blue as the conversation with the sheriff, and Blue kept looking out the dark window thinking about how he'd gotten himself into this situation. None of it felt right.

CHAPTER 27

Tucker County High School
West Virginia

Stacey pulled over a chair and shimmied right up next to Tyce as he busied himself with the charts and maps. He crunched on some leftover crackers and drank a cold cup of coffee from the day before.

"You know, I just had an idea?" she cooed close to his ear. She stared intently at the small hairs on the earlobe that moved from her breath.

"Yeah?" Tyce said absently. He had a list of names of all the wounded and fallen soldiers and Marines in each unit in front of him and was completely absorbed in his morbid task. "How to find that mole?" He ran the tip of his pen down the roster to review next of kin for his letters to their families.

"No," she said. Inside, she was wondering just how long it was going to take to seduce him. It usually wasn't much of a challenge. Ever since she was sixteen, she had known that boys, and later men, could hardly contain themselves around her. "Which way the train is going to go."

Tyce stopped looking through the charts and turned toward her. He pulled his face back, only just now realizing how close she'd gotten to him on the operations center map table. "Uh, well, what do you think, Petty Officer?" He blinked. After many nights on only a few hours of sleep, propped up by multiple pots of coffee, his mind was not functioning at its highest level.

She backed off a little, too, as if she had just been looking at one of the maps. He'd used her rank and not her name, so she recognized she was going to have to slow things down. But only just a touch.

The confident ones take longer, she thought. *That's okay. He is going to be* such *a prize once I make it happen.*

And even better, it was going to be right under the nose of that bitch, Victoria. Something ticked off her insides at the thought of that woman.

She couldn't put her finger on it, but she knew conquering Tyce was going to be much sweeter than killing Captain Blake. But only half as good as killing Tyce out on the battlefield was inevitably going to be.

One thing at a time, she reminded herself. She shifted a half inch closer to Tyce on the bench, ostensibly to reach some highlighters on the other side of him. She could tell he was groggy. *Time to turn up the sweetness and hit him where he's vulnerable; he likes to plan a successful mission.*

"I still have some contacts back there at our last headquarters," said Stacey. "Back at the Omni Homestead Hotel. You know, I think I once saw you swimming there." She gave him a brief smile and shrugged her shoulders, then went back to explaining, "I had gotten in good with a few of the employees there, and if I can get in touch with them before the train goes through, I might be able to persuade one of them to go out into the Shenandoah Valley where the train tracks split north and south and get him to relay back to us. It'll save a hell of a lot of time, and then we can better vector Lieutenant Bryce in on the train."

"Do you trust the person?" Tyce asked. He didn't know intelligence work other than in passing—he gave them information from his reconnaissance missions, and they sent him the refined intelligence products.

"Oh, for sure. He'd do anything for me," she said.

Tyce raised his eyebrows. "Jeez. That's a hell of a good idea, Petty Officer Van Andersson. I mean, really good work."

"Thank you," she said, "I feel like, maybe, since we're gonna be working with each other for some time, it would be okay to drop the formalities . . . What do you think, Tyce?" she asked playfully.

Tyce's brain was still a step behind, but his expression changed. "What? No. It's still Colonel Asher and Petty Officer Van Andersson." His tone was slightly shocked, but his sleep-addled brain was still chewing on what would be needed to intercept the train once Stacey's contact found it. "But I think you really may be on to something big. This will make *the* difference in our operations for the next seventy-two hours. How soon can you place the call?"

"Right away . . . sir." She smiled. She bounced upright to a slightly childish version of attention and saluted. "I can probably have something within the hour."

"Excellent. I'll get Gunny to have Lieutenant Bryce check in by radio in an hour, and we'll relay any news you can get us."

Stacey wagged her finger at him and said, "Stay off those radios, Colonel. Remember, the big Russian Bear is listening." And she went off to make the call.

Tyce's gaze followed her as she went, unconsciously homing in on her shapely backside, apparent even through her Navy uniform. Was it just his imagination, or had she just now come on to him? *Nah, she's a real trooper. The girl is all work*, he thought. *Troops just want to make friends with their bosses, and in tight quarters, the first thing they want to drop are ranks and last names.* It was all natural—Tyce had seen it a lot before, especially given the stress they all go through. He had spent almost his entire Marine Corps career around males, but he respected every trooper, every dedicated American who cared enough to sacrifice during this invasion. Especially ones who could help him solve clever tactical problems. Anyone who helped give him the edge it took to get the job done right was a bonus, in his experience. In combat, seconds were king; in operations, hours made the difference between a mission's success and catastrophic failure.

Tyce's mind was still stuck on Stacey when Gunny arrived a moment later.

"Sir, Bryce and his guys are ready. Should I send 'em?"

"Immediately. They can get a head start. But tell him to stay up on his radios. We may have some message traffic for him on the train in about an hour's time. Something really good, I hope."

"Great." Gunny seemed surprised. "Do we know something?"

"We'll if Sta—uh." Now she had him saying it. "If Petty Officer Van Andersson can hook it up, we may know soon whether the train is going north or south."

"Holy crap, sir. That'd save us hours. Probably a whole day, and a lot of nail-biting. If we get the direction, we can set up a fully prepared ambush." Gunny thought about it for a second. "I'll go brief Lieutenant Bryce quickly so he knows, and I'll come find you when I'm done. Where are you gonna be?"

"I'm headed over to the battalion surgery to check in on the wounded Comanche men, then over to the mortuary for a bit."

"Got it, sir. I need to visit there, too. Meet you there in a bit." He was about to go, then he added, "That girl's got some brains, and ain't too tough on the eyes, either. We really would be at a loss if it weren't for Petty Officer Van A. Damn well-trained intel specialist and has proven her worth in gold."

"You got that right, Gunny. At least we know one person who isn't the mole."

Morgantown, West Virginia

Wynand pulled the car over to the side of the road for the fifth time and cursed the Russians. They'd been driving around for over an hour avoiding Russian patrols but found every bridge over the river was blocked and manned by Russian checkpoints. "Goddamn. How the hell are we gonna make it like this? Gonna be damn daylight soon."

"At least we got closer. Look." Victoria pointed above a house to their right. The blinking red lights atop a tall building were visible in the distance. "That's the hospital."

"It's still across the river," Bill was quick to point out.

"I'll get us closer," Wynand said, "but we gonna have to swim."

No one in the car relished that fact, but there it was. If they wanted to get to the hospital, they were going to have to swim across the freezing-cold Monongahela River.

Ten minutes later, Wynand pulled the car over in a quiet spot and parked behind an autobody shop. The three disembarked, slung their rifles, and pulled out their empty rucksacks. The thickets and brambles tore at their hands and faces as they made their way down to the banks of the river.

"Strip down to our skivvies," Victoria said, "and we can put our clothes in our bags so we at least have dry clothes to change into on the other side."

Without a word, everyone started pulling off jackets, shirts, and pants and stuffing them away.

"What if we look for some kind of boat?" Bill asked.

"A little late for that suggestion," Wynand said.

Victoria was still angry, and though she'd had that same thought a half hour earlier, she didn't want to talk to the two men anymore. She'd been looking for a boat ramp or a boat repair shop as they drove, but she'd lost patience with the other two.

And why wouldn't I? she thought. *They treated me like shit.* She knew she wasn't a natural-born-leader type, but she didn't need to be degraded or have her loyalties questioned. It was times like this that she just wished she could have an ounce of Tyce's courage, or even just his usual male bravado. She wanted so badly to put both men into their place, but she also knew from many years of experience that when women spoke up on matters of imminent leadership, the men ganged up on them. Better to just keep going and do her job.

Victoria put her naked foot in the water, and a shiver went up and down her spine. She looked back at the other two, who were still changing out of their clothes, and caught Wynand ogling her.

Creep. She plunged farther into the freezing water. Once she was more than waist deep, she looked back and saw both men standing half naked on the rocky beach.

"What are you waiting for? Let's get going." Turning around, she lifted the pack above her head and plunged up to her neck in the water. She didn't look back until she'd gotten halfway. Behind her, she could see Wynand struggling against the currents and Bill still back on the other bank. She finished her swim and was already into her pack pulling out her clothes as Wynand came panting up. It looked as though he had struggled the whole way.

"Where's Bill?" she asked.

"I . . . I . . ." He was completely out of breath. In the moonlight she could see his pale, skinny chest heaving from exertion. Combined with his scraggly hair and droopy, wet moustache, he looked like he'd nearly drowned. The image of the usual tough country boy was gone and she couldn't help but giggle a little.

He caught her laughing at him as he pulled over his own pack and started yanking out clothes. "What's so frickin' funny?"

"You," she said, laughing. "You look like a wet rat."

"Well, you look like . . . like . . . like a WonderBra commercial." It was apparently all he could muster on the spur of the moment, but it sent Victoria into semi hysterics.

"A *bra* commercial? What the hell does that even mean, *tu idiota*?" She laughed at him, her hands on her hips. She was about to give him more ribbing when she realized Bill still hadn't arrived on their side of the river and in the dim moonlight wasn't even visible out in the river. "Hey, I can't see Bill."

Wynand stopped pulling on his shirt and looked back over his shoulder. "You think he went under?" he asked.

"I don't know."

"Well, we can't wait." said Wynand, angrily.

"What are you saying?"

"I mean we're leaving. We can't wait no longer. It'll be daybreak in less than two hours."

Victoria looked out onto the cold river. There wasn't a hint of daylight yet—just the opposite, the quarter moon looked like it was setting, and soon it would be pitch black for at least another hour.

Wynand put on his pants, did up his belt, gathered his pack, and started up the bank.

"You coming?" he asked. Behind him, he heard a gentle splash. He turned in time to see Victoria's head come up in the water as she swam back out into the cold darkness.

Charleston, West Virginia

The suburbs of Charleston didn't look much different from when Blue had seen them last, the only other time he'd been through the city. The houses and porches were lit and, oddly, people were visible. Almost all of his recent experiences with civilians had been in the eastern half of the state, where everyone still hid in their homes and mostly kept to themselves. Here, there were cars driving on the road, and some of the business seemed to be operational. At least, the gas station and several greasy-spoon restaurants had their signs turned on, and people were walking in and out. Charleston was not a big city, but there were plenty of eight- and ten-story buildings downtown. As they crossed out of the suburbs and started across a bridge to enter downtown, Blue noticed the buildings and even billboard advertisements were well lit.

As they crossed, Blue also spotted a Russian checkpoint on the other side of the bridge. The sheriff turned to him. "Now, don't you say nothing. Let me handle this." As they drove up to the checkpoint, they waited in line as a few cars in front of them passed through. When it was their turn, the sheriff rolled down the window of his squad car and handed the Russian soldier a piece of paper. To Blue's surprise, the man saluted the sheriff and waved him through.

"Okay, now you listen good. I'm going to drive us into the parking lot behind the Capitol building. We'll go into the Department of Education building and we'll head inside, then up the stairs to the roof together. That's where you're gonna set up your sniper position. Any questions so far?"

Blue shook his head.

"Good. Now, we'll only have about an hour to wait. The governor is giving his live broadcast on the back steps in"—the sheriff looked at his watch—"about one hour. Put your rifle into this bag," the sheriff pulled a long black nylon gear bag out of the back seat. "Inside is a state construction worker's jacket and helmet. Go ahead an' put those on. Any Russian guards will ask fewer questions. Now, suit up and let's go."

Blue put on the yellow jacket and helmet and squeezed his trusty Weatherby into the bag. They both stepped out and proceeded up to the building. Two Russians were there, but they glanced at the sheriff's uniform and Blue in his construction clothes and waved them through without even checking their IDs. Once inside, they found the stairway and headed to the top, where the sheriff produced a key that let them onto the roof. The visibility to the capitol steps was excellent. Even at night, it had a clear and unobstructed view. The sheriff pulled out a package of cigarettes and lit up. He offered one to Blue, who declined.

"Hey. We're supposed to call the mayor soon. Unpack

your rifle, get situated however you need to be, and then we'll let her know we've made it."

Blue started to set up his rifle. He watched out of the corner of his eye as the sheriff leaned against the wall, smoked his cigarette, and messed with his phone. As Blue checked things over, he noticed the sheriff had drawn his pistol and laid it atop the wall. The sheriff took a long drag on his cigarette and looked down at Blue. He gave Blue a big, toothy grin and blew the smoke down toward his face.

CHAPTER 28

Russian Pentagon
Washington, D.C.

"General, we just got another radio intercept. It's centered exactly on that high school where the SPETS-VTOR predicted it would be," said a watch officer.

"Excellent." General Kolikoff's spirits had picked up immensely in the past few hours. Things were really playing out.

"Sir, Agent Panther just checked in," said Major Pavel. General Kolikoff got up and went over to Pavel's computer screen. A message had come over the secure satellite digital uplink. It read:

> AMERICANS PLAN TO ATTACK TRAIN
> VICINITY, WINCHESTER VIRGINIA. THEIR
> COMMANDER REMAINS AT THEIR BASE.
> ESTABLISH COUNTER-AMBUSH AT
> CEMETERY, LAT/LON 39.182, -78.161. DO
> NOT TRY TO CONTACT ME.

"Good. Send the location to Captain Shenkov and tell him to take off immediately. He can get there well before them if he leaves now. They won't get through our ambush this time."

"Agent Panther has been very valuable," said Pavel.

"Yes, we have a great asset . . ." *and another who needs some work, Captain Shenkov, should take her as an example.* Kolikoff thought. "That part about their commander. That's the man named Lieutenant Colonel Asher. Sounds like we'll be able to kill him in the process. Cut the head off the proverbial snake."

"Do we have a dossier on the enemy commander, sir?" asked Pavel.

"Not yet. We tried to get into the military file systems in St. Louis, but someone destroyed all the digital records before we could recover them. Some fool executed all the Veterans Affairs personnel out of anger, and now we don't even have anyone to unlock the records we have recovered. No worries, though. Moscow has made a deal with China. Apparently, they stole all the U.S. service records a year ago, including active-duty personnel, and we've made an agreement to buy portions we need."

"Should I send her an acknowledgment of receipt?"

"No. She said no contact."

"What about the bombing run? We have confirmation on your request from the 79th that six Sukhoi Su-24 short-range bombers will hit the target at daybreak and 0752 hours. Does she need to know about that?"

"No, she's nowhere near there. Just make sure Shenkov has the comm links so he can link up with her when we ambush the Americans in Winchester."

Victoria swam ashore, dragging Bill Degata behind her in a practiced rescue swim maneuver. She stood on the shore, dripping wet and shivering from head to toe.

"What the fuck?" Wynand said.

He had her civilian shirt and pants out of her bag and ready for her. She pulled the pants on with some effort, her teeth chattering. It wasn't until she'd gotten her sweatshirt on that she caught her breath enough to answer, "He hadn't made it more than a few feet." She panted, "He doesn't know how to swim."

"You're kidding." Wynand stared at Bill, who lay on his back, so tired he could barely move.

"No." She turned to Bill, "Change. Now. Or you'll die." It was said with such force that Bill immediately used whatever reserve strength he had to weakly roll over and try to claw the now-sopping clothes out of his pack. His hands didn't look to be grasping anything very well, so Wynand bent down and helped him.

"They're all wet," Wynand said.

"I know. That was the only thing keeping him afloat for any time at all. He was all the way under when I got there. The only thing visible were his hands holding on to his floating pack."

"You . . . you dragged him up?"

"Look, no time for screwing around. He's got the beginnings of hypothermia. I need to get him to a warm spot or he'll die."

"How do you know?" Wynand looked at her.

Victoria glared at him. "I just said I don't have time to explain, or do you want me to quote *Stedman's Medical Dictionary* to you? Just help me carry him. The more he moves, the better chance he has for survival."

The two pulled on their clothes and half walked, half dragged Bill over the bank and onto the street. It was only a few blocks before they were both winded and had to stop.

"There." Victoria pointed to an all-night laundry facility.

Wynand didn't argue, and they both went inside. It was open, but there was a girl in there who leapt up when they came in.

"It's okay," Victoria said. "He just fell in. Can you help us? We need to get his clothes dry while we, uh, run some errands. And we need to leave some rifles here, too."

The girl eyed them up and down, but seemed to understand and was eager to assist. Anything to stick it to the Russians. "Sure thing," the girl said, helping Bill sit. She tugged his wet outer clothes off and promised to keep him dry and warm.

Victoria and Wynand left Bill and their weapons, trusting the girl, and walked the remaining few blocks to the hospital.

"That was quick thinking back there."

"Yeah."

"I mean at the river. You saved his life."

"Just shut up. We have two more blocks, and we haven't even gotten to the tricky part."

"What do you mean?"

"What, you think the Russians aren't guarding every hospital? They'll have at least a platoon of men there round the clock. It's the same in every occupation. Not only does owning the hospital give you the power of access to healing, but you can spot any insurgent who shows up. A gunshot wound will get good treatment, that's the doctor's oath, but the Russians will interrogate and arrest anyone who looks suspicious."

Wynand thought about that for a while but kept silent.

When they arrived at the entrance to the hospital, Victoria said, "Listen, you just follow my lead and keep your fat mouth shut."

Wynand nodded and stayed quiet as they approached the

hospital's ER entrance. As they neared, Victoria supported Wynand under the arm. He played along, dragging his feet a bit. Two Russian soldiers with AKs were sitting on stools smoking cigarettes and watching them approach. One stood and held up his hand.

"You must show me paper," he said in halting English.

Victoria turned up her Italian accent and didn't skimp on her rapid-fire tempo, "Yeah, great, listen, I'm Doctor Seno, this man's having a grand mal seizure with acute and violent muscle contractions. His O_2 saturation levels are in the blue. We gotta get him to the ER stat or his hypopharynx will seize up."

Wynand went full bore and started twitching and spitting up. He croaked loudly, rolled his eyes back and kicked and flailed his arms. Victoria made a motion to hand him off to the soldier and indicated for the other soldier to help her carry him. The man tossed his cigarette and grabbed Wynand by the shoulders. Victoria physically placed the other man's hands on Wynand's ankles and yelled at him, "Get his legs." The man looked confused but understood her gesture. The two Russians carried Wynand through the sliding glass doors, following Victoria into the hospital.

CHAPTER 29

Morgantown, West Virginia

Stacey jogged onto the high school basketball court wearing a form-hugging sports bra and spandex work-out pants. Not unusual for the unit, where troopers looked to get some exercise any chance they could around the clock, but a little out of place now that the court had been turned into a makeshift hospital. She ran over to Tyce, who was quietly praying at the bedside of one of Ned's Rangers along with a few of the unit's men. The man had lost both arms and was about to be taken to a local hospital, along with a few others who were well beyond the capability of the surgery Victoria's people had available to them.

"Hey," she said gleefully, tapping him on the shoulder. "I got news on the train."

Tyce held up a finger and finished the prayer, his eyes remaining shut: ". . . even when I am afraid, I may put my whole trust in You; through our Savior Jesus Christ. Amen."

He stood slowly and looked down into the man's eyes. "Don't you worry about a thing, Sergeant Spicer. The docs got you one hundred percent stabilized. They told me you're gonna be A-OK." The man smiled weakly, and the other Marines grabbed the sides of his stretcher and hoisted him up. "I'm guessing that morphine has hit you pretty good about now. Just remember we're all with you and praying the whole time. I know Captain Blake would be damn proud of you, as am I."

"We got him from here, sir," one of the others said, and they headed off to the school's loading bay, where there were already several ambulances waiting to take the severely wounded away.

"Okay, Petty Officer Van Andersson, what do you have?" He glanced at her, just now noticing her formfitting civilian exercise attire.

"Um, well, not here, sir. I have some intel on the train. Follow me."

Tyce looked around at all the wounded men. "I don't have many secrets from these men," he said.

"Sir, I'll respectfully remind you that you have a mole."

"*We* have a mole. Remember, you are the one who's going to help me root him out."

"I remember, and I also know the first few procedures include plugging all your leaks. That means not talking about highly classified intelligence details in a wide-open basketball court in an uncleared high school." She put her hands on her hips and half-turned her head, giving him a reproachful look.

"Okay." Tyce was still somber from talking to Ned's wounded men. It was a melancholy visit, but he'd had a chance to lift a few spirits and hear the men tell him firsthand about some of their acts of bravery fighting the Russians. He hadn't intended that the visit lift his *own* spirits, but remarkably, saying a few prayers with the living and a few more over the dead had been strangely therapeutic. In each case, the fallen and the wounded had two or three caretakers who'd spoken to Tyce about the man's deeds or how he had fallen. He was reluctant to leave them, but like most commanders, he needed to be in four places at once.

Tyce followed Stacey up through the school. He was a little surprised when she didn't turn in at the command post offices but kept going and entered the area they'd designated as the female's quarters.

"Hey, let's do this in the CP," he said as she lifted up a camouflage poncho that led into her bunk area. Being in the females-only area was a no-no that even Tyce couldn't violate. Whatever people saw, they immediately suspected more, and Tyce didn't intend to be a part of the barracks gossip.

"Oh, relax. All the girls here are medical types, besides me." She smiled. "And they're all busy back down in the hospital. Besides"—she held the poncho for him to step in—"you aren't afraid I'll bite, are you Colonel?" She giggled.

When Tyce didn't immediately step in, she ushered him in and said, "This is where I keep my secret stuff, Colonel, and I don't like to leave secret cell phones, maps, or even lists of contacts in your CP." She winked at him. "After all, that's where moles go for their information."

Tyce came inside. The 150th hadn't been in the Tucker County high school long, but already Stacey, like most of the troops, had tried to make things as comfortable as possible. All around there were sheets and ponchos set up as makeshift walls. A small mirror and a towel hung from nylon paracord. Her bed had a fuzzy comforter with a big panther on it; who knew where she had acquired it. But most notable was another paracord line hung with all manner of a lady's delicates. Tyce could feel his face flush.

"What's the matter, Colonel? Never seen a bra before?" Stacey delighted in Tyce's embarrassment. She took out a locked Pelican case from under the bed, then made him turn around as she undid the two big combo locks. "No peeking, top secret, eyes only." Tyce obeyed, pivoting about and coming face-to-face with several leopard- and other animal-patterned underwear and a sheer, bright red nightie.

"You can turn around now, sir. Unless you're enjoying the view."

Tyce turned around. Stacey had laid out several maps, cell phones, and notepads of handwritten notes across the panther bed spread.

"Okay." She knelt down and smoothed the map. "Here's what I've gotten from my sources." She pointed to Lexington, Virginia, on the map. "The train has already started to turn north. It's left Clifton Forge and is on its way through Staunton. It'll be in Winchester in about four hours. I calculated Lieutenant Bryce's men can make it up there to Winchester in less than two. That gives them more than two hours to set up an ambush and take out the train. I picked a wide-open spot here." She pointed to the Mount Hebron Cemetery in Winchester. "Here he will have a clear view of the entirety of the train as it passes, and he can take out the engine with ease. Should be a snap." Stacey snapped her fingers for emphasis and smiled.

Tyce knelt beside her and looked over the map. "This is really good, Petty Officer Van A." He squinted his eyes at the map and leafed through her notes. "No, I mean it. *Really* good work." Tyce smiled from ear to ear, he was so pleased. *Maybe, finally, my luck is turning*, he thought. He read over her calculations, all written in perfect cursive, paying special note to the timetables she'd drawn up.

The news seemed to make him completely giddy; Stacey could hear it in his voice. She smiled back, genuinely glad he'd dropped his guard and shortened her name. She maneuvered closer to him, pointing out the most important data then cautiously leaning her head against his shoulder and sighing very softly. He was too engrossed in the intelligence and didn't notice.

She liked seeing him happy. Or maybe it was the exquisite feeling of stealing another woman's boyfriend? Whatever, it didn't matter. She had carefully planned everything, and he'd already fallen for the first few opening moves. Now it was time for her to turn up the heat. He would ask her some more questions and she would answer, but he would be so happy that he wouldn't even really register the gentle neck rubs she was about to give him. He would enjoy it, of course. He was stressed, and men secretly loved the gentle touch of a woman rubbing their necks and temples, and then more. She had even sprayed a very special perfume on the comforter. Just a touch, which he would already have caught a whiff of when he knelt beside her. She had composed a meticulously crafted albeit subliminal battlefield. One he didn't even know he'd wandered into.

The scent of a real woman, she thought. Men couldn't resist it at all. He would fall uncontrollably for her devices.

"I estimated a ninety-percent certainty of this routing." she said, slowly dragging her finger along the map. She squished herself even harder up against him. As she spoke, she blew gently on his ear again, once more delighting as the little ear hairs twitched. Her mind dallied through what was going to happen next, savoring every notion.

"Just one problem," he said, interrupting her thoughts. He abruptly folded her map and stood up.

"What?" she said, completely taken aback.

"We're not going to launch an attack in Winchester," he said.

"*What?*" She was practically shouting.

Startled, he said, "Hey, tone it down," His brow furrowed in genuine concern over her suddenly odd behavior.

Stacey's whole face had changed. Her sweet expression vanished and she turned practically demonic.

"Look, it was a good suggestion, but it makes no tactical sense."

"How do you figure?" she forced through clenched teeth.

"Well," he said, unrolling the map on the bed, bending and pointing to Winchester, "that's not a bad spot. I mean, for someone who dwells in the intel world and not the tactical world."

It wasn't intended as an insult, just an observation, but Stacey tightened her jaw and glowered at him. He didn't notice. He seemed too eager to explain the tactical play of the problem as he saw it. "You see, there's several gas stations, and two large subdivisions of houses right here and here. Civilians, all across near where the train will travel. The 25mm cannon on Bryce's LAV can go over two thousand meters, even on a flat trajectory. If we start firing there, any overshoots and we'll be inadvertently killing noncombatants left and right."

"So?" she said.

"*So*, I don't aim to kill civilians. Also, there's a bigger problem. What if those chemicals get broken open, the entire town is going to look like the Bhopal disaster."

"The *what*?"

"Um, never mind. A big chemical disaster over in India."

"Who gives a shit," she said, realizing a little too late that her emotions at being blown off were almost as strong as her anger at his blowing apart her scheme.

"Well, me, for one." He stood straight up again. "Hey, that was some truly amazing intel. Really saved the day. Possibly changed the whole outcome." He looked her up and down once, as if just now remembering she was in skimpy exercise gear. "Ah, go ahead and get changed, then come on up to the CP, ASAP. I want to brief everyone on the news, then get to work on a new plan."

She glared at him but nodded.

"Way to go, champ!" he said, chucking her on the shoulder like an old pal. He spun about, pulled back the poncho and jogged out quickly.

"Motherfucker," she said quietly, scowling at his wake.

Five minutes later, Stacey entered the command post in uniform. First Sergeant Hull, Gunnery Sergeant Dixon, and a smattering of NCOs from across the unit were looking over maps and talking in animated tones. She walked over to Gunny and jabbed him in the ribs.

"What's going on?"

"The boss just finished briefing them on your intel about the train. Good stuff."

"Uh huh. Well, where are we goin'?"

"Not sure yet. Big decision brief. We reconvene in ten minutes. Colonel Asher said for me to tell you to grab your maps and timetables and come right back."

Stacey was walking out of the room when one of the Navy Petty Officer nurses named Bartlett walked up to Stacey and held onto her arm as she tried to exit. The room was still a loud rumble of troops talking over their parts in the upcoming action. Even so, the girl leaned in close so she wouldn't be overheard.

"Heard you in the women's quarters. Sounds like you're trying to get the colonel in the sack." She shook her head at Stacey and clenched her grip. "We respect the colonel around here too much for that shit." Bartlett glared at her, then added, "Whore."

Stacey's mouth fell open.

"Better set your sights a little lower, girly," the woman said. "He's got eyes for the top shelf anyhow, and I am talking about my boss, Commander Remington. Besides, I'm sure you don't even have what he wants." Bartlett looked at Stacey's chest, smirked, and quickly walked out.

If she had stuck around even one second more, she would have heard Stacey hiss, "I'll kill you, you fat fucking bitch."

CHAPTER 30

Morgantown, West Virginia

Victoria stopped at the hospital admissions table. She went into doctor mode and apparently talked the talk so well, or Wynand's schtick was so believable, that in moments the night nurse had a crash cart brought over and even had someone bring a spare doctor's white coat for Victoria.

Wearing the lab coat and wheeling a still flopping and foaming Wynand through the corridors seemed to forestall any questions or interference from the night staff around the hospital. The sight of someone running and pushing a gurney was not new, especially these days. In less than five minutes, Victoria had navigated them over to the office of medical affairs. It was closed.

"What are we doing here?" Wynand stopped flopping long enough to stare up at her.

"Getting us an all-access badge. These guys always leave their badges on their desks. I'm assuming you still know how to pick a lock." She pointed to the door of a closed and darkened office. Wynand pulled the sheet off and leapt up. He examined the door for a second, then went to where Victoria had stuffed the packs under the cart. He rifled there a second or two, then came up with a set of devices that looked like lockpicks.

"How messy can we be?"

"Here?" She looked around; no one was about. "Messy."

Wynand looked at the picks, shook his head, and grabbed the sheet from the gurney. He wrapped it around his fist and punched the small glass windowpane. Reaching in, he undid the latch from the inside.

"Boom," he said, opening the door wide for Victoria. She went in and was back in several seconds holding up a shiny, stolen, red-striped all-access badge. She pinned the zip cable on to the stolen white coat.

"There, now we're official." She patted the badge.

"Official thieves," he said. "We really need that?"

"Where we're going, yes. Now get your butt back on the cart."

Once Wynand climbed back on, she raced off down another corridor and took them up a long ramp to the second floor. As she ran, Wynand had stopped his flopping and saw the pharmacy go by. He whispered to Victoria, "Hey, we're passing by it." He pointed though the sheet and up to the sign.

"Do I need to strap your ass down? Shut up!" Victoria said.

Two men in hospital scrubs stood to the side of them, both frowning at Victoria's harsh tone toward her patient.

Finally, a few corridors and badge swipes later, they stopped outside a large steel door. Hazardous-material placards adorned the door, and a sign bordered in red and yellow read:

EXTREMELY HAZARDOUS MATERIALS
FEDERAL EMERGENCY STOCKPILE
CONTACT ANESTHESIA
OR LEVEL-SIX PERSONNEL FOR ACCESS

Victoria stopped. "Okay. We're here."

"Where's here?" Wynand asked, trying to make sense of the sign.

"Let's just say, this is where they keep the good stuff."

Wynand jumped off the gurney and looked around.

"So what's next?"

"Next is you pick that lock, and we have about a minute to grab what we need."

"Seriously?" Wynand looked at Victoria incredulously. "Can't you just swipe that badge."

"No. That's what got us this far. It won't work anymore. This section is coded for only a select few, and we don't have the time to go searching for the badge that opens this door. How long until you can get it open?"

"About ten seconds, why?"

"Because as soon as you pick the lock, the keypad will trigger, and a few seconds later an alarm will go off, and the magnetic pads will lock down the door."

"Shit."

"Not done," she continued. "Then the central alarm will sound all over the hospital. I estimate the hospital security guys will arrive about a minute later. That is, if the Russian guards don't beat them here."

"How do you know all that?"

"Because I'm the one who runs that drill for our hospital. Sans Russians, of course. It's a pretty big breach for the hospital."

"*Pretty* big?"

"I lied—the biggest. Only stealing a baby from the maternity ward compares."

"So what the fuck is in there? Babies?"

"You know what remifentanil is?"

Wynand shook his head.

"Ten thousand times stronger than morphine and a hundred times more potent than fentanyl?"

Wynand's eyebrows raised.

"Yeah. Catch your breath, you crook, then get your ass to work. You'll only have a few seconds to open the door before the magnetic lock goes, so . . . no pressure."

Wynand wasted no more time. He grabbed his lock-picking tools, sorted through them, and jammed the electronic device against the lock. As soon as his electronic mechanism entered the lock, the keypad next to the door started beeping. Wynand's tool whined briefly, then stopped. He pulled it out, shook it, stared at it, then pushed it back in. It still did nothing, but the electronic beeping from the PIN pad now started picking up the pace.

"Problems?" Victoria glared at him, wide eyed. "'Cause this is a pretty crappy time to have performance anxiety, buster."

"Working on it." He tossed the electronic picks back to Victoria and pulled out a set of steel lock picks. "Just have to go analog."

"What the hell does that mean?" Victoria was looking around nervously. As yet, and probably because of the early hour, no one was in their hallway.

"A few seconds longer than planned." Wynand worked furiously on the lock. The keypad went from beeping to a continuous whine.

"The alarm is going to go off." Victoria squinted and started to think about the quickest route to get out of this corridor.

"I know," Wynand snapped back. Then he stepped away from the door.

"Shit. Can't get it?" Victoria asked.

He shook his head and pulled the door handle. A

screeching alarm went off, and red lights flashed above the door, but it opened. Right at the same time, they both heard a loud thud from around the door frame. The magnetic lock had just engaged, but the door was already open.

"I did it." Wynand stared at the door incredulously.

"Congratulations, con man. You just graduated from common thief to full-blown bandit." She pushed him aside and ran in. "Hustle up!" Wynand started following her, and she yelled, "Don't forget to leave it open, or we'll be locked in."

Wynand caught the door with his foot just before it closed, then wedged the crash cart in the entryway. He turned and stared around at the all the shelves, cabinets, steel doors, and glass cases like a kid in a candy store, then stopped in his tracks. "What do I grab?"

Victoria was frantically racing around the room searching for something. She stopped briefly and pulled open a cabinet labeled "Surgical Narcotics." "Grab anything with a red label in here." Then she continued flinging doors open, quickly searching inside and moving on.

Wynand stuffed everything with a red label into the backpacks on the crash cart in the doorway, then grabbed some bottles and vials with blue and green labels for good measure.

"Thirty seconds," Wynand yelled back to Victoria.

"I know," came Victoria's voice from a behind a shelf.

Wynand looked inside a few other cabinets and contemplated taking what was inside. The trouble was everything had a medical name on the outside, none of which he understood. Victoria ran up and dumped a load of medicines on the cart, then glanced at what Wynand was holding up. "Those are industrial-grade laxatives. Leave them alone unless you want explosive poo. Won't sell well on the black market, anyhow." She raced back between the shelves.

"Ten seconds. What else do you need?" he said, loading the medicine up into the packs and shoving one bag under the cart. Four or five bottles dropped out and rolled under the cart. He lay down to fetch them.

Victoria came back with several small vials, breathing heavily. "Got it," she said, her eyes lit up.

Wynand was still stretching to get the lost vials. From his position on the floor, halfway under the crash cart, he looked up and watched as Victoria's face change from joy to dread. "What now?" he asked, half out of his wits.

Victoria just shook her head. She was looking out the doorway. Wynand twisted around a bit farther, and through the legs of the cart, he saw two pairs of high-topped leather Russian boots and the tips of two AK rifle barrels.

First light was starting to show its face, and Blue watched as workers assembled a podium, speakers, and microphones. Others wheeled floral arrangements and large plants up and set them around the speaking venue.

Blue looked up at the sheriff. He stood, dispassionate, looking out at the cool morning scene. He picked up the phone, dialed a number, and started talking.

Blue's heart sank to rock bottom. It was about to happen. He understood that he was about to assassinate an American, but it felt surreal now that he was here. It seemed as if he was in another man's body, or like he was in a nightmare in which he knew he was about to commit a terrible crime but could not stop himself.

All of a sudden, some words of one of his teachers, Mrs. Nevarez, started to come back to him. He churned them over in his mind trying to make sense of them. He could even see her there in her homely but authoritative plaid skirt and turtleneck. He had respected her. Like his mother, she spoke about things deep in the heart that his head couldn't make sense of. Those women brought order to what Blue saw as an otherwise chaotic world.

But so did the mayor, Blue thought. *Didn't she?*

"Yeah. We're in position." The sheriff looked down at Blue. "Okay, here he is." He held the phone out to Blue. "She wants to talk to you."

Blue took the phone. "Hello. This is Blue."

The sweet Southern voice of the mayor came back. "Mr. Blue. I am forever grateful to you and your state, and nation will be, too. Right about now, you are wondering if what I told you is true. If it is righteous and correct. You may even be wondering if what I am asking from you is legal, or more importantly, if it is right. And I do mean that in a patriotic and a Biblical sense."

Blue nodded but didn't speak.

"Mr. Blue, when we spent time with each other last night, you looked deep into my eyes. And your eyes asked me to be truthful, and you hoped that I was trustworthy. Ignore your head for a minute, and tell me what your heart told you."

Blue was silent a moment more, then he answered, "That you were right."

"Good. Now, I want you to listen to something else. When the governor speaks this morning, I want you to listen carefully to his words. Your heart is convinced now to do this thing for me, but when he speaks, I need you to listen to what he says. Then your head will ultimately tell you what your heart already knows. Can you do that for me, Mr. Blue? Can you listen to the governor?"

"Yes . . . yes, ma'am. I can do that."

"Good." She hung up.

The sheriff snickered and reached for the phone. He popped a stick of gum in his mouth and chewed with his mouth open. "All right, hotshot. Looks like we're in business." He looked out at the small crowd that had begun to arrive and now was milling around, getting snacks and hot drinks from a side table and chitchatting. Blue got back behind the rifle and watched the men and women gathering there. They all had little name tags and were arriving from the other buildings around the capitol. Blue could see they were other government employees. They laughed and joked freely, and for a moment, even with the Russian occupation, Blue could see they were in genuinely good spirits. He couldn't remember the last time he'd seen civilians laughing and joking.

Was it possible people could get back to normal under Russian rule? Blue's head was starting to swim, just like it did back in Mrs. Hewitt's algebra classes.

CHAPTER 31

Tucker County High School
West Virginia

Stacy went back to her quarters, grabbed her notes, and pulled the Pelican case out from under her bed, undoing the locks. She pulled out the encrypted comms device and hastily typed a new message:

> AMBUSH LOCATION CHANGED, NEW
> LOCATION: UNDETERMINED.
> UPDATE IN 30 MINS.

She didn't have to wait long. A message came back almost immediately.

> UNDERSTOOD. ASSAULT FORCE ALREADY
> EN ROUTE TO OLD LOCATION. UPDATE NEW
> AMERICAN AMBUSH SITE IMMEDIATELY.
> BOMBING RUN ON ENEMY CP
> COMMENCES IN 10 MINS.

Stacey paused in confusion and reread the message. *Bombing run? What the hell kind of bombing run are they talking about?* she thought. They couldn't mean *this* command post. *They don't have this location—because I didn't give them this location.* She sent a text back.

INTERROGATIVE: WHAT BOMBING RUN?

The response took more than a minute. Her mind was racing. *What the fuck are they doing back there? Are they suddenly starting to make decisions?* She had gotten very accustomed to being able to outthink the higher-ups at both her American and Russian headquarters. *Damn it!* It was a hell of a time for her stupid headquarters to be growing some initiative. She heard the main door open, and a voice called out from behind her near the entrance to the room.

"Petty Officer Van A, you in here?" It was Gunny Dixon. "We need you back in the CP, the CO found us a perfect ambush spot for the train. Don't forget those maps and timetables."

"Oh." She tried to calm her voice. "Be out in a minute." After a pause, she called out, "Where's it gonna go down?"

There was a second's hesitation, then Gunny yelled back, "Just hustle. Can't say it here—remember, OPSEC," he said, using the military term for "operational security."

God damn it, so now the Marines are finally following operations security counterintel protocol, she thought. *Why can't everyone just follow the fucking plans I've laid out for them?*

"M'kay, be right out." She listened for the click of the door so she knew Gunny had gone out, then whispered to the cell phone, "Come on, hurry the fuck up." Finally, it buzzed, and a message popped up that looked like a cut-and-paste by the watch officer from a squadron attack time line. She knew their attacks were hardly ever on time, and she hoped that would be the case this time. It read:

UNITS: 6 SUKHOI SU-24
ACTIVITY: BOMBING RUN ON ENEMY
COMMAND POST.
LOCATION: TUCKER COUNTY HIGH
SCHOOL, VIC: THOMAS, WV.
TIME: 0752HRS

Stacey's eyes grew at the last line of the message. An instant later another message came in:

REPEAT: GENERAL SAYS HE NEEDS NEW
ENEMY AMBUSH SITE, NOW!

"*Mat' ublyudok*!" she said out loud. "Motherfuckers!" She contemplated texting "fuck off," then calmed herself with a few deep breaths. Her plan was going to pot, and in eight minutes there would be bombs blasting the school into bits, with her in it. She reached farther into the case and pulled out her father's Soviet-era red handkerchief and held it against her cheek to try to calm herself further.

Then a voice came from behind her.

"So what's all this now?"

Stacey turned to see Bartlett, the female Navy corpsman who had confronted her earlier. Stacey realized she'd probably come in with the Gunny and overheard everything. She pointed to the red hammer-and-sickle handkerchief and said, "Who the fuck *are* you?"

Victoria pulled out her badge and showed it to the Russians. They were the same two soldiers who had helped them at the entrance. Both men stared at her and the scene inside the room in stunned silence. One looked at Wynand's kicking legs from under the crash cart and said something in Russian.

Victoria snapped her fingers in the two men's faces and pointed to Wynand, shouting in her best angry, urgent doctor's voice, "*Avariynyy*, damn you, *avariynyy!*"

The men stared a second more, trying to take it all in: the whoopie lights, the sirens, Wynand kicking, and the obviously angry doctor yelling at them. Victoria could see they were trying to decide what was going on. She decided to make up their minds for them. She jumped the few feet between them and shoved the badge on its zip string holder directly in front of their faces. She had been a military surgeon long enough to know how military men thought and acted. She was gambling that her knowledge of human nature was better than their understanding of hospital alarms.

She yelled, "*Avariynyy!* You bastard, *avariynyy!*" This time, her words contained a real note of stress as she pointed to Wynand's prone form on the ground. Wynand had gotten the gist of what was going on and was busy flopping his arms and legs around again. As the soldiers rolled the cart out of the way, he even managed to whip up some foam from his mouth. He doubled down and rolled his eyes back a few times, barking out incoherent noises.

The Russians had seen enough. They grabbed him by the arms and legs and threw him back up onto the gurney, quickly strapping him down. Victoria indicated for one of them to pick up the pack still on the floor. Then she took the handles of the cart and started running down the hallway, all the while yelling, "*Avariynyy! Avariynyy!*"

With considerable effort, his heavy boots clacking on the polished floor, one of the soldiers jogged beside Victoria and gave her a thumbs-up. The other dropped behind them, and together they hastily made their way through the corridors and down the ramp to the ER, with Wynand now flailing and gurgling loudly. The soldiers waved their rifles and yelled, albeit in Russian, at the few hospital personnel who had started to trickle in and the sleepy looking night crew coming out of their offices to see what was going on. The hospital workers all stuck close to the side or gawked from doorways as they spotted the oncoming Russians brandishing their AKs, yelling and waving.

The alarm was still sounding at full blast when they made it to the ER. A different nurse from the one in the reception area stood up from her desk, looked at Wynand, the two armed Russians, and then to Victoria and her red-striped, all-access badge.

"No time. Gotta transfer him to . . ." Victoria tried desperately to remember the name of the other, higher-level trauma hospital in the region. "Uh, WVU Berkeley."

The nurse nodded, pointed to the exit door, and said, "Just go, Doctor. An ambulance is waiting outside. No airlift available. I'll take care of the transfer paperwork."

"Great," Victoria said, but she had already started running for the ER loading bay, where she burst through the flexible double doors. Two EMTs helped her load Wynand into the ambulance. In seconds, the driver indicated he was ready.

Victoria turned and shook both Russian soldiers' hands, then kissed one of them on the cheek and smiled, giving him a look she hoped conveyed genuine relief and thanks. She added in Italian, "*Ragazzi, siete degli stupidi,*" then hopped aboard the ambulance and closed the door behind her. Neither of them understood Italian. She could see both soldiers high-five each other through the ambulance window as they pulled away, not realizing she had just called them idiots.

"Hey Doc, where to?" the ambulance diver yelled into the back compartment.

"The laundromat to grab a friend, then across the river to administer this"—she fished out a vial labeled levothyroxine—"to a little boy. Then over to Tucker County High School."

The driver looked back at her face to see if she was serious. "Okay, you're the boss. Lights and sirens on or off?"

"On," she said, smiling and wondering how she was going to explain hijacking their ambulance to the EMTs in back who stared at her with shocked expressions.

CHAPTER 32

Tucker County High School
West Virginia

Tyce was on an unsecure line with the vice president when Stacey ran into the busy briefing room. Her hands and face were splattered with blood. "We have to get the fuck out of the command post!"

Everyone started at her in stunned silence.

"Right fucking now!" she screamed.

"Hey, what the hell is going on? We're in the middle of something important," Gunny said, holding up both hands for her to slow down. Then seeing the blood added, "What happened to you. Are you all right?"

Tyce hastened the end of the call, "Yes, send them. They will be a huge help today, but I'll have to call you back, Mr. Vice President." He hung up and stared at Stacey.

"No time to explain," she said. "Get out of here, *now!* We have about five minutes before Russian bombers demolish the building."

Tyce didn't hesitate further. "You heard her—everyone get out. Grab what you can. All free hands go immediately to the gym to assist the wounded." He turned to Gunny. "Close down the CP. Grab the maps, and have the men get the radios and as many weapons from the armory as they

can carry, then join me in the gym assisting the wounded."
Gunny nodded and started barking orders at the radiomen.

The room erupted as everyone raced out. Tyce grabbed
Stacey, "Do I need to know how you figured this out?" He
looked at her blood soaked uniform.

"I found our mole." Stacey held up what looked like a
small iPhone with a strobe light on top. "I caught her
trying to set up a beacon for the aircraft." She flipped it
over and showed him Russian Cyrillic writing across the
bottom.

"Holy crap. What did she say?" Tyce said.

"She told me about the attack." Stacey looked at the
blood on her hands and arms. "It took some persuading."

Tyce gritted his teeth. He did not condone torture, but
this didn't seem like the time to mention it. It appeared that
Stacey had again saved the lives of his entire command.

I guess we'll find out soon enough, he thought.

He grabbed the school's PA system microphone and
thumbed the switch. "All hands, all hands. Be advised,
Russian bombers are about to hit the building. Evacuate
the building immediately. Assist the wounded. Grab what
you can, toss it into the vehicles, and drive along the firebreak and into the woods to the west. Get as deep and as
you can, as fast as you can. You have four minutes." He
turned to Stacey. "How sure are we of their attack time
line?"

"We're not. Could be earlier," she said. "Russian aircraft
attack time lines are unreliable, uh, but the information is
solid."

"Did you get your maps and notes?"

She patted the Pelican case. Tyce nodded and ran out to
help his men.

Charleston, West Virginia

Blue zeroed his rifle in on the podium. There was a fair amount of commotion as three large SUVs pulled up onto the grass near the venue, escorted to the front and rear by state police cars. In moments, two Russian armored personnel carriers arrived. Machine gun turrets on top started scanning the area. Several squads of Russian soldiers got out of the armored vehicles and ran to set up a wide perimeter. A few soldiers pushed those in attendance tighter together and closer to the stage. Blue glanced at the sheriff, who was kneeling next to him, chewing on another piece of gum.

Sensing Blue's eyes on him, the sheriff said, "Don't worry, big guy, it's all gonna go down just fine. Just stay focused on your target, he'll be out in a minute."

"I was wondering something."

"Yeah?" said the sheriff, who was watching the activity below intently. "Shouldn't do that. Just do what you're told."

"Respectfully, Sheriff, I'm just wondering about this mission?"

The sheriff stopped chewing and turned to Blue. His lip curled up, and he said, "Listen here, you punk. You agreed to this, don't go getting cowardly on me now."

Blue wasn't scared or intimidated by the sheriff, but he'd arrived at an important thought, and he felt he deserved an answer. "It's not that. I've killed men before, when they deserved it. I'm wondering how come Mayor Holly didn't ask you to do this."

"Now you listen closely. You've been given a job to do, mister. You agreed to it, and you're gonna follow through. There's no backing out now."

Blue fell silent and looked back through his Leupold rifle sights to view the scene down below. The Russian perimeter had been established, and the state police went over and opened the door to one of the sedans. A few important-looking people got out, and a tallish man in a dark suit and grey overcoat walked confidently up to the podium. There was brief but muted applause from the people gathered around, and then he began to speak.

"My fellow West Virginians." He spoke with an upbeat and confident tone. "We are facing difficult times, but we need not despair."

Blue could see the TV cameras around the area sweeping over the crowd, filming both the governor's speech and the people in attendance. He looked through his sights, panning across the crowd. As he did, he spotted someone sitting in the small VIP area behind the governor who he recognized immediately. It was Mayor Susanna Holly. She was in a light red suit with an elegant, fur-lined overcoat, and she sat with her legs crossed. He watched her for a moment while listening to the governor's speech pounding out over the big speaker systems and across the central square. He couldn't be certain, but it looked like she glanced their way a few times.

The governor continued. "Today I announce a new agreement that will make West Virginia the great state we were always meant to be. This pact is called the American New Deal. My fellow West Virginians, we are entering a new era, one in which we can finally trust that our government will do what's right for us, the people. On behalf of you, the great people of West Virginia, I have forged a partnership between Russia and America that will provide for our needs better than ever before. In this modern day and age,

I believe strongly that a wealthy society should not be one in which anyone is too poor to live. This new partnership will level the playing field and spread the wealth from those who have it to those who don't.

"Moving forward, we will be a peaceful nation, with all guns eliminated. The new Russian-American policy is an initiative that will improve the safety of all Americans."

Blue had an unconscious thought, which he accidentally said out loud: "Shall not be infringed . . ."

"What's that? Stop mumbling, and get ready," said the sheriff. Blue noticed he had placed his hand on his pistol.

"But perhaps most importantly, this agreement will eliminate the need for political parties. These same parties that have plagued us all these years since our founding fathers, forcing us to make devil's bargains and preventing true equality. They will be dissolved and made into one. This new pact will do away with party bickering and replace it with solid and much more speedy decision-making. Finally, the American New Deal will consolidate the courts and include them directly in the executive branch."

Another line jumped into Blue's mind. "A government of laws and not men . . ." Blue said quietly.

"What's that you say?" the sheriff said.

"The committee of five," Blue said quietly.

"What the hell are you talking about, kid?"

"Um . . . nothing, sir. Something Mrs. Nevarez said."

"You just shut your mouth and focus."

The governor paused his speech and chuckled a little, telling what sounded like a pre-staged joke. "Think of it, folks. We can finally enact legislation with zero debate, and I know y'all will be thankful not to have a bunch of God-damned lawyers running the state." A few laughs went up among the crowd. "Yes, folks, it was time we grabbed that broken document, the state constitution, and rewrote it to work for today's citizen." A small wave of applause broke out.

"Fire," said the sheriff quietly. "Now, son. Fire your rifle and kill that man."

Tucker County, West Virginia

Tyce and Gunny waved the last Humvee to turn off the firebreak and into the woods. The driver spotted them and turned hard, boxes of equipment and MREs spilling out the open back canvas flap. The vehicle skidded to a halt a few meters from where Tyce and Gunny were squatting and looking back toward the high school, which wasn't visible through the tall trees even though the sun was up.

Gunny looked over at Tyce. Both men were panting heavily. "What if this is all BS?" said Gunny.

"I was thinking the opposite," said Tyce. "What if we didn't get the men far enough away?"

"Do you trust her, then? What if it's some ruse to get us into the open? Make us better targets."

Tyce frowned. "I don't have any reason not to. Didn't you see her? She was covered in blood, she must've tortured the info out of the other girl. Her data and intel have saved our bacon more than a few times already. I thought you trusted her too?"

"I don't mean Petty Officer Van A. I mean, what if the other girl, the mole, played a final hand. You know, knew she was cornered. Get us in the open so they could strafe us."

Tyce's eyes widened, "Oh, shi—"

Smack-boom! Smack-boom!

The far side of the forest erupted in two giant balls of

red flame. An enormous shock wave tossed Tyce and Gunny flat to the ground on their backs. Several nearby trees snapped in half, and branches rained down all around them and onto the Humvees. A huge cloud of pine needles and debris followed, blowing through the woods like a sandstorm and slamming a wave of heat into them.

Tyce sat up and looked over at Gunny, who was holding on to his chest and trying to catch his breath after getting the wind knocked out of him. Gunny took a few labored breaths and pointed at Tyce's leg. The force of the blast had knocked the prosthetic at an odd angle. Tyce reached down and adjusted it, then started his routine for standing up.

Smack-boom! Smack-boom!

Another double blast, and everyone was knocked flat again. Both men lay there a second, then turned to each other before looking back at their troops. There were big clusters of men and vehicles spread out all through the woods. All of them seemed to have fared about the same—flattened but, for the most part, unhurt.

"You okay?" asked Gunny.

"Yeah, you?"

"Good, sir. I saw your leg, and for a second I thought it was your good leg, all fucked up and broken." They both laughed and patted themselves to make sure they had all their other parts. Several troops looked on, puzzled that their leaders were laughing at a time like this.

First Sergeant Hull was the first to run up. He helped them both to their feet. "Hey gentlemen, you okay?"

"We're good, do you have a count?" Tyce asked.

"I do, sir. Sixteen men absent, but some of the men think they just ran out a different side. Went east instead of west. We have all our medical cases accounted for, though. No telling how they'll do now. We had to manhandle most of them, and it probably opened up their wounds. We'll need priority medical support."

"Got it, First Sergeant, that's your first task, then. You and Schmalcs that medical section to set up a temporary hospital."

Charleston, West Virginia

Blue pulled the trigger. The Weatherby made a loud *bang* that echoed across the government square. As soon as Blue fired his rifle, the sheriff jerked his pistol toward him. Blue had been ready for this and swung his rifle upward, slamming the barrel hard against the sheriff's gun hand. The pistol discharged, and the bullet creased Blue's shoulder, tearing off an inch of flesh. Surprised, the sheriff stood all the way up, quickly switched his pistol to his opposite hand, and readied for a second shot. But Blue didn't hesitate. Still prone, he rolled and pointed the barrel of the Weatherby at the sheriff's head and pulled the trigger. Simultaneously, a cascade of machine gun bullets blasted the parapet to pieces. The Russians had a clear line of sight and fired at everything in view. The sheriff disappeared as a hailstorm of bullets ripped him to shreds.

The Russian armored vehicles were now firing full force up at the roof. Blue got up to a low crouch, clutching his rifle to his side and racing for the roof door. In seconds he had it open and was down the stairs without giving the sheriff's remains a backward glance.

Near Tucker County High School
West Virginia

Fifteen minutes after the attack, Tyce and Gunny had already set up a makeshift command post and were getting reports by both runner and radio. Most of the radios had made it out, thanks to the actions of the quick-thinking communications NCOs. The school was smoldering, a reminder of how close they'd gotten to losing the entire 150th.

Men raced to bring reports of new injuries and damage to equipment. Some of the men had gotten so separated from the group that there was still a question of finding everyone. Although open to the elements, the woods were a good temporary HQ. They only had what they'd been able to grab at the last minute, but it afforded them some cover from any aerial reconnaissance Tyce was sure would be coming. They had maps and several status boards set up, and the men were manning the radios—just as they'd drilled a hundred times before.

A civilian ambulance pulled into the parking lot near the demolished high school. It pulled straight past onto the firebreak and followed the small packs of Marines and soldiers looking through the wreckage and salvaging equipment to take back into the woods. To Tyce's surprise, it pulled up nearby and Victoria and Wynand got out and walked over to him.

She didn't pause for niceties. "How bad is it?" she asked.

"We're still getting a count, but so far we have four men missing." Victoria looked back toward the still-smoldering ruins of the school. "It could have been a lot worse. Catastrophic, even. Petty Officer Van Andersson's intelligence saved us." Victoria turned back to Tyce with a quizzical look. "She found the mole. It was one of your sailors."

Victoria's eyes widened. "Who?"

"Petty Officer Bartlett."

Victoria frowned. "What? Couldn't be. The girl from Jersey?"

"No idea, but she didn't make it. Van A killed her."

Victoria's frown deepened at Tyce's shortening of Stacey's name. Then she looked around for her. "Where is she?"

"She helped us get the big antenna up so we could pass the new ambush location to Lieutenant Bryce, but she had to go. She's following a new lead."

"Really? Tyce, I'm not so sure of her. She's kind of a bitc—"

"Hey!" Tyce interrupted Victoria and pulled her away from the command post area to where they could talk privately. "Look, right now I have four missing men, a platoon of LAVs headed to attack a train full of chemical munitions, and we just got the crap bombed out of us. I am gonna need you to get your medical section on top of taking care of all the wounded special forces men. A lot of them got reinjured when we pulled them out. Can you do that for me?"

Victoria's azure eyes bored into Tyce's but quickly softened as everything settled in. "*Fatta!* You got it, boss."

"Thank you, Victoria."

"Yeah. By the way, we got the meds for the general. And a bunch of other stuff we could probably put to good use now."

"Excellent. Everything else go smoothly?"

"Yeah, rescued a kid, saved Bill from drowning, kicked Wynand's ass—the usual."

Tyce gave her an odd look, but didn't have time for details, "Get your folks ready for more. Me and Gunny are headed out soon to try to join Lieutenant Bryce at the ambush."

Victoria pursed her lips and furrowed her chin. Her eye's scanned Tyce's face. This wasn't welcome news, and her feelings were once again deeply in conflict with her duties. She slipped her hand down and gently touched his palm with the tips of her fingers, drew closer, and whispered, "Be safe, and go give 'em hell, *Amore mio*." Then she walked off to go take charge of her surgical team.

CHAPTER 33

Russian Pentagon
Washington D.C.

Major Pavel looked up from the Russian tactical messaging computer. "General, Panther has reported in. We have the enemy's new ambush location pinpointed. A city called Strasburg."

"Good," said Kolikoff. "How long to get Shenkov rerouted?"

"He says he can be on the ground in there in fifteen minutes."

"General." Major Quico held up the watch floor's tactical telephone. "It is General Tympkin. He requests a status report."

Kolikoff did some hasty mental calculations, then picked up his own tactical phone. "Give me the 184th Guards Heavy Bomber Aviation Regiment. I have an urgent strike mission." Kolikoff wasn't going to take chances this time. Shenkov would still get his chance, but he was going to back him up with a heavy bombing run.

A voice came back on the phone. "Colonel Barbarov."

"Donni, this is your old friend calling."

"Viktor! Er . . . I guess it is General Kolikoff now. How are you, old man?"

"Listen, Donni, not much time for pleasantries today. I have an urgent strike request for you. I need an immediate heavy carpet-bombing run in a place called Strasburg, Virginia."

There was silence on the other end of phone.

"It is in the American Shenandoah Valley."

"Yes, I know the area, but this is very short notice, and the improper channel for a strike request, General."

"Yes, yes, I know, my dear friend. But I seem to remember you have a fondness for American whiskey. I have a case of the best—really premium stuff—if you can help us out."

"I'm listening."

Finally, thought Kolikoff. *We'll get these hillbilly bastards out in the open.*

Wardensville, West Virginia

The six Humvees and four civilian pickup trucks tore down Route 48 at a reckless speed. Tyce had ordered the men to drive as fast as humanly possible to try to make a link up with Lieutenant Bryce before the train arrived at his location. One understrength platoon from the 150th was all that he could spare to join Bryce's LAVs, which were already at the ambush position outside Strasburg, Virginia. They grabbed their gear and tossed in all the heavy weapons and spare ammo they could scrounge from Tyce's mostly demolished armory.

Gunny was loading loose ammo into rifle magazines and stopped to look over to Tyce, who had his face buried in a map. "Are we gonna make it, sir?"

"Barely. Train will be there in thirty minutes, and we're thirty minutes out from the target area," said Tyce. Just as he said it, their vehicle slowed to a halt, causing Tyce to look up angrily from his map. He called over the radio, "Hey, what's the damn holdup?"

The report came back at once. "Sir, there's a street barbeque outside a small bookstore. There are civilians standing all over the road."

"Crap, this is all we need." Tyce felt like he was about to have a heart attack. His chest was pounding from the adrenaline. He keyed the radio. "Tell them to get the fuck out of our way."

"We're all good, sir," came the report, and the vehicles were already starting to accelerate.

Tyce looked at Gunny. There was sweat beading down both men's faces even though the temperature was only in the forties.

"Can we have any more trouble?" Tyce said. Gunny shook his head and went back to loading rifle magazines.

South of Strasburg, Virginia

Major Uintergrin walked up and down the line of new infantrymen. He'd been ordered to pick up two full platoons of men and three armored combat vehicles when they reached Lexington, Virginia. Communications had been spotty through the mountain ranges, but he'd managed to get several messages from the Pentagon. Intelligence had located an ambush along his route, and rather than give him a detour through the coastal cities, they'd beefed up his forces and told him to fight.

It really is the golden mission, he thought. The one that would vault him up to lieutenant colonel. He'd been given two additional fighting platoons, a group of tough soldiers who had been putting down a mixed bag of local militia and students at the Virginia Military Institute.

Uintergrin looked back through the glass at the two new flatbed train cars they'd added, but mostly he looked appreciatively at the reason for their addition, the three BTR-90 armored battle wagons. They were packed with the latest in Russian military hardware, from a 30mm chain gun to several 7.62mm machine guns, a 9M113 Konkurs anti-tank missile launcher, and even a 30mm automatic grenade launcher. He was to receive air support, at a critical point in the battle, from a flight of four Tupolev Tu-95 four-engine turboprop strategic bombers. But what really made him grin was that he'd been handed the exact coordinates of the enemy ambush.

He'd always wanted to be an infantry officer. His grandfather, father, and uncles had all been infantry officers, but he'd scored too high on the entrance exams. Or maybe he didn't look or act the part. Either way, he was made a chemical officer with little chance for advancement and next to no chance for glory on the battlefield. He'd watched men with half his mental acuity rise up in the ranks with great success. Successes that weren't their due. But this mission had changed everything, and he'd known it from the beginning. Known it even when that rat-faced colonel of his had tried to hold him back, maybe even stop him from success. Just like all the stories his father and uncles had told him, everything important happens on the battlefield.

Uintergrin went into his new operational planning room, barely able to suppress a smile. It was now his command car. His boss had regrettably suffered gross exposure to a chemical leak caused by the American attack. At least, that was the way he'd filled out the digital report to his headquarters. Naturally, he'd been able to advise his headquarters that he had no trouble taking on the role of commander. The extra troops weren't even his idea, headquarters had just told him to pick them up on the way through Lexington and to expect all the support they could manage at short notice. It had caused a delay, but he now had the equipment and personnel to spring a classic counter-ambush. Just like his grandfather had at the Battle of Kursk, and just like he'd studied in school.

He entered the command area, and five men plus two infantry lieutenants sprang to attention. The room contained the dining section of the Amtrak train but had been converted by pasting maps on the walls and stacking military grade radios on the tables. Crude, but effective.

"At ease," he said confidently, relishing the concept that he now had officers, real fighting infantrymen, under his authority. He'd commanded bean counters and chemical nerds all his career, but from now on, things would be different. He extended a radio antenna as a pointing stick and slapped it against the ambush site on the map. "Prepare to receive your mission orders. I will now brief you on how we will crush an enemy ambush. Take out your notebooks."

A truly golden mission, he thought to himself as the train raced on.

West of Strasburg, Virginia

Twenty minutes later, Tyce was within radio range of Lieutenant Bryce's ambush position. He started calling him over the radio using his call sign. "Dragoons, Dragoons, this is Iron Horse six, do you copy?"

A faint crackle came through, then nothing. He tried again. Another crackle, and nothing else.

"I think he's reading you, sir, but our radios aren't powerful enough to hear him."

Tyce tried a few more times as they sped toward the site. Then finally, he heard "Iron Horse, we read you."

"Thank God," Tyce said. He keyed the radio. "Hey Bryce, we're inbound to your poz. Be there in about ten."

"Copy, sir. Be advised . . . already . . . see the train." Any other words were lost to the crackling radio.

Tyce's heart went into overdrive. "Damn it." He banged his elbow against the armrest, then immediately regretted it. Stinging pain went through his arm. He rekeyed the radio, his voice sounding more desperate than he wanted it to. "Say again, Dragoons. Did not copy." Tyce hoped to God he had heard the lieutenant wrong.

"I say again, we already see the train." This time the transmission came through, clear as day.

Tyce gritted his teeth. "I copy, the ambush is yours. Hit the engine and get it to stop. We'll be there in"—Tyce looked at his watch—"six minutes."

"Commencing ambush, time now," came the response. On the last two words, Tyce could hear the *thump-thump* of Bryce's 25mm rounds.

Or so he thought. Another transmission from Bryce followed quickly. "We're under heavy fire—" *Boom-boom*. Tyce could hear the background noise of explosions and the rattle of machine gun fire. "There are two, no, three enemy vehicles firing on our positions. They've dismounted troops. We're being hit from two sides."

Tyce sat up straighter in his seat and grabbed what the troops called "the Jesus bar" because you grabbed it when the vehicle was going so fast or over such rocky terrain that you cried out and grabbed the bar to keep yourself from being flung from the vehicle. He was preparing himself.

"Corporal Dunworthy, I don't care what you have to do, but make this thing go faster, and get us to Lieutenant Bryce."

The corporal already had the throttle almost all the way open, but on Tyce's command, he gave it the last bit of gas and locked his arms out to hold the wheel steady. Gear was bouncing all around the Humvee, and Tyce's vision was obscured by the back of the next Humvee.

Tyce called out on the local squad radio. "Pick up to maximum speed, everyone get ready. It sounds like Lieutenant Bryce is in a shit sandwich." Holding the radio in the crook of his neck, the map with one hand, and the Jesus bar with his other, he thought up a quick tactical scenario. "We'll approach from the north and act as a counterattack force. The enemy will be attacking from the rail lines at about the intersection of Route 55 and Interstate 81. If we hit them with enough force, we can split his forces. They'll be focused on Bryce. Get all weapons locked and loaded, we hit the ground running." The men in his vehicle must have been listening, too. Tyce heard the .50 cal machine gunner on the top turret rack his charging handle back. The two other Army National Guard troops who were squeezed in the vehicle back seats locked a magazine and started checking over each other's gear. One of them was a grenadier and had a 40mm grenade launcher attached to his rifle's barrel. He opened his pack, pulled out a bunch of extra 40mm rounds, and started talking his buddy into carrying most of them.

Gunny was looking over Tyce's shoulder. "Hey, sir, there's a civilian housing development right near there." He tried to point out the location on Tyce's map as the vehicle bounced around crazily.

"I know. Can't be helped. It'd be a lot worse if we tried to go around him to the south. That would mess up Bryce's geometry of fires. It's the best option." He switched back to the radio. "Dragoons, Dragoons. Give me a SIT-REP if you can."

"Heavily engaged," came the report. "Stand by."

Tyce hated getting a "stand by" from one of his field units. It meant they were so heavily engaged that they couldn't even take the time to talk. The situation must have gotten even more dire. Of course, Tyce imagined the worst, but he had to ensure he projected calm confidence to his man. "Copy, fight and report when able."

Tyce briefly let go of the bar to load a magazine—right when they went over an enormous bump. Even though he was buckled into his seat, he flew up and smashed his head against the roof of the Humvee. He had his helmet on, but his neck seared in pain. He looked up and saw why Corporal Dunworthy had suddenly gone off road.

Ahead of them, in a valley just below the highway, an immense volley of tracer fire zigzagged across an open dirt construction site. Tyce could see the train engine stopped just under five hundred meters in front of them. The engine looked very much intact, and, in fact, Tyce could see it had stopped at a perfect location to dismount its troops next to a long, low berm. The Russians were able to remain in cover while raking Bryce's men from his right flank and keeping him pinned from the front.

"There, there!" Tyce pointed to a collection of newly constructed houses at the edge of the field. "Get us over to those houses. No terrain around to mask us, so artificial terrain will have to do for getting close." Then, over the radio, he said, "Each of you, pick a house." Tyce held on for dear life. The seat belt wasn't enough to hold him steady as the vehicle careened over curbs and bounced across unfinished sod lawns.

"There." Tyce managed to point at a house. "Go fast." Tyce knew better than anybody that they had the element of surprise. If the BTRs saw the new arrivals, they'd train their 30mm guns on them and open them up like tin cans.

"Roger!" was all Dunworthy said. He didn't let up on the pedal until they bumped up the lawn and smashed straight through the front of the house. Tyce heard the top machine gunner grunt loudly as he dove back into the Humvee just in time. It was fortunate that none of the houses looked occupied yet, but Tyce had a feeling Dunworthy wouldn't have let any occupants stop him. Dust and debris fell through the top turret opening. and Tyce grabbed his rifle, radios, and combat pack.

"Out, out, out!" yelled Gunny.

The men threw the Humvee doors open, pushing away aluminum siding and splintered wood, then raced for the stairs. As Tyce ascended the stairs, he could hear Gunny yelling at the machine gunner to stop and go back to get his .50 cal unstuck from where it had become lodged in the ceiling of the front room.

CHAPTER 34

Russian Pentagon
Washington, D.C.

"Sir, they've made contact. The enemy was right where Panther said they would be. They are in battle now," said Major Pavel.

"Excellent. What is Shenkov's progress?" asked General Kolikoff.

"He's ten minutes out, Comrade General."

General Tympkin entered the operations room and, spotting Kolikoff, walked over to him. "Give me an update."

Perfect timing, thought Kolikoff. *The old man gets to see success as it unfolds.*

Kolikoff stood up and went through a quick report. "Major Uintergrin reports he has unloaded two of his three BTR-90s and all of the infantry. Agent Panther Chameleon sent us the exact coordinates of the enemy ambush, and right now Uintergrin is maneuvering on the enemy from two sides."

"What the hell is Uintergrin doing giving reports? What happened to Karataev?" said Tympkin.

Kolikoff barely knew who Uintergrin *was*; after all, Tympkin had kept the mission a secret even from him until a few days before. Since then, he'd not really been given control of the train except that they'd gotten in touch with them and provided them answers and redirected area troops to support. "Uintergrin has assumed the role of acting commander on the death of his superior last night."

Tympkin's eyes widened, but he seemed to appreciate that things were moving along well in spite of the setback.

The room was getting livelier now, as a Russian UAV had shown up on the battlefield and was providing a live feed. Tympkin glanced at Kolikoff. "Your call for reinforcements?"

"Yes, General."

"Good work," said Tympkin.

Strasburg, Virginia

Tyce couldn't see the men in the other houses but knew his squad leaders would be instructing their squads to do about the same as he was directing the squad with him. His Humvee machine gunner had knocked out a section of wall and was now setting up the tripods for the .50 cals. The other 150th cavalrymen were sprinting around collecting construction material. Bags of dry cement and cinderblocks acted as sandbags and barricades, and two-by-fours became aiming rests.

The battlefield was completely visible to him from the vantage of the second story, and with his tactical experience, he instantly sized up the situation. An entire cleared section of forest just off the railroad tracks had been opened up to build a new housing development, which was now the epicenter of a massive exchange of cannon and small-arms fire. From there, it was a gentle dirt slope down to the tracks, with neighborhood blocks mapped out, some yards done, and even a few foundations dug and bricked in.

At the train, several gravel berms providing erosion protection for the railway gave the Russians near-continuous masking terrain. The train and what looked to be about a company of Russians had excellent cover and near-perfect fields of fire, including up to Tyce and Lieutenant Bryce's LAVs in the woods off Interstate 81. Bryce could probably hit the engine at maximum long range, but it was a chancy target, and the BTRs were keeping him pinned. If he was going to get a clear shot on the engine, or anything else besides the approaching BTRs, he'd have to sacrifice the cover of a good position for a completely exposed one. The BTR was a stronger and more heavily armored vehicle than the LAV, and eventually, the basic math didn't add up in the LAVs' favor. A Russian BTR with a 30mm cannon and turret mounted anti-tank guided missile versus a light armored semi-amphibious vehicle meant for speedy reconnaissance and carrying only a 25mm cannon? No question. The big part of that equation was Tyce could see that realization dawning on the Russians, too.

He used the squad radio. "Look, you can see the enemy is preparing to advance up the field and close the distance on Lieutenant Bryce. Once they get close enough, that 30mm is going to hurt. Report to me when your guns are set. We'll commence firing at the same time. I want to hit them when they get halfway across the field advancing on his Dragoons."

The squad radio was more like a walkie-talkie, less formal than military radios, but fortunately, each squad "rogered up" that they understood.

* * *

The report that came in after the men had begun their advance caused Major Uintergrin some confusion. "Wait, there are enemy spotted where?"

"Sir, we have a report that there were Americans spotted in the houses on the other side of the field. The BTR man wants to know if you have any change of orders? He's passed on his concern that they have shoulder fired rockets."

A prickly sensation crept up Uintergrin's neck, a twinge that he might be out of his depth. He willed it away and looked at the map. Then realized he could see those buildings from the train and walked to the window. He held his binoculars up and stared at the houses. Sure enough, there seemed to be some activity on the second floor of a few of the buildings, but it didn't look like anything much to him. "It is probably construction workers, trapped by the battle. Can't be helped." Then, momentarily, doubting himself due to his own lack of infantry experience, he took another look through the binoculars. "Besides, there is no firing coming from there."

"The BTR commander advises that in his contact with the regular American infantry, they always carry anti-tank rockets."

"I've been assured those enemy vehicles are National Guard, third-line troops, and hillbillies. Just tell the men to continue their advance," Uintergrin said with annoyance.

"Now!" yelled Tyce, both to the machine gunner set up next to him and over the squad radio.

Brack-brack-brack-brack went the heavy-barreled machine gun. It belched out round after round at a rapid rate. Coming from experienced men on the .50 cals at five hundred meters and their tripods, the fire was immediately accurate. It caught the BTR-90s in the flank. Although it was not a big enough round to penetrate the vehicle's armor plating, it did kick off some of their explosive-reactive armor. Their ERA was a kit of explosives, almost like land mines, placed in a carefully designed array across the sides of the vehicle that would detonate when struck by an incoming American anti-tank missile. Tyce didn't have any of those, but knocking the ERAs off gave Bryce's LAV's 25mm cannons a better chance to penetrate the vehicles on the sides where they were the weakest. The sharp pings of constant suppressive fire gave the Russian vehicle crews and the infantry onboard a hell of a headache, adding to their confusion.

"There you go, pour it on," he said over the radio and to the men around him. Although they were at their maximum range for effectiveness, they were also getting into the action.

Tyce could see the tactic was working already. One of the BTRs stopped, and the other two slowed its advance considerably. The only trouble was now the BTRs were using their turrets to search for the source of the incoming fire. Tyce saw the trail vehicle searching widely around them; the other two seemed a little more fixed on Bryce in the wood line. It was difficult while under fire and but-toned up inside a vehicle to tell from which direction you were being shot at. Tyce was banking on it. It would take just a few minutes of fire dominance to get all the men into positions in their respective houses.

Finally, the trail BTR must have seen a few muzzle flashes or the source of some tracer fire. The Russian turret gunner didn't hesitate; he spun onto the houses and opened fire with his 30mm cannon.

Boom-boom-boom! Huge chunks of ceiling, drywall,

and segments of wood framing showered around them. One of the men screamed. Tyce turned and saw a rifleman kneeling behind a stack of cinderblocks, an eight-inch piece of splintered wood sticking through his bicep with blood pouring out of the wound. A buddy pulled him down into cover and went about removing the giant splinter.

Tyce could see the BTRs had divided their fires between his positions and Bryce's. He'd definitely gotten their attention.

Tyce heard Gunny running up the stairs behind them. "Hey sir, the other houses are starting to take heavy-caliber fire. How long do you want to keep these positions?"

Tyce now had to walk a delicate balance between robbing the initiative away from the enemy and assuming too much risk of losing a machine gunner or his gun. His gunners had opened up with a steady, cyclic rate of fire, but were now backing it down to conserve ammunition. There was no chance the .50 cal would penetrate at that distance, and they knew they needed to save some ammo for whatever Tyce ordered up next.

Tyce picked up the squad radio. "Fix fires on the trail vehicle. Aim for his tires."

Gunny was still waiting patiently with Tyce behind the stack of cement bags. "Don't those BTRs have run-flats? You can puncture the tire, but he can still drive. How long do you want to keep this up, sir?" Gunny sounded eager to get on the move and was probably worried Tyce was making a mistake in keeping their positions too long. He wasn't going to come out and say it, but senior enlisted men had their own way of prodding their leaders into action when they thought they were getting sluggish.

"Until I see them cracking, Gunny," Tyce said bluntly. "Look over at that trail vehicle. He isn't so sure that our heavy guns can't penetrate him. When a few shredded tires cause steering problems, he'll reverse."

Boom-boom-boom! More incoming cannon fire. Tyce and Gunny ducked flat, and the machine gunner had to stop firing. A huge hole opened up in the wall in front of them, and the roof over their heads cracked, partially caving in on top of them.

"How long, sir?" Gunny's voice betrayed some doubt.

"Wait," said Tyce, firmly. Then, to the gunner, "Pick him up again, aim for those tires."

The machine gunner wiped sweat and dust from his face, yelled, "Roger!" got behind his gun, and began firing again. He'd been shaken by the sound and the fury around him, and his shots were falling wide, but Tyce could see through the new hole that the other three machine guns were making their marks. Chunks of rubber and a few as-yet-unexploded ERA boxes blew off the trail vehicle. The other two were still moving forward at a slow but steady pace and seemed to be concentrating mostly on Bryce. Either the trail vehicle had to change belts of ammo or there was a debate inside the vehicle, because even though it had their range and was landing rounds practically in their lap, it stopped firing. In moments, there was a cloud of black smoke from the exhaust, and it began to reverse.

"How could you know that?" Gunny asked, watching in wonder as the other two BTRs also began backing up—slowly at first, then faster.

Tyce didn't answer. He called over the squad radio, "Keep the fire on them. Five more bursts apiece, then break down your positions and get down to the first floor." Tyce knew when he had the advantage, but he also knew the best-kept secret of the infantry was displacement.

When you were buttoned up in an armored vehicle, you had the advantage of speed, but you never had the simple tactical agility you gained from ducking into cover, then popping up somewhere else. That ability to keep the enemy guessing was the experienced infantryman's best weapon.

"Uh, sir." Gunny pointed to the two lead vehicles. They were still reversing, but now they'd both turned their turrets toward the houses.

'Oh shit." Then, after a pause, he yelled to the room and into the radio, "Get ready for some heavy incoming!"

"Sir," said the Russian radio operator, "the vehicle commander said they had to pull back. They were losing tires, had lost traction, and were about to get pinned down in the field. The American LAVs had found their range, and they'd had a few penetrations of their hull armor."

"Damn it, Tell them to—"

Another radio operator interrupted Major Uintergrin. "Sir, Captain Shenkov is inbound on final approach and requests to know where he can land to get into the assault. He's requesting a a position report on the Americans."

How sweet the small tactical reversals, Uintergrin thought. "Tell him to land behind those houses. They will take the enemy by surprise from behind."

"Sir, won't that interfere with the fires from your BTRs?" said the new infantry platoon commander he'd received that morning.

"What? Why?" said Uintergrin angrily. He may not be an infantryman, but he hated being corrected by one.

"The dynamics of fire, sir. If the Spetsnaz captain lands behind the four houses, he will be behind the direct line of the BTR fire. If they shoot, he will receive any wide rounds, and vice versa."

Uintergrin flashed an angry look. "Don't tell me how to run the battle, Lieutenant. I know perfectly well what we need to do. Give the order, radio operator, and inform the BTRs to maintain their fires and hold their positions. We will squeeze the enemy in between our forces. This is a classic maneuver. It's called a, ah . . . well, in the manual it's a form of killing maneuver."

All military radio operators in every military the world round listened to discussions held in their command post. It took a thinking man to be a radio operator; they must always be listening so they could quickly anticipate what information needed to be passed. Uintergrin's radiomen were no different. They had been operating with their own infantry unit for some time and trusted their lieutenant over their new major. They glanced between the two officers with some doubt as to what to do. Ultimately, one made the radio call. "Wolf six, Wolf six, you are to commence your assault from grid location two-seven-nine, two-one-one. Your targets are the four houses at the edge of the construction site. The enemy is facing away from you, and you will have the element of surprise. Orders are to attack immediately."

"Understood. We will land in seconds. We have heavy guns and rockets and will commence the attack immediately on touching down," came the response over the radio speaker system.

The volume of fire over their heads was unbelievable. Large spans of the roof had fallen in on them, adding to the confusion. In the cramped quarters, the reports of the rifles and machine gun were magnified, making normal discussion impossible.

Tyce had to yell in Gunny's ear over the din to be heard. "Time to go. Help the gunner. I'll get the rest of the squad out front where we can regroup and displace." Gunny made an "okay" gesture with his thumb and forefinger and slapped the gunner on the helmet to get his attention.

Tyce was halfway down the stairs when he heard a strange sound. One he had heard only once in recent months. The *whoop-whoop* of a helicopter's rotor blades could be heard, even above the noise of outgoing and incoming gunfire. Tyce raced to the front of the house, where the back of the Humvee still stuck halfway out the smashed front room. About a hundred meters away, six helicopters were landing. He recognized them right away; they were Kamov Ka-60 assault helicopters. Tyce could see Russian troops spilling out as the first aircraft touched down.

CHAPTER 35

Strasburg, Virginia

A withering cross fire blasted from the tree line as the Russians assumed positions, forming a lengthening line in the north. Red tracer fire from light machine guns, looking like dozens of laser beams, rattled from among the bushes and ripped through the houses' wood and tin siding. The men had just made it to the first floor, but now they were all lying completely flat around Tyce. Tyce knew that if the Russians were given the time, they would bring up medium machine guns and grenade launchers and start chewing the houses to shreds.

The radio operator screamed in his ear, "Sir, second squad wants to know if they should try to make their way over here."

Tyce slashed his hand across his neck. "Negative, negative. Tell him to remain in place. Tell all squads to hold fast and get into the basements. The brick foundations will give them cover."

The Marine indicated he understood and radioed the command. The noise of incoming fire again made verbal commands nearly impossible. Tyce low crawled over to the squad leader and pointed downward with his thumb. Tyce and the man looked around and spotted the basement stairwell. The majority of the interior drywall wasn't up yet, so it was easy to spot. Tyce and several others crawled to the front windows. Without needing to coordinate, they immediately fell into their unit's SOP and used a pop-up technique. Three Marines and Tyce each went to a different front window, and one man popped up at a time, firing rapidly but accurately onto the Russian's muzzle blasts. Tyce hoped the squad leaders were communicating to one another on their own and doing the same. If they didn't pick up some fire, the Russians would have them thoroughly pinned and advance on them a few at a time until they could toss grenades in the windows. Tyce recognized the danger because he had done it himself many times in Iraq and Afghanistan against terrorists and ISIS.

When he saw the last pieces of the .50 cal disappear along with the final soldier's boots, he got up and dashed down the line of mixed Marines and soldiers furiously pumping out rounds into the woods. He tapped each man on the shoulder, then ran to the next, dodging between construction beams and wall studs until he'd gotten the last man. He fired once more from the last window, then made a mad dash for the basement stairs.

Uintergrin looked out the train window through his binoculars and watched the battle as it was unfolding. Around him, the men were running in and out of the train car, delivering messages, offloading crates of ammo, and retrieving supplies.

God, the din out there is horrendous, he thought. He didn't care to go outside, instead sticking by his radios.

The noise was overwhelming enough inside the train car as it was.

"Sir, BTR commander reports he isn't receiving any more incoming from the Americans at the house cluster. But he's still a sitting duck in the field. It's only a matter of time before he loses one of his vehicles to the American LAVs."

"Nonsense, they have thick armor, and the American vehicle has a weak gun. Tell him to keep his position and divide his fires between both targets."

"Understood, Comrade Major."

Was it just Uintergrin's imagination, or did the radio-man just say "Comrade Major" in a tone of disrespect? Never mind, he'd consider that later. Yet he was feeling an apprehension in the air that he didn't like. The men were tense, and he wasn't sure why. He'd always been taught that you should use a three-to-one ratio when fighting, and with the arrival of Shenkov's men, he was at two-to-one. The odds were not decisive, but he calculated that they were still in his favor.

The Marines were panting from heat and exhaustion. A few drank from canteens, draining the liquid down in one big gulp with half the contents splashing down their flak jackets.

"Sir, what are your orders?" said Gunnery Sergeant Dixon.

Tyce looked around. Twelve men crowded in a base-ment stared back at him. "Okay, listen up. We're going to take a calculated risk based on my assessment of the battlefield geometry. The LAR guys are going to keep those BTRs busy. I want two men on the back keeping an eye on the BTRs. One fireteam of four men use the small windows or make a mousehole in the bricks, and keep fire on the Russian dismounts. Have the grenadiers lob an occasional grenade on any pockets you see advancing. The rest of you are going to grab whatever construction stuff you can, and you're going to construct a platform for the .50. On my command, you're going to open up at the same time as the other two squads. We're going to pour it on them."

Gunny looked at him and blinked. He understood the tactic Tyce was setting up immediately. "You're gonna counterattack, aren't you, sir?"

"We're gonna motherfucking counterattack," Tyce said flatly, and with the hint of a grin. He rarely swore, but sometimes it felt appropriate. This was the time.

Cries of "hell yeah!" and "damn straight" went up among the men.

Gunny looked around the room. "Well, what the hell you bastards waiting for? You heard the colonel. Time to show those sons of bitches what the 150th is made of."

Whether it was from Gunny's booming battlefield voice or confidence in Tyce's experienced and reasoned tactic, the men complied with gusto. They bolted in different directions. The radio operator relayed the orders to the rest of the platoon, then passed them on the field radio to the LAVs. Gunny put together a team of two volunteers to go back into the fire-ravaged upstairs to gather ammo from the Humvee still stuck in the wall.

Captain Shenkov could see the enemy pocket. He watched as his men landed and raced to the edge of the woods, picking rough ground and clusters of trees to take cover and start setting up their arsenal of light machine guns. He could see the enemy taking positions in the basements of the four houses. They were firing mostly small arms, but their bursts of fire were generally inaccurate, and the volume of fire was not enough to prevent his men's freedom of movement.

He looked back and saw his secret weapons moving up. He knew the American mindset; they would dig in their heels and try to achieve fire dominance. He'd seen it before in videos from Iraq and Afghanistan, and in his own experience recently against their special forces outside Huntington. They were well-trained marksmen, but this tactic only worked when they had air superiority. Something the Yankees had had bred into them that came with a flaw: they no longer had air superiority. Without their illustrious air forces, they were just another light infantry unit.

Better yet, Shenkov had a foolproof plan. He was going to root them out of their basements, and he could either kill them out in the open or let them die in place. He looked back and saw one team of men surging forward bringing two heavy 82mm mortars. The tactic he was going to use he'd learned from reading his Marine counterparts' field manuals and after-action reports. They were stupid to post them all online; democracies gave out their secrets too freely.

He was about to paste them with a huge volume of RPK-74 light machine gun fire, then slam them with mortars and rockets. Four pairs of men, the last to offload from the helicopters, raced up with the PG-29V Vampir anti-tank rockets, steel crates of extra ammo swinging between them. Platoon commanders down the line yelled and grabbed the rockets, putting them right into key positions where they had clear shots at each of the four houses.

It was excessive force, and Shenkov knew it. The massive 105mm rockets were designed to defeat heavily armored American main battle tanks in a conventional war. They would blow giant holes through the basement brick facade and collapse the buildings with overpressure. The PG-29V was a tandem warhead. Its armor penetrator would turn to liquid metal and ricochet around the room, while the explosive heads would detonate in their midst. The men would experience all of the air being sucked out of the room, bursting their eardrums and making eyes pop out of their sockets. Or they would die when chunks of steel magma melted huge holes through them.

But there's no such thing as overkill in war, Shenkov thought to himself, *just victory and defeat.* He yelled the old Soviet battle call, "*Uurah!*" as rocketeers ran past. The war cry was picked up along the line, strengthening his men's resolve.

CHAPTER 36

Strasburg, Virginia

"Sir, Lieutenant Bryce is on the hook. He says he just lost a vic. Sounds like the one LAV was hit hard. He's also down to about one-third of his ammo load. He wants you to know he cannot advance. The BTRs have a 30mm cannon, and every time he tries to displace a vehicle, they take a heavy volume of fire."

Tyce ran to the back windows. There was a lot of shrapnel, and 7.62mm machine gun fire hitting the upper stories of the house and the ground out back. It wasn't accurate, but every burst tossed chunks of earth or big pieces of roofing material in front of the narrow basement windows. He looked to the southwest, where he could see Bryce's burning LAV. There was a massive roar of flames coming out the top, like a flamethrower.

There's no way anyone survived that, Tyce thought.

He ran back to the front of the basement and yelled, "Boys, you have seconds, not minutes, to get that .50 cal up and ready. Everyone not assisting the gun or keeping up fire, follow me. We move now. Squad leader, call over to the other two squads, and tell them to have their men ready."

"You going house to house?" asked Gunny, with a look that told Tyce it was practically suicide.

Tyce gave Gunny a reproachful look. "You have the guns, Gunny. I'll call as soon as we're at the last house and need you to turn on the heavy guns. I'm banking on that guy being light, special forces. He's never been smacked around by .50 cals before, and we're going to hit him with three."

Gunny smiled. "Nothing like getting hit by a *heavy* machine gun. I know from experience." Gunny gave Tyce a fist-pump arm shake, then Tyce ran halfway up the stairs in a low crouch with two squads of sweaty Marines and soldiers following him.

Stazia parked the rusted blue Ford pickup off of Route 55. She could see the battle raging in an open area of what looked like a half-built housing development. She now understood why Tyce had picked the location for the train ambush. There were open fields of fire and the train lay exposed, though she could see it was partially obscured by the trees where it had halted. Men had dismounted from the train and were firing at extreme long range at a cluster of houses where she presumed Tyce was located. Beyond them, she could just make out machine guns firing into the houses. In the middle of it all were three BTRs that seemed trapped, for some reason reluctant to use their speed and mobility.

That's fucked up, she thought. The Americans were certainly trapped, too, stuck between the BTRs and what she assumed were Shenkov's men, but why were the BTRs and Shenkov firing into each other? *Oh well. Not my matter to worry about.*

She glanced a moment at the dead body of the West Virginia man whom she'd flagged down for a ride. He had stopped quickly for the solitary and striking blond beauty only to be rewarded by her climbing in, then knifing him in the back and stealing his car. She had been about to push him out when she reconsidered. He might still prove useful.

She'd not decided yet whether to use an advanced sniper tactic of setting up her hide position inside the vehicle or to dismount and find a more stable shooting platform. She pulled out her father's red hammer-and-sickle handkerchief and unfolded it on her lap. Outside, the continuous chatter of machine guns, the constant *snap-snap* of rifle fire, and the deep *boom-boom* of heavy cannon fire filled the air. She looked at the Soviet flag and all the faded signatures of her father's men, a gift to him upon his retirement from the service.

What do you think, Papochka? She stroked her face with the fabric, then, as if she heard an answer to her question, she responded out loud, "Yes, I agree—a good tactic, and one that offers me full mobility. Just have to remain incognito. Like you did in Chechnya, right Papochka?"

She pulled the dead man roughly forward so his head was against the dashboard, like someone assuming the crash position on an airplane, then rolled down her window. She kept the engine running and turned up the radio she had tuned to a good 80s rock station. It wasn't good old-fashioned Russian 80s pop music, but she knew all the American songs by heart. Her father always loved to tell her of the time he met the American band the Scorpions in the Kremlin while on a detail with President Gorbachev. A weak president—not strong like the current leader, President Kryptov, but she loved Father's little stories to her.

She propped the bipods on the dead man's back and looked through the Marine Corps compound rifle sight. It was not as good as the one she had mounted on her old Orsis, but it was more than adequate for her needs today.

She zoomed all the way in on one of the basement windows. A soldier or Marine, she couldn't exactly make out which, popped up with regularity to look at the BTRs. Obviously some kind of lookout. She'd rather have her first shot be an officer, a radioman, or a medic. *But what the hell; sochnaya mishen' pokazyvayet sebya! A juicy target presents itself.*

She propped the rifle on the dead man's back, then aimed out the window. She choked up the little stadia lines in the sight to get the range, pulled out a pencil, and wrote her firing tables. There was virtually no wind, but it was cooler than usual. She stuck the barrel out the window to try to reduce the echo in the car and put in two earplugs. Now, with a well-calculated trajectory and a stable but concealed firing platform, she began her breathing and waited for the man to pop up.

Bang!

The sound and concussion of the rifle was louder than she expected inside the vehicle, but the shot did the job nicely. She pushed the barrel out of her way and tried to get a glimpse of her handiwork. When the man didn't appear, she smiled and looked for a new target.

Shenkov angrily grabbed the radio from his operator. "Hey, Uintergrin, your BTRs are firing at me. I am receiving incoming 30mm rounds." Shenkov pulled out his map and traced his finger from him through the enemy's position and to the BTRs, confirming the unacceptable fire geometry. "Tell those bastards to check their fires."

As he spoke, six 30mm cannon rounds burst in the trees

overhead, raining small, razor-sharp pieces of shrapnel down on him and his men.

"What's that son of a bitch trying to do?" When no response came, he took matters into his own hands and dialed in the frequency assigned to the BTR unit. "*Bronetransportyor* commander, *Bronetransportyor* commander, this is infantry commander. Your fires are hitting my position. Either advance north or retreat south to change your angle of fires."

The response was instant. "I copy, infantry commander, we will halt all fires. Be advised, we were ordered to hold position and continue firing."

A third voice came over the net. It was Uintergrin. "Do not cease your 30mm fires. We have the enemy caught in the middle. Reduce him to shreds. That is my order."

Although Shenkov was only a captain, he was also a Spetsnaz officer from the famed Russian Spetsgruppa V, or Vympel, and he didn't have to take orders from Uintergrin. "Negative, Major, that is a bad order. BTR commander, you will cease your fires now!"

The next radio transmission blew up Shenkov's ear as Uintergrin shouted loudly, "Now you listen to me. I am the on-scene commander, and you will obey my orders. Continue your fires!"

Shenkov dropped the radio handset, put his AK-15 to his shoulder, and let loose a burst of fire at three Americans running between buildings. "Stupid fucking rat," he said. Then he fired another burst. "This is not the way to run a battle."

The squad leaders had established good coordination, and as Tyce and the others ran, the stationary men had picked up their volume of small-arms fire, keeping the enemy's heads down. Tyce sprinted between the last two houses. He and two other men were the last ones. They heard the pings and zips all around them as they dove through a bashed-in wall and into cover.

Inside the broken building, he caught his breath and looked around. Two squads were assembled, half lying spread out prone around the first floor. The other half of them were taking shelter in the basement until Tyce gave the signal. Tyce crawled up to the front of the house, weaving between the half-constructed walls. He poked his head up to see the Russian lines. They had established solid positions, about one hundred meters away and one hundred meters long.

Tyce pulled his squad radio off his belt and thumbed the transmit button. "Gunny, give me fifteen seconds, then unleash hell."

"Got it, sir," came Gunny's response.

Tyce turned to the assembled men. "Men, once the heavy guns kick off, follow me out of the house. We'll circle wide left, get into the woods, then roll down the Russian flank. One thing is vital on a flanking maneuver, so listen closely: don't stop. You got me? Whatever happens, keep going."

A rumble of assent went up from the men, As it did, a burst of tracer fire shot over their heads and directly through the house. If anyone had been reluctant to follow Tyce on his charge, this removed all doubt. Staying put looked to be just as deadly.

Stazia had moved her position to get a better look at the LAVs. They were clumped together on Interstate 81, facing south. One of the vehicles had been badly hit and was completely in flames. The other three had good cover from the BTRs' 30mm behind the berm on the interstate and clumps of trees. It had only taken her a few minutes to drive behind them on the opposite lanes, and now she was close enough to see the backs of all three LAVs. Men were running in and out of the back hatches, exchanging ammunition and coordinating their shots. She looked around for the lieutenant.

What's his name again? she thought. *Brance? No, Bruce?* Yet she didn't really care. She'd already begun her breathing; it was now just a matter of picking her target. None of the Marines had detected her presence.

This was a good rifle she'd acquired. At the right range and with the right ammo, she could reach up to 1,200 meters easily. Shooting at that range took some additional sniping measures, but those were unnecessary here. She could see almost every Marine in the unit at less than eight hundred meters.

She watched as a youngish man with blond hair jumped onto the back of the middle LAV, climbed up to the turret, and put on his intercom helmet. She leveled the barrel and sighted in.

Ah, there you are! She was so close that she could read the stitched name tape on the back of his body armor through her optic. *Bryce. See, I knew it started with a B.*

Bang! The sniper rifle exploded with another shot. The round penetrated the back of his head, blasting a fist-sized hole and continuing at an upward angle, and through the far side of his helmet. Bryce's body was flung all the way forward onto the front of his LAV, where he lay motionless atop the driver's hatch.

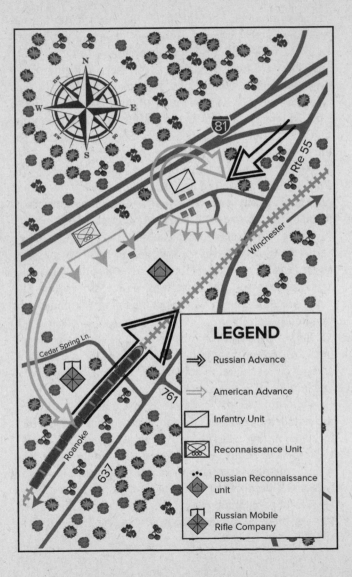

LEGEND

⇒ Russian Advance

⇒ American Advance

▱ Infantry Unit

⊠ Reconnaissance Unit

◈ Russian Reconnaissance unit

⬒ Russian Mobile Rifle Company

CHAPTER 37

Strasburg, Virginia

Suddenly, the woods shattered around Shenkov. Massive chunks flew off the trees. Clods of earth and rocks were being tossed through the air.

"What the hell? Where is that coming from?" he yelled.

"Sir, the enemy has heavy guns. They are firing heavy machine guns from the basements."

Shenkov could barely hear the soldier over the noise. Up and down the line, he heard only loud yelling, the content of their shouts utterly lost to the sound the American heavy guns were making. Three men clustered around a tree were blown apart as the heavy bullets struck them in spite of their cover. The American heavy guns were actually penetrating all the way through the trees.

Shenkov looked back at the 82mm mortar men. They had just finished setting up their equipment when the enemy guns had started. They dared not sit up now to drop a round. Anybody who popped above knee height was being cut to pieces. Two ammo men who had gone back to the helicopter LZ to pick up ammo got cut in half in an instant.

At great personal danger, one of the radio operators crawled over to him and shouted in his ear, "Sir, enemy have been reported on our right flank. They are attacking on our side."

For the first time, Shenkov felt a nervous feeling creeping up his spine.

"Sir, it's General Kolikoff on the line. He says the flight of Tu-95 Tupolev bombers have arrived on station and are ready where you need them."

Uintergrin used one of the Amtrak hand towels to wipe sweat from his forehead and neck. He had just received a report from Shenkov that some enemy forces were flanking him, and the BTRs seemed to be disregarding his orders and had refocused their fires back onto the LAVs. They also looked to be creeping backward from their positions in the middle of the field where he wanted them. He was so pissed he could hardly see straight, but the news of the bombers' arrival was welcome. "Excellent, excellent. Tell him to have the bombers hit the houses. Now we decimate the enemy. We will blow them sky-high."

One of the headquarters sergeants who had the duties of fires-NCO moved a pin on the map put his finger on the houses and made a pencil circle with a compass around them, drawing the radius for the KAB-500S-E guided smart bomb. His job was to coordinate all the indirect fires, artillery, bombs, et cetera, but also to make sure they didn't inadvertently kill their own men. The KAB-500S had a yield of 195 kilograms, and, not even calculating for a missed drop, which happened frequently, the blast radius still covered Shenkov's men in the woods entirely. The sergeant looked back over his shoulder at Uintergrin. "Comrade Major, if you target the houses with heavy bombs, you will hit Captain Shenkov."

"Don't tell me how to do my job, boy!" Uintergrin hissed. He was sick and tired of the tone and comments the men were giving him. He was almost positive they were because he wore the chemical symbol on his collar, not the plain collar or insignia of a Russian infantry officer.

One of the new infantry lieutenants spoke up. "Comrade Major, I must protes—"

Uintergrin interrupted the man. "Shut your mouth, and hand up the coordinate for the buildings. We have the enemy in a classic move. It's called a kill box. I don't expect you to understand advanced infantry tactics."

The infantry lieutenant paused to stare at the major. He had seen a kill box established before, and this wasn't it. Nevertheless, he nodded to the radio operator to send coordinates back to the Russian Pentagon.

Tyce felt two bullets impact his flak jacket. They knocked him back onto his ass, but a cavalryman picked him roughly up by his arm and stood him up. The wind was still knocked out of him. He put a hand to his chest. He could still feel the bullets embedded partway in his jacket; the ceramic plate underneath had prevented their penetration, but he was certain his healing ribs had re-broken. The other man looked at him as he stood unsteadily. His good leg was wobbly, but his prosthetic leg held him up straight. He nodded at the man, and together, they continued racing forward.

Tyce had been practically the lead man before he got shot and had now dropped back only a few steps behind the two lead teams. He watched the lead team overrun a Russian light gun position. The men fired their weapons into the two Russians and continued without stopping. He saw the looks of surprise on the Russian men's faces when they died. They had never expected anyone to show up at their sides. Tyce ran forward, firing at every pocket of Russians as he went. Adrenaline was pumping so fast now, he felt like his feet weren't even touching the ground. He leapt over a long, unburied metal drainpipe and was surprised to see two Russians half covered under it. He was about to turn to fire on the Russians when two Marines and a cavalryman behind him leapt over behind him, firing downward and killing the Russians.

Tyce had seen a lot of combat, but the intensity that came with catching the enemy by surprise and rolling up their flanks was something he'd only read about. He turned back and ran to catch up with the lead men.

"Fire the damned rocket!" Shenkov yelled, but he could not be heard above the din of the battle. After a few futile attempts to get their attention, Shenkov brazenly stood up and ran over to the rocket men. He dove into their position, crashing among them. He saw that one of the men was clutching at his ankle, and at first, Shenkov thought he had landed on the man's leg. Then he glanced at it and saw only meat and bone where the man's foot had once been.

He pushed the man aside and picked up the big 105mm rocket, sighted in, and aimed at one of the buildings. He set the shoulder brace and stared into the flip-up sight. He'd used one of these rockets before, just not under the withering fire he and his men were under now. Rounds were kicking up all around him, and at least one of the enemy riflemen had noticed his kneeling form. He squeezed the trigger. The rocket launcher let loose a thunderous roar, dirt and leaves jumping into the air all around him, and the warhead blasted downrange, leaving a trail of white smoke. The shot was perfect. It connected right against the basement's short stone wall.

Boom!

A tremendous explosion erupted, spars and timbers vaulting skyward in a cloud of black smoke. Through the dirt and debris, Shenkov could see the house had collapsed in on itself, and one of the American heavy machine guns was now silenced.

Tympkin listened to the exchange, then looked back to the live UAV feed. Before he could say anything, Kolikoff grabbed the radio handset. "Listen to me. Get Major Uintergrin on the radio, right now."

Uintergrin came onto the radio. "Comrade General, very good of you to call. The battle is unfolding to plan. We have the enemy exactly where we want them—"

"According to whose plan?" Kolikoff interrupted. "Now you listen to me. The coordinates you passed will directly impact your men. That bombing run is denied, and I want to know how you intend to change the tide back to your favor."

There was a moment's pause. Then Uintergrin came back on. "Comrade General, I think you can understand we are stressed by the sting of combat, but we still have the upper hand. Any reports to the contrary are just absurd."

Major Pavel was manning the radios to the bomber squadron and looked at both generals. Kolikoff shook his head. Pavel understood and told the bombers to hold position and wait until they developed the situation further.

Tympkin pulled Kolikoff aside. "Viktor, things are going badly for your man on the ground. He is beginning to sound unhinged. We need to resolve this thing now and get my train moving."

Kolikoff was acutely aware that the man was actually part of the unit General Tympkin had hand-selected for his own nefarious mission, but there were more important problems to worry about. The counter ambush had been a plan handed to him by Stazia, but he had jumped at the chance to kill the American mountain unit. So now he owned this mess. Fine, then he would fix it.

"General, when this is done, I need to know what's on that train."

"Fix this, and we'll talk. Maybe even have something to show for all this chaos after the war is over."

It looked like he was going to remain in the dark for the moment. In Russian terms, ignorance wasn't necessarily bliss. Whatever Tympkin was caught up in would probably filter down to him eventually.

"Pavel," Kolikoff shouted gruffly, "they are too close to engage with smart bombs, and I will not risk it. Tell the bombers I want them to switch to precision, low-level passes. Have them set up gun-runs from the north to the south. One bird at a time."

"Low passes?"

"Yes, Pavel, you dunce. They have the Afanasev Makarov AM-23 autocannons. If they can't use their bombs, they can strafe the targets. They can save the bombs until we find a chance to use them."

"Aren't those guns on the back?"

"Pavel, you do not need to personally instruct each and every pilot how to maneuver his aircraft. They are trained for this. Tell them what we want, and let them do the rest."

Tympkin beamed at Kolikoff. "Viktor, you are still one of my best in a pinch."

Kolikoff would normally be proud to receive the comment, but he hardly believed that this would be enough to stop what looked like a rapidly unraveling situation.

Tyce stopped mid-stride and watched as the house Gunny had been fighting from blew sky-high. He couldn't help but stare at the ruins that once held his senior enlisted man, someone he considered a good friend. The smoke hung in the air like a white mist, and big chunks of the building began to fall all around. Chunks of concrete, bricks, and pieces of wood all came down with a clatter. The sheer noise of the explosion was enough that everyone in the area, both American and Russian, momentarily ceased their fire across the battlefield to watch the spectacle. Then, almost as quickly as the explosion happened, the small-arms fire resumed.

Tyce felt an uncharacteristic rage boiling up in him. He had been in enough battles that he was usually able to keep his animalistic instincts at bay, but this felt different. He'd just lost someone close to him, an old vet whom he'd counted upon and trusted for many years, along with a full squad of men. The pain of the loss was gut-wrenching.

He felt himself surging forward, rushing ahead. His mind was a blur. Suddenly, he was among the first team. They had stalled; the Russians had noticed them and were turning toward their flanks, trying to adjust their lines to counter this new threat. Tyce wasn't going to let that happen. He heard a roar, a guttural noise like something he'd heard in a Hollywood Viking movie. It was coming from him. He was bellowing and running and firing. He ran and jumped over Russian fighting positions, shooting at everything on the ground. Everything before him was enemy, and he wanted to kill them all. A part of his rational brain told him to stop, let the others catch up with him, let the .50 cal gunners shift their fires. He might even be racing directly into his own machine gun fires, but something inside him didn't let go, wouldn't let up.

He took a big leap over a stand of bushes, but then he realized his rifle was dry. The two men on the other side saw his wild-eyed, frenzied look and stood up to confront him. Something hammered into his prosthetic leg. He felt the leg get ripped off of him, and he fell forward, catching both of the Russians in the chest with his rifle. The three men wrestled on the ground. One Russian reached toward his belt for a fighting knife while the other tried awkwardly to short-stock his rifle to get a shot at Tyce at point-blank range. Tyce took his rifle by the barrel and bashed the Russian trying to shoot him. The buttstock skipped off the Russian's face and slammed against the man's AK-15 rifle, driving the barrel into the dirt while it discharged. One of the bullets caught Tyce in the front of his body armor, the other two hit the ground behind and in front of him. The brute force of the blow knocked the Russian to the ground, a massive gash across his nose and mouth gushing blood.

The second Russian had his bayonet out and up at the ready. He got to his knees and leapt on top of Tyce, leading with the knife like a cobra striking its prey. He held the knife downward, his other hand making a fist behind the hand that held the knife. The weight of his body helped plunge the knife deep, driving it through Tyce's flak jacket and all the way up to the hilt and into Tyce.

* * *

Stazia had rebalanced the Barrett and was looking for another target among the LAV men when she heard the sounds of big aviation engines. She watched the first giant Russian bomber descend into the Shenandoah Valley from the north. She could see another a ways back, lining up behind the first.

"What the hell are they doing?" she said.

It was just too big an aircraft to be that low. It looked out of place. For a moment, she got the feeling that she was in its path and might get caught up in its fires, or bombing run, or whatever it was up to. It was an optical illusion, of course, but there was an undeniable fear factor inherent in the arrival of such a great force among what, till now, had been a relatively two-dimensional fight. One that she'd enjoyed immensely, driving around and seeing from every angle. She watched the aircraft as it seemed to hover in midair. Then, in a flash, it was overhead, and a stream of heavy gunfire spewed out the back, blasting into the middle of the remaining three houses. The rounds also impacted in the woods where she'd seen Tyce and Captain Shenkov's men fighting. The streams almost looked like two firehoses, except these were setting fires and not putting them out. The broken, caved-in roof of the middle house was smoldering, and she could see the flicker of a yellow flame. Two or three more passes, and the civilian houses in which she'd seen Tyce's men would all be gone. She lay down her rifle, shifted the car into gear, and floored it back along Interstate 81 to a spot on the overpass where she knew she'd be able to better see the battle.

My work here against Lieutenant Bryce's men is done for now, anyhow, she thought.

CHAPTER 38

Strasburg, Virginia

Now it was Tyce's turn. Though his left arm and shoulder hung uselessly, he had a knife in his right. In one swift motion, he whipped the blade up and directly into the man's neck. There was no protection there, and the man had been so focused on driving the knife into Tyce that he'd left his neck completely exposed. The violence of Tyce's upswing was so powerful that the knife penetrated, slicing cleanly through the man's windpipe and out the other side. The man gurgled, his body spasming. He let go of the knife in Tyce's arm and reached for his neck.

Tyce kicked the man off. He was still moving, but Tyce knew he didn't have long left to live. Out of the corner of his eye he saw the other Russian. This man lay in the dirt, his nose bashed in and blood covering his face, but he was only wounded. He let out some labored breathing and reached for the AK. Tyce was still on his back, so now it just came down to the matter of who was fastest. Tyce dropped his knife and drew his pistol from its holster just as the other man grabbed his AK and turned it to fire. For the briefest of instants, Tyce prayed that he'd remembered to chamber a round. There was no way he'd be able to rack a round into the pistol one handed—if he even had time to try. He aimed loosely for the man's head and shoulders and squeezed the trigger.

The first round ripped into the Russian's neck, the second grazed him across his back, but the third hit him squarely in the head. He fell where he lay, his finger curled around the trigger of his own AK. He had been just a little too slow.

Tyce let out a loud groan, balanced the pistol on his stomach, and reached his right hand up to the knife in his chest. Under his arm in the small gap in his flak jacket, he could feel the point of the Russian's bayonet. The Russian dagger had penetrated his flak jacket, but the jacket and a rib bone in his chest had partially deflected the blade, so it had gone through his pectoral muscle and out his armpit. When he breathed, he could feel the cold steel rubbing against the ribs and between the muscles.

"Shit," he said, lying and listening to the sounds of the battle still raging around him.

He watched as his men stormed around and past him. They took up temporary firing positions near logs, the big, unburied drainpipes, and what remained of grenade-felled trees. The rate of fire had died down considerably, and the .50 cals were now mostly silent. Tyce wanted to call out, but he'd used up all his energy and lay silent for a few seconds, feeling his heartbeat and wondering what to do next.

"Hey, sir, there you are. Dragoons is on the radio and wants you to know the train is starting to move. He wants to know what you want him to do."

Tyce looked at the radioman weakly, then signaled for him to come closer.

"Dang, sir. You got a fucking knife sticking outta you." The man knelt down to get a better look. He looked around at Tyce's smoking pistol and the two dead Russians, one with a knife in his neck, then yelled, "Medic! Medic!"

Tyce took the handset. "Dragoons six, Dragoon six, this is Iron Horse six, do you copy?" It was hard to breathe, but he could feel adrenaline still coursing through his veins.

"Iron Horse, good to hear from you. Dragoon six is . . . a fallen hero," Tyce recognized the voice of Staff Sergeant Peters, Bryce's platoon sergeant. "Be advised, I have assumed command and I need instructions. The train looks like it might start to move again."

"Roger, Darkhorse five. You take control, but I need you to get fire on that train. Hit that engine, but only the engine. It's still got chem on board, and we don't want any leaks. Same rules apply."

"Understood. We'll do our best, but those BTRs are making life pretty tough on us."

Tyce looked around for the radioman, who was standing up and signaling for a medic to hasten over. "Get your head down, son."

"It's okay, sir. We got them mostly on the run. The guys followed your insane charge all the way up their flank. The Russians are hightailing it out to the east. There's a few pockets, but we're cleaning them out."

Tyce thought, *How on earth . . . ? It worked!*

It was a testament to the American spirit; the guys just didn't let up. As he'd told them, once you have the element of surprise, don't stop. The enemy will see you raging and think he's defeated, even if he still has greater numbers. Tyce caught sight of a long steel ammo crate near the detritus and the two dead Russian. He couldn't read Cyrillic, but he recognized the Roman numbering. It was 105mm. He knew that could only be a rocket.

"Hey, trooper."

"It's McClotsky, sir."

"Got it. Belay that corpsman or medic and go grab me an a sergeant or a staff sergeant. We gotta get things going. We have the upper hand, but it won't last long if we don't do something now." The soldier eyed him but got ready to leave him to go find a leader. Tyce looked around. "Uh, before you go, help me find my leg."

Uintergrin was in a complete panic. The BTR men were starting to withdraw, there was no word from Captain Shenkov, and the Tu-95s flying at treetop level and blazing away with their tail guns made a hellish noise that made him cringe.

"Sir, General Kolikoff is on the line. He wants a situation report."

Another radio operator leaned back. "Major, the BTR unit leader says he is running very low on ammo. He also reports seeing the Spetsnaz forces retreating from the woods and moving to the east. They are not stopping."

Uintergrin was aware of a man standing in the doorway. It was one of the guests, the former FBI traitor. "What do *you* want?"

"Our guards ran. We didn't know what was happening, and we've been encased in these infernal suits for hours. When is someone going to let us in on the plan?"

"Go back to your car and wait for instructions," said Uintergrin. His voice was so high-pitched that everyone in the operations car turned to stare at him. FBI Agent Hanson looked at him curiously, then turned and walked out.

Uintergrin's brain was exploding with the overload of information and decisions he needed to make. He rubbed his head in his hands, then he said to no one in particular, "We have to get out of here." He looked up and around him, wild eyed, "Somebody get this fucking train moving."

"Grab two fire teams and collect up the Russian rockets. Get over to the clearing and find a spot to fire on the BTRs."

"Got it, sir." The cavalry staff sergeant stared at the knife that had been sticking out of Tyce's chest the entire time Tyce spoke. Tyce felt like telling him, *My eyes are up here, not on my chest*, but figured humor was not in order at the moment. Maybe it was the meds the field medic had just jammed into his arm, but he was starting to feel A-OK.

The soldier ran off to execute his command, and Tyce, still hopping on one leg, watched the medic examining the knife.

"Sir, I don't want to take this thing out of you. If it's hit an artery and I pull it, you're gonna be down for the count. How's your breathing?"

"Well, it hurts every time I breathe, but . . ."

"Okay, well, you're not coughing up blood, so it missed your lungs. Overall, I'd say you were extremely lucky. I'm going to tie your arm up to hold it immobile, then we'll get the knife out of you when we have some more . . . ah, breathing room."

"Got it. Thanks, ace."

A voice from beyond the grave came out of the woods. "Hey, Iron Horse." It was Gunny Dixon. Tyce watched, bracing himself against a tree, as Gunny emerged from the woods. His uniform was burned and his face was blackened, but for the most part, he looked okay. He smiled as he walked up, then frowned on seeing the knife. "For Christ's sakes, what the hell?"

"As if we have time. How did you—"

Gunny interrupted. "Likewise, time for that later, sir. I got word about your plan to hit the BTRs. The men have already found the rockets and are headed over there now. We also found a Russian 82mm mortar and a bunch of ammo."

"Jeez, okay. Maybe we need to start using Russian weapons. Easier to get ammo. Have the men turn the mortar on the fleeing infantry. I'm betting some of the men know how to shoot it. If the Russians start to cluster or look like they're readying a counterattack, drop some mortars on them."

The nose of the beaten-up blue pickup truck stuck out into Route 55. Stazia had the huge sniper rifle balanced on the hood now, with her father's red handkerchief tied onto the stock. She'd finally pulled the dead man out of the passenger side. The corpse lay in a heap halfway across the road. Occasionally, a car passed by, swerving to avoid her car and the body, but the explosions, burning fires, and constant gunfire kept all but the truly foolish out of the way. They stared out the window at Stazia, but when their minds even partially caught up to the gory truth of what was taking place, they inevitably gunned it and sped off.

Stazia ignored it all. Civilians held no interest for her. Fighting men, on the other hand, and battle were exhilarating. Especially her role in battle. Killing anyone she wanted, being able to shift the tide of battle in one direction or another—that was positively breathtaking.

"There you are!" she murmured. Her intuition as to the

best angle had proven right, once again. There among a cluster of trees was a man talking on a radio. He was about a kilometer away, but Stazia knew she was good for the shot. One arm was strapped to his chest in a sling, but his hobbling around was all the proof she needed. It was Colonel Asher.

"Mmmmmm." She looked him up and down, appreciating his masculine form. It was pretty far, but she could still make out his features—his chiseled jaw and good looks. His helmet was off, and she could see his dirty-blond hair.

"Fucking idiot, taking your helmet off in battle again . . . especially when there's still a sniper threat nearby. Of course, you don't even know there *is* a sniper threat, do you?" She actually licked her lips as she balanced the rifle on the hood of the pickup and sighted in on Tyce's head.

"So fucking delicious," she said, swinging her butt back and forth while maintaining a tight aim on Tyce's head. Her instinct and training told her that the tide of the battle had changed yet again. The Americans had driven Shenkov off the battlefield, and even though they looked to have taken some hits, they were starting to regain the upper hand. Stazia started running through the variables and found herself wondering what was going to happen once she pulled the trigger. How long would it take for the battle to shift again? She would, of course, move to another angle and see if she could make it last even longer. Then she'd watch with glee as the men tired themselves out even more, sweated, bled, maybe even cried for their losses or out of despair. All because of one lone phantom on the battlefield.

"Or, in my case . . . a *chameleon*," she said, smiling even more and thinking of the origin of her code name. She loved when she stole men's secrets and got into their minds. She loved it even more when she could do it right under their noses and watch them twist and turn. She began her breathing routine.

Odin . . . dva . . . tri . . .

Some crashing sounds nearby pulled her momentarily out of her concentration. She had gotten used to civilians racing around the area like scared rabbits, so she didn't immediately look up. When she did, she saw a line of Russian Spetsnaz men hoofing it across Route 55, about fifty meters away from her. They spotted her and saw the rifle on the hood. A few stopped and stared. Then she saw him. Captain Shenkov was in a cluster of men about ten deep and getting ready to cross the road. She could see instant recognition in his face. She smirked, swung the rifle at him, and, without aiming, squeezed the trigger.

Tyce heard the first rocket go, only a few hundred meters away. The burst and brilliant white flash on a battlefield always reminded him of a thunderclap.

Like the Norse god Thor just briefly visited the battlefield, he thought. It was a familiar sound, as was the slackening of fire across an entire area after the shot. It took remarkable skill and experience *not* to look for the source of a rocket blast and take a peek.

And, just as quickly as it stopped, the gunfire picked up again. He heard a whoosh and a dull boom a little way off. The detonation was a sharp, smacking sound, and without looking, he registered the sound of a rocket striking naked metal. He also knew it meant the men had hit their target.

If they'd have missed, it would have been another sound, a diluted kind of blast that meant they'd hit short or long and just blasted a big hole into the earth.

He heard the dull *boom-boom-boom*, then again, *boom-boom-boom*. It was the LAVs firing on the train. The *clang-kang-bing!* noises told him they were causing some damage. It was the sounds of LAV-25 cannon fire against metal, mixed in with the sounds of the train engine trying to get fired up and moving.

Then he heard the roar of a plane's engines. The Russian bombers were coming in for another low pass. They seemed to have gotten the word that any juicy targets in and near the houses were the ones on which they should concentrate their efforts. They were making low passes with their twin 20mm with a murderous effect. Tyce had given orders for the surviving men to get out of the houses and come over to the woods. He had been watching and listening intently as more and more men arrived from the houses by the minute bringing gear and weapons. Hopefully by this point, the bombers' runs were ineffectual. The best way to defeat enemy air support was to keep moving. He'd learned that from the Taliban in Afghanistan and was relearning the same lesson under fire from Russian air superiority.

The radioman had found his leg for him, about twenty meters away in the woods. It was a pretty mess, a tangle of metal hinges and fake rubber skin. There was no way to salvage it, but he stuck it into his waistband by the foot and grabbed the man's shoulder to help him hobble over to a cluster of logs. He called for another radioman so he could talk to the LAR guys, and pretty soon, the men started to set up a hasty command post around their wounded leader. Medics and corpsmen used his position as a rally point, bringing in wounded men from around the area.

The 82mm mortar arrived, and the men found two soldiers and a Marine who knew how to work it. Tyce started to give them some brief pointers, but they seemed distracted, just staring at the knife sticking out of his chest, so he left them to figure it out. In minutes, someone on the hasty observation post to the east had spotted the Russians on Route 55 near some civilian vehicles. They worked up a firing solution and began tossing a few rounds at them. Tyce listened to the calls for fire, then watched them shoot the mortar. Everything from the bipods to the sight were in Russian, but all mortars worked about the same. He had no doubt the rounds were inaccurate, but given time and a few "practice" rounds, the men would be plenty deadly.

"Hey!" Tyce heard shouting nearby. A sentry was yelling. "There's a sheriff's car coming toward us with his lights flashing."

"What the hell?" Tyce said. The battlefield always brought new oddities.

Before he could address it, the radio operator reported, "Sir, the LAR guys say that one BTR looks to be a kill." He handed Tyce the radio.

"Sir," said Staff Sergeant Peters on the radio, "the rocket hit, and at first it didn't look like a penetration. But it's smoking badly now, and all three BTRs are retreating."

As Tyce listened to the report, another rocket blasted. *Boom-whoosh-crack!*

"Nice shot, nice shot!" Staff Sergeant Peters said. "You got another one. That's one BTR total K-kill, and one limping back toward the train. The third is firing furiously, but you're in his head, he's retreating, too."

The sheriff's vehicle pulled between the woods and the

smashed houses. Tyce was about to yell for someone to stop the driver. He'd seen a ton of crazy stuff on the battlefield, but why in the hell a sheriff would think it was safe to roll in with his lights and siren on was a new one.

Then Blue stepped out. He had his rifle, and when he spotted Tyce waving at him furiously, he waved back and started walking his way.

"Run, Blue, run!" Tyce yelled.

Blue looked quizzical, but then every soldier and Marine in the area started yelling the same thing. Blue was stuck out in the open, the sirens and lights still going behind him. As they frantically waved and yelled at him to run, Blue realized there was some danger he couldn't see and raced at breakneck speed, tumbling into the forest and crashing in a heap in the midst of the Marines and soldiers.

It was a good thing, too, because the next Russian Tu-95 seemed to have caught notice of the red and blue lights of a vehicle right in the middle of his designated target cluster. Maybe it was just too fun of a target for a young Russian tail gunner to pass up, but the sheriff's car caught a full burst of air-delivered gunfire. Everyone watched as the car was torn completely to pieces by heavy-caliber, explosive-tipped cannon rounds.

Blue looked up from his spot in the dirt and smiled a foolish grin. "Hey, Colonel."

CHAPTER 39

Strasburg, Virginia

Uintergrin was like a cornered rat. He scampered back and forth in the command post, clutching his hands to his head. He grabbed up several of the radio logbooks and flipped through them, as if looking for answers to his predicament written inside, then put them down again. The train lurched forward and halted, lurched again, then stopped hard and didn't move any farther. When the sounds of the LAVs incoming fire rang out against the train's engine, he hit the ground. A report came back from the front of the train: the engine was damaged beyond repair.

"Sir, the BTRs have taken catastrophic damage. They are returning now," yelled a radio operator.

"Why . . . what do they return to? We are taking fire here, too, don't they know that?" Uintergrin said.

"Sir, they report the American LAVs are advancing. He is out of ammunition and says he must retreat."

"Tell him to hold position," Uintergrin said, still lying on the floor.

"I will relay the message, Major." The soldier stared for a moment down at Uintergrin, who seemed unable or unwilling to move off the floor. After a few tries with the radio, he said, "Major, he does not respond now. He is not answering on the radio."

One of the NBC soldiers came into the car dressed in his full chemical suit. "General, the prisoners have taken some weapons and refuse to leave their railcar." His appearance in the chemical suit at the height of the battle served to greatly increase the level of panic in the command post.

Another radio operator said, "Major, General Kolikoff is calling. He needs you to tell him what adjustments the aircraft need to make on their strafing runs."

Uintergrin seemed unable to process this much information at once. He propped himself up slowly but remained on the floor. Suddenly, a terrific whoosh sounded outside. Everyone looked up and through the big café car's window in time to see two jet fighters flying directly overhead. The sounds of a raking gunfire followed, then two thunderous booms.

Tyce looked up and saw two McDonnell Douglas F/A-18 Hornet jet fighters streak overhead. They were racing up the Shenandoah Valley at maximum speed. Directly above them, the jets, which were not more than a few hundred feet off the ground, launched laser-guided smart missiles. Everyone around Tyce could actually see the missiles take off from the Hornet's wing pylons. They shrieked loudly, forging blazing white contrails, superseding the Hornet's own speeds and making the jets look as if they were standing still in a matter of milliseconds.

"What the hell was that?" someone asked.

"At least they're not shooting at us," said another.

Tyce forced a painful shout. "They're Royal Canadian Air Force."

"How do you know?" said Gunny.

"I caught a glimpse of their wing markings. That, and I spoke to the VP before we left. When the train turned north, Canada said they'd help, apparently. Didn't know how before, but now I do. That red maple leaf never looked so glorious," said Tyce.

"Oh, Canada!" Gunny yelled up and into the wind. Others picked up the chant until it echoed among the men throughout the forest.

Stazia had a great angle to see the woods, but she couldn't find Tyce anywhere amid the mix of soldiers and Marines running around. They had beaten Shenkov—or, as she thought of it, *she* had beaten Shenkov, given them an unexpected boost by shooting him as he retreated.

She knew there were going to be questions asked, but it was an instinctive, snap shot with her rifle. And it was worth it.

Deal with it later, she told herself. *Something will present itself.*

Shenkov's men had taken the truck under fire, but she managed to limp it over to another location. There must've been a few hits to the engine or the radiator or something because there were now wisps of white smoke coming from under the hood. Whatever happened next, she was now on foot.

The Americans looked about ready to close the deal and move in. Two LAVs were maneuvering up to the train, the infantry had reestablished their heavy guns, and it sounded like they'd even gotten ahold of one of Shenkov's mortars.

They were dropping rounds on his retreating men. Stazia could still see a few of them slinking away into the bush.

They're effectively out of the picture, she thought. Still, she didn't like seeing the Americans win. Plus, she'd wanted to string the battle out at least a few more hours. And she definitely needed to leave this fight with one more head on her wall.

"Colonel Asher . . . where have you gone? Come out and play," she said.

She scanned the rifle sight over the American machine gunners and rocket men. She could even see occasional puffs of white smoke—the mortar firing. All juicy targets. She contemplated taking one of them out. In a normal, conventional situation, a sniper would jump at the chance of any of those targets. But they'd just replace any man she took out and keep fighting.

"Nah, not good enough," she said.

Besides, telling General Kolikoff that she'd personally shot Colonel Tyce Asher might just be the bonus she needed. She'd get promoted, of course, but she could also probably ask for a new, better sniper rifle. That thought kept her busy as she scanned for signs of the American commander.

Time was ticking; the battle would probably only last another thirty minutes. She checked her ammo pouch and was shocked to see only five rounds left.

She made a decision, "Ah, fuck it." She began her breathing and chose the mortar team leader. "I'll find Colonel Charming later."

Odin . . . dva . . . tri . . .

Tyce was actually watching the mortar team do their work when the shot came. He was proud of their efforts.

A Marine named Sergeant Mascenick was running the tube, like clockwork, when his chest exploded like a red firework. Gore sprayed all over the rest of the team, and he fell lifeless to the ground.

It took a few seconds. No one reacted immediately. Then, as if someone had hit pause in a movie scene and resumed play, everyone hit the dirt.

Blue crawled over to Tyce. "Hey Colonel, it looks like we got ourselves another sniper."

Tyce nodded at the big mountain man and sighed heavily, staring at the lifeless body of Mascenick and his men struggling to move the tube while staying low.

"Mind if I take a look?"

Tyce nodded again. "Don't mind at all, Blue. Go to work on him and see what you can do."

Blue slid his rifle over his shoulder and started crawling over toward the edge of the woods while Tyce low crawled in the opposite direction to help the men drag Mascenick's lifeless body over to the medics. There would be nothing they could do for him, Tyce knew that. Tyce also knew it would give the mortar team enough peace of mind to keep fighting.

Staff Sergeant Peters watched the Canadian jets fly up the valley. He was trying to maneuver his LAVs against the train while the remaining BTRs attempted to slow his progress. When the Canadian jets appeared, both BTRs turned and fled, one limping slowly behind the other. Peters gazed up for a second to watch the sky show. The Canadian missiles easily caught the first low-flying bomber completely by surprise. Two missiles slammed into it, one hitting the wing and the other the tail. The big aircraft nosed down and crashed somewhere out of sight. A plume of red and yellow flame burst into the sky, followed by a column of dark smoke.

The fighter jets then streaked directly upward, made an Immelmann maneuver, and faced the other three bombers, who were awaiting their turn to enter the valley to begin their strafing run. Till now, they had been operating with impunity. When the attack jets came, they scattered like gazelle fleeing the savannah when lions appear.

Peters was just appreciating the comfortable feeling of his side owning the skies again, like the old days, when a bullet penetrated his crew helmet and passed cleanly though both sides of his head. His body went limp, and he fell straight down into his turret.

For a second, the gunner thought his boss had just come down to help him work the gun, but then he saw splattered brain matter oozing from the man's helmet. He turned and retched over the side of the turret.

Stazia resented it, but she figured it was finally time to report to her superiors. *I'm having too much fun, but it's time to call the boss.* Her latest spot was only two hundred meters from the train. Here she could watch the Americans take their trophy, then report all the gory details of Shenkov's latest failure back to General Kolikoff.

It's always better to be the first to report, she said, re-calling one of her father's favorite axioms. *He who checks in with HQ first controls the story.* She also knew Shenkov's troops' account might damage her carefully sculpted reputation with the top brass.

Without her encrypted satellite beacon, she had to rely on her backup radio. She unlocked her Pelican case and carefully removed a civilian cell phone. The phone number was one that the Russian Pentagon would recognize, even though it wasn't her regular device. She tapped out the message:

> SHENKOV'S MEN ROUTED.
> AMERICAN FORCES HAVE SEIZED THE
> TRAIN. I HAVE PERSONALLY KILLED TEN
> MEN, BUT I CANNOT PREVENT INEVITABLE
> MISSION FAILURE. REQUEST ORDERS.

It was disgusting to her to have to toady to her command, but there really was no other way. It was this or let Shenkov's troops tell HQ that she had been discovered on the battlefield and had shot Shenkov.

> DO NOT COMPROMISE YOURSELF.
> CONTINUE REPORTING. WHAT IS SHENKOV'S
> SITUATION AND DISPOSITION?

Hmmm, they seem in the dark and greedy for information. Good—means no one else has reported in, and their eyes in the sky are gone.

She'd watched the Tu-95s getting hit, and she knew there was probably one or more UAVs up. But when the command was truly in the dark, they grasped at any reports given. Then a moment later:

> DO AMERICAN'S HAVE PRISONERS FROM
> TRAIN?

Ah, so they were more worried about the train. Excellent. Okay, let's give them what they want.

She typed in her response:

AFFFIRM. RUSSIAN OFFICERS AND
SEVERAL OTHERS.

The next response was delayed. They must be thinking things over, perhaps how to salvage something from this fiasco. She looked through her rifle scope across the battlefield, still hoping she might spot Tyce.

If I can't make you a notch on my bedpost, I sure as fuck am gonna make you a notch on my rifle.

She scanned the train, impatiently waiting for a response, and watched the procession of Russian POWs being loaded into Humvees and into the backs of civilian pickup trucks.

"Sucks to be those guys," she whispered into her red talisman handkerchief.

Georgia-Blue caught something out of the corner of his eye that his brain didn't like. Kind of like when he was hunting mountain lion. The mountain lion was one of the hardest species to hunt. Like their tiny, house-trained relatives, they went where their whimsy took them. Their camouflage patterns, even the way they slunk across a field or mountain forest, was so in tune with their natural surroundings that often a hunter could lie in wait a whole day and not see them, only to pick up to go and see the great cat's fresh paw prints mere meters away. So Blue relied on an instinct he'd earned the hard way. He didn't usually hunt a cat for sport, just in competition for resources. How many times had he been as hungry as the cat, or hungrier, and found that one of the beasts had moved into his area? Then it was all about survival. Whomever won that struggle got to eat in the evening. And the loser either went home hungry or not at all. Blue had spent half his life hungry and struggling, and the other half prowling around to keep things that way.

It was just a shadow of a movement, a cluster of foliage that moved counter to the wind. Blue had taken his time getting into his position. Unlike what a civilian imagines about a sniper, much of the time getting into a good location involves melding with the environment and taking in what the nature there was trying to tell you. Watching and understanding the eternal, flowing patterns of the day on that specific ground.

His eyes remained fixed on the spot, and he waited patiently.

The Canadian jets had never gotten in touch with Tyce over the radios—too difficult to find their frequency, and Tyce hadn't thought to bring a ultra–high frequency radio, the kind they would be talking on. Still, their arrival had been very much welcome. They had driven the Russian bombers away and even taken out a high-flying drone no one had seen until the thing fell like a duck shot out of the sky by a hunter.

The LAVs had done most of the rest of the work, covering the ground to the train and blasting every Russian still left guarding the objective. The cavalrymen and Marines of the 150th set up a perimeter to ensure the Russian Spetsnaz or the limping BTRs didn't try to mount a counterattack, but the reports said they were long gone.

Tyce and Gunny had extracted their Humvee and driven

over to the train, where the LAV men had taken a line of prisoners. Most were men in NBC suits, but there were a few regular soldiers, too. What took him by surprise was what he'd been asked to come over and resolve a situation. There was a standoff of sorts happening at the café car. Tyce hopped out of the Humvee with Gunny assisting him, and they went over to an NCO in charge, a Marine sergeant from Lieutenant Bryce's LAVs who was still whopping mad at the loss of both his platoon commander and sergeant and wanted to shoot everyone inside.

"He's in there, sir. Refuses to come out. He's got a pistol, but I'm pretty sure I could kick his ass in a few seconds. Thing is, he speaks perfect English."

"Okay, hold fast." Tyce looked down the train. A line of Russian prisoners was being led off toward some nearby construction trailers. It was the safest place to take stock of them. Since they had not really expected to take prisoners, it was a hell of a hassle, but Tyce had ordered them to be treated exactly in accordance with the Geneva Conventions. Probably why the LAR sergeant hadn't just rooted the men out of the café car.

The train's engine was smoking, but the rest of the train looked relatively intact. He hoped to hell nothing had spilled. As of yet, no one had taken ill. Gunny had issued the orders to use chemical sniffers they'd gotten from Chief Wheeler, and no one had to be reminded to stay close to their NBC suits.

Gunny helped Tyce hop over to the train car's entrance and called out into the open doorway. "Hey, you in there. What's the word?" He tried to mask the sounds of pain evident in his voice.

"Are you the commander?" came an American voice.

"I am. To whom am I speaking?" It sounded silly, speaking so formally, but the words just came out.

"My name is George Benson. I am a civilian captured by the Russians. I have their major here, under my control. I was worried someone might shoot me by mistake if I came out. But I offer the prisoner as proof."

Tyce had had enough, and blood loss was making him angry. He fearlessly hopped up the steps, using his right arm on the railings. Gunny stood directly behind him, ostensibly to provide fire support, but mostly to prop him up if he fell. Once inside, Tyce took a moment to get his breath and take in the sights. The train car was mostly intact. Maps hung over the walls, and Russian radios had been abandoned in their place. Russian weapons and equipment lay in disarray. Tyce couldn't help it, but his first thoughts were what to do with this windfall of ammo, grenades, and food. Gunny came in close behind him, propping him up.

Tyce now fixed his gaze on the man. He was older, mid-sixties, and clean-shaven but wearing an ill-fitting shirt and pants. He held a pistol against a Russian soldier's head. The Russian wore the rank of a major and had his hands behind his head. Tyce recognized the collar tabs of a chemical officer. He was shivering and only looked up when Tyce spoke.

"FBI Agent Hanson?" Tyce pulled his pistol and trained it on the man. Hanson was completely shocked. Hearing his name was clearly not what he was expecting. Tyce could see him wrestling with thoughts of turning the pistol and shooting Tyce. The lines of Marine and soldiers trooping by outside the big picture windows were probably enough to dissuade him, but being confronted by two obviously battle-hardened, battle-scarred troops was what really halted him in his tracks. Both Tyce and Gunny looked like death warmed over, Tyce knew, and there was a completely no-nonsense aspect to them that said they might not mind just gunning him down in cold blood.

Hanson dropped his pistol. "You got me." He raised his hands over his head.

Whatever had just happened here, Tyce didn't care for theatrics. Tyce called for the LAV sergeant to come in and take charge, "Tag these idiots, zip-tie them, and put tape over their mouths. There's nothing we need to hear from either a traitor or a coward. And I'm really not sure which one is the more detestable."

Then he turned back to his prisoners. "You, sir, are under arrest. You will remain in my custody until such time as I can put you back where you belong—the strongest and worst jail I can find."

Hanson seemed about to protest, but Tyce cocked the hammer back on his pistol and aimed it squarely at his head. "Give me an excuse, asshole. It's been a long day, and no one likes a traitor."

The man gulped and remained silent. Tyce turned his attention to the major, still cowering on the floor in front of Agent Hanson. "And you, Major, are under arrest for violating the Geneva Convention on chemical weapons. You will stand a fair trial when we can find the time and the place. But I should warn you, I will bring every citizen exposed to your fucked-up chemicals from here all the way back to Huntington to kick your fat ass." Tyce knew the major didn't understand, but it felt good to say it anyways.

As Tyce and Gunny brought the two men outside at gunpoint, one of the 150th soldiers came over to them. "Hey, sir. We captured two more. Both Americans, and they fit the profile of those scumbags we got from your description."

"Okay. Let's bring them over here and put them in the back of my Humvee. Those three Americans and the Russian major are going to be our guests for a while."

Stazia's phone buzzed in her breast pocket ruining her concentration. *Really . . . now?*

> URGENT MISSION UPDATE. KILL ALL
> AMERICAN POWS. KILL MAJOR
> UINTERGRIN, RUSSIAN COMMANDER
> ON TRAIN.
> DO NOT ALLOW THEM TO TALK.

Stazia didn't know all the details wrapped up in this whole train endeavor, but she knew that by cleaning up their mess, she would come out smelling like a rose.

Suits me fine, she thought, looking up and down the length of the train and contemplated how she was going to accomplish everything with only three bullets left.

Blue saw it. A small movement. Someone was looking at a cell phone. Behind it was a figure, well concealed in the woods not far from the train. It was a pretty long shot, but he was good for it. He could see the outline of the rifle barrel. Oddly, the shape looked familiar—and feminine.

A woman? he thought. That didn't sit well with him, not at all.

Ever since he'd shot the governor, he'd had a lump stuck in his throat. One that wouldn't go away. All the killing in recent months seemed to be taking a toll on him. At first it had been easy; all the troops around him were doing it. Now he was hearing his mother's voice. The same disappointed voice she would use when he'd done something bad. Like the time he'd taken the Lord's name in vain. On a Sunday. Something hurt inside in a way he really didn't understand.

I know, Momma, he thought to himself. *I ain't forgot the Good Book. But this is different. She's aiming to hurt my friends.*

Bang! the first American civilian went down. A nerdy, skinny kid. Normally, Stazia would slow down, enjoy the thrill of watching the target's look of surprise at being shot. It was usually priceless. But right now, it was all business. Had to be.

The prisoners were all clumped together near a Humvee. All of them, except the Russian major, were wearing civilian clothes with orange hazmat pants, which stood out amid the sea of U.S. troops in camouflage uniforms. Identifying the targets was not a challenge, though her vision was bothering her. Just a twinge, but her one, brown eye had started watering and was overly sensitive to the bright light. *Am I getting tired? Can't be, just have to concentrate even harder.*

Bang! Down went a stuffy looking man with glasses.

For a brief second, she felt a little sick to her stomach. None of these kills mattered much to her, but it was physically painful to shoot them. Was it because they were prisoners? Because they were civilians? Or because they were tied up and presented no challenge?

Nah, she thought, *they just don't matter to me. The prob-*

lem is they don't affect the battle one way or the other. But now, here was a different thought. Was it coming from her father's red handkerchief? She felt like it was. *What's that? Only one round left, Papa? Oh! You're right. Crap. And still two targets left.*

She could see the Russian major and the tall, well-built civilian man. They were both near a Humvee, too, but a little farther from the others. Near some Marines she'd not really scanned yet. She took in the target area. Then she caught sight of Tyce. She recognized him by the drastic limp. He was in a crouch, crawling rapidly over toward the remaining two prisoners.

You look foolish, Colonel, like a crab scurrying on the beach. She could see him yelling something. She noted the knife sticking out of his chest, but her gaze lingered, admiring the shape of his backside as he moved. Yes, just shoot him, and it would be all good. *One round left, and it's meant for him.*

There was the mission to consider. But that was unattainable now, anyhow, with only one bullet left. Or was it?

What should I do, Papochka? She tapped the remaining bullet against her teeth. Then seeming to hear an answer, she loaded the big round into the chamber of her sniper rifle. *Yes, you are right, that opportunity can only arise with patience. Give them a moment and watch how they move about. It will be a matter of perfect timing though. The new rifle is powerful, and I certainly am good enough for that.* Suddenly, her spirits were lifted. She watched intently and began her breathing.

Tyce recognized sniper fire almost as instinctively as his snipers did, just in a different way. He'd been under sniper fire so many times himself, he knew what the single shot ringing out across the battlefield sounded like, even amid all the others. But his instincts were born from the Marine SOP and his own battle drills to his men. It was a grim thing, being under sniper fire. By the time you found out there was a sniper, it meant one of your compatriots was already dead. A sniper rarely missed their first shot. The actions were always the same: accept the fact that the sniper had killed someone, but also accept the fact that it wasn't you, or you'd already be gone and running your fingers over the wheat fields in Elysium.

The next steps were simple. Move immediately. Get out of the kill zone. Head to whichever side you knew shielded you from the sniper's field of view. Then, last, call out the danger, start to send a large volume of fire, and try to advance. Tyce always thought snipers were either cowards or cold blooded at heart, and when they took heavy fire or were confronted by advancing forces, they usually broke and ran. The only other methods of response were calling in a precision artillery strike or guiding an air-delivered bomb directly onto their forehead.

The latter SOP didn't apply in this case. Tyce had prisoners to concern him, civilians he'd placed out in the open. And someone was taking them out, one at a time. He didn't know why, he didn't care, but he had taken them prisoner, so they were his duty to pull from danger. Even if he despised them, and who they were, they were his responsibility. So Tyce threw his normal procedure out the window and made a new one up on the fly. He high crawled toward them, yelling at them to get behind the Humvee. The first two took bullets to their chests, and Tyce knew they were goners, but he could still save the other two.

* * *

Blue watched the chaos this sniper was causing. But it just wasn't right. It just wasn't right, and he knew it. And with that certainty, he felt the awful weakness pass out of his system.

Momma, some things ain't right in the Book but still gotta be done.

Blue aimed at the female Russian sniper and squeezed the trigger. *Bang!*

Tyce thought he heard two gunshots. He knew one sniper was to his right, and he'd been expecting another shot from that direction. Maybe the one off to his left was an echo. What surprised him though, a mere two meters in front of him, the Russian major's head exploded out its right side, and Agent Hanson doubled over, a bullet tearing into his chest.

Tyce stopped crawling and stared for a heartbeat at the gory scene. The major crumpled to the ground like a sack of potatoes, then lay in a heap, motionless. Hanson gasped, looked straight into Tyce's eyes as both arms instinctively reached up and held onto the gaping chest wound. Bone and muscle had been torn apart.

It was enough. Hanson was a goner. There was nothing more he could do. Tyce managed to roll over the tracks and out of the way, but only by enduring excruciating pain as each roll drove the knife deeper. He lay himself flat against a trestle and listened to three more loud, gasping breaths coming from Hanson. Then nothing more.

Tyce forced himself to remain unemotional. He'd witnessed a lot worse on the battlefield, but though he could slow his heart rate and steady his nerves, he really never got used to the many in-your-face experiences that war threw at him.

Two snipers? thought Tyce.

"Boys," he yelled, "who's got the shots? I got one at our five o'clock from the tracks. About two hundred meters."

"Same!" came a shout.

"Everyone, light his ass up!" Tyce yelled.

It started slowly, a steady pop-pop from the men who felt they were out of the danger zone. Then a few more. Pretty soon, Tyce and the men with him inside the kill box felt there was enough lead going downrange at the sniper that they could get up and take better cover.

Before Tyce could attempt to move on his own, Gunny was on him and half dragging, half running with Tyce's arm over his shoulder. Tyce turned and sprayed a few rounds from his carbine with his one good arm as they went. Gunny jumped up, then yanked Tyce aboard the train, and they both collapsed into the dining car.

"Well," Gunny panted, "saving an officer under sniper fire. That ought to at least be a Silver Star."

Tyce was weak from the pain, but it was times like this that he appreciated how really experienced men did what Gunny had just done—inject a little humor. A sick, battle-field sense of humor. Tyce laughed hard, winced in pain, and crawled to the window, where he propped himself up on his missing leg and started pumping rounds in the direction of the sniper. The metal sides of the train were probably not bulletproof, but it wasn't over until it was over. Gunny grunted loudly but came right up to join his commander.

In between firing, Tyce yelled, "I might be able to do a Navy Commendation Medal. If you can scare up some tequila." They both laughed, quite literally in the face of danger, and continued laying down a base of fire as the men maneuvered toward the sniper.

General Kolikoff looked at General Tympkin and shook his head. There were no further communications from Stazia.

"I will try her later on her other device."

"Okay, Viktor," said General Tympkin. His eyes had changed from his usual look of self-assurance to one of uncertainty. "This is a grave setback. Very grave, Viktor."

Kolikoff nodded but stayed silent. What came next was not clear to him. He'd never seen Tympkin look distressed. He always seemed to have plans within plans, but that look had vanished. Tympkin must have sensed it himself, and not wishing to display weakness in front of his subordinates, he turned and quickly walked away.

Kolikoff was left to clean up. He knew that even a case of America's best bourbon was not going to be enough to placate his old pal Colonel Barbarov and the rest of the 184th Guards Heavy Bomber Regiment for the unexpected—and grossly unacceptable—losses.

The firing even on the far end of the battlefield had died down to zero. The Marines and soldiers had thoroughly blasted the area and were now combing the trees to find the sniper's body. Tyce had given orders for the remainder of the men to consolidate a perimeter and pack up as quickly as they could. "Do whatever it takes and prepare to move out," Tyce said.

A few volunteers were found, and they approached the open chemical railcar with caution. They captured two

Russian soldiers, still alert and at their posts. It took some coaxing, but once they explained to them that Major Uintergrin was dead, they seemed more than willing to turn the volatile chemicals over to the Americans. After a few Marlboro cigarettes and some coffee, they even began helping the Americans by explaining the chemical cargoes, their inventory, and their further safe handling.

Somehow, the American rail engineers had survived the whole ordeal. They offered up that there was a whole rail depot ahead of them in the nearby town of Winchester, and if anyone could get them up there, they could be back in a half hour with a new engine. As long as the first one could roll, they could tie the second up to it and push it all the way back to wherever Tyce needed it. It hadn't taken more than a few minutes to get one of the rail workers in a pickup and the other working over the damaged engine to unhook its gears and basically stick it in neutral.

Gunny sat down next to Tyce and picked grit and black ash out of his hair and off his face. A ridiculous trifle of vanity after a battle, especially after what he and Tyce had been through. The smudged dirt covering Gunny's face and his raggedy uniform made his attempts to clean up look all the more humorous to Tyce. But then again, Tyce knew he looked a mess himself—leaning against a captured train, still missing his prosthetic leg, a Russian knife sticking out of his chest. The two leaders of the 150th were a hell of a sight, and as men hastened to the assignments given to them, they all slowed down to stare at Tyce and Gunny. Every one of them down to the last man gave them both either a loud Marine "Oorah," an army "Hooah," or a navy "Hoorah" before going back about their business.

"We've got some shit to do," said Gunny.

"Yup," said Tyce, tiredly. His wounds, the pain meds,

and the loss of adrenaline were catching up to him. He looked at his watch. He didn't fully know the Russian Bear's reaction times, but he knew a battlefield. He figured they had maybe two hours before the Russians sent additional forces, and he didn't want to stick around.

Down a few cars, they heard someone shouting. "Hey, is the colonel around?" Someone else answered yes and directed them to the café car. Two men in NBC suits ran over to Gunny and Tyce. They took in the scene, stared for a second at Tyce's knife wound, then said, "Hey, sir. You're gonna want to come see this." Their voices were muffled from the masks.

"What is it?" said Tyce.

The soldiers looked at each other, then said, "You really better come with us. Put on your suits, though."

Ten minutes later, Tyce and Gunny were in NBC suits and had climbed into the open side cargo hatch of the last car and were staring down into dozens of big metal cases. The troops had smashed all the locks off and flung the top covers open. A brilliant pattern of reflected sunlight danced a scintillating array of colors through their masks and across both men's faces. At first, neither man was really sure what he was looking at.

"Sir, we, uh, broke open the others. You know, just to check them," said the Marine, his beaming smile visible inside the gas mask. "They're all the same."

"That's . . . that's . . ." Gunny stammered, "gold!"

"A whole shit ton of it," said Tyce, wondering just what the hell the Russians had been up to and, what's more, what he was going to do with it all now.

CHAPTER 40

New River Gorge Mine, West Virginia

Tyce watched as the coal mine's enormous banded and bolted iron doors slammed shut with a loud clang. Much of the long train had fit down inside the mine shaft and would remain safe for the time being. The heavy industry rails were all compatible, and the unneeded cars had been easy to ditch. Gunny and Victoria came over to Tyce, clapped him on the shoulder, and sat down beside him on a pile of railroad spans. A cool spring breeze blew in a hint of the summer to come.

Trigger trotted over, his tail wagging, and flopped down at their feet. He glanced at the big mine door, then back at them, puzzled as to why three of his buddies were staring at a door. He had been sitting by Staff Sergeant Diaz's side almost continuously, so Victoria had brought him with her just to get the dog out for some exercise. They had failed to get Diaz a new limb, but Trigger's constant presence had kept her spirits high.

The three humans contemplated things for a few minutes, each lost in their own thoughts. Gunny was the first to break the silence. "What do we do with it all, sir?"

"I was just wondering that same thing. What do you think?" Tyce asked.

"Head out to Vegas," said Gunny with a tiny hint of humor in his voice.

Tyce tried to stifle a laugh. "Not a bad idea, but it all still belongs to the American taxpayers. Besides, it's contaminated, and I'm pretty sure the Russians control Vegas too. "

Even though he'd turned down the suggestion, he felt Victoria's pointed elbow bash him in the ribs for considering it. She was careful to avoid his left arm, which was still in a sling, but even still, he winced noticeably and grunted. It was a lot more painful than she knew. He still hadn't told her about the other busted ribs from the sniper shot. The same ribs he had rebroken when he'd caught two rounds in the flak jacket at the battle of Strasburg. Victoria had cursed him out so badly while she stitched up the deep knife wound that Tyce decided not to mention the ribs. He knew the meds she'd prescribed for the pain would run out soon. Then, maybe, he'd find the courage to bring it up with her.

"Yeah, I figured you'd say that," said Gunny, "but me and the commander here think the taxpayers owe us pretty good for all we've been through, and that gold in there just about pays us off. Might even get us a bunch of new weapons or some decent chow."

Tyce grimaced. He knew Gunny was joking and trying to get a rise out of him, but he couldn't resist the bait. He was about to speak, but before he could say a word, the other two said in near-perfect unison, "We're not mercenaries for hire." Then they both laughed at how easy it was to predict Tyce's thoughts. They had all now been together long enough to be cohering as leaders as much as the men were melding into a battle-hardened unit.

"Took the words right out of my mouth," Tyce said, standing up and wiping gravel off his hands, "but none of it replaces the men we lost." His last words resonated in everyone's ears. For a moment, no one said anything.

Tyce's words had reanimated the names and faces of those they'd lost. He realized he'd better break the mood; it didn't need to be a somber day. That would come later, when they held the services and tried to contact the families. "I'll be honest, I think with all the other mess the Russians left behind from Huntington all the way up to Strasburg, NBC Chief Wheeler has his hands full trying to do a good cleanup and warning and moving the people away from the dangers. It's a hell of a mess. It's going to be a while before we have time to decon the gold."

"At least we know no one will fuck with it. And things coulda been a lot worse," Gunny said.

"Yes, it could have," Tyce said, thinking about how close they came to seeing the Russians gas an entire army division, and maybe several towns worth of civilians with them. "By the way, sixteen of our men from the 150th have returned," he said, trying to further change the topic.

"They did?" Gunny said. "How come I didn't hear about it?" He looked incensed, as he probably should be.

"Well, as the acting sergeant major for the 150th, you're supposed to already know all that troop-level stuff," Tyce said, teasingly.

Gunny knew now he was the one being baited, and he quickly changed the subject. "To what do we think we owe the honor of their return?"

"People heard 'bout you all," said Wynand, startling the three as he came up from behind. He rarely interjected himself into military discussions but had watched the gold go into the mine from nearby and was sticking around to see what the bosses were up to. "I heard out in town that folks, civilian folks, now want to come on over and join the unit. They've been calling the 150th the 'red mountain wolves.' A beast that's so tough but elusive in this region that they have become a bit of a local legend. Just like y'all."

"*Us* all," Victoria corrected him. She still had not reconciled his and Bill's bullying behavior in Morgantown, but this was her team.

"And with that fortune down there"—Gunny pointed to the big iron doors "and the good fortune we had back there on the battlefield, maybe comes a little bit of fame."

"Probably why some of the troops returned. Wanted to serve in a well-led and honorable unit." Victoria added.

Tyce glanced at the assembled hodgepodge of a crew, and it seemed for a second that he was about to get emotional. Instead, he said, "We're in it to win it. I'm not quitting until the last Russian is kicked off our soil. That's my promise to you." He walked around to each of them, one at a time, and shook their hand with his good arm. He looked them in the eye and said, simply, "Thanks." When he was done, he walked off.

They each got up and solemnly followed Tyce back to the old mine buildings that now hosted the new headquarters of the 150th West Virginia Cavalry.

Bill Degata walked in just as Victoria was finishing up a Marine's knee surgery. He waited patiently in a far corner and watched as she nodded to her surgical assistant to close for her and stitch up the wound. She walked to a table, stripped off her nitrile gloves, and sat down to fill out some paperwork.

"Did you need something, Bill?" she asked, scribbling notes on the patient's paper chart. It was hardly fun work, but she knew the continuity of care meant a lot to the men.

"Yes. I have something to say to you," said Bill. Victoria looked up, unsure of which direction this conversation with Bill was going to go. "We—that is, Wynand and I— uh . . ." he stammered.

"Bill, get to the point. I have a lot of work to do," she said brusquely.

"I know, I know. That's kind of what this is about. I wanted to come and apologize. What I, err, what me and Wynand said, you know, what we, um . . . You are a good person, Commander. I just wanted to say that. Also, to ask if there is anything we can do to make it up to you."

Victoria was conscious that the rest of the surgery was listening in on their conversation. While her Italian side wanted to yell at Bill and ask where the hell Wynand was, anyhow, she tried to remember how important it was to heal wounds—of both body and soul. Combat made people say and do things they shouldn't. No one really knows what they are made of until the time comes. Besides, she often said stuff in the heat of the moment. It let everyone know where they stood and vice versa, and she was too strong-willed to go around regretting it.

"Tell you what," she said to Bill. "You just keep calling them as they come and keep a good eye on the general. I'm pretty sure we couldn't manage without either of you. *Capisce?*"

Bill nodded his assent and walked out.

"Certified badass," Petty Officer Purvis whispered to his buddy, the words slightly muffled by his surgical mask.

* * *

The general was still confined to a bed and a wheelchair, but Bill brought him into the command post every day. The general had asked Tyce if his visits were a nuisance, but Tyce had taken it upon himself to insist on the visits, even going so far as ordering Victoria's folks and asking Bill to make sure he came by. It was a tremendous comfort for Tyce to have him there. Sometimes they didn't do more than clear the maps off the central table and lay out a game of chess. Tyce had lost every time, but the general had let him get close on a few games.

Today, Tyce picked up his rook, began to move it, and said, "Rook moves to . . ." He stopped himself when he saw the general shaking his head slightly. He put the piece back with frustration and looked over his other remaining pieces. "Do you think the people will ever get used to us being here? I mean, actually support us with things we need?"

"Do you mean Governor Holly, or the populace?" said the general.

"Both, I guess." Tyce moved his piece and stared at the general's sightless eyes. "Queen to C-seven."

"So it's the job of the populace to feed its army during times of war?" said the general. His fingers gently felt across the tops of the pieces, then moved his own queen. "Queen to C-six."

Tyce looked at the new move with glee. "Queen to B-six, and check, General!" Though it wasn't a checkmate, it was the first time he'd ever gotten the general's king in real jeopardy, and he was thrilled with himself. "I guess, in dire straits and without a functioning supply system, the 150th is at the mercy of the Russians and at the mercy of the people. Couldn't we just take a few things we need to keep on fighting?"

"Hmmm . . ." the general seemed to be contemplating more than just the chessboard. "That's very Napoleon of you, Colonel Asher. He said 'Make war pay for war,' and he ravaged the villages he conquered and made captured towns pay him in food and treasures. It didn't go so well for him. King to F-one." The general moved his king to safety, nullifying Tyce's last move. "And I'm pretty sure there's an amendment to the Constitution that says we can't. But, to your question, I'm not sure they are one and the same. Oftentimes, roosters fight, even when the fox is in the henhouse." The general scratched at the bandages on his forearms. Tyce hadn't seen the wounds the general had gotten from all his blisters, but Victoria had filled him in on a little bit of it, and he knew they were very painful. "I still can't figure out what happened with that assassination, but something about how it went down doesn't make much sense."

"They said the assassin was the sheriff from Parsons."

"Where did that come from? The Russians? I'd take it with a grain of salt," said the general. "There's more to that story we don't know about."

Tyce was staring intently at the board. He began to make a few moves but reconsidered each in order. "I knew him. He didn't seem like the assassin type. More a hick who hated the federal government and was probably lining his pockets, even during a time of war. But I'm more concerned about where we are going to get food and ammo."

"Tyce," the general said gently, "this war is not about you or me. And it's everything about the people we are fighting to protect."

Tyce picked up his rook and started to move it, saying, "Rook to"—The general gave another of his not-so-subtle headshakes. Tyce sighed heavily and moved the piece anyway—"B-eight."

"You're nothing if not persistent," the general said. Then, perhaps trying to ease the inevitability of Tyce's now-looming loss, he said, "You do realize you are the richest Marine in the history of the world. That gold—"

Tyce laughed. "Most poisonous substance known to man." He pushed back from the table and stood up. The sudden motion woke Trigger, who leapt up and followed Tyce on his short walk over to the fridge, where he grabbed two beers, and back. When Tyce returned to his seat, Trigger snorted a few times to indicate his displeasure at being awakened for nothing of substance, then curled back up on the small office rug.

Tyce was pretty strict about the troops not drinking while on duty, but he turned a blind eye at other times as long as the NCOs kept everyone in line. It was now well past midnight, and he was pretty sure there were no more duties that needed his attention tonight. Things had gotten pretty peaceful over the past few weeks in their new command post. He handed a beer to the general, who popped it open and took a small sip, sighing with satisfaction.

"I figure that you're well enough now to have a beer," Tyce said.

The general seemed to eye him up with his white, sightless pupils, then said, "Or you know, like I do, that alcohol conflicts with my new medication, which could double or even triple the effects of the alcohol, giving you the advantage on the chessboard."

"The thought never even crossed my mind, General." Tyce laughed. "But it won't be the first time a Marine outdrank a soldier so he could beat his ass."

They both laughed now. Tyce was grateful for the

banter, but mostly he was just grateful for the general's wisdom about all manner of things. "You know us Marines are half sailor. Our service was started in a tavern."

A radio operator looked in through the doorway, seemingly reluctant to interfere with the chess game. Nevertheless, he stepped in after clearing his throat and said, "Hey, sir. There's a call for you on the mine company's telephone."

"Okay," said Tyce, quickly hiding his beer. "Be there in a minute." Then he added, "Can you find out who it is?"

The Marine acknowledged and went back to the radio room. Tyce could hear him talking over the phone.

The general shook his head and let out a tsk-tsk. Tyce was used to the general's persona and knew this to mean he was about to execute the killing blow. He reached out to pick up a piece.

Before the general could finish his move, the Marine came in again. "Hey, sir. The guy says he's Eagle six. Said you would know what that meant."

Tyce looked up him in astonishment. "*Eagle six?*"

The general stopped mid-move and sucked air through tight lips. "There is only one Eagle six."

"Gotta be a joke," Tyce said, jumping up from his seat and spilling his beer, waking Trigger as he raced into the other room.

Trigger woofed toward Tyce through the doorway, then came over and rubbed up against the general, who reached down and scratched him on the crown of his furry head and stroked his ears. The general turned toward Trigger and said, "Rook to A-six." He moved his piece, then said, "And I believe with that, my loyal canine friend, your boss has just lost the game." He patiently petted Trigger and waited for Tyce to return. He had become extremely attuned to any sounds, even though before his blindness his hearing had been declining with age, and he listened with interest to the conversation unfolding in the next room.

"This is Colonel Asher . . . Yes? I mean, yes, sir . . . I am listening closely, sir . . . Yes, we caught a handful of Russian soldiers too. I can do—I mean, the 150th can do that, sir . . . It's just—you have to understand, we all heard you were dead, Mr. President."

CHAPTER 41

Russian Pentagon
Washington, D.C.

General Kolikoff sat in the back of the morning's operations and intelligence briefing in silence. Major Pavel was droning on about the 8th Guards' setbacks against the 10th Mountain Division in New York. Such negative effects were to be expected after their last mission failure, but they seemed to be occurring noticeably sooner than he would have expected. Kolikoff reflected on the past several days of operations. There was more to the train affair that Tympkin was not willing to divulge. Perhaps he'd get more from Captain Shenkov's men once they were able to limp back to base.

Near the end of the brief, two men in dark suits arrived and sat in the back. They waited patiently until the briefing was over, then walked over to Kolikoff.

"General Viktor Kolikoff?" one said.

"Yes, that's me."

They both flashed badges. "We've been sent by the Kremlin to ask some questions about your most recent operations," the first man said. Kolikoff's eyes grew wide. "Can you fill us in on a certain hijacked train?"

The other said, "Who, exactly, authorized the mission?"

"And what do you know about sixty million U.S. dollars in gold?"

Near New River Gorge, West Virginia

Georgia-Blue walked up to the 150th's new armory, which was set up in the mine's cavernous old tool room. Giant hydraulic jacks and pipes still hung on the walls, and hundreds of meters of spooled cable were stacked against a wall. Blue was a known regular in the armory, well respected by the men there—mostly due to his uncanny shooting skills, but also because of his friendly, polite nature and deep knowledge of all things marksmanship.

"Hey, sir," said Blue as he approached the locked gate.

The Marine armory chief was too busy filling out paperwork to look up. "You don't gotta keep calling me sir, Mr. Blue. In fact, I think most of the men have been calling *you* sir."

Blue flushed a bright red hue and felt thankful the man didn't look up. "I'd rather y'all didn't. Watching Colonel Tyce and the others, I'm pretty sure I ain't built to make an officer's decisions." For the briefest of instants, Blue's heart skipped a beat, and a wave of guilt passed over him. "Least, not regularly."

The armory chief finally looked up, unlocked the steel fence-like door, and let Blue in. "We worked on your rifle trigger for you, like you asked," he said, leading Blue through. "Your sear spring was pretty old, but nothing major. The boys replaced it with a non-OEM. You're gonna need to replace your ejector pin soon, though." He shut and locked the door behind them.

He led Blue to a side storage room that had become the unit headquarters' weapons storage room. Many weapons were left behind and destroyed in the Russian attack on their command post back at the Tucker County High School, but what remained still needed to be cared for and maintained between missions. Colonel Asher had also asked the units to store weapons for troops not on duty, patrol, or alert status after the locals had started to complain that the troops had practically hunted the forests clean of all deer, bear, and rabbit. He didn't have enough ammo for the men to be wasting bullets on filling their plates and had made the unpopular decision in order to, as he had said, "save some ammo for the Russians."

In the back room, two Marines were sitting on stools in front of a long, low workbench, busily repairing a heavy machine gun damaged in the last battle. The armory chief told the men to assist Blue, then headed back to the front to complete his paperwork. The men opened up the weapons cabinet, pulled out Blue's Weatherby Mark V Deluxe, and handed it to him to inspect. Blue took the rifle lovingly in his hands and looked it over, then found a clear spot on the table and began to disassemble and clean it with rags and gun oil.

Blue knew all the weapons in the armory almost as well as the men there did. He looked around as he was cleaning his own rifle and was surprised to notice the unit's Barrett M1A2 .50 cal sniper rifle was missing. Blue frowned and stared for a moment at that one empty spot among all the unit's other sniper rifles. The snipers always took him when they went out for training, and all their other rifles were there, where they belonged. He was about to ask someone if it too was destroyed in the attack on the school when the armory chief poked his head back in.

"Oh hey, Mister Blue, just one more thing. My boys had a helluva time getting all that gunk out of your Weatherby.

I understand you and the top brass must have a good reason to be firing blanks through the rifle, but could you let us know next time you're gonna use blank ammo? It causes a lot of carbon buildup in the chamber and inside the trigger mechanism. My boys had to go to town on it with the chemicals and the solvents before they could even get to the fixes it needed. I don't mind repairing your rifle, but I'm low on solvent, so let me know when you're gonna use blanks again, deal?"

"Blanks?" said Blue, genuinely baffled.

EPILOGUE

February 3, 1945
Berlin, Germany

Shredded Nazi flags still hung from the blasted Reich Chancellery building. The People's Court and the Gestapo headquarters, along with pretty much everything near *Oranien Strasse*, had been mostly reduced to smoldering rubble. The explosions had leveled almost everything, and Goering's promise that "no enemy bomber will ever reach the Ruhr" was an obvious lie. The tally was an unimaginable 1,000 heavy bombers. That figure, unlike quotes from the Reichsmarschall of the Luftwaffe, was believed. They had struck with impunity and they struck during daylight, demonstrating the power of the Allies coming onslaught.

Two men walked farther, past the blackened skeletal remains of a streetcar, wading through knee-deep water from a burst water main. Fire still raged from a building, pouring out of the upper-story windows while fire brigade men in heavy canvas cloaks and steel helms baring axes and hooks ran around trying to control the blaze.

A disheveled and pimple-faced, too-young policeman bade them to halt. Flashing their identity badges, the two men pushed past.

"Look," said the younger man, "our building is intact, *Doktor*. Mostly."

The *doktor* shook his head in disbelief but led them both inside, up the narrow, twisted stairs and into their offices. Shattered glass was everywhere. The outer windows had all burst inward with such shock that thousands of shards were embedded in the opposite walls. The sheer force from the overpressure of the bombing had been such that every interior door was blown from its hinges.

The men stepped over the remains and into what had once been their office. Inside, they surveyed the damage: papers and mechanical and electrical tools were strewn everywhere, but both machines seemed relatively unharmed. Of course, there was no power to confirm that the delicate array of wires and switches were still functional, but the outer casings looked intact.

"Nestor," the doktor said in a dry, sullen voice. He stared at his young protégé a moment. "It is no longer safe for me to keep the rest of the team and their families here."

"What will you do, Doktor?"

"Continue the program. Develop the next-generation computer. Perhaps it is time to finally use those vacuum tubes you seem to think so highly of." He smiled briefly, but it quickly faded.

"What shall I do, Doktor?"

"You will remain here. You must continue to feed data to Von Braun, or all his *wunderwaffe* will fall from the sky. I am entrusting my greatest inventions to you."

The older scientist, Doktor Konrad Zuse, inventor of the world's first working computer, surveyed his apparatus one last time. He pulled a key from the drawer of a toppled wooden desk and unlocked the steel hatch of one of the machines. He ran his fingers lovingly over the wiring, the cold metal scaffolding, and harnesses, then closed the lid with a clang.

"Most importantly, never let them fall into Soviet hands. If they do . . . then God help us all."

"They will turn them against Germany?"

"The Soviet behemoth will not stop now that it's rolling. They will use our computers for exceedingly advanced military calculations against anyone who gets in their way," said Doktor Zuse, prophetically.

Outside came the sounds of the enraged fire, then an earsplitting crack and crash, and both men turned in time to see the front wall of the building across the street collapse away.

ACKNOWLEDGMENTS

Many thanks: To *all* my friends and family, who continue to encourage me in my new(ish) career in writing. Special thanks to my wife and kids for ensuring I have the time to write, but also for being forgiving when I'm truant in my number-one duty as husband and father. To my mom, for all their help, support, inspiration, and thoughtful recommendations. To my good friend and mentor, Mark Greaney. My incredible agent, Mr. Scott Miller, and the team at Trident Media. My author-mentors and pals: Captain Dale Dye, Marc Cameron, Mike Maden, and Sean Lynch—I'm humbled daily by the breadth of their writing knowledge and their willingness to impart it. To my comrades in arms: Josh Smith, Colonel Al Bryant, Lieutenant Colonel Dave Pinion, Lieutenant Colonel Ben Papas, Commander Scott Boros, Lieutenant Colonel (Select) Donnie Barbaree, Mr. Pete Frost, Josh Hood, and Ward Larson for their reviews and advice. To my fabulous editor Gary Goldstein and all the great folks at Kensington. To the amazing bookstores who aren't afraid to support the little guys: Barbara Peters with The Poisoned Pen in Arizona, The Tattered Cover in Denver, and Novel a Bookstore in Memphis. As always, to my favorite writing haunt, the Elden Street Tea Shop. To my buddies and pals, the Cerratellis, the Hoang/Friedmans, the (O')Scannells, the Westbrooks, and to the principal, administrators, and teachers of DTES. You guys all rock!

Keep reading for a special excerpt!

ASSAULT BY FIRE
by H. Ripley Rawlings

In the thrilling tradition of Red Dawn *and* The Dirty Dozen, *this action-packed page-turner from Lt. Col. Hunter Ripley "Rip" Rawlings IV brings together insider military expertise with riveting suspense, as special ops fighters must foil a surprise attack on American soil in a daring novel fans of Brad Thor and Tom Clancy will love!*

ASSAULT BY SEA
U.S. Marine Tyce Asher knew his fighting days were over when he lost his leg in Iraq. He thought he'd never see action again—but when he hears secret espionage intel that a potential attack from Russia is imminent, Tyce knows he has to do everything he can to stop it.

ASSAULT BY LAND
With his history in the Middle East and connections to other veterans, Tyce is enlisted by Homeland Security to coordinate reserve fighters and special ops teams to help prepare the nation for an uncertain future . . .

ASSAULT BY FIRE
It is a full-fledged potential invasion orchestrated by a Russian military mastermind hellbent on destruction. With no time to lose, Tyce has to enlist every American he can find—seasoned vets, armchair warriors, backwoods hunters, even mountain moonshiners— to help protect their homeland.

Look for ASSAULT BY FIRE, on sale now.

PROLOGUE

When Premier of the Soviet Union Joseph V. Stalin died in 1954, the Russian Executive Command finally received permission from the presidium to alter the grand Soviet national military strategy from one focusing on the defense of *Rodina* (Mother Russia) to something completely new—one that could be summed up by saying that a series of lightning offenses are the best defense in the modern, nuclear era. In these new war plans, a successful invasion of Europe was given as a foregone conclusion. Russia was completely confident they held the upper hand on the Continent.

But the invasion of the continental United States, without the use of strategic nuclear arms, remained a vexing problem for Soviet military planners. Three major obstacles prevented the generals from supporting an invasion.

The following pages are an excerpt from the original Soviet War plan.

Union of Soviet Socialist Republics

War Plan 90X-54 (Invasion of the United States)
Combined Assault of America
by Russian Ocean and Air Forces

<u>Para 18-01</u>
1. Invasion of the contiguous forty-eight United States by sea is determined by the leading Soviet naval planners in Leningrad to be impractical at this time. Achieving our doctrinal and desirable five to one troop ratio via undetected large transport ships and across the Atlantic/Pacific oceans is not feasible with current technology.
2. Invasion of the United States is <u>unlikely to be sustainable</u> due to wanton and massive U.S. practice of private firearm ownership. The American Second Amendment means conflict within the continental United States will devolve rapidly and inevitably into a bloody house-to-house conflict. Insurgencies will consist chiefly of remnant military interspersed with willing, patriotic, and well-armed civilian insurgents—who will arise shortly after (or during) the planned Soviet "Assault Phases" and after our forces' initial seizure of the U.S. coast(s).
3. The U.S. policy of Mutual Assured Destruction (MAD) means an invasion would be <u>costly,</u> as any surviving U.S. nuclear force command and control architecture will retaliate with strategic nuclear weapons.

SOVIET MILITARY EXECUTIVE COMMAND
CONCLUSIONS

<u>Para 18-02</u>
Any invasion of the U.S. will be cost prohibitive in
both materials and personnel, and any estimates for
victory in a land invasion of the continental United
States offered to the Supreme Soviet in War Plan
90X-54 should remain marked as merely
"feasible," until the three listed factors can be
removed or mitigated.

Finally, it is the estimate of my entire staff that
invasion should only be considered in the event of
an existential threat against Mother Russia herself.

Signed,
Colonel General I. V. Magyv
Soviet General Staff Headquarters
Offensive War Plan 90X, April 1990 Revision

CHAPTER 1

Twelve years ago
Fallujah, Iraq

He was being dragged backward into a building by the scruff of his flak jacket. As his heels left marks in the sand and dirt, he dazedly stared up and admired the beautiful blue-grey smoke eddies in the air. The near-constant fighting had left a cloud of swirling gas from the guns. Still deafened by the explosion, Lieutenant Tyce Asher looked around, bewildered. His face and hands were singed and burning in agony, but he couldn't remember why. He scrambled to his feet, wobbling and taking in his surroundings. His Marines had taken up positions at the windows. As things became clearer to Tyce, he could feel a thumping, a dull pounding against his face and chest, the bass of booms and pops reverberating through his body even in his still mostly silent world. Nearby, a machine gun was going full bore out a narrow window.

Good! The men are letting them have it, he thought, somewhat proud of himself for making his first coherent thought through the haze in the room and the fog in his brain.

Three grenades had been used to clear the room of militant fighters, and now the formal, antique-style office furniture was ripped and shredded. Charred and torn, the filing cabinets leaked Iraqi government paperwork out onto the floor. A painting of Saddam Hussein, sliced by shrapnel, hung off-kilter on the wall.

Tyce was starting to remember the detonation that had torn up and through the bottom of his Marine Corps Humvee. Shards of searing-hot steel shrapnel had spiraled through the air, slicing and tearing everything in their path. The two Marines in the front seats were spared the hell of being chopped into a hundred pieces by the ricocheting metal: Both were vaporized, disappearing in the fireball that engulfed the Humvee.

The shock wave from the underbelly IED had blown out all four doors, catapulting Marine Lieutenant Tyce Asher from the back seat and out of the vehicle. His heavy body-armor-clad frame was ejected and thrown in a somersault. He landed on his head with a sickening crunch.

He had lain in a heap atop a twisted Humvee door. His brain pounded, displacing all rational thoughts. Sitting partially upright, he fixed his gaze on the vehicle he'd occupied only a moment before. Now flames roared out the top and sides of the contorted wreckage. It took a major effort, but with a shaky hand, he reached up to his head. His helmet was gone, splintered on impact with the concrete. Thankfully, it had done its job—breaking into pieces so his head didn't.

He'd sensed a shape next to him—Sergeant Dixon kneeling over him. Tyce could see the sergeant's mouth moving, but no sound seemed to be coming out. There wasn't even a ringing in Tyce's ears, just dead silence. That and the feeling that every inch of his body had been beaten with a lead pipe.

After a few seconds of screaming in his ear, the sergeant had given up and dragged him toward a nearby building by the handle built into the back of his flak jacket. Tyce's legs kicked weakly at the baking-hot noonday pavement, his body automatically trying to assist even in his near-insensible state as he was manhandled across the street.

Emerging from the memory, Tyce grabbed his platoon sergeant by the shoulder. He pointed at the building down the street, presumably the one from which the enemy had initiated the IED. Tyce motioned for him to assemble a squad and follow him. Deaf or not, the time had come to take the fight to the enemy. His platoon sergeant looked him up and down and seemed to be saying something, probably telling Tyce to go get checked out by one of the navy corpsmen. Tyce just shook his head and told him to hurry up. Or at least, Tyce hoped that was what it sounded like. He still couldn't hear his own voice.

Not long after, Tyce was leading the squad out into the acrid air, past the still-burning wreckage of his Humvee. He picked the middle of the group. A good place from which to lead—he could see everyone and contribute to some accurate fire, if need be. Tyce was an expert marksman with both his rifle and his service pistol.

Youngish by most standards, but considerably older than most of his men, Tyce was twenty-six. Taller than average, about six-three, lean and with sandy blond hair. Marines used every tactic in the book to maintain order and discipline, but the most important of all was respect. And that could only be earned. Tyce had done pretty well in the eyes of the men over in these last months in practi-cally nonstop combat. He never shied away from a firefight and never ordered his men to do something he wasn't personally willing to do himself.

When they reached the building, the men hoisted each other up through two blasted-out corner windows.

Never clear a building through the front door. Tyce recited the maxim to himself, then thought, *or any door, for that matter.*

He'd learned that in his first fifteen minutes of combat. Anyone who didn't went home in a body bag.

Once the men's eyes adjusted to the gloom and smoke inside, Tyce pointed at each squad leader, directing them to start clearing the building from room to room. Rifles short stocked, up and at the ready. Grenadiers in the middle, machine gunners bringing up the rear. Adrenaline and blood pumping.

Each squad received some quick instructions from their sergeants, then raced off to different parts of the building. Tyce dashed a note onto a scrap of paper for his radioman to transmit back to their company commander.

As the squads passed by on their assignments, a few men gaped at him openly. A few minutes before, they had seen him blown clean out of his Humvee, and here he was, standing tall and issuing orders. Tyce waited next to his radio operator in the empty room, weapon at the ready and every muscle tensed and straining for any sign of action from the squads.

Five blasts from upstairs. Even in his deafened state, Tyce felt the concussions.

Corporal Clausen's squad. He bounded up the stairs after his men, realizing as he did how foolish he was to do so without anyone to assist.

No time, he thought, *gotta attack. I'll just have to rely on my other senses*.

Bullets and fragments of wall skittered by him as he ascended the stairs. When he got to the top, the smell of gunpowder was strong—and mixed with something else. He smelled the air. In his deafened state his other senses were already taking over.

Cooking oil and cardamom? he thought.

Dull, pumping sounds of adrenaline-fueled blood rushed through his ears.

As he reached the top of the stairs, his heart sank. In a flash, he realized he'd sent his men into a trap. No one had survived. The small room was a bloody scene of death, booby-trapped. A veritable kill zone.

Holy shit . . . my orders killed them, he thought.

Two flashing shapes caught his eye. Two figures moving at the exact same moment. In a heart-bursting instant, he made a decision born of combat experience to target the one he assessed as more dangerous.

He chose the terrorist at the door, balancing an AK-47 assault rifle against his hip and blazing away at full auto as he tossed a grenade into the room with his other hand. Directed by instinct, Tyce pulled the trigger twice. Accurate and controlled, both rounds met their marks. The man fell in a heap, motionless.

The choice was a good one, but out of the corner of his eye, he saw another movement down by his feet. A wounded terrorist with a knife. Tyce swung his carbine around—too late. He felt a searing pain in his leg as the terrorist's wicked blade cut deep into his calf. The wound and his body armor brought him crashing heavily to the floor. The fighter jumped on top of him, weighing him down, trying to drive the deadly knife into Tyce's neck. Tyce blocked it and tried to reach for his own Marine Ka-Bar fighting knife.

This was the wrong move. By shifting one hand, he was rewarded with a wicked downward slash across his face.

He had reduced the threat from two to one, but now he was in a death struggle on a floor slick with blood, battlefield debris, and cooking oil. And somewhere in the smoke-filled room, a hand grenade ticked silently.

Tyce had to do something—anything—or he was going to die. In one swift, calculated movement, he wrenched the wounded terrorist fully on top of him like a shield. It was the right move. The man kicked and clawed at Tyce, but it was too late. The grenade exploded in a huge blast. Shrapnel filled the air of the small room.

Tyce went deaf again.

Twelve years ago
St. Petersburg, Russia

Colonel Viktor Kolikoff paced up and down his large, new, oak-paneled office, lost in thought. He'd worked twenty-two years to earn this place in the army head-quarters building in Saint Petersburg. Twenty-two long, industrious years.

The best years of my life, he thought, and he felt he'd earned this corner office, one with enormous floor-to-ceiling Empire-style picture-frame windows overlooking the Moyka River. It afforded him wondrous views of the Bolshoi Theatre and the Fabergé art museum.

The building was once a grand palace of Tzar Nicholas II. Kolikoff had occasionally tried to guess what the office had been used for, just about a hundred years ago. It was his now, along with his vaunted new title, Chief of Staff of the Western Military District, and all the duties attendant to that position.

As one of the Russian army's quickest and brightest rising stars, Kolikoff had made full colonel in less than twenty years—a meteoric rise only achieved by less than one percent of all Russian officers. He was absolutely certain of himself, and certain that he was destined for greatness.

That is, he had been . . . until just that moment.

At a slight squeak of over-polished shoes behind him, Kolikoff tore his gaze from the beautiful views and equally ripped himself away from any remaining thought of grandeur.

Everything had changed in the blink of an eye a few hours before. With just a few words, the general had placed him in charge of the worst assignment Kolikoff had ever heard of. Hell, worse than he could dream of. He couldn't think of a more career-killing project if he tried.

He pivoted sharply about and glared at the three lieutenants standing at attention, as if they were to blame for spoiling his grand dreams of climbing to the very top of the military ladder. "A fucking computer?!" he shouted.

The officers stared blankly back at him from the same spot on the worn red carpet.

Colonel Kolikoff didn't bother waiting for an answer; he continued his tirade. "The Victory Day parade is one month away. Every military district will come with their fighter jets, tanks, troops, all polished to the last brass belt buckle"—he inhaled deeply and boomed again—"and quite literally, you *fools* have nothing to show for your *months* of preparation except a stupid computer?"

Of course, Kolikoff knew basically what this computer was. The so-called SPETS-VTOR computer. In the closing days of World War II, the Soviets had gone out of their way to capture a bunch of Nazi computer scientists, just as they had captured German rocket scientists for their missile program. Ever since, some of these scientists had been toiling away with first Soviet and now Russian Federation computers to make them do something. Well, finally, they were supposedly doing something.

Sighing heavily, Kolikoff resigned himself to his fate. He lowered his voice and spoke slowly. "Okay . . . go and issue the order. Every man below the rank of major will march in the parade. I want every baker, cook, and mechanic in this command to polish their boots, clean their rifle, and drill every day from now until then." He went back over to the window, trying to gain some solace from the view overlooking the bourgeoisie—*Just as*, he thought, *maybe the Tzar did.*

His anger rising again, continuing to stare at the bustling streets of Saint Petersburg, he shouted, "Ev-er-y day!" Then, simmering down, he said, "And last—and most importantly—I want something big on that computer. Something enormous. If we have nothing but this *stupid computer* as our centerpiece, I want it to calculate something immense in scope and grandeur."

One of the lieutenants opened his dry mouth, about to ask a question.

Kolikoff interrupted before the junior officer could speak. "Have it calculate the plans . . . the battle plans to invade the United States of America." And with a wave of his hand, he dismissed the men, who gladly hurried off.

Kolikoff suddenly noticed that the huge windows he'd

been looking through so proudly—windows that framed a view he'd admired immensely these last few months—had iron bars on them. The converted Tzar's palace was just a pathetic, worn-out army headquarters. As drab and confining as all the other offices he'd had before.